Crown City by the Sea

Jennifer M. Franks

KONSTELLATION
PRESS

Konstellation Press
San Diego
October 2018
www.konstellationpress.com

Crown City by the Sea is a work of historical fiction. Some names, characters, places, and incidents are historical, while others are the product of the author's imagination and are used fictitiously.

Author photo by Julie Licari Photography at: JulieLicariPhotography.com
Book design by Scarlet Willette
Cover image: Hotel Del Coronado, courtesy of San Diego Historical Society
Back cover: Hotel Del Coronado, courtesy of Coronado Public Library
Cover image:

ISBN: 978-0-9991989-0-2
ISBN-10:0999198904

For my family.

"Those who do not find Coronado a paradise, have doubtless brought with them the same conditions that would render heaven unpleasant to them did they have the chance to gain admittance."

~L. Frank Baum
Author of *The Wizard of Oz*

CHAPTER 1

San Diego, California
November 1885

What are the odds a railroad executive, a piano salesman, and a banker with a cattle ranch could build the largest, most extravagant hotel resort in the America? *Very high*, Elisha Babcock calculated, sidestepping vendors and tourists along the busy San Diego harbor. He kept a brisk pace, his mind reeling at the prospects of such an undertaking. Tall, lean, and not yet forty, he showed no signs of being under a physician's care. In fact, he had never felt better since moving from Indiana to San Diego. The crisp ocean air had done wonders for his health, and his coughing fits had become scarce. He kept a handkerchief in his pocket just in case, but it had been months since he'd seen one tinged with blood. Mr. Babcock halted for a lady to cross his path. From beneath her parasol, she smiled obligingly, her bustled dress swaying in tiers to the ground as she walked. Mr. Babcock pinched the rim of his top hat, tipping his head. "Good day, madam!" He flashed a charming smile from under his waxed mustache.

Now, how to overcome the obstacles? he pondered, finding his stride again. Firstly, he would have to persuade his colleagues that it *could* be done, although neither he nor they had any experience in the hotel industry, nor the means to finance such an endeavor. Grim as the prospects seemed, he could not push the grand vision from his mind. From its inception, the idea of a building a seaside resort had combusted like a struck match, lighting the possibilities of his imagination. It consumed him day and night. He even dreamed of his opulent creation.

Regardless of the slim odds, he had to inspire his partners to take the risk. As Mark Twain once said: "Why not go out on a limb, that's where the fruit is." And a long limb the endeavor would be. If their resort failed, they would face certain financial ruin. But if they succeeded . . . they would have accomplished the unimaginable—and profit handsomely for doing so. The challenge so thrilled Mr. Babcock, it gave him a heightened sense of purpose. His warm brown eyes blazed as he looked over the blossoming city. Bricklayers were adding yet another building to the skyline. San Diego was experiencing a boom, and he meant to capitalize on its inevitable climb.

Mr. Babcock paused to look over the harbor, resting his hands on the wooden railing of the safety barrier. Below him, train tracks ran the length of the pier, where cargo could be efficiently offloaded from ships to meet the insatiable appetites that accompanied prosperity.

"Whatever you can do, or dream you can, begin it. Boldness has genius, power, and magic in it," Mr. Babcock recited, inspired by a quote he'd read that morning by the poet Goethe. He followed with another quote from his favorite, the wise Aristotle. "There is only one way to avoid criticism: do nothing, say nothing and be nothing."

Elisha Babcock would not succumb to such a dismal lot. He believed life was to be lived, pushed, and tested to the limits. His fragile health served as a catalyst rather than a hindrance, embracing those ideals. He would not live the remaining years of his life avoiding criticism or settling for mediocrity. With bolstered resolve, he made his way down a wooden ramp to the docks. He had a proposal to make and his colleagues awaited him.

❧❦

Mr. Hampton Story and Mr. Jacob Gruendike—both dressed in dark suits and black top hats—greeted Mr. Babcock, and the three men promptly boarded Mr. Story's steam-powered yacht the *Della*. The crew eased the boat away from the dock, coiling her bowlines on the deck. The wind was calm and the water an emerald mirror, disrupted only by the vessel's gentle wake. The *Della* puffed into the open bay, where tall ships tacked lazily into port. Slacked lines drooped from their square sails that luffed in the morning still. Not a cloud roamed the pale blue sky, signaling another summerlike day, even for late autumn.

"I can see it already, the largest hotel in the world, right here in San Diego. Think of the possibilities, gentlemen." Mr. Babcock could scarcely contain his enthusiasm. "We could promote it as a destination health resort. The most elegant hotel in the world, where the sun always shines year-round. A place to play, relax, and rejuvenate even in the winter season."

"Haven't we just retired, Babcock?" asked Mr. Story, his keen blue eyes twinkling with humor. The men erupted in laughter. Hampton Story was a tall, distinguished gentleman in his early fifties. An avid sportsman, he spent his days hunting and fishing when he and his wife, Adella, weren't circling in San Diego's blooming high society. Since his days in the Union Army during the Civil War, his disposition was that of a man who had been dealt a lucky hand. He was quick-witted and laughed the loudest when a good joke was told.

"Retired to newer possibilities, my good man," Mr. Babcock replied. "I'm far too young for retirement. My physician merely *recommended* I winter in warmer climates, not give up on life entirely, and I daresay San Diego suits me exceedingly well. Mrs. Babcock and I are quite settled here." He waved a hand toward the city's growing skyline across the bay. "What San Diego lacks is a world-class hotel. Without one, I'm afraid she'll remain a small port city, destined to ambiguity. Think of it, San Francisco has the Palace, with all its city charm. Monterey has the Del Monte, but have you ever summered in either place? Both San Francisco and Monterey can be quite cold, even in summer, and the fog is simply not conducive for one's health. New York and Rhode Island have their fine establishments, but occupancy in both locales is limited by the seasons. Europe is a fine destination, of course, but involves a tiresome journey. During one of my sojourns to escape the Indiana winter, it occurred to me . . .Why not build a destination resort here that isn't limited by the season? By train, it only takes six days to cross the country now. We could entice patrons from the East Coast and all over the world for that matter." His eyes burned with conviction. "We could capitalize on the clientele of guests who spend their winters dallying from one resort to the next." He waved his hands like a puppeteer pulling on strings. Mr. Story and Mr. Gruendike laughed, amused by his antics.

"Everybody knows California is the next great destination to live, work, and play in. That is why it was admitted to the Union," Mr. Babcock continued." Well, apart from all that gold they discovered. At any rate, we could build a resort that would be the crown of the Pacific! I am quite certain of it, and the time to do it is now."

Mr. Story became serious. "I've only just retired from my piano company, Babcock. Imagine me telling my dear Adella I'm planning to open the largest resort in the world." The men chuckled.

"Not just *any* resort, Hampton, but an entire community in support of it," Mr. Babcock replied as he fiddled with the tips of his walrus-like mustache. It was a bad habit his wife, Isabella, dismissed as *incommodious*.

"An *entire* community you propose?" Mr. Story clarified. "I tell you, it may not be enough for me to have named this boat in honor of my wife—I may have to name a street after her, too, just to keep the peace." The men threw their heads back with laughter.

"I assure you, Hampton," Mr. Babcock said, "our new resort community will incorporate both of our loving wives in gratitude for their enduring support. We can even let them choose where *Isabella* and *Adella* Lanes will be most happily situated."

Mr. Story tipped his hat. "Very well. Proceed with your proposal—we await the details most fervently."

"I'm delighted to both oblige and persuade you, gentlemen," Mr. Babcock quipped.

"Pray tell me, Babcock, where do you have in mind to build this resort anyway?" Mr. Gruendike interrupted. He wore boots with his suit and spoke with a slight Southern drawl. "Because we appear to be leaving San Diego entirely."

"Ah! Very astute of you, Mr. Gruendike, which is why you are here. We need partners with such acumen as yours. Additionally, it is a matter of great convenience that you happen to work for the bank." More laughter ensued. "Do you see that spot of land across the bay?" The men turned in their seats to look. "It's a peninsula, really, but at high tide, it's an island at its northern end, or at least it was when the cartographers first mapped it. To that end, we can still call it an *island* and technically be correct. The land is fallow, as you see, and filled with game. Story and I were hunting there recently, when we got the idea that a resort would do splendidly," Babcock explained. "You see, it wasn't simply my idea, as he would have you believe."

Mr. Story raised his hands as if to signal an admission of guilt. "As soon as the railroad lines reached Barstow, we knew it was only a matter of time before everyone could access Southern California. I believe you are right, Babcock, the time is now. San Diego is already in boom. Alonzo Horton is buying and building everywhere. People arrive daily by coach, train, and ship. Builders can scarcely keep up with the demand for homes and new establishments. The city of San Diego is projected to expand from five thousand to upward of thirty thousand within two years' time."

Mr. Gruendike whistled. "That's an astounding rate of growth!"

A burst of steam hissed through the smokestack of the *Della,* followed by several loud puffs. Unable to hear one another, the three men observed the island's coastline in silence, taking in the shrubs, yucca, and sagebrush. With his brow furrowed, Mr. Gruendike calculated the improbable odds of transforming a barren wasteland into a paradise resort.

Mr. Babcock noticed his colleague's troubled expression. "Do not yet draw your conclusions. Let me first show you the island!" he said, assuring him loudly through his cupped hands.

The *Della* coasted to a makeshift ferry landing where the crew secured her lines to the dock. A two-horse carriage awaited the men as they disembarked. "Good morning, Mr. Story. Watch your step, sir," a friendly coachman said, flashing a bright white smile that contrasted against his dark skin.

"Thank you, and good morning, Mr. Thompson. Excuse me, *Gus*," Mr. Story quickly corrected himself, remembering the coachman preferred to be called by his first name.

"And a fine morning it is!"

"How is Mrs. Thompson these days? Faring well I pray?" Mr. Babcock asked, following Mr. Story up the steps to the carriage.

"She sure is! The baby's due any day now, and I just know it's a boy this time, Gus replied. "I plan to have an assistant coachman soon enough." Gus laughed robustly, and his lively eyes gleamed.

"Excellent! Be sure to let us know when the baby arrives. Mrs. Babcock has a gift to send round—she's been knitting for weeks."

"We feel blessed! Thank you, Mr. Babcock—that's awfully kind."

Mr. Babcock halted on the final step. "And Gus, I do hope you'll take me up on my offer to expand upon your business, should you so desire. We expect a lot of growth in the coming year. You should consider the possibility—it could be very profitable for you."

"I sure will, sir."

When the men had taken their seats in his carriage, Gus urged the two horses into a canter. They headed northward along the waterline. The carriage was unyielding on the trail. The men swayed, jostled, and bumped along, all the while admiring the skyline across the bay.

When they reached a marshy, shallow body of water, the carriage halted. "This they call the Spanish Bight," explained Mr. Babcock. "It separates the island into northern and southern ends, if you will. I suppose it could be filled in with sand to make it usable land someday, but it certainly isn't suitable for a foundation. It does, however, provide a lovely prospect of Point Loma." He pointed across the narrow channel to a long stretch of land, dotted with trees and jutting out to buff-colored cliffs that slipped into the sea. "All of the ships that enter the harbor pass through this channel, which makes for pleasant observation, but I have a finer location for our resort in mind."

The carriage moved onward to the western side of the island. Startled jackrabbits bolted from the shrubbery as the carriage passed by. From a safer distance, they sat tall, pointing their ears forward warily. "Incidentally, there is a bit of a jackrabbit infestation here," Mr. Babcock commented, causing more laughter. Gus chuckled from the driver's bench up front, shaking his head. "And that's the truth, Mr. Babcock. I've never seen more rabbits in all my life!" he said over his shoulder.

The rutted terrain gave way to rippling white sand on a beach that stretched for miles in a wide, gentle curve. The carriage wheels sank into the sand, spinning in place before catching in the firmer pack near the waterline. Picking up speed, the carriage ran smoothly again, stirring up sea gulls that ran ahead before stretching their wings and taking flight. They circled curiously above, crying out in protest.

Sapphire waves crested, crashed, and rolled along the shore in a foamy reach. The water swirled, pooled, and then slipped back into the ocean, leaving behind groomed sand that sparkled with golden flecks. Sandpipers chased the receding waves, poking holes in the sand with their long, curved beaks, nibbling as they went. With every wave that rolled ashore, they darted away, keeping just ahead of the frothy wash with their stilt-like legs.

Mr. Babcock had Gus stop the carriage on the southern end of the island, just before the land narrowed to a long strip that continued for miles. He called out to the men, telling them to step down and walk along the shore. A breeze had picked up, which allowed the sea gulls to soar lazily overhead, flapping their wings occasionally to sustain flight. The men observed a small sea gull as it swooped down to the waterline, snatching up a clam in its beak. Alarming cries rang out as the gull resumed flight, followed by a harrowing aerial pursuit. Larger sea gulls swarmed, trying to steal the clam from the smaller bird, which outmaneuvered them as they chased it in dizzying circles. Despite fearful screeches, the smaller bird managed to keep hold of the clam in its beak and thwart the other gulls' advances. The larger birds created a flying barrier around him, but when an opening presented itself, the younger bird took the advantage, rising through them and on to safety. Eventually—their agitated cries abating— the larger birds abandoned their efforts and returned to soaring.

"I'd say that was a risk worth taking." Mr. Babcock commented. "There are always lessons to be learned from nature. Wouldn't you say, Gruendike?"

"Your eternal optimism is contagious, I must admit," Mr. Gruendike replied.

"What I find interesting is this beach actually faces *south*," Mr. Story interjected. "Most would assume a beach along the Pacific was westward facing, but that is a faulty notion."

"How interesting," admitted Mr. Gruendike.

"And you see those islands over there?" Mr. Story pointed to two jagged, rocky protrusions on the horizon, dotted by three smaller ones between them. "Those are the Coronado Islands. They belong to Mexico and are not inhabited at present. They're inhospitable, really, but there's great fishing to be had in the waters around them. I tell you, the yellowtail and barracuda are as plentiful as the sea gulls." Mr. Gruendike squinted, raising his hand to shield his eyes from the sun's glare. "They don't seem very far away."

"They *aren't*—maybe forty miles or so. And you see that hill in the distance?" Mr. Story now pointed south, beyond the beach. "That's Mexico. You're looking at the city of Tijuana." Smoke billowed from hazy structures on the hillside. "We're a border town. It's only a short ride to the crossing."

The men kept walking, taking in the fresh, salty air, invigorated by the beauty of the sea. When they reached a marker in the sand, Mr. Babcock turned them around. "Now, gentlemen," he said, "may I present to you the finest prospect on the island for our resort?" He extended his arms wide, as if embracing the view he hoped to capture. The city of San Diego beckoned across the bay to the northeast, the crest of Point Loma loomed to the north, the Pacific Ocean to the southwest, and Glorietta Bay to the southeast.

"Absolutely glorious! Stunning vision, Babcock!" Mr. Gruendike exclaimed.

"Is it not?" Mr. Babcock grinned triumphantly. "I picture a massive hotel right here, a Queen Anne Revival design—wooden, not stone or brick as one would find on the East Coast. It has to be an architectural masterpiece, something unique that will draw people from everywhere, something whimsical and spectacular to behold! I imagine multiple turrets and towers with little dormers. Turrets so tall they can be seen from miles away. Perhaps even red."

"A red hotel?" asked Mr. Gruendike.

"No, just the turrets. A *white* hotel." Mr. Babcock chuckled. "A massive white hotel, with red turrets and a red-tiled roof. And electricity. Think of it? The first hotel with electric lights running throughout, and every modern amenity and luxury." Mr. Babcock's hands moved through the air like those of a maestro as he described his vision. "Incidentally, I've had this land surveyed, and I believe we are standing over bedrock, which makes this location ideal to build upon. So what do you think, gentlemen? Shall we venture into the realm of hoteliers?"

Mr. Story and Mr. Gruendike became quietly pensive.

At last, Mr. Story spoke. "I think I need to tell my wife about 'Adella Lane' straightaway." The men erupted into laughter.

"It is wildly ambitious yet unmistakably appealing!" Mr. Gruendike admitted. "But how would we proceed? I own a cattle ranch for heaven's sake and know nothing of hotels."

"Let me speak with my attorney at once, Major Levi Chase, from town," Mr. Babcock replied. "We will need to see if the land is for sale, firstly. If it isn't, we must ensure that it *becomes* available for sale. After which, we will make an offer to purchase it . . . all of it."

Mr. Story whistled, and Mr. Gruendike gasped, "*All* of it? You mean the entire island?"

"Why yes, of course. How else will we find the capital to build our resort?"

"Providing we secure the substantial loan for the property, how could we possibly have the remaining funds to build a world-class resort?"

"My good Mr. Gruendike, I have solutions to all of your questions and subsequent vexations," Mr. Babcock assured. "Trust me, gentlemen, I have a detailed plan for how we can purchase the island in its entirety, and build our resort, with little capital—initially, that is. Meet me in the office of Major Chase tomorrow afternoon, three o'clock sharp."

"I'll be there," promised Mr. Gruendike. All three men shook hands firmly.

"Count me in!" said Mr. Story.

Mr. Babcock grinned. *These men*, he thought, *are willing to go out on a limb—where the fruit is.*

.

CHAPTER 2

Cynthiana, Indiana

December 1885

Ava Hennessey slid the strings of her bow across amber-colored rosin. She pushed it along an inch at a time, reversing direction as Mrs. Bosworth had instructed. "Get as much rosin as possible, Ava, this will help your bow stick to the strings, and your violin will make a *usable* sound."

Mrs. Bosworth turned the pages of the music book, squinting through the rectangular spectacles perched on the end of her sharp nose. Ava snuck a peek to the dining room, where her brother, Owen, and sister, Lydia, were covering their ears. They grinned at each other over schoolbooks strewn across the table. *So they think it's funny, do they?* Ava thought, narrowing her eyes at them. She put down the rosin and picked up her violin. Mrs. Bosworth pressed open the page of "The Butterfly," a Celtic jig. She wound the metronome on the table and then raised her hand, motioning for Ava to begin. The metronome clicked in steady beats as the pendulum swung from side to side. *Tick! Tick! Tick! Tick!* Four beats per measure.

Ava blew away a loose strand of her brown hair from her eyes, lowered her chin, pinched the violin against her shoulder, and placed the bow. The fingers of her left hand fell into first position, and she found her place on the sheet music. Holding her breath, she dragged the bow slowly downward. A screeching sound rang out. Wincing, she quickly ran the bow upward, hoping a more pleasant sound would result, but the screeching only worsened. She began bowing at a frenzied pace. Quarter notes became sixteenth notes, and she outpaced the metronome. Giggles erupted from the dining room, and Mrs. Bosworth threw her hands up in protest.

"Too fast? Was I too fast?" Ava cringed. "I sped up too much, didn't I? Oh, I couldn't help it, Mrs. Bosworth, I just got so carried away, and the notes started blending together!"

"Count, Ava. One and two and three and four!" Mrs. Bosworth clapped her hands for each beat, matching the ticks of the pendulum. "You mustn't rush the timing, and keep your elbow fixed. Only your forearm should move as you bow."

"Yes, Mrs. Bosworth." Ava stole another peek at her younger siblings, who had clamped their hands over their mouths to stifle giggles. She shot them a fierce, threatening look, causing more muffled laughter. *It is funny*, Ava had to admit. She bit her lower lip so she wouldn't laugh, too. Distracted, she lost her place on the page and asked to start over.

Mrs. Bosworth pursed her lips and promptly closed the music book. "Perhaps we should work on your scales before moving into song. Without a solid foundation, I'm afraid you'll only perpetuate your bad habits. Begin with the C major scale. At least we'll not suffer from flats and sharps today."

"Yes, Mrs. Bosworth."

Ava had regained her focus by the time her father entered the house. From the corner of her eye, she saw him stride into the kitchen, find her mother, and hand her a yellow piece of paper. A telegram. She turned it over immediately and read it with interest. She looked at him, surprised. He smiled. Ava returned to her scales because Mrs. Bosworth tapped her foot impatiently. The pendulum ticked. One bow per note. *How many scales can there be?* Ava wondered, suffering. She was curious about the telegram. They never received telegrams. The last time they got one had been a year ago, when an uncle was in trouble. He had been robbed on a train and needed money. But Ava's mother had smiled, so *this* telegram had to be good news.

When the clock in the hallway finally chimed, Ava let out a sigh of relief—and Mrs. Bosworth began packing her belongings.

"Will I be seeing you again next week, Mrs. Bosworth?" Ava smiled sheepishly, revealing dimples on both cheeks.

"It's a good thing you are so charming, child. Otherwise my answer would be a resounding *no*. Practice, practice, practice! One can never improve without practice. You're now twelve, I expect greater focus from you."

Ava's bright hazel eyes gleamed. "I promise to focus and I'll practice every day! I do truly love the violin."

"That's encouraging to hear. Let us hope to see all that practice reflected in your progress. Good day, Miss Ava." Mrs. Bosworth let herself out the door, riding away on her bicycle with perfect posture and a sour expression.

෨ඊ෧

That evening, over supper, Father finally made the announcement Ava was waiting for. "So I've received a telegram today from Mr. Babcock, my old employer. He's asked if I would be willing to relocate and work for him again."

"What does *relocate* mean?" Lydia looked from her father to her mother. Her large green eyes filled with worry.

"It means 'to *move*,'" Ava replied, her heart quickening.

"Move where? What about our ponies and my donkey?" Lydia demanded.

"We'd move to California. Bring the ponies with us, and your donkey—sell the farm." Father put a forkful of food in his mouth and began chewing slowly. Mother smiled at him when he winked. Whatever this exchange meant, she was already amenable to the idea of moving.

"Well, where's California?" Lydia put down her fork. Although she was just four years old, Lydia was clear as to how she felt about change: she didn't like it. An oversized green bow sat on top of her mass of wavy blonde hair, a cheery contrast to her wrinkled nose and pouting lips.

13

"On the Pacific Ocean," Mother said, "Do you remember where the Pacific is in our atlas?"

"I remember where it is!" Owen blurted. "It's on the West Coast. I learned it last year in third grade."

"That's right."

"Will we get to go to the beach?" Ava asked. She had never seen the ocean, but she had read about it in textbooks. Her excitement was mounting.

"We might be living *on* the beach, or very near it from the sounds of it. We'd be on an island, near San Diego," Father replied. All three children gaped. "It's not certain yet, but Mr. Babcock wants to know whether we'd be willing to run the stables for him if his business plans work out."

"How would we get there? California is far away from Indiana." Owen started counting off the states that fell between them. "There's Missouri, Kansas, Colorado . . ." He frowned because he couldn't recall the others.

"Utah and Nevada or Arizona and New Mexico," Mother added. "It depends on the route we take across the country. Would we go by stagecoach or train?" she asked her husband.

"Train. Would you like to take a long train ride?" Father looked at each of the children. Ava felt a lump rise in her throat. Trains got robbed by outlaws. "Didn't Uncle Anthony get robbed on a train?" she asked meekly.

"I would love to ride a train!" Owen interjected, drowning out Ava's question.

"Me too!" Lydia cried, suddenly changing her mind about relocating.

Ava imagined outlaws on horseback, their faces hidden behind handkerchiefs and with guns shooting in the air.

After eating, they all sat in silence as the news settled over them. Owen smiled dreamily, gazing up at the ceiling, Ava looked stricken by the thought of being robbed at gunpoint, and Lydia started lining up all the green peas that remained on her plate.

Father finally spoke. "All right, it's time to wash up and get to bed, then. Off you go." The children rose quickly, clearing their plates and taking them to the kitchen.

That night, Ava was restless in her bed. She wondered what the ocean would be like, recalling books she had read. Images of Robinson Crusoe sailing through rough seas came to mind. But then so did his shipwreck and his trials living as a castaway on a deserted island. She abandoned *Robinson Crusoe*, focusing instead on *The Swiss Family Robinson*, but there again was a shipwreck and hardships for the family and its livestock. *Aren't there any happy stories about sailing across the ocean?* Ava wondered, relieved they'd be traveling by train—outlaws or not.

Father said they would know within a week if the job in California had come through. Ava didn't think she could wait that long to find out. The thought of moving and beginning their own adventure thrilled her. All of a sudden, Cynthiana, Indiana, was too small for her. She imagined racing their horse, Ambrose, down a long sandy beach. She hoped she wouldn't have to sit sideways in the saddle, like proper ladies were expected to do. Her mother was always teaching her ways to be "ladylike"—and none of them were fun. Her mother's lessons floated back to her: *A lady always sits quietly, straight and tall, with her ankles crossed, hands in her lap, looking disinterested.* And: *When a lady walks, she's so steady she can balance a book upon her head.* Ava would rather *read* that book while sprawled on the floor than balance it on her head. What a waste of a good story! Mother said feminine qualities like these made a lady *prepossessing*. That meant people would like you right away, before you have even had a chance to talk. Ava couldn't sit still long enough to act disinterested, and there wasn't a chance she could go even one minute without chatting. In fact, she couldn't think of anything worse than being prepossessing.

Tossing and turning, Ava pulled a blanket up around her. She imagined waves crashing endlessly on a sandy shore. She could almost smell the salty air and hear the sea gulls screeching overhead. But the images that engulfed her weren't her own—they were Robinson Crusoe's. And in that moment, Ava decided she had to experience and interpret the sights and sounds of the ocean for herself. She determined that if her family didn't move to California, her life would be positively ruined. Fretful for the next hour, she finally drifted off to sleep..

CHAPTER 3

Messrs. Babcock, Story, and Gruendike arrived promptly at the office of Major Levi Chase, attorney-at-law. Introductions were made, hats and coats hung, and everyone took their seats, politely declining beverages. Major Chase had the documents prepared and spread out on his large oak desk. He shuffled through the papers, and finding one in particular, he placed it on top of the others. Leaning back in his desk chair, he addressed the three men.

"It appears your little island has changed hands many times, gentlemen," Mr. Chase began. "First, it was owned by a Señor Pedro C. Carrillo, excuse my poor pronunciation, who sold it to a Mr. Bezer Simmons, who in turn sold it to Messrs. Peachy, Billings, and Aspinwall. There are a number of other names in the mix, but ultimately these three gentlemen sold the land to a Mr. Charles Holly, who eventually sold it to a Mr. George Graniss, who owns it today." He paused to look up from the documents. "The good news is, Mr. George Graniss is willing to sell and is open for negotiation. The bad news is, there is currently a land boom in California, and the value of the land has increased dramatically since its first purchase."

Messrs. Babcock, Story, and Gruendike nodded to signal they understood the situation.

"Well now, where was I? Oh yes, I have been in negotiations throughout the day with Mr. Graniss, and he has reached his final offer."

"Go ahead," urged Mr. Babcock, perched on the edge of his seat. Major Chase swiveled from side to side in his chair. "He will sell the deed to you for a sum of $110,000, nothing less."

The three prospective buyers shifted uncomfortably in their seats.

"Can we secure a loan from First National Bank?" Mr. Babcock asked Mr. Gruendike.

"We could try to secure it, but it would be high risk," Mr. Gruendike replied. "They'll likely keep the interest rate very high."

"What if we brought in more partners?"

"How many?"

"I can promise two more, both prominent businessmen I know very well. My brother-in-law, Mr. Heber Ingle, and another named Joseph Collett. Both live in Indiana, but I'm certain of their interest as junior, silent partners. They could perhaps share a quarter, leaving us with a quarter each."

"Would they relocate?"

"Certainly, but would they have to?"

"Perhaps not," said Major Chase. "It may not be necessary."

"That would cover the land deed, but what about the loan to build the property? How would we pay for it?" Mr. Gruendike asked.

"What we do is this," Mr. Babcock said, leaning forward. "Purchase the land and then *sell* the land."

"Come again?" Mr. Gruendike replied, clearly startled by the wild notion.

Mr. Story joined the conversation. "We have a land auction. We recoup our loan money, create a surplus, then use that toward building the resort," he clarified.

"Precisely!" Mr. Babcock broke into a wide grin. "That is after we heavily advertise our luxurious resort, of course. We need to drum up investors first."

"Oh, I see." Mr. Gruendike looked as if a light bulb had flashed in his head. "It's brilliant!"

"Is it not so?" Mr. Babcock asked, beaming.

"I think I know just the man we need to drum up investors for us," said Mr. Story. "His name is Colonel Holabird. William Hyman Holabird. He's an advertising genius. They call him the Father of the Boom in California."

Mr. Babcock scribbled down his name on a notepad. "Excellent. We will need to contact him in due time. Be sure we have his current information, will you?" Mr. Story nodded.

"What about infrastructure?" Major Chase asked. "You'll need roads, water, housing, and laborers. With all the building in California, skilled labor is hard to find."

"Yes, we'll have to find laborers first, won't we? We'll also need to lay railroad tracks, create a ferry system, pipe in fresh water, start an electrical company, and build living quarters for the laborers . . ." Mr. Babcock began scribbling feverishly. "With an established rail system, we can import laborers and the materials we need to build." He scribbled some more.

"We will also need to designate a larger company to oversee all of the development," Mr. Story added.

"Quite right. Can we file articles of incorporation with you?" Mr. Babcock asked Major Chase.

"As soon as the land is purchased, absolutely. We'll need a company name."

The three men looked at each other thoughtfully.

"Why don't we name the company after those Mexican islands?" Mr. Story suggested. "The Coronado Islands. We could call it something like . . . the Coronado Beach Company."

Mr. Babcock and Mr. Gruendike pondered this possibility. "Excellent name, Hampton," Mr. Babcock said at last. Mr. Gruendike agreed.

"Now, before we get too far ahead of ourselves, let us have Major Chase first secure our land deed," Mr. Babcock said. "What do you say, gentlemen, are we all in agreement to move forward? It is a grand undertaking to be sure." Mr. Story and Mr. Gruendike nodded. "That settles it!"

"Very well, then I shall inform Mr. Graniss that you agree to his price." Major Chase set down his pen.

The men rose and shook hands, planning to reconvene as soon as the loan was funded and the documents were ready to be signed.

"When should we have our land auction?" Mr. Gruendike asked.

"As soon as the whole country knows about our health resort, where one can convalesce under constant sunshine and in ocean air," Mr. Babcock replied with a laugh. "After we unleash Colonel Holabird on the nation, we'll start a bidding war."

"Capital, Babcock! Capital!" Mr. Story exclaimed with a full-bellied laugh.

The men slipped on their long coats, placed their top hats on their heads, and left the building, chatting amiably.

"Who do you propose is the best architect in the country?" Mr. Story inquired on their way out the door.

"Richard Morris Hunt, but he's building a 'cottage' in Rhode Island for Vanderbilt. He's just recently completed a Fifth Avenue flat for him as well. It would be difficult to retain him," Mr. Gruendike answered.

"No, I don't suppose we could steal him from Vanderbilt," Mr. Story said with a chuckle. "I've heard the Astors are looking to retain his services as well."

"He's certainly out of the question, then," Mr. Babcock admitted. "They say 'The Mrs. Astor' is not to be trifled with. We don't want to meddle with her on any level! I do know of an architect back home in Indiana—he's young but extremely talented. James Reid is his name. He works with his brother, Merritt. I'll send him a telegram straightaway, upon your approval, of course."

"If we can secure them, do so. Meanwhile, we should consider the next matter at hand, which is a rather large obstacle," replied Mr. Story.

"Pray tell me, good man, what is it?"

"Beyond the labor issue is the lumber issue. Neither of which can be found readily in Southern California."

"Not to worry. I have solutions to all of these issues," Mr. Babcock assured Mr. Story. "Let us first secure our land deed. When it is in our hands, I will share with you what I have in mind."

Feeling optimistic, the men tipped their hats and parted ways. Mr. Babcock walked home, greeting everyone he passed along the way. His dream of building an island resort was starting to take root. *Boldness has genius, power, and magic in it*, he repeated to himself. Whatever lay ahead, he was ready to risk everything for it.

CHAPTER 4

"All right, Lydia, I'm going to lie on my stomach. What you need to do is stretch across my back and balance yourself like a seesaw, but raise your arms and legs." Lydia did as she was told, giggling. Ava read from a book opened before her on the parlor floor. "It says here, all you have to do is kick your legs and move your arms in wide circles, making sure to take deep breaths." Lydia began kicking in the air while also swinging her arms and gasping.

"Okay, try to relax or, it says, you will tire and sink," Ava said, struggling not to laugh. "Try again."

Lydia flailed about, but she couldn't maintain her balance while giggling.

"Have my daughters gone mad?" Father asked, entering the room with an amused smile.

"Ava is teaching me how to swim!" Lydia replied.

"'How to Swim If You Don't Live Near a Body of Water,'" Ava said, pointing to the chapter title in the book. There was a photograph of a classroom filled with children spread out, flailing on the floor, practicing their lesson.

"I see." Father laughed good-naturedly. "Well, you won't be needing that book anymore." He waved another telegram in his hand. The girls jumped up, trying to snatch it from him, but he raised it over their heads.

"It's time for a real swimming lesson. We're moving!"

Lydia squealed so loudly, Father clamped his hands over his ears. With the telegram now within reach, Ava grabbed it. "Got it!" she cried. She opened it and began to read aloud:

Dear Mr. Hennessey:

The Coronado Beach Company would like to extend an offer of employment to you for the management of livery at the Coronado Stables. Upon your request, a contract will follow.

We hope you find the terms most agreeable, and that your relocation to California will be trouble free should you accept.

Sincerely,

E. S. Babcock

Ava looked at her father, her eyes shining brightly. "Did you answer already?"

"Of course I answered. I told them to send me the contract at once."

Lydia shrieked again, and Ava pressed the telegram to her heart. Owen and Mother entered the room, both already aware of the good news.

"When will we go?" Ava asked.

"It could be as soon as three weeks," Father said. "Believe it or not, we already have two families interested in purchasing our farm. I think this move *is meant to be.*"

Mother stood beside him, looping her arm through his affectionately. "Your mother can open a schoolhouse, and you can help me run the stables when you're not in school. There will be plenty of work to do on an island. I expect tourists by the hundreds to visit. We'll need every carriage available to transport them."

"Will we get to run the carriages by ourselves?" Owen asked, looking incredulous.

"More than likely, yes. I'll need you and Ava to manage on your own. I'll also need to find someone to be in charge of treats for the horses."

"Oh, I can do that, Father!" Lydia insisted. "I know just what they like! I'll give them carrots, apples, sugar cubes, maybe some blueberries—well, no, not the blueberries." Lydia's fondness for blueberries, when left unchecked, had led to many an episode of sour belly.

"Excellent!" Father replied. "You are hereby hired!"

Lydia grinned radiantly.

ॐ◈ॐ

One month later, the Hennessey family sat aboard a train that puffed a trail of gray steam from its smokestack. Their six horses and donkey were stowed five boxcars behind them, along with two carriages, a buggy, and everything else they valued. Ava watched from the window as all that she had ever known slipped by like the images in a deck of photographs flipped in her hands. The town's only grocery store, the church, a field where she used to ride her horse, and the brick schoolhouse quickly disappeared from view. Cynthiana had become too small overnight, as if a veil had been ripped off, revealing all the town's shortcomings. Ava pondered her years growing up in the small, sleepy town. She and Owen used to watch the workers lay the tracks for the Evansville and Terre Haute Railroad that ran through the center of town. She never imagined those very tracks would one day lead her to a new life. She pressed into memory all that she loved, somehow knowing she would never return. She would miss the springtime, with its wildflower bloom, and the country roads and fields of wheat. But she wouldn't miss the insufferably long, bleak Indiana winters, which brought leafless trees with pointed branches stabbing at the sky. She was happy to leave horrible weather behind for good and almost felt she was getting away with cheating Mother Nature—guilt she was sure would quickly melt away.

She had a few childhood friends, and they had shared farewell tears. Her friends agreed Ava was lucky to be leaving Cynthiana behind. They doubted they'd ever get the chance. A spirit of adventure was replacing any sadness Ava may have let linger. When the last image of town, a weather-beaten sign that read Cynthiana slipped by, Ava smiled to herself. This chapter of her book was closing, and she was turning the last page to a new blank one.

After miles of staring at frostbitten fields and icy rivers, Ava closed her eyes. She listened to the rumble of the train as it moved along the tracks, smelled the scent of oil that greased the levers, heard the hiss of steam pumping the pistons that turned the wheels and the quickening *chug-chug-chug* as the engine gained speed. Like the characters in her books, she was embarking on her own voyage. *If only the voyage didn't take six days!* Ava wished. She would have to learn patience. Unable to nap, she opened a book, hoping to be diverted.

Two hours later, Ava closed the book, her eyes weary and watery. She found Lydia napping, her mother knitting, and her father reading a newspaper. Owen pushed a small wooden train car along the cabin's floor. "Father, can Owen and I check on the horses?" Ava asked.

He looked up from his paper, nodding. "Be careful passing between the cars."

Ava and Owen ran down the narrow corridors that snaked through the train's cars, both giggling as they struggled to keep their balance. They passed through a pair of doors, the wind whooshing around them, and then slowed to walk through a cabin with tables set for tea. The next cabin was filled with copper-studded trunks that smelled of saddle soap and new leather. After bravely leaping over iron couplers in a windy gap between boxcars, they finally reached the car designated for livestock. Goats bleated from pens, and chickens clucked nervously from their crowded cages. Ava offered the chickens a few comforting words, but they eyed her warily. "You'll have a new henhouse before you know it," she said. The rooster stood tall, and his red comb and wattles quivered as he cocked his head from side to side, ever watchful.

Penelope, their donkey, stood beside the horses, which were motionless except for their tails swishing. Ava took a handful of hay and fed the four mares, stroking their necks in a comforting manner. Ambrose, her favorite of the stallions, looked beseechingly at her with his large dark eyes. "Just a few more days, big boy," Ava said to soothe him. She pulled a sugar cube from her pocket and placed it gently in his mouth. Over the crunching, Ava heard a loud thump coming from the next boxcar, and then a muffled voice. There was another thud, and the voice rose angrily. The words were harsh: "I'm warnin' you, Twilah, don't you start gettin' cross with me!" Curious, Ava and Owen left the horses to investigate the commotion.

Owen opened the cabin door to find a boy racing toward them. A large, wing-flapping ostrich followed, fast on the boy's heels. Its long neck stretched forward as it nipped at the boy with its beak. "Shut the door!" the boy screamed. "Save yourself!" Owen moved to slam the door, but Ava stopped it with her foot. The boy's arms pumped at his sides as he sprinted toward them, keeping just ahead of the ostrich. He dropped to the floor, sliding on the straw scattered about. Once the boy was through the door, Owen slammed it shut. A frightening thud shook the cabin. "Holy cow! Did that wild ostrich crash into the door?" Owen asked. Panting, the boy looked up with a grateful smile. "No, she kicked it. That was Twilah, and she has a bad attitude." All three of them burst into laughter.

"You certainly are brave!" Ava said, reaching out to help the boy to his feet. He was thin but scrappy, with dark brown hair and friendly eyes. It occurred to Ava that he needed a haircut.

"Brave or stupid. My pop says there's a fine line between the two. Thanks for keeping the door open for me. You shouldn't have."

"What would have happened if we shut it?"

"Well, you'd still be alive for certain, and depending on how I took that last turn, I maybe would be, too." He laughed. "Ostriches are strong, mostly disagreeable, and really good at escaping their pens."

"I guess we got lucky," Ava replied. "I've never even seen an ostrich before. I had no idea they were so mean!"

"Not all of them, just some. We have twelve of them. Twilah's been mean from the day she hatched."

"And you're her keeper?" Ava was curious about the boy and didn't hesitate to pry.

"Yeah. My pop and I aim to run an ostrich farm in California—that's where we're heading."

"What do you do on an ostrich farm?" Owen asked. "Do some people eat ostriches?"

"No. Really, we just raise them for feathers. The ladies like them for their hats, and sometimes they even put them in their dresses, or something like that. I guess it's fashionable. It's not easy to pluck their feathers, though—I'll tell you that. You have to be real quick! But some people just like to see ostriches, like a tourist attraction." He wiped his hand on his trousers and held it out for a proper handshake. "My name's Nathan—Nathan Beckman."

"I'm Ava Hennessey, and this is my brother, Owen. Nice to meet you. We're going to California, too."

"No kidding? Where to?"

"A new town—it hasn't even been built yet. It's near San Diego."

"That's where Pop and I are heading, too! We're setting up the farm there."

"For Mr. Babcock?"

"The very one. Pop used to work for him before."

"Our father did, too. We're going to run the stables for him."

"I'm glad to hear it. Pop wasn't sure there'd be too many youngsters on the island. He said there'd be lots of work, and I won't have time for making friends."

Ava frowned. It seemed a sour thing to say. "Where are you from?"

"New Orleans. You?"

"Indiana. Why don't you don't have an accent?"

"I used to. Guess I lost it along the way—we move around a lot."

"How old are you?" Ava asked. She noticed the boy's pants were too short, and his shoes were bulging at the toes. She knew what it felt like to wear shoes that were too small. Your big toe always ached, and the blisters never healed properly. If you were lucky, you'd get a callous.

"Thirteen."

"I'm twelve, Owen is ten."

"Almost eleven," Owen corrected her.

"And where are you and your father riding on the train?" Ava asked.

"We have a little place in back. Pop said it'd be best if we kept an eye on the birds. It's not bad, really, I made myself a bunk out of hay bales. At least Twilah can't kick me up where I am, although she tries." Ava burst out laughing, causing Nathan to smile.

"You're welcome to come up to our cabin if you'd like, and have some supper with us. You can meet our folks and our little sister." Ava could tell by the way his shoulders slumped that he wasn't going to accept her invitation. He started kicking at the straw on the ground awkwardly.

"Aw, thanks. That's real nice, but I don't want to leave my pop, and he's already making supper for us."

"All right. Owen and I are going to head on back, then. We're five cars up if you change your mind."

"See you around." Nathan stuffed his hands in his pockets and watched them go.

Owen raced back to their cabin; he couldn't wait to tell their father about Nathan and the ostrich farm. Ava took her time, wondering whether Nathan had a mother. He hadn't mentioned her, and he looked a little unkempt, even a little small for his age. *What are the chances we'd be going to the same town?* she thought. Ava felt certain she and Nathan would be fast friends, maybe even *great* friends. It would be nice to pass the time on the train getting to know him better. She decided to visit him again the next day.

CHAPTER 5

The assembled gentlemen signed their flowing signatures on the land deed placed on the oak desk of Major Chase. "Congratulations!" he bellowed, "Sold for $110,000 dollars and not a penny more."

The buyers shook hands and clapped shoulders—champagne was poured. "As much as I would love to celebrate this momentous occasion," Mr. Babcock said, "we do have some pressing matters to attend to. Let us get right down to business before the champagne affects our better judgment. Are the additional documents ready, Major Chase?"

"Indeed! I have your articles of incorporation for the Coronado Beach Company, Coronado Ferry Company, Coronado Water Company, the Coronado Railroad Company, Coronado Brick Company, and finally the Coronado Beach Stables." Major Chase produced the documents from his leather attaché case and placed them on the desk.

"Excellent! Your organizational skills are second to none," Mr. Babcock said. "We are ready to sign these here and now. In particular, the Coronado Beach Stables, as I've taken the liberty to hire someone. Good fellow, Hennessey is his name—he arrives from Indiana next week with his family." Mr. Story and Mr. Gruendike signed their names below his. "Now, for our second order of business, our task list, which is rather long. We'll need to clean up the island, remove the shrubbery, then map out the streets and assign names to them." Mr. Babcock rolled out an empty map of the peninsula on a nearby table. A red X marked the spot for the proposed hotel site. "What do you think gentlemen, street names by numbers or letters?"

"Both," replied Mr. Gruendike.

"I prefer straight streets, personally," admitted Mr. Babcock, "for ease of navigation."

"I prefer irregular streets like spokes on a wheel," Mr. Story offered.

"Then I suggest we incorporate both straight and irregular streets. We can even name streets for the trees that line them, which would be quite appealing." Mr. Babcock took his pen and began marking up the map. "Here's a logical place for our ferry landing, directly across the bay from San Diego. We could have our main street running from here straight to our hotel." He drew a long, straight line connecting the two points. "But we shouldn't call it Main Street, that's far too common, and what should we plant along it? Something edible and delicious?"

"Oranges grow very nicely in this region," suggested Mr. Story.

"Very well, Orange Avenue will be our main street, and we'll plant citrus trees on either side for its entire length. Our guests can pluck oranges right from the trees if they like!" Mr. Babcock drew a grid, and the gentlemen agreed upon First Street through Tenth Street, which ran perpendicular to Orange Avenue. The parallel streets they approved to be alphabetical, from A to K Avenues, and Mr. Babcock marked them as such.

"It would be nice to have a few diagonal streets as well. We could plant olive trees and palm trees and name them each accordingly." Mr. Gruendike said, pointing at the map. "Perhaps here."

"Very well, done!" Mr. Babcock added the additional streets to the map with a few strokes of his pen.

"And over here would be ideal for Adella and Isabella Avenues, closer to our hotel," suggested Mr. Story, tapping the map with his pen.

"Another ideal choice." Mr. Babcock scribbled down the names. "We'll line them with roses and every sort of lovely flower. The ladies will be delighted." He flashed a radiant smile, his mind racing with excitement.

"And what of this one?" Mr. Gruendike pointed to a small, curving lane with no name attached to it.

"Any suggestions?" Mr. Babcock asked.

"Now that I think of it," Mr. Story replied, his eyes twinkling with amusement, "the workers made a street request. It seems there's a gentleman from Long Beach who has a lovely daughter named Tolita, with whom they are quite besotted."

Mr. Babcock tapped his pen to his chin thoughtfully before answering in an earnest tone. "Never underestimate the importance of a muse," he said. The men laughed. "Any objections to Tolita Avenue?" No objection was raised, so Tolita was added to the map.

"Moving right along, we will also need a railway line coming through the center of town to bring our building supplies and future guests." Mr. Babcock drew heavy double lines to show where the tracks should be. When the map was completed, the men agreed upon it and set about creating lots to sell at auction.

"Any word on the arrival of Colonel Holabird, our advertising genius?" Mr. Babcock asked Mr. Story.

"He's due to town next week," Mr. Story replied. You'll know when he's arrived. He's a colorful fellow, hard to miss."

"I think we should have him advertise our lovely daily temperatures in the New England papers." The men laughed.

"How about this . . ." Mr. Story said, raising his hands. "A brochure that states: 'A spot on Earth where doctors have little employment, where all year is summer and every day has sunshine and gentle, balmy breezes.'"

"Poignant and poetic," admitted Mr. Babcock.

"What about this," suggested Mr. Gruendike, "We could list what there is and what there is *not*. For instance, we could start by stating what there is not: malaria, hay fever, a heated term or cold snap, or any languor in the air whatsoever." The men mulled this over.

"A little dour, but I like it nonetheless." Mr. Babcock scribbled down the idea in his notebook.

"Pray tell us, Gruendike, what is on the There Is list," insisted Mr. Story.

"The most equitable climate in the world, cool nights, and plenty of sunshine."

"Both lists are excellent," said Mr. Babcock, "Let us flesh out our brochure and have Colonel Holabird distribute copies to as many newspapers and cities as we can possibly reach. He should do so as soon as possible. And we'll continue to update our brochure regularly."

"Babcock, you haven't shared with us your plan to overcome our lack of lumber and labor force?" Mr. Gruendike said. "Most laborers are already committed to building projects in San Diego."

"Ah yes, you are quite right. The solution is that we'll simply bring down additional laborers from Northern California by train. We'll import the Chinese, who so skillfully laid our railway lines across the country, and also gather any local men in need of work. There are plenty of craftsmen in Old Town and at the Mission de Alcalá."

"And what of the lumber shortage?" asked Mr. Story.

"The lumber will have to be brought in as well. They have massive quantities of redwood and pine in Northern California. Since we will need an extraordinary amount, perhaps we can float it down the Pacific on large rafts."

"Are we to expect day laborers to know how to build a hotel? I would imagine the skills for laying rail lines are markedly different than those required to construct a hotel."

"Quite right," Mr. Babcock conceded. "They will have to acquire the skills necessary as they progress." Undaunted, he smiled confidently. "I have in mind that we should first build a boathouse to resemble our hotel, on a much smaller scale, of course. Our builders can then apply what they learn to the construction of our hotel."

Mr. Gruendike whistled. "You lack an aversion for risk, Babcock. To be sure!"

Mr. Babcock took this as a compliment. "I am of the belief that determination and optimism can turn a dream into something real—and magnificent. Notwithstanding obstacles, and there will be many, we can prevail. There are no precedents here, gentlemen. We are the innovators, and our steadfast conviction will be the order of the day."

Mr. Story agreed, adding, "Along with a boathouse, we should build an interim pavilion along the shore. A place where we can host parties to bring in potential land buyers, thereby providing a location from which to observe the construction. Adella suggested we procure an orchestra and promote symphony and dancing."

Mr. Babcock ran his fingers over his mustache. "That is a capital idea! I had not thought of that. Please encourage the ladies to continue making suggestions—we are open to all of them."

The gentlemen adjourned their meeting, thanking Major Chase for the use of his office and legal expertise. They placed their hats on their heads, buttoned their long coats, and stepped out into the sunshine. "Say, Babcock, what of any language barriers among the laborers?" asked Mr. Gruendike. "You mentioned mixing locals from Old Town and the mission, in addition to the Chinese. Mixing Spanish, Mandarin, and Kumeyaay dialects will be highly complicating."

"Not to worry, good man, we'll just show them a sketch and let them go to it."

Mr. Gruendike gaped, until he realized Mr. Babcock was jesting. Mr. Story burst into full-bellied laughter.

"I assure you, communication is the least of our barriers," Mr. Babcock added. "It will be easier to pull jackrabbits from our hats than execute our plan, but fear not—solutions to problems will materialize as needed. We are going to make history, gentlemen. Our hotel *will* be the finest the world has ever seen."

"With you at the helm, I'm certain we can build this resort *whilst* pulling jackrabbits from our hats," joked Mr. Gruendike.

The men were still laughing when they climbed into their carriage. "Good day at the office?" Gus asked.

"An excellent day at the office, Gus. Couldn't have been better." Mr. Babcock beamed at the driver. *Whatever you can do, or dream you can, begin it,* he thought, and they had only just begun. How they would pay for it all remained a mystery, but he'd never felt more optimistic.

CHAPTER 6

Ava was bored to tears. It was the fourth day of their journey, and she was out of books to read. She had tried to find Nathan a few times, but nobody answered when she knocked on the door to his cabin. She found this troubling but vowed to try again the following day. *What else is there to do? Except die of boredom or watch Lydia and Owen squabble.*

Having read the few the novels she'd brought, she picked up a collection of poems in *A Child's Garden of Verses* by Robert Louis Stevenson. In the table of contents her eyes rested on a title called "Good and Bad Children." Mildly interested, she flipped to the page and began reading:

Children you are very little,
And your bones are very brittle;
If you would grow great and stately,
You must try to walk sedately.

You must still be bright and quiet,
And content with simple diet;
And remain, through all bewild'ring,
Innocent and honest children.

I can write better than this, Ava thought, unimpressed. She closed the book, sighing. *Children* didn't rhyme with *bewild'ring* at all, and she didn't like the poem's message. Father gave her a pitying look and suggested she play her violin on the caboose of the train. "You shouldn't disturb any passengers back there."

"I think I'll do that. Anything is better than taking another nap." She gathered her violin, leaving the sheet music behind, and left the cabin.

Walking along the corridor, she braced herself against the sway of the train car, tucking her violin case under one arm. She couldn't help but peek into the windows of other cabins. *After all, they could have drawn the curtains if they wanted privacy.* Ladies sat knitting or reading from leather-bound books, which they held far from their gaze with one hand. Others sipped tea. Gentlemen read the daily newspaper purchased from the paperboy who had hopped aboard at the last station. "Extra! Extra! Read all about it! Five cents a paper! Extra!" the boy hollered up and down the corridors, jumping off the train just as the whistle blew and the pistons started pumping again.

Ava was surprised to see the door to Nathan's cabin door was ajar, and she felt a jolt of excitement. "Nathan?" she called tentatively, nudging the door open a little. There was no reply and no sign of Nathan. The ostriches watched her with dark, unreadable eyes under their oddly long lashes. Ava hurried away, fearful of the strange creatures although they were locked up in pens. She made her way to the caboose.

Once she reached the caboose, a feeling of freedom washed over her. The landscape had changed dramatically from the lush greenery of Indiana to the desolate desert of Nevada. Jagged mountains loomed in the distance, speckled in the afternoon light like a rainbow trout in shades of chocolate, vanilla, and peach. The air was dry and the sun bright in a cloudless sky. *How can something as barren as the desert be so beautiful?* she wondered. There wasn't a single flower or tree to be seen, just an occasional hardy shrub clinging to life. A hawk soared overhead in a wide, slow circle. Ava watched its shadow glide over the earth, its shape shifting in sync with variations in the terrain. She feared for the little critter that would lose resolve and bolt from its hiding spot, becoming the hawk's prey.

She leaned over the brass railing of the caboose and looked out over the tracks. To think that countless laborers had nailed every wooden beam so evenly into place was unimaginable—yet there the tracks were, stretching as far as she could see. Father had called the beams crossties and said there were over thirty-five hundred of them per mile of railroad track. Only the day before, the conductor had given Owen an iron spike, and they all had marveled at its weight and size. Ava couldn't imagine the strength it took to drive a single spike into the earth, or whose miserable job it was to lay all the crushed stones beneath the beams that held the tracks in place. She had to admit, she was as impressed by locomotives as her brother was. The rhythmic *chug-chug* of the smokestack reminded her of a metronome clicking along at an accelerated pace.

Feeling inspired, Ava knelt down, placing her case on the caboose floor. She opened it, taking her violin out, and stood, leaning against the railing for stability. She placed the bow across the strings, sweeping downward with a fluid motion. She wiggled her fingers with vibrato. She began playing "The Butterfly" just as Miss Bosworth had instructed her. Something about the lonely desert pulled the song out of her, and she played the first half with few errors. She switched songs when it became too difficult, vowing to master the technical measures of the song at another time.

"That was really beautiful, Miss Ava," a voice said from above. Startled, Ava looked up to the roof of the caboose and saw Nathan's head popping over the edge. He smiled down at her.

"What are you doing up there, Nathan, and where have you been? I've been looking for you."

"Ah, you know . . . hiding from Twilah. I come up here to think."

Ava couldn't help but grin back at him. Nathan had such a funny way about him.

"Come on up," he said, motioning toward the ladder.

"Is it safe up there? Will I tear my stockings? My mother will be sore with me if I do. She wants me to look like a proper young lady when we arrive."

"Sure, it's safe. Just duck if we go under something low. I can't make any promises about your stockings, though."

35

Ava handed her violin case up to him and ascended the ladder. It was gusty on the roof, and the tremor of the train rattled her every bone. To the front of the train, Ava counted thirty train cars wiggling as the locomotive pulled them along, pumping an endless stream of thick gray smoke from its stack. She sat beside Nathan, tucking her long, gray skirt beneath her feet. He gave her a reassuring smile. She was glad to be on the roof, although she was certain her parents wouldn't approve. Perhaps she wouldn't tell them.

Nathan motioned for her to play again, and she obliged him. He pretended to play an imaginary fiddle while she linked everything she could remember about playing into one song. Every time she made a screeching error, she would cringe and he would laugh. "It's still music, isn't it?" he yelled. "Doesn't have to be perfect!" Ava played until she ran out of songs to play, even partial ones. She put her violin back in its case, and they watched the desert stretch out around them. Nathan pointed to a roadrunner racing across the desert floor, and they watched the hawk swoop down to the earth, pinning down its prey with its talons under wings opened wide. Ava pouted, making Nathan laugh. "It is lunchtime, right?" he said. "Let's head back down—it's getting too warm up here."

Nathan led, and Ava followed him down the ladder.

"Would you like to join my family for lunch?" Ava asked as they looked out over the tracks.

"Nah, my pop and I have some work to do. Next stop is home, you know?"

"I know. I'm so excited I can't stand it! I can't wait to swim in the ocean."

"Can you swim well?"

"Not very well, no. There was a creek by our house, but it was freezing cold most of the year. We went to a river a few times each summer, but I never really got good at swimming."

"You best be careful," Nathan warned. "The ocean waves will be bigger than you are. We can't have you getting carried out to sea."

"How would I get carried out to sea?"

"Rip current."

"*Rip current?* I've never heard of such a thing. Does it rip you apart?"

He laughed. "No, it doesn't rip you apart! A rip current is a strong current that pulls you out deeper in the ocean and makes it hard for you to swim in to shore." Ava gaped at him, horrified. "Just remember this, if you're caught in a rip, swim parallel to the beach and you'll break free," Nathan warned. "Everybody panics and tries to swim straight in, but it just wears them out. People drown trying to swim through a rip current. My pop told me all about it."

"What a horrible way to go."

"It is." He grew serious. "I probably just saved your life."

"You did *not* just save my life!" She swatted him playfully on the arm and he burst into laughter, his brown eyes twinkling.

Suddenly, the breaks began to squeal and the train shuddered hard. Nathan grabbed onto Ava's arm so she wouldn't lose her balance. "Why are we stopping?" she exclaimed. "We're in the middle of nowhere!"

They leaned over the railing as the train came to a full stop. The locomotive hissed and steam vented upward from the stack and outward from the wheels. Passengers peeked curiously from open windows and leaned from doorways. Minutes passed without an explanation.

"Well, that may have something to do with it," Nathan said, pointing along the track to where a small railcar was fast approaching. "It looks like it's trying to catch up with us."

Ava began to panic, clutching her violin case protectively. "Are they bandits? What do we do?" she cried.

"Don't worry," Nathan assured her, putting his hand on her shoulder to settle her. "Bandits wouldn't chase us in a car that fancy."

He was right. As the railcar approached, Ava could see it was sparkling new—blue, with swirling gold embellishments and gleaming brass trim. A single-engine locomotive pushed from behind, and the car came to a stop when it reached them. They had an up-close view as two train technicians quickly hitched the fancy car with an iron coupler to the hook at the bottom of the caboose. The technicians then signaled the engineer, who blew the whistle and put the train back in motion. Pistons pumped and metal shrieked as the wheels ground slowly forward again.

"Well, how do you like that? They just added another car to our train," Nathan said, amazed. "You have to be important for them to do that for you."

"Why didn't they just attach to us back at the last station?" Ava asked.

"They were probably running late, and they can afford to run late—that's a Pullman sleeping car. Finest train cars ever made. People pay the railway companies to couple onto big trains so they can travel across the country in luxury. I have a friend back home, Reginald—he told me all about Pullman cars. Boy, would he love to see this one. She's a real beauty!"

A curtain rose in the window of the Pullman car, and three people peered out. A woman wearing a flowerpot hat stood in the center. Next to her was a blond-haired boy in a pale suit. He looked to be in his early teens. His hair was parted neatly to the side and slicked down with wax. Next to him stood an older girl, perhaps his sister. Her blonde hair was swept up in a loose chignon. She wore the sour expression of one who was easily bored and not easily impressed.

Ava waved at them and the woman balked, reaching for the curtain pull. The blond boy stepped toward the window, studying Ava and Nathan with quick interest until the curtains dropped.

"Well, that was very rude!" Ava scoffed." Why are they so unfriendly?"

"We're nothing to folks like them. Don't let it hurt your feelings. I don't," Nathan said. Ava huffed, feeling slighted.

A gruff, inpatient voice called from a cabin window, and Nathan's smile faded. "That's my pop. I guess I better get on back to work. I really liked your music," he said. "See you in California?"

"Thank you . . . and yes, see you in California. Unless you do your disappearing act again." Nathan flashed a crooked smile.

Ava watched him go, sad that they had to abandon the fresh air. It had done wonders to lift her spirits, in spite of the awful occupants of the Pullman car. She studied the car one last time, looking for any motion behind the curtains. Seeing nothing, she turned and stepped into the caboose. A small corner of the curtain fell back into place. The blond boy had been watching.

CHAPTER 7

The evening sky glowed from small, blazing fires on the island across the bay. Those walking along the waterfront wondered what was afoot. *Who is cleaning away the brush on the island? And for what purpose?* It was a mystery that grew with each passing day, making it into the local newspaper, the *San Diego Union*. Word began to spread that the island had been purchased and something extraordinary was to be built. When an architect from Indiana came to town, a Mr. James Reid, who let a room at the Brooklyn-Kahle Saddlery, the mystery intensified. Then two train cars arrived, carrying Chinese laborers from Oakland. Shrouded in mystery, they promptly boarded a private yacht and were transported across the bay. The dockhands reported that the yacht was the steamship *Della*, owned by Mr. Hampton Story, formerly of Story and Clark Piano Company. None of this made any sense, so the narrative lit like a match in a haystack. Articles in the newspaper were updated daily, climbing from page three to a headline on page one.

Building materials and tools arrived by train cars that pulled up to the end of the wharf; barges transported their cargo to the island. Laborers came and went, housed in small white tents that popped up in the cleared fields. It wasn't unusual for a train car to be filled with laborers speaking Chinese, Spanish, English, and Native American dialects. *A common language* was listed on the There Is Not page in Mr. Babcock's notebook. Still, he was undeterred.

Before long, the citizens of San Diego could see a ferry landing under construction across the bay. There were whispers of a magnificent hotel being built there, but nothing had been publicly stated or confirmed. The buzz around town was just what Mr. Babcock had hoped for.

&⸰⸱

Mr. James Reid, a young man of sturdy build, left his hotel room and walked down Market Street with a white scroll tucked under his arm. He weaved through several young ladies out for a day of shopping, tipping his hat to each of them. "Good day, ladies," he said. They giggled bashfully at the handsome stranger, hiding their smiles behind their gloved hands. He halted a carriage on Fifth Street so a mother pushing a pram could safely cross.

"And such a gentleman," one lady whispered to another, who quickly agreed. Mr. Reid had become the subject of great interest since his arrival, particularly among the single ladies in town. Public sightings of him were discussed at length over tea.

The ladies watched Mr. Reid walk to the office of Major Levi Chase, attorney-at-law, knock on the door, and enter, removing his bowler hat.

"Ah yes, our architect has arrived at last! Welcome! May I take your coat, James?" Mr. Babcock said eagerly. Mr. Reid's coat and hat were hung, and he was ushered to a seat around an oblong table were a number of gentlemen waited. Mr. Babcock made introductions and the meeting commenced.

"What we have in mind is something extraordinary," Mr. Babcock began. "In the Queen Anne Revival style, but unlike anything you've ever designed before. It is to be the largest hotel in the world." Mr. Babcock stretched his arms wide in a show of great dimension.

"Tell me everything you're thinking." Mr. Reid said, taking out a charcoal pencil from his pocket and unfurling the white scroll on the table.

"We are looking for a design that is asymmetrical, whimsical, and fantastical—something that will delight the eye!" Mr. Babcock sat up in his

chair, his expression passionate. "We want turrets with little dormers, and tall towers, and cupolas of all sizes.
We'd like every bedroom to have a private bathroom, and as many rooms as possible to be ocean facing. We'd like to have a number of verandas that overlook the water, and a large, round ballroom lined with windows for a full ocean view."

Mr. Reid began sketching rapidly. "Keep talking. Just let the ideas flow."

"We plan for our resort be the very first hotel to have a sprinkler system for fire prevention and the first with running electricity," Mr. Story added.

Mr. Reid paused from sketching. "Can we do that?"

"We've already asked the world's preeminent expert on the matter, Mr. Thomas Edison," Mr. Story confirmed.

"Oh yes, of course, the creator of the light bulb. I know all about his work. Fascinating man," Mr. Reid replied.

"Mr. Edison believes it's a brilliant idea. Pun intended, of course." The men laughed. Mr. Story continued, "Most hotels burn to the ground by accidents from their gas lines. Mr. Edison believes we might be able to run electrical lines through the gas lines, decreasing the risk of fire with the added benefit that should the electricity fail, we will have the traditional gas line system as an alternative."

"And by what manner do you intend to produce the power?" Mr. Reid inquired.

"We are already building a steam-powered station to supply enough electricity to serve the entire island," Mr. Gruendike reported. "With the ability to power lights, we can structure our laborers to work day and night, in shifts, thereby wasting no time for construction."

"Will you be using Edison's current, or his rival, Tesla's? A terrible feud is brewing over currents as we speak," Mr. Reid commented.

Mr. Babcock cleared his throat, "Tesla hasn't filed for patents yet, but they say the tests on his alternating current are showing promise."

"You still have time. I've heard the AC current might be safer than

DC, anyhow. How many rooms?" Mr. Reid returned to his sketching.

"Three to four hundred. Give or take," Mr. Babcock replied.

"Materials?"

"Red shingles for the roof, white wooden tiles for the rest. Oregon pine and redwood, maybe even some Douglas fir."

Mr. Reid looked thoughtfully at the ceiling, rolling the charcoal pencil in his fingers while he let his imagination flow. He began sketching more rapidly, making erratic strokes on the page.

"We'd also like a central courtyard," Mr. Babcock added, "where we can plant a tropical garden. We've already contacted the renowned horticulturalist, Miss Kate Sessions, who will see to it that we have an amazing collection of exotics."

"And the projected cost for the project?" Mr. Reid didn't so much as glance up as he sketched.

"We will spare no expenses. Whatever you need to secure the finest materials, you will get. There will be no finer establishment than our resort, Mr. Reid. We will be importing the best management, staff, glassware from Belgium, linens from Scotland, china from Paris. The menu will be exquisite, the service second to none. If we hope to draw patrons from all over the world, our hotel has to be spectacular and nothing less."

"I would agree." Mr. Reid moved his pencil in a circular motion, using his thumb to smudge the lines here and there. After he had sketched intensely for a few more minutes, his brows relaxed and he blew away charcoal dust from the page. "How about something like this?" He raised the sketch for the men to see. They leaned forward in their chairs, taking in the design. Mr. Babcock's eyes grew wide and then narrowed as he scrutinized the sketch. A slow, triumphant smile widened across his face. "That's it! That's more or less what I had in mind. *More* in fact!"

"It's marvelous!" Mr. Story declared. Mr. Gruendike gaped.

Pleased with the men's positive reactions, Mr. Reid placed the sketch on the desk them to further peruse. "This is obviously just a preliminary sketch. With more time, I can go into finer detail."

The sketch showed a tall, sweeping structure with several floors, numerous windows, balconies, towers of differing heights, and a great round room topped with a massive turret studded with dormers. The adjacent ocean was depicted by four squiggly lines.

Mr. Babcock reached out to Mr. Reid for a congratulatory handshake. "I knew you were the man for the job. How on earth did you capture my imagination so perfectly?"

"I could clearly see it. I'd be honored to take the job if you find me a suitable fit."

"The position is yours!" bellowed Mr. Babcock after the others nodded their agreement.

"How much time do I have? My brother Merritt and I are just finishing up a hotel in San Francisco—not to worry it's a small one, not a competitor to yours," Mr. Reid said. The men chuckled heartily.

"We won't need you on-site right away, but we're hoping you can begin designing as soon as possible. We still have to section the lots and prepare them for auction. We hope to have the auction by fall and start building shortly after."

"Complete architectural plans take time. Will you need finished plans to begin?"

"No," Mr. Babcock replied.

"And if construction outpaces the development of our design plans?"

"Then we improvise."

Mr. Reid smiled—he liked Mr. Babcock's spontaneity. "Very well. I can work within those parameters so long as we have a mutual understanding."

"We do," replied Mr. Babcock. "The Southern California land boom is now, and we need to capitalize on this opportunity without a moment's delay. We do, however, wish to proceed with proper order. We wouldn't want to 'put the cart before the horse' as they say."

"Haste makes waste," agreed Mr. Reid. "Might I make a suggestion?" The men nodded. "It is my understanding that your laborers are unskilled, and the turnover rate is high. Is this the case?"

"To be honest with you, yes, they are unskilled at present, and the turnover is very high. But I've found a solution to keep our workers on the job," Mr. Babcock confessed.

"Pray tell me! What is the solution? We have a similar issue in San Francisco."

"Beer." The gentlemen erupted into laughter. "No, really," Mr. Babcock insisted. "At the end of every day, we allow the workers one glass of beer. Needless to say, they have been highly satisfied with their current place of employment." Mr. Babcock grinned impishly. "Might I remind you that we are to be a moral community, however, desperate measures are required in cases such as these." The men continued laughing.

"I shall not draw a line in the sand," Mr. Reid replied. "On past projects with intricate architectural designs, the builders begin with the simple side first. Might I suggest we do the same? By the time the laborers reach the heavily detailed design plans, they usually have become quite proficient."

"Great minds think alike!" agreed Mr. Babcock. "We have discussed the very thing and determined the need for a boathouse to service our hotel as the solution. Perhaps you can design the boathouse first, preferably in the same fashion as our hotel, and we can use it as a template of sorts."

"That would be an ideal way to begin," said Mr. Reid.

"And by all means, please feel free to share any pearls of wisdom you have garnished with us, Mr. Reid. As you know, none of us have any construction experience."

"I run a cattle ranch back in Oregon," piped in Mr. Gruendike. "Unfortunately, I have plans to return soon, so expect me to be a very silent partner in this venture. I trust your decisions on my behalf."

"And I was in the piano business of all things!" added Mr. Story. "I thought I had retired."

Mr. Reid chuckled heartily.

"Fifty is too young for retirement," Mr. Babcock chided Mr. Story. "Don't hear a word of it, Reid. If Story's wife allowed for it, he'd be traveling the back roads of America on foot!"

"It's still on my list to do, should I live long enough. Providing this hotel isn't the end of me," replied Mr. Story.

"Oh nonsense!" said Mr. Babcock good-naturedly.

Mr. Reid was amused by their friendly banter. "I daresay your vision for this hotel exceeds anything I've ever seen. One need not experience if one has the determination to see the thing through."

"No dream has ever been met, nor accomplished, hindered by fear," Mr. Babcock added.

"Who said that?" Mr. Story looked at him, puzzled. "I've never heard that one before."

"I just made it up. I'm still working on the verbiage." The room erupted into laughter again.

"Then shall we have Major Chase draw up a contractual agreement?" suggested Mr. Babcock, returning to the matter at hand.

"I am most eager to begin this project," admitted Mr. Reid. "I'll get the boathouse designs to you as soon as possible. Afterwards, I'll start designing the hotel. Merritt and I will plan to relocate here to commence with construction after the land auction."

"That sounds like an ideal course of action." Mr. Story said. "We'll have the auction after summer."

"When are we going to share our secret with the world?" asked Mr. Gruendike.

"Not yet . . . but soon." Mr. Babcock replied. "Let's let our resort's intrigue build a while longer. Do we have an update on our brochure?"

Mr. Gruendike flipped through his notes. "Yes, here it is, in the What There Is list, I've added: *perfectly pure water*—since we will soon have it piped in, and also, *perfect sanitation*."

"And in the There Is Not list?"

"*Any loss of appetite or sleeplessness*."

"Excellent additions. I do so enjoy your word choices," said Mr. Babcock, "Has Colonel Holabird arrived yet?"

"Had a slight delay in Phoenix, but due in tomorrow," replied Mr. Story, shrugging.

"Odysseus made better time. Very well. Soon enough, we will start a national advertising campaign, creating demand before we've even broken ground."

Major Chase presented the legal documents to retain the services of Mr. Reid, and all the men signed the contract.

"Did you know that genius has boldness, and power and magic in it?" Mr. Babcock asked Mr. Reid as he signed his name.

"No, I did not."

"Yours again?" Mr. Story asked, raising his eyebrows in response to Mr. Babcock's words.

"Johann Wolfgang von Goethe. I've quoted him before, Hampton, do try to remember."

"He was my obvious second choice," Mr. Story said sarcastically.

"You see, retirement doesn't suit you, Hampton. Look at what you'd be missing? I'll loan you my book of inspirational quotes. It's highly transformative."

"Making your acquaintance has been all the transformation I need, Mr. Babcock," he quipped.

Mr. Babcock laughed at this, before changing the subject. "Are we fishing this evening?"

"Absolutely," Mr. Story replied.

"I'm out," said Major Chase, "I have a dinner engagement."

"Count me in," said Mr. Gruendike. "I'd like to reel in one more beast before I return to Oregon."

"Care to join us, Mr. Reid?" Mr. Babcock asked.

"I thank you but no, I'm catching the afternoon train to San Francisco. As soon as I can wrap up that project, I'm all yours."

"Perhaps next time, then. We are thrilled you are joining our team and anxiously await your creation."

"I will think of nothing else. I'll have the boathouse plans to you by the end of this month, or by early February at the latest."

"Splendid."

When the gentlemen departed the office, a number of young ladies stood idly by across the street. They peeked from under their parasols, giggling among themselves.

"I believe this gathering is on your account, Mr. Reid," Mr. Babcock suggested.

"San Diego girls certainly are lovely," he admitted with a wide grin.

"Do we need a Reid Avenue on our island?" teased Mr. Story. "And why is there no demand for Story Street?" The gentlemen laughed.

"My wife tells me I get more handsome with each passing day," joked Mr. Babcock. "A reflection of the effect of San Diego sunshine and fresh air on one's disposition—perhaps affecting her more than me."

"Are you reading quotes from Narcissus, Babcock?" Mr. Story bantered.

"Casanova." The men looked shocked. "I'm teasing, gentlemen! I would not entertain such moral depravity."

Before the men parted ways, Mr. Babcock tasked Mr. Story and Mr. Gruendike with a challenge for their next meeting: determining a name for their hotel. "If we can't reach a consensus, we'll put the issue in the newspaper and let the public decide. It's a fantastic way to stoke the fire of interest among the populace, as well as gain a suitable name."

Mr. Babcock could not have known that putting the decision to the citizens would cause untold consternation—and fail miserably.

CHAPTER 8

Ava, Owen, and Lydia pressed against the window as the train slowed to a stop at the depot. They could see the blue water of the bay beyond the station. "Oh, look—I see the Pacific!" Ava exclaimed.

"Not yet, that's San Diego Bay," Father corrected her. "Do you see that island across the water? We're going to take a ferry over to it. The Pacific is on the other side."

"Yes, I see it, but it doesn't look like an island. It's so flat." Ava furrowed her eyebrows.

"The northern end is an island, but the rest is a peninsula."

"Ah, so it's connected to the mainland. But there aren't any buildings or houses," Ava noted. "I only see tents."

"It's brand-new," Father explained. "Isn't it exciting to be here from the very beginning?" The children nodded, wide-eyed with excitement.

The whistle shrieked, the train hissed, and smoke from the stack billowed as the train sputtered to a stop. A second whistle blew, signaling for passengers to disembark at the station, which was small and partially under construction. Father checked his timepiece, then slipped it back into his coat pocket. "I need to find Mr. Babcock and get our permits. Go ahead and take a look around. Walk down to the wharf but stay together."

San Diego was a sprawling and clean city, with tall buildings made of new, bright red bricks. The children crossed Broadway, which was unpaved and rutted with tracks from horses and carriages that moved along it. Shops lined either side of the street, promoting their wares in display windows under striped awnings. Finely dressed gentlemen and ladies strolled along the sidewalk, milling about to peer in windows and venturing inside if enticed. Scaffolding for new construction lined Atlantic Street, which ran along the waterfront. The city pulsed with energy that stemmed from growth and promise. Father said San Diego had gone from a sleepy seaport town to a burgeoning metropolis, virtually overnight. It was a city in boom and its citizens were in good spirits, living comfortably on more than luck. Ava had only just arrived and already she decided she liked San Diego very much.

The children reached the wharf and looked out over the water. Tall ships tilted from wind in their sails as they crossed the bay that was shaped like an hourglass—narrow in the center with bulbous ends. Ava could see the barren island they would soon call home. Smoke trails rose from the land. She guessed it was less than a mile across the water, less if you measured from the end of the piers.

"I count nine sails on that ship!" Owen exclaimed, pointing to one of the larger vessels. "And they are raising up another sail. I think it's a schooner."

"It looks like a schooner to me," Lydia agreed, squinting to temper the sunshine.

"How do you know what a schooner is?" Owen asked.

"I don't. I just like to say it. *Schooner.*" She giggled.

"Or is it brigantine?" Ava suggested. "What's the difference between a schooner and a brigantine anyway?"

"I think it has to do with the number of masts they have," Owen replied. "Some have two or three—also the type of sail. Some sails are square and others are like long triangles. We'll have to ask Father. I know it isn't a sloop. Sloops only have one mast."

"*Sloop!*" Lydia repeated, giggling again, "I like sloops better than schooners. Sloop! Sloop!" She skipped happily, the sun shining through her bouncing blonde hair.

They watched the ships for the next hour, fascinated by the manner in which they traversed the bay. They could see sailors duck under the boom when it swung across the deck, before the sails bulged with wind again. When a ship changed course, the sailors hustled, pulling in thick lines. Ava could have watched all afternoon, but Mother came to fetch them and they had to return to the station.

They passed the Pullman car along the way. It had been disconnected from the caboose of their train and sat alone on a separate track. The door was open. Ava slowed her pace so she could peek inside without her mother's notice. The car looked vacant, and she could see a platter of purple grapes on a small, round table. *How could anyone leave those behind?* she wondered. She fell farther behind, letting her siblings and Mother walk ahead. She could see her father removing a damaged wheel from a carriage. She had a little time . . .

Ava slipped into the Pullman car, climbing the stairs nervously. She knew she shouldn't be doing this, but she had to see it for herself. Nathan had said it was the finest train car ever made. An acanthus pattern swirled in the lush green carpet that lined the parlor floor. Everything sparkled, shined, and smelled like new—with a hint of cigar. Damask curtains were held open by golden rope ties with frayed tassels. A stately claw-foot sofa, fashioned from tufted and buttoned burgundy upholstery, stood against the parlor wall. A reading light was mounted above it. Beyond the parlor was a small dining table, with a crystal chandelier above. In the kitchen, cabinets of dark lacquered wood studded with gleaming brass handles lined the walls. An empty brandy snifter poked up from the sink.

Fascinated, Ava dared to venture farther. She had never seen such opulence, and she ran her fingers lightly over various items she passed. A master suite revealed a round bed covered by a floral quilt, as well as a vanity with a matching chair and gleaming mounted mirror. A silver hairbrush lay on the table next to a porcelain powder box with a ballerina figurine festooning its lid. Floral perfume hung heavy in the air. In the next room, twin sets of bunk beds lined the walls. Ava stepped inside, too enthralled to remember she was trespassing. She spun slowly around the room, her gaze falling on the blond-haired boy sleeping on a lower bunk.

Ava froze, not wanting to take another breath lest she wake him. *Why did they leave him here?* she thought, panicking. *Oh, I shouldn't have come!* But he looked so peaceful, she found herself stepping closer to him. His nose was straight, his lashes long, his lips finely formed. He looked like a sleeping angel. Ava watched him breathe in relaxed, even measures. Then he opened his eyes. Ava gasped, which caused him to notice her. They locked eyes. His were a piercing bright blue. "Hey!" he shouted but Ava was already fleeing from the beautiful Pullman car.

෧෯

"Ava, what kept you?" Mother asked.

"I had to lace my shoe." The explanation was a half-truth. Racing down the stairs from the train car, Ava had stepped on one shoelace and nearly tripped. Her fingers trembled as she yanked the two ends of the lace taught, tying them into a bow. The boy from the train had yelled after her, "Come back here!" But Ava ran, pulling up the hem of her long skirt.

Father loaded the horses, donkey, carriages, and their belongings onto a barge that would ferry them across the bay. As they pulled away from the dock, Ava glanced at the Pullman car, relieved that it looked still. She hoped the boy wouldn't report her for trespassing—and that she'd never see him again.

The ride to the island took a long time for such a short distance. Ava peered into the water, seeing her warped reflection on its glassy surface.

"Over there is Old Town," Father explained, pointing north of the city, where chimney smoke trailed into the sky. "San Diego is New Town."

When the barge bumped to a stop at the ferry landing the horses became restless, tossing their heads and sidestepping. Only the donkey was content to stare blankly ahead. Ava could smell smoke, and she saw bonfires burning near fields that had been cleared recently. The island was wider than she'd imagined, also dusty and flat. Not a single structure or tree stood upon it. It wasn't the island she had envisioned, with swaying coconut palm trees and crosswinds, but she wasn't disappointed.

"Father, where are we to live?" Owen asked. "There's nothing here."

"In a tent," Father replied.

❧❧

In a dirt field sat a square white tent, its flaps tethered open for windows. There was a firepit for cooking nearby, and a makeshift corral for the horses. Father pointed across the field to a group of laborers hammering planks of wood. "They're just beginning the framing for our stables, which should be completed in six months. Our home will be above the structure."

The children gaped. "They can build the stables that quickly?" Owen asked, looking doubtful.

"You'll see everything go up quickly here, my boy."

Movable canvas walls sectioned the tent into a living room, with three small sleeping quarters. The tent was simple but clean and new. Ava wondered where Nathan was going to live. She hoped his home would be nearby. She hadn't seen him depart from the station, and she wondered where he was as she unpacked the trunk filled with cooking utensils.

When everything was settled, Father took the children to explore the island. Mother stayed behind, preparing dinner. Two horses were saddled, but Ambrose was left saddleless. "Ava, leave Ambrose unsaddled," Father instructed. "A saddle won't take well to seawater. Owen, you ride Tina. Lydia will ride with me."

"Why do I always have to ride Tina?" Owen complained. "Tina's as old as the hills. I can ride Ambrose as well as Ava can," he grumbled, climbing into the saddle.

"Tina's not that old and she's steady," Ava replied, hopping up on Ambrose.

They cantered to the north end of the island along a shallow, stagnant body of water Father called the Spanish Bight. They followed it across the island. The land had been cleared of rocks, and blackened spots dotted the earth where vegetation had been scorched away. Small white flags protruded from the ground, marking lots where houses would be built.

They reached a narrow strip of land, not more than a hundred yards wide and bordered by water. "At high tide, this area gets submerged, creating North Island—you can see it there." Father pointed. "And across the channel is Point Loma." Ships passed through the channel entering the bay. Dotted among them were smaller vessels, each with a single, oddly shaped sail that looked like a square fan.

Lydia eyed the strange ships. "What are those?" she inquired.

"Those are *junks*," Father explained. There are a lot of Chinese here—you'll see them selling fish in the market."

Turning south, they halted to take in the view. The great, blue Pacific Ocean and a pristine white beach stretched out before them. Lydia shrieked. Ava held her breath. The view was more breathtaking than anything she had imagined. Waves barreled and washed upon the entire length of the beach. Just as one crested, another perfect wave formed behind it, crashing with a thunderous roar into a white mass of churning water. Ava marveled as the waves rolled upon the beach, pooled, then slipped back into the ocean. A brown pelican glided just above the water's surface, out beyond the waves where the water was smooth. The odd-looking bird rose, hovered in the air, and then dove headlong into the water below, tucking in its wings at the last instant. A splash erupted, and the pelican surfaced again, bobbing like a cork. It shook its head, gulped, and the lump in its beak disappeared down its gullet. Lydia was delighted. "How I love pelicans! Father, did you see it dive?"

"Yes, of course, dear." He laughed. "Ava, are you going to run that horse or not?" he asked, turning to her.

Ava grinned, realizing what he was allowing her to do. She loosened the reins and dug in her heels. Ambrose charged forward, racing down the beach. Ava leaned low, gripping his mane to keep the wind from unseating her. She giggled as he picked up speed, striding into a smooth gallop. She steered him to the water's edge. She felt free, light, untethered. She laughed into the wind, tasting salt in the spray that drenched her.

❧

At the far end of the beach, Ava raced by two gentlemen standing on a bluff. They were reading from a large map.

"Was that a young girl on a rather large stallion?" Mr. Story asked, turning to Mr. Babcock.

"Your eyes do not deceive you. I meant to tell you our stable staff arrived today."

"Capital! We must add that to our brochure at once."

"The stable staff?"

"No, the idea: a place where one may take a constitutional along the beach."

"I'd call that a mad dash rather than a constitutional."

"Are you suggesting it doesn't constitute a constitutional?" They laughed heartily. Mr. Story clarified, "We can include both: Take a constitutional, or enjoy a horseback ride at breakneck speed along the beach."

"Delightful! I'm quite certain you missed your calling selling pianos. You have a brilliant mind for marketing, you know?" Mr. Story laughed.

When the girl on the stallion passed again on her return, she grinned and waved. "Spritely little thing!" commented Mr. Babcock, raising his hand to wave back to her. "And so, our island has its first family. I could cry tears of joy!"

"First of many. Which reminds me, we should build a schoolhouse right here." Mr. Story pointed to a spot on the map. "A school will certainly draw families to the island."

"At Sixth and D? Excellent idea."

CHAPTER 9

"Mother, the Pacific is the most beautiful ocean on Earth! I know it's the only ocean I've ever seen—but wait until you see it! Ouch!" Ava yelped as her mother struggled to pull a comb through her hair. She sat in a chair before a small vanity with a mirror on a stand. Mother frowned in the mirror's reflection. "Good Lord, child! If I haven't told you a thousand times to wear your riding bonnet."

"Nobody wears riding bonnets anymore." Ava winced as her mother tugged at her tangled mess.

Lydia sat on the bed nearby, swinging her doll from side to side, lost in her imaginary world.

"Father says we can go swimming tomorrow."

Mother finished detangling and began braiding Ava's hair, tying a white ribbon to the end. "The horses need grooming first thing in the morning. We also need to polish the carriages and get them presentable for service. I'm going to the market, so I'll need you to watch Owen and Lydia, but once I return, you should have plenty of time for an afternoon swim."

Ava eyed herself in the mirror, her face drooping with disappointment. "Will you ask about my friend Nathan when you're in town?"

"Is there cause?"

"I'm just worried. I'm surprised I haven't seen him yet. Do you think his father changed their plans? Maybe they aren't moving here after all."

"I'm sure he'll turn up. It's best not to worry." Mother smiled at her reassuringly. "I'll inquire. It shouldn't be hard to find a boy with a dozen ostriches."

Ava brightened again. "Can he come to our school when it opens?"

"Of course. Every child will be welcome."

"Will there be enough children to open a school?"

"There will be soon enough. Isn't it exciting to be the first family?"

"I suppose so."

Mother frowned "You *suppose?*"

"You're right, I really love it here already. I'm never going back to Indiana, and I won't miss the snow. Not one day of it."

"Sunshine does wonders for the spirit. It's past your bedtime." Mother tucked Ava in next to Lydia, kissing each girl on the forehead before blowing out the candle.

Ava was tired but she couldn't sleep. She could hear the faint roar of the ocean. She imagined the days she would spend sitting on the beach, watching the waves swell and roll in. She liked the way the spray lifted off the top of cresting waves. She thought about rip currents, wondered about Nathan, and before long, she fell fast asleep.

ॐ

Ava awoke with a jolt. Morning light was shining through their tent. *Did the night pass so quickly?* She couldn't remember ever sleeping so soundly. Lydia was still sleeping, her doll-like face tranquil, her breathing even. Ava got up, dressed, and tiptoed out of the tent. She went about feeding the horses and donkey, then started polishing the brass handles on their finest carriage. Owen joined her, and when the work was done, they made breakfast for Lydia.

Father returned from town unexpectedly, telling them to ready their finest carriage and change into their Sunday-best clothing straightaway. Mr. Babcock and Mr. Story were coming to meet them. The girls hurriedly put on matching full-length blue dresses with a wide, white sash around the waste. They pulled on stockings, shoes, and white hats with blue ribbons that tied below their chins. Owen wore tan knickers, long socks, polished shoes, a tweed jacket, and a bowler. They were ready in minutes.

At the ferry landing, they waited as the *Della* docked, then watched as two finely dressed gentlemen disembarked.

"Mr. Babcock and Mr. Story, may I present to you my children," Father said, removing his hat respectfully. "My daughters, Ava, Lydia, and my son, Owen." He smiled proudly. "Ages twelve, four, and ten."

"Pleasure to make your acquaintances," said both men, shaking Owen's hand. The girls curtsied.

"Say, aren't you the young lady we saw riding so adeptly along the beach yesterday?" asked Mr. Babcock.

"Yes, sir, I am," Ava replied, her face lighting up. She liked him right away. He had a friendly way about him, and his eyes were warm and happy.

"We have never seen a young lady ride with such command! We were very impressed, weren't we, Story?"

Mr. Story agreed. "We'll certainly need your help when the island becomes populated."

Ava grinned. "I look forward, very much, to working for you at the stables."

"And what about you, Miss Lydia? Do you ride horses, too?" asked Mr. Story.

"I ride ponies, and I can pull a buggy behind my donkey all by myself."

"Did we not say we'd like to have a donkey-drawn-buggy to transport children, Babcock?"

"I believe we did. We were looking for someone who could do the job."

"I'm sorry, Mr. Babcock, but I already have a job," Lydia confessed.

'Lydia!" Ava blurted while Father coughed quickly into his fist.

"Is that so?" Mr. Babcock squatted down to Lydia's level, amused by her honest response. "I like your loyalty, young lady. Pray tell me, what is your current employment?"

"I'm going to feed treats to the horses and my donkey," she added matter-of-factly.

"Well, maybe if you have time—and if you want to, of course—you can do both."

Lydia's eyes lit up at the possibility. "And get a fair day's wage?"

"I believe it's only fair," Mr. Babcock admitted, winking at Father.

Ava turned to Lydia, her eyes boring into her, but Lydia took no notice of her sister's warning stare.

"Can I, Father?" Lydia asked.

"Lydia dear, I'm sure you can do both," Father managed to say.

"Fine, Mr. Babcock, I'll do it." she said.

"That settles it. The job is yours."

"But I need you to shake on it." Lydia stuck out her hand expectantly. Ava thought she would faint; Mother would be mortified. One at a time, the men solemnly shook Lydia's hand.

"I daresay this has been one of the toughest negotiations yet!" said Mr. Babcock with a hearty laugh. "Perhaps you will entertain hotel management for us one day."

"She would do a fine job of that, too, I assure you," Father interjected, wanting to move the conversation past his opinionated young daughter. He put his hand on Lydia's shoulder.

"As for you, Mr. Hennessey, can we count on you to help your sisters and assist your father as his right-hand man?" Mr. Babcock asked Owen.

"Absolutely, sir." Owen stood up tall, his face serious.

"Very well, you too are hired. Everyone will be paid hourly wages." Owen grinned sheepishly. "Thank you, sir."

"Now that we have our additional staff in place, let us get on with it, shall we? Mr. Story and I need to take a few more measurements," Mr. Babcock said. The gentlemen climbed into the carriage and Father closed the door behind them. He let Ava take the reins, and Lydia and Owen took seats on a bench meant for luggage at the rear of the coach.

"Miss Ava, please take us south, along Glorietta Bay, if you please."

"Yes, sir, Mr. Babcock!" She prodded the two horses forward.

Mr. Babcock pointed out where the boathouse, power station, and resort would be. They stopped along the way to let him place more markers in the sand. He pulled out a long chain from his satchel and took additional measurements, with Owen's help.

"How long is this chain, Mr. Babcock?" Owen asked curiously.

"Sixty-six feet, my boy. Invented by a farmer named Gunter. Ten chains make a furlong, eighty make a mile."

Mr. Babcock and Owen took a few more measurements while Mr. Story made corrections in a notebook. Then they returned to the carriage.

"What are your estimates for how long it will take to build the hotel?" Father asked.

"With a natural stone foundation, she'll go up quickly. We're hoping for one year," Mr. Babcock replied.

"Is that all?"

"It's all we can afford, by our estimates. We'll be building around the clock."

"Thus the need for a power station?" Father clarified.

"Precisely. Day and night, there will be no rest until the hotel is completed. We aim for greatness. Is there a quote for that, Story?"

"'Be not afraid of greatness,' from *Twelfth Night*."

"Was that not a love triangle following a shipwreck? Good heavens, no! Let us avoid Shakespearean tragedies at all costs."

"I believe it was classified as a comedy of sorts," Mr. Story said, correcting him

"All the more reason for avoidance!" The men burst into laughter. Ava didn't understand what they meant, but she found their friendly banter amusing all the same. She was already fond of both gentlemen and reluctant to return them to the ferry landing a short while later.

After Mr. Babcock and Mr. Story departed, Father announced they were all free to enjoy the late afternoon at the beach. Mother packed a picnic.

"Did you see Nathan?" Ava asked her mother.

"Nobody has. I'm sorry," she replied sympathetically.

"It's best not to worry unless I have to—you're right. Thank you for asking about him for me."

Ava changed into her swimming attire. It seemed odd to be putting on a dark dress, pantaloons, stockings, shoes, and a hat to swim in, but Mother insisted it was proper attire for a lady. *If not for the white stripes on my hem, I'd be fit for a funeral,* Ava thought.

When everyone was ready, they headed on foot to the beach. Mother unpacked the picnic basket, setting it and the food on a quilt she and Father had spread on the sand. Lydia began making sandcastles with a tin cup while Owen started digging a great hole in the sand. Ava walked to the ocean's edge and waded in up to her knees. Father reached for her hand. "No, I can do this," she said shakily, stepping in deeper up to her waist. The water was chilly, and something slippery scuttled away from beneath her shoe. *What was that? Maybe shoes and stockings aren't a bad idea,* she thought. Gathering courage, she took another step.

"I'm right here if you need me," Father said.

"I'm all right. I'm not afraid." Ava's voice trembled as she inched in deeper, hopping over smaller waves that nearly pushed her off balance. Before long, her shoes could no longer touch the sandy bottom. She began waving her arms in wide circles and kicking her legs. A wave built up, coming toward her. It surged, toppling her. Father caught hold of her hand, bringing her back up to the surface. Sputtering, she grabbed her hat just before it floated away.

"Hold your breath and duck under the waves," Father instructed as a larger wave approached. She dropped below it just as the wall of water started to curve over her. Below the surface, currents pulled her in all directions. She could feel the wave pass over, pulling her into a somersault. Tiny bubbles rose from her mouth, getting larger as they ascended. When she surfaced again, she was laughing and salt stung her eyes.

"Here's another one, duck!" Father warned. Ava's laughter turned into more bubbles that rippled along the sides of her face. She closed her eyes and let the wave roll over her again, tugging her by the hair.

After an exhausting "swim" Ava stretched out on the quilt, basking under the warm sun. She let her mind wander. *Where is Nathan?* Worry washed over her like the waves that had tumbled her. She couldn't shake the feeling that something bad had happened to him. But the sand beneath her blanket emanated a steady heat. And it wasn't long before Lydia's prattling, worry about Nathan, the sea gulls crying, and the crashing of waves blended together into one sound, lulling her to sleep.

CHAPTER 10

"Isabella, thank you for inviting us to dine with you this evening," Adella Story said. "We haven't had a chance to catch up. We need to talk about our husbands' latest preoccupation." She glanced out from the spacious dining room to the patio where the two men stood chatting.

"We should compare notes," Isabella Babcock replied, "This new resort has been quite diverting, and I daresay Elisha's health has improved considerably. He scarcely suffers from the maladies that plagued him before we moved here." On the dinner table, she lit two candelabras that flickered to life. Set between them was a floral bouquet that spilled onto a lace tablecloth studded with four place settings of delicate china bordered with rosebuds. Crystal stemware gleamed in the candlelight. Each silver spoon, fork, and knife had a cursive letter *B* engraved on its round, flattened handle. A fire raged in the hearth nearby, warming the room with glowing embers that crackled and popped.

"I've never seen Hampton so agreeably engaged, either," admitted Mrs. Story. "I knew his retirement would be difficult for him, and I feared his descent into a state of melancholy. What would he do with all of his free time? But then he came home one day, enthusiastic after speaking with Elisha about this resort—and I knew right away this was just what he needed. I have since put my full support behind their endeavor."

"As have I," Mrs. Babcock conceded. "I know it is a grand undertaking, but I am confident that our husbands can accomplish whatever it is they put their minds to. If one cannot aspire to large dreams, one simply cannot hope to achieve them."

"Well spoken, Isabella. Meanwhile, I have been thinking of ways we might assist them."

"Yes, we should help them in every way possible," Mrs. Babcock said, rearranging a flower in the centerpiece. "As women, we are naturally inclined to such things as party planning and the like. Though surely, we can contribute in bigger ways. I was thinking that while the men are preparing the land for auction, we could help drive interest through social events. For instance, we should have a celebration for our nation's Independence Day. We could invite local dignitaries, military personnel from Point Loma, and citizens of San Diego to come over to the island and participate in an inaugural celebration, perhaps even start a tradition."

"I think that is a fantastic idea! It calls for a parade of sorts," agreed Mrs. Story. "I have proposed an idea to Hampton, that they should build a pavilion for symphony performances and dancing. We could host events in a pavilion to court potential land buyers. Perhaps we can offer free ferry passage and carriage rides for the land auction, and provide lunch for those who come to see the lots."

"That's brilliant, Adella!"

"If the land auction is scheduled for this November, might I suggest we host engagements throughout all of September? The nights are balmy that time of year. All we need is a little music—and ideally, a full moon rising over the ocean. How could anyone resist?" The ladies broke into laughter.

"And whilst the hotel is under construction, perhaps you and I should go on a shopping trip to Europe," Mrs. Babcock added. "It's imperative that our resort has the finest linens, flatware, stemware, and china we can find. Elisha said so himself."

"You are quite right. We cannot leave the delicate decisions of taste and elegance to the men alone. I believe our expertise will be much needed."

"Ah, here they come now." Mrs. Babcock smiled affectionately as the men entered the room. "Adella, and I have been very busy planning the manners in which we may complement your efforts."

"Behind every great man is a great woman, as the saying goes, and we are in full agreement," replied Mr. Story. "Elisha and I are wise enough to know the superiority of opinions bestowed by our wives. We certainly welcome all suggestions, complements, and epiphanies. Compliments are acceptable, too." The couples laughed lightheartedly.

"My Hampton is as charming as the day we married!" Adella said, reaching for his hand.

"As are you my dear!" her husband replied, and she smiled as he kissed her fingertips. "What ideas did you and Mrs. Babcock come up with?"

"We are already planning parties and parades to draw the masses to your island."

"And there we were, Hampton, discussing the social ramifications of a groundhog's ability to predict the weather," said Mr. Babcock." Meanwhile, our lovely wives have been busy doing all the heavy lifting."

"A groundhog to determine the weather?" repeated Mrs. Story with a giggle as the four of them took their seats at the table. "How absurd!"

"I received a letter from an old colleague who lives in Punxsutawney, Pennsylvania," Mr. Babcock explained. "He wrote about the accuracy of a groundhog to predict the duration of winter, or early arrival of spring. The city has plans to make the event an official occasion."

The women continued to giggle at the idea of a groundhog playing a pivotal role in any prediction, including the weather. "Do tell us all about it," insisted Mrs. Story.

"Certainly!" Mr. Babcock replied. "It has been a tradition carried on by Dutch immigrants to America, whereby the prognosticator—which in this case is a groundhog—appears from his burrow every February. If the prognosticator should happen to see his shadow, he returns to his burrow to resume his nap—and winter will continue for another six weeks. If by chance the prognosticator fails to see his shadow, he remains outdoors with the obvious conclusion that he feels the climate will be moderate moving forward. It's quite accurate they say," Mr. Babcock explained as he tucked his white napkin into his shirt collar. The two couples began their first course: a bowl of split pea soup.

"What a delightful tradition!" exclaimed Mrs. Babcock, "A bit of amusement to lighten the winter doldrums is a welcome notion."

"The good news is, the groundhog just saw his shadow and returned to his burrow. A long winter will make our island climate more appealing."

"Perhaps we need to add this to our resort's brochure," suggested Mr. Story. "We can safely say a groundhog would not resort to his burrow if he were to winter here at our resort island. Instead, he'd be relaxing in the California sunshine."

The women continued to laugh. "Oh, this is too much fun!" gushed Mrs. Story.

"Speaking of the resort," said Mrs. Babcock, "have you decided upon a name for it?"

The gentlemen's merry expressions fell. "Well, we had a naming contest in the paper as you know, but it turned into a debacle, so we've decided to name it ourselves. We hope you'll offer your thoughts on the matter," replied Mr. Babcock.

"What debacle? You never mentioned a debacle, Hampton—pray tell us what happened?" Adella inquired.

Mr. Story wiped his beard with his napkin. "I didn't want to bother you with it, dear, but here it is: We put a naming contest in the *San Diego Union*. The response was heavy, but the most popular name stirred up controversy and dissent among the applicants."

"What was the name? What caused such dissent?" Adella asked.

"Miramar."

"*Miramar?*" Adella looked puzzled. "But that's a fine name. I quite like it."

"In Spanish it means 'sea view,' more or less. Sadly, the applicants did not find Miramar so agreeable, and they were very vocal about it."

"What were the alternatives? What did you decide upon?" Mrs. Babcock asked.

"There were many: Belvedere, Belulah, Estrella, Bella Marine, Corona,

Villamar, Welcome City, and Shining Shore to name a few."

"Belulah?" Mrs. Story puckered her lips, causing Mrs. Babcock to giggle. "Belulah is dreadful."

"Ultimately, we decided to maintain the Spanish origins of the peninsula and we thought we would use a Spanish name. As you know, we've incorporated the Coronado Beach Company, whose namesake is taken from the nearby Coronado Islands. With the help of our attorney, Major Chase—who secured for us the proper Spanish translation—we thought we'd call it: the Hotel del Coronado."

"It turns out, *del* is the contraction for *de* and *el*, which in Spanish means 'of the,'" added Mr. Babcock. "Like the Del Monte in Monterey, for example."

"The 'Hotel of the Coronado' is the direct translation, then?" Mrs. Story clarified.

"Providing, of course, that Major Chase is accurate," Mr. Babcock said. He and Mr. Story chuckled. "And in simpler but resonant terms, our grand resort could become known around the globe as the Hotel Del."

The women pondered this for a moment. Mrs. Babcock sipped from her wine, then announced, "I believe it is a fantastic name for a resort! It exudes elegance and finery."

"I agree. It is both exotic and appealing," said Mrs. Story. All four of them began the main course, a braised pheasant with pumpernickel bread.

"What a relief that it is to your liking," admitted Mr. Story.

"As we've said, we value your opinion," Mr. Babcock concurred. "Although, we *have* questioned your judgment for marrying fools such as ourselves." The ladies laughed.

"We are delighted to share solicited opinions for a change," bantered Mrs. Babcock.

"Do share with us your ideas," Mr. Story chimed in.

"Firstly, Isabella and I thought there should be a Fourth of July celebration. Something sensational! Can we accommodate a crowd by July?"

"With the blessings of our wives, we can accomplish anything," replied Mr. Story, with a wink to his wife.

"We would need transportation to bring visitors to the island, bandstands to seat them, a marching band, a parade of dignitaries, and perhaps a military demonstration from our local troops at Ballast Point," Mrs. Story added.

"It's a tall order," admitted Mr. Story. "But it is possible if we start planning now. And I think it's an excellent idea."

"I agree," said Mr. Babcock. "We'll find more laborers to begin paving Orange Avenue right away. We also need to start laying tracks to establish a railway route. It won't be ready by July, but we can ferry our guests over for the day. We've already begun drawing plans for the pavilion where we could hold such an event. We'll need to advertise heavily. That reminds me, has Colonel Holabird arrived, Hampton?"

"I'm happy to report, he arrived yesterday."

"Very well. The time has come for him to share our secret with the local and national papers. Colonel Holabird is our advertising genius we've hired to circulate promotional brochures and start our advertising campaign. Ahead of his efforts, I've already leaked a story to the *Los Angeles Times*."

"You *leaked* a story?" Mrs. Babcock looked surprised.

"Yes, as a matter of fact, I did." Mr. Babcock grinned. "To the effect that our hotel would cost over six hundred thousand dollars to build. That should drum up interest and intrigue."

"You sly devil you, Babcock!" said Mr. Story.

"Thank you." Mr. Babcock pulled a folded paper clipping from his pocket. "I have it right here: Harrison Gray Otis—editor and publisher of the *Los Angeles Times*—wrote, and I quote: 'The hotel would be the finest thing, not excepting the Del Monte at Monterey.' End quote."

"Effective marketing, and yet we have to build upon our first stone!" Mr. Story exclaimed. "We had better speed up construction so we can capitalize on all of the free publicity."

"Yes, we're in dire need of more laborers." Deep in thought, Mr. Babcock stroked his mustache. "How can we secure more laborers and get started sooner rather than later? Ladies, may we prevail upon both of you to shovel?" Mr. Babcock asked, his expression serious.

"*Shovel?* Shovel dirt? Have you lost your mind?" Mrs. Babcock replied, astonished.

"We didn't tell you?" Mr. Babcock tried not to laugh.

"Heavens no! I had heard you say you were short on day laborers, but I daresay Adella and I will not do very well at all in their place. We would be a hindrance to your progress—we are quite certain of it!" The women gaped at each other across the table.

"My darling Isabella, we mean for you to shovel dirt only at the groundbreaking ceremony," Mr. Babcock explained, laughing.

"What a relief! I was suddenly overcome with dread! I might have needed my smelling salts to bring me round again. Are we available to break ground, Adella?" Mrs. Babcock asked.

"I believe we are."

"Then it is settled. We have no need of a groundhog to make that determination, based on temperate weather." More laughter erupted.

Mr. Babcock poured champagne for everyone. "Tomorrow, we give orders to begin building the boathouse, followed by the pavilion. We then host a few fabulous parties. Soon thereafter, we auction the land, and last but not least, we build our resort. The liberty of party planning and otherwise showcasing the Hotel del Coronado is hereby delegated to the ladies, and we, of the Coronado Beach Company, vow to trust their judgment implicitly."

"One more idea did come to mind," Mrs. Babcock said, broaching the subject tenderly. "We thought it imperative that we—Adella and I, that is—travel to Europe to purchase all of the required furnishings. Perhaps Paris."

Both men blanched and the two women held their breath.

"What say you, Hampton? It would be demanding for us or anyone else to shop on such a large scale, with the pressures of exhausting such an enormous budget. Should we place this tiresome burden on our lovely wives?"

"At the risk of such an arduous task reducing them to frailty?" Mr. Story shook his head. "I'm not certain." The ladies eyed both men anxiously.

"We have planned for most of the furniture to be manufactured by craftsmen in Pennsylvania, but everything else will likely need to be imported. Could they rise to such a monumental task, Story?" Mr. Babcock said.

Mr. Story frowned.

"'Tis the very thing!" Mr. Babcock confessed at last. "We had thought to impose upon you ladies this very task. We cannot imagine anyone more qualified to do all of our purchasing."

Relieved, the ladies exhaled, grinning at one another.

"Here! Here!" said Mr. Story, raising his flute of champagne. "A toast! To the Hotel del Coronado!" Champagne swirled among the four of them, bubbling gently in the candlelight.

"May she be the crown of the Pacific!" Mr. Babcock proclaimed. Four crystal flutes clinked together. "And the finest resort in the nation."

CHAPTER 11

Ava fed the horses, raked the corral, then saddled up Ambrose. It was noon, and the sun was beginning to break through the clouds. Some mornings were thick and gray with cloud cover—the marine layer that dispersed to a clear blue sky. Ava liked the marine layer. It made it easier for her to get the heavy work done while the day was still cool. She also appreciated that there weren't any biting flies or mosquitoes like those in Indiana. They had been living on the island for only two weeks, and already she had formed the opinion that no pesky insects were allowed to live here.

When her work was finished, Ava changed into a tan-hued riding habit with a brown short-rimmed top hat. She wanted to look for Nathan. As she headed for the door of the tent, she grabbed her violin case. She figured that if she didn't find him, she could at least explore the island and find a quiet place to practice—away from the relentless sawing and hammering sounds of construction. She fastened the violin case to the back of the saddle, hoisted herself up, and eased Ambrose through the gate of the corral.

Across the dirt path, the framing for the stables was well underway. Freshly cut planks fastened by nails lined a long, rectangular foundation. The air smelled of sawdust and curly wood shavings littered the ground. Father said it wouldn't be long before the stables were completed and they could at last settle the horses. It didn't seem possible, given the size of the stables, but everything was built overnight in this town. The rhythmic sound of hammers striking nails was constant. Ava guessed it was easier to build on empty flatland. Back in Indiana she had watched an old barn get torn down and removed piece by piece. It had taken an awful long time to remove the rubble—and each section had to be dragged away behind mules. Here, in Southern California, one had only to clear the shrubs, measure, and start building.

Ava headed south, along the street slated to be called Orange Avenue. She surveyed the land, seeing neither ostriches nor a corral to house any. There was nothing but empty, freshly groomed land with white flags staked into it. Nathan wasn't in sight. A sluggish feeling churned in Ava's stomach. *Why didn't he send word? Aren't we friends—or am I mistaken?* Her eyes began to well with tears, and she blinked them back rapidly. She realized that if a tear didn't fall, then she wasn't crying. She bit her lower lip. *If he doesn't care about me, then I won't care about him. That's just how it will be, then.* She spurred Ambrose along, resolved to fret no more about Nathan. Better to spend her time studying the island than looking for an inconsiderate boy she wished were her friend.

Besides, Mr. Babcock had said she could drive her own coach filled with tourists around the island if she knew her way, so she intended to learn every inch of her new home. Ambrose snorted deeply, rocking his head as he plodded along. His hooves made muffled clopping sounds on the earth.

Ava stopped at the southern end of the island, where San Diego Bay became Glorietta Bay. She watched the wind make tiny ripples across the surface of the water, disturbing its mirrorlike surface. Chimneys smoked from homes across the bay, clustered around the city's skyline of brick hotels and other business establishments. Beyond the city were rolling hills that comprise rocky formations and acres of farmland.

Although Ava found the bay to be beautiful, to her it lacked the thrill of the ocean—a thrill she couldn't get enough of. She instead headed instinctively toward the beach. The waves were like giant claws reaching along the shore and dragging everything with them back to the sea. How seaweed got left behind to rot in the sun was a mystery to Ava. There were heaps of it stranded along the beach. Leaves, stems, and bulbs the color of molasses, all tangled together into mounds.

Ava dismounted from Ambrose and walked to a pile of seaweed, pulling out a long branch with a bulb the size of her head. She jumped on the bulb and felt it burst beneath her boots with a loud *Pop!* Ambrose startled at the sound but stayed near her. Ava pulled on another strand of seaweed that had two bulbs. She popped both, laughing at the sound. She popped a few more bulbs before noticing a shadow had fallen over her.

A carriage had pulled up beside her. Its passengers included two ladies wearing wide-brimmed feather hats. Two familiar gentlemen were perched on the driver's bench.

"Why, good afternoon, Miss Ava!" Mr. Babcock said, looking amused.

"Oh, umm, good afternoon, Mr. Babcock!" Ava stammered. "You startled me."

"Enjoying some amusement, I see?" Mr. Babcock replied.

Ava flushed with embarrassment. "I know it's childish, but have you ever popped one of these bulbs? It's fun actually."

"I can't say that I *haven't*," Mr. Babcock admitted with a wry smile. "I concur there's something inherently fun about popping seaweed bulbs! Allow me to introduce Mrs. Story and Mrs. Babcock to you." He nodded, one at a time, toward the women.

Both ladies smiled and waved, their hats, which rustled with feathers.

"And this, of course," Mr. Babcock added, "is my partner, Mr. Hampton Story."

Ava removed her own hat and curtsied in the general direction toward all four of them. "I'm very pleased to meet you," she said. "Hello again, Mr. Story."

"Good day, Miss Ava," he replied.

"Ava is the young lady I was telling you about," Mr. Babcock explained to the ladies. "She's a superb rider and will be running our stables with her family, which was kind enough to relocate from Indiana." He turned his attention back to Ava. "We were just showing the ladies around the island."

"You picked a fine day for a tour," Ava said, dimples appearing in her cheeks as she smiled.

"Miss Ava, I think we need to employ you on our welcoming committee to the island," suggested Mrs. Story.

"We may be in need of a young lady with your expertise," agreed Mrs. Babcock.

"She will be the eyes and ears of the island to be sure," Mr. Babcock chimed in.

"I would be very pleased to assist you in any way possible," Ava replied.

"Let's hope your father can spare you from time to time. Do you have any progress to report?" Mr. Babcock asked.

Ava didn't hesitate. "They've begun paving Orange Avenue, and the gardener, Mr. Kipling, has planted orange trees. On the bay, they're dredging and building a pier, and they've just started construction for the boathouse. Progress is being made on the steam-powered generator, and the pavilion is going up right behind us."

"She may need to be on our staff, Babcock. Leave the ladies to fend for themselves," teased Mr. Story. The ladies giggled.

"I told you, all eyes and ears this one," Mr. Babcock replied. "Thank you for your thorough report, Miss Ava. We'll be sending a gentleman over soon, Colonel Holabird. I would like you and your father to show him around. Tell him everything he needs to know about our island."

"I'll keep an eye out for him, sir." Ava said. She thought to ask about Nathan but decided against doing so.

"Very well, then. We will let you be on your way," Mr. Babcock said. Give our best to your parents."

Ava nodded.

"We will call on you soon, dear. Come for tea sometime with your mother and sister," said Mrs. Story.

"We'd be delighted," Ava replied

The Babcocks and Storys departed, with the feathers in the ladies' hats billowing in the breeze.

Ava guided Ambrose to the narrow strip of land that led to North

Island. Wild grouse and jackrabbits darted around her, frantic for shrubbery to hide under. She steered him to the water's edge, where large boulders provided a natural water break. She then brought Ambrose to a stop and dismounted, untying her violin case from the saddle. Ava leaped from stone to stone, bridging the gaps before reaching a flattened stone. Opening the violin case, she retrieved her instrument and stood tall. She nestled her violin between her shoulder and chin, drawing the bow across the strings. As she wiggled her fingers on the fret board, a sweet sound rang out. She played "The Butterfly" until she made an error, then started over. Repeating the same error, she started again, her frustration mounting. She was out of practice and it showed.

"You're never going to get through that piece playing it like that," a voice said from behind her.

Ava whipped around to find a boy sitting on the rocks with a fishing pole in his hands. *How did I not see him?* she thought. His blond hair was parted to the side and slicked down with wax. She recognized him instantly as the boy from the Pullman car.

"You startled me! Um . . . have you been sitting there for long?" she stammered.

"Maybe," he replied.

"Why didn't you announce yourself?"

"I didn't know you were coming, and before I could tell you, you started playing," he countered sharply with a frown. "If you want to call it *playing*."

Ava gaped. "You are certainly rude!"

"I was here first, and I'm not the one who spied on me while I was sleeping. So if anybody is *rude*—it's you!"

"Well, had I known you were here, I would have chosen a different rock to play on," Ava huffed, jutting her chin out defiantly. "And I didn't know you were sleeping on that train. Now I can see why they left you behind."

He scoffed at this. "I happen to like that song you were playing, even though you were destroying it."

Ava gasped, "I was *not*!"

"Were, *too*."

She couldn't believe his unflappable nerve. "You are just a disagreeable boy!" She felt her face reddening.

"Well, you're like a fractious, stubborn horse! I'm going to call you that, *Fractious*!"

Ava scowled at him. He wedged the fishing rod between two rocks and stood up, leaping over a rock to reach her. Ava stepped backward defensively.

"I'm not going to harm you, Fractious." He laughed. "Hand it over."

"Why should I? And my name *isn't* Fractious!" His eyes were the same startling blue she remembered from first seeing him on the Pullman car. She guessed he was a year or two older than she, only because he was taller. His tweed coat, matching knickers, socks, and polished-brown shoes looked new.

"Look, I'm sorry about the way we started off," he said, his tone softening. "I'm sure you have a very fine name. I just want to show you something, then I'll leave you alone to practice." Ava took another step backward, clutching her violin possessively.

"Geez, I'm not going to throw it into the ocean!" he said, laughing. "It's the way you're holding the bow. It's all wrong—let me show you." Ava looked him squarely in the eyes, squinting. Her father always said you can tell if someone's not shooting you straight if he or she can't hold your stare. She stared and he waited.

"You done squinting at me?" he asked at last. "I haven't got all day."

Reluctantly, she handed over the violin. He looked it over disapprovingly. "How old is this thing anyway?" Before she could answer, much less protest, he raised it to his shoulder and began to play. The notes lifted from the strings with perfect ease. Ava couldn't help but admire his skill as he maneuvered through the most difficult measures of her song. His features relaxed, and he almost looked handsome. But when the song ended, he bounced right back to being the obstinate boy he had been before.

"You won't get through the faster measures with that grip of yours. You have to be lighter and extend your little finger for balance. You master that technique, and you'll master the bow."

"I wasn't *gripping*," she argued.

"You most certainly were." He demonstrated her rigid grip to show how impossible it was to make fluid movements with her clenched approach. "You bow like this, right?" She knew he was right. Mrs. Bosworth had tried to correct her many times, but the way she held the violin felt more natural to her. "Fine, I'll extend my pinky next time," she conceded.

"You do that." He handed back the violin, flashing a perfect white smile. "Try it."

"I don't want to play anymore."

"Oh, come on! I've already heard the worst of it."

Ava shot him a sour look and placed the violin between her chin and shoulder. She positioned her fingers on the bow as he'd suggested and began to play. Still glaring at him, she ran the fingers of her left hand along the fret board. Picking up speed, she easily played through the difficult measures until she reached the end of the song. She looked shocked.

The blond-haired boy clapped slowly. "You play better when you're cross, which I'm sure is all the time."

"I am *not* cross all the time," she countered.

"What's your real name anyway?" he asked. "I saw you in the back of the train, with the ostrich boy."

"I saw you, too, before you shut the blinds on us."

"Oh, here we go again!" He sighed heavily. "My name is Wallace."

"Is that all? You don't have two middle names and a number behind your last name?"

"Actually, I do—it's *the fourth*, as in Wallace Jessop Gregory the Fourth."

"Lucky guess."

"And yours?"

"Well, it isn't *Fractious*—I can tell you that."

He rolled his eyes and sighed again. "Can you just tell me your name, or does everything with you have to be difficult?"

"It's Ava—Ava Sophia Hennessey . . . *the First*," she said with a small laugh.

"Nice to meet you, Miss Ava Hennessy the First." Wallace lifted an imaginary cap as he bowed.

She was curious why he was alone. "What are you doing here, anyway?"

"My father is out fishing and I didn't go."

"Why not?"

"Because I get seasick if you have to know."

She grimaced.

"I'll tell you about my one fishing trip sometime—and mind you, it's not for the weakhearted."

"Where are you staying?" she asked.

"We're at a hotel across the bay, the Horton House."

"Where are you from?"

"New York City. My sister has a bad cough, so her doctor thought it would be best for her to winter here. There's a sanatorium in La Mesa. Hopefully, she won't need to go there." His expression darkened.

"It's a terrible thing to have a bad cough," Ava said.

"It is. So why are you here? My turn to ask questions."

"We moved here to run the stables."

"My father says they might be building a hotel. Is that true?" he asked.

"Maybe." Ava eyed him suspiciously.

"Don't worry—you aren't spilling any secrets. My father knows everybody in town, and there's an awful lot of talk about the new hotel already. He says it's a big risk to build that big and fancy hotel here, and he's not sure if he wants to invest in it."

"Well, my father says Mr. Babcock is a brilliant businessman—and if anybody can do it, *he* can."

"He may very well be just the man, but I guess we'll just have to wait and see, won't we?" Wallace picked up Ava's violin case and handed it to her.

"Where did you learn to play?" she asked, gently placing the instrument inside and snapping the clasps shut.

"I've been taking lessons since I was four, but the pianoforte is my favorite."

"We never had room for a piano, but I've always wanted to play one."

"To be honest with you, I think the piano is easier to play than the violin. If you can remember a melody, you can play the piano on your first day. You can't accomplish that so easily on a stringed instrument. It takes practice to make a clear note. I'll teach you how to play the piano sometime if you like."

"You *will*?" Ava's eyes flashed.

"Sure. I'm not going anywhere all winter. I'll find a piano. There has to be one around here somewhere."

"I would like that very much," Ava admitted, smiling at Wallace for the first time.

Wallace picked up a few pebbles and hurled them into the channel, settling into silence.

Ava put down her violin case and did the same. "So did you catch a fish?" she asked.

"Nah, I think I'm too early. Sunset or early mornings are when the fish are biting. I lost my bait, though."

"That's a good sign."

"Oh, they're out there all right. It just wasn't my day. I would love to catch something bigger than what my father brings in." He skimmed a stone across the water—it skipped three times before it sank.

"Hey, you called my friend the ostrich boy. How did you know he had ostriches?"

"Because I saw him yesterday."

"You did? Where?"

"Old Town, working at a cantina."

"What's a *cantina*?" Ava felt panicked.

"It's a Mexican bar. Old Town isn't far from here—it's where all the action used to be, before Mr. Horton started building near the water."

Ava's mind was spinning. "His name is Nathan, and he can't work at a bar—he's supposed to be opening the ostrich farm with his father." Ava was visibly upset. "I knew something bad must have happened!"

"He didn't look so good, either," Wallace added.

Ava gasped. "Why? What's wrong with him? Tell me!" she said.

"For starters, when I saw him, he was filthy and running for his life."

"Running from *what?*"

"An ostrich. Mean old thing. It kept nipping at him—it got him a few times, and the crowd loved it!"

Ava raised a hand to her mouth. "Why on earth is he doing this? Oh, this is awful! Did he get hurt?"

"Relax! He's fine. He got out of the ring just in time—and he got paid handsomely for all the drama! I have to admit, the kid's pretty fast. I'm not so sure he's smart, but he can *move.*"

"He did it for money?" Ava veered from worry to anger, her cheeks burning.

"He made an even bigger bet for tomorrow. He says he can outrun the meanest bull in town. They shook hands on it and made him sign a waiver. A lot of people are keen on winning back their losses from the ostrich bet."

"What? We have to stop him, Wallace! He could get himself killed—if I don't kill him myself!"

"Well, he's about to. I'm going to watch tomorrow afternoon, and I can take you if you'd like."

Ava's bit her bottom lip as she recalled her family's plans. "We'll be in town for church in the morning. I can go right after if I bring my brother and sister along. Is that all right?"

"Yes, but can we keep the plan a secret?" Wallace's clear blue eyes held Ava's as he waited for her answer.

Why does it have to be a secret? Ava wondered. *And a secret from whom?* She didn't have time to be suspicious. "Yes, fine. I need it to be a secret, too. What time?"

"One o'clock, at the train depot."

"I'll be there. You'd better not be teasing me, Wallace the Fourth!" she warned.

"It's Wallace *Gregory* the Fourth." He rolled his eyes.

"Whatever it is!" she huffed, throwing her hands up in the air.

"Take it easy, Fractious! I'll take you to see him—I promise."

"And do you keep your promises?"

"Always."

They shook hands on the deal, and Ava squinted at Wallace, causing him to burst out laughing. "Not that again!" he said.

Suddenly, his fishing pole rattled and the reel began to spin.

"Look! You've got something!" Ava cried, pointing over his shoulder.

The pole pulled out from its lodging between the rocks and started sliding toward the water's edge. Wallace ran and leaped for it, catching it just before it plunged into the water. Ava clapped as he cranked on the reel, causing the pole to bend severely.

"It must be enormous!" she squealed, envisioning the fish at the other end as he struggled.

Wallace raised the rod high, arching backward, then spun the reel as fast as he could to take up the slack. Holding his breath, he yanked on the rod, reeling in the line to collect his gain. Ava peered into the water, looking for any sign of a great fish. After five minutes, she spotted a shadow switching back and forth along the sand below. "I think I see it! Keep going, Wallace—you almost have him! It's really big, too!"

Wallace doubled down on his effort, his hair becoming all the more disheveled from the struggle. Seconds later, a splash broke on the water's surface—and the fish swam sideways, trying to gain traction and submerge again. Wallace grinned as he reeled it in. When he and Ava laid it out on a flat rock, the fish wiggled, gasping.

"What is it?" Ava asked, her brows furrowed. The fish was gray and several feet long, with a triangular head, flat underbelly, deep-set dark eyes, and a sharklike tail.

"It's a skate," he replied at last. "It's in the stingray family." Wallace knelt down beside it. The fish thrashed from side to side, pausing with fatigue.

"Do we eat them?" Ava asked.

"The Chinese do."

Wallace held the fish down, twisting the hook from its mouth and pulling it free.

"Wait until your father sees it. He's going to be so impressed!" Ava said.

Wallace frowned. "No, he won't. Better to let him live." He lifted the fish by the tail and flung it back into the bay. After a splash, they watched it wiggle, submerge, and disappear with a flick of its tail.

Ava studied Wallace with a sideways glance. He was a boy who seemed to have everything, yet she sensed he was sad. "Well, maybe the next one will be a sea bass, and you can bring it home for supper," she offered.

"Sure, Fractious, the next one. And you can help me reel it in."

"Not if you're going to toss it back in."

"If it's a bass, we'll keep it."

"Deal," she replied with a broad smile.

"So, you smile?" he quipped.

"It depends on the inducement."

He laughed. "You use big words for a young girl."

"I'm an avid reader."

"I can't argue against that," he admitted.

"That's the wisest thing you've said all day. Do you need a ride to the ferry? It's getting late. I need to go back home."

"A coach is coming for me later, thanks anyway. I think I'll cast in one more time and try my newfound luck." He walked her to her horse.

"See you tomorrow, one o'clock?" She pulled herself up and into the saddle, choosing to sit sideways. She didn't want Wallace to think she wasn't ladylike.

He smiled up at her, nodding.

"Don't be late."

"And suffer your wrath? Never."

She smirked, satisfied with his answer.

After she had gone, Wallace cast his line, sitting down on the rocks again. He started whistling a tune that evolved into the melody of her song, "The Butterfly."

CHAPTER 12

Ava faced the congregation, singing hymns with the choir. She wondered what time it was. The service was running late because the pastor, in his zeal, kept prompting the choir into more song. She worried she would be late to meet Wallace and hoped he'd wait. She had to stop Nathan. The choir director tapped on the podium, and Ava became aware the congregation was staring at her. "I'm so sorry!" she pleaded, quickly raising her violin for a solo. She could see her mother's grim expression over the top of her music book. Luckily, Ava played the piece without errors, and her mother smiled proudly at her when it ended.

They filed out of the church at a painfully slow pace, exchanging greetings with other families. Ava's palms began to sweat. She was happy to hold her violin case; doing so gave her an excuse not to shake anybody's hand. She nodded, curtsied, smiled, and inwardly fretted. "That's a lovely blue dress and hat you're wearing," Mrs. Slaughter said. She was a new friend of Mother, and had just moved to town from Virginia. "My daughter Emma loves that shade of blue. She calls it blue-jay blue, but I find it to be more indigo bunting. My dear Emma's not here today—she wasn't feeling well. Have you ever seen an indigo bunting, Miss Ava?"

"No, Mrs. Slaughter, I haven't." Ava inwardly cringed, with the minutes ticking by. *I beg you not to explain indigo bunting, Mrs. Slaughter!* she thought.

"The indigo bunting is a lovely little bird with a delightful little chirp,"

84

Mrs. Slaughter continued, her voice rising and falling merrily.

Ava forced a weak smile. "I have a book about birds," she said. "I'll have to look that one up." Ava changed the subject. "My mother made this dress for me. Thank you for saying you like it." Lydia wore a matching dress with a yellow hat.

"Your mother sews?" Mrs. Slaughter asked, brightening. "How I love to sew! I have a pattern for a gown from the coming season in Paris!" Mrs. Slaughter whispered, holding her hand to her mouth to hide her secret. "I'll share it with your mother!" She giggled.

"That's very kind," Ava replied.

"Oh dear, we're late for our appointment at the saddlery," Mother said, realizing the time at last. "We must go. Ava, look after your brother and sister. Meet us back at the ferry landing in two hours."

"I will. Go on ahead, Mother, not to worry."

Ava quickly said goodbye to the pastor and Mrs. Slaughter, then hurried Lydia and Owen along the sidewalk away from the church. She stopped to face them squarely, her violin case tucked under one arm. "All right, you two, I need a big favor. Can you keep a secret?"

"Yeah, I can keep one." Owen stuffed his hands in his pockets, lifting his chin to the challenge.

"A secret about what?" Lydia said, looking uneasy. "Mother doesn't like secrets. She says they're very, very bad." Ava gave her a stern look and Lydia changed her mind. "One time I told a secret to my dolly," she confessed.

"So, we have a deal?" Ava asked. They both nodded. "All right, follow me."

They hurried down Fifth Street, passing ladies who peered into the window display at the George W. Marston department store. Each week, the display was changed to another expensive gown that young ladies dreamed of wearing. Ava spotted the Yuma Building, a three-story, narrow structure that looked oddly out of place beside its one-story neighbors. She knew not to go farther south. or they'd end up in the Stingaree district, a place of rowdy bars and houses of ill repute. It was said a night in the

Stingaree could sting you like a stingray in Mission Bay. Ava made a mental note to avoid both experiences, guiding her younger siblings onto H Street, the only paved street in town. They happened upon a trolley car pulled by two horses. "Need a lift?" said the friendly driver. "Hop aboard—it's a slow day. Everyone's out for a stroll."

"Train station, please. Thank you," Ava said, handing the man a few coins. The three of them took seats on a bench.

Ava tried to settle her nerves, wishing the horses would gallop rather than canter. She guessed she was over twenty minutes late and prayed Wallace was still waiting.

At the train depot, she spotted him glancing at his timepiece. When he looked up and saw Ava, he smiled broadly, slipping the timepiece into his pocket.

"Wallace, I'm so happy you waited! I was so worried you wouldn't," Ava confessed.

"I told you I keep my promises."

Ava thought he looked remarkably well in a blue coat, knickers and hat. "This is Owen and Lydia, my brother and sister," she said. "We haven't got a lot of time, only two hours. Can we be back from Old Town by then?"

"*Old Town?*" Lydia repeated, looking nervous. "We're going to Old Town?"

"Sure," Wallace replied to Ava, grinning. "I'll have you back in half the time. It's nice to meet you, Lady Lydia," he said bowing to her. She curtsied and giggled, quickly forgetting her protest. "And a gentlemen's handshake," Wallace added, taking Owen's hand firmly. "Hop on up!" He held out his hand to help Ava. "My lady, might I say you look lovely in blue, and your hat is very fine." She took his hand and bunched up her long dress in the other so she could step up into the coach, with Wallace guiding her.

"Aren't you charming today," Ava said flatly.

"At your service, my lady." She smirked, causing him to laugh.

In the coach, Lydia looked apprehensive. Ava tried to console her, "We'll be fine. We're just going to go find Nathan and see that he is safe.

I'm worried he's going to get hurt. It's a quick trip, and we'll be back before you know it! Mother and Father will understand, I promise. They would want us to help Nathan." Lydia fought back the tears welling in her eyes, nodding.

"If it's any consolation, I have my chaperone, Mr. Thompson, with us," Wallace said, motioning to the coachman sitting up front.

"You're Mr. Babcock's coachman, Gus, aren't you?" Ava said.

"That's right. It's nice to meet you, Miss Ava," Gus said. He turned to Owen and Lydia, smiling warmly. "Don't you worry now, children. I'll get you there safely and in no time at all." His voice was deep and comforting.

"Thank you, Gus," Ava said appreciatively.

Gus started humming a hymn as he urged the carriage forward.

The road to Old Town was unpaved and bumpy. Dirt clouds swirled behind them as they pick up speed. Ava fought to suppress her fraying nerves, feeling a tightness in her chest. She realized Wallace was watching her. She looked away, feeling awkward under his heavy stare. She fiddled with the violin case on her lap, then pretended to study the landscape.

"Do you want to know a little of the history around here?" Wallace asked. Ava turned back to him and nodded, prompting him to share.

"On the top of that hill is the old Presidio," Wallace said, pointing to a building with a red-shingled roof and white dome. "That's the very first European settlement on the Pacific Coast. Ahead of it is a valley where you'll find the first California Mission. It was founded by a Spanish priest, Father Junípero Serra, back in 1769. He's built missions every twenty-one miles all the way up the coast, along the El Camino Real."

"How did you learn of it?" Owen asked.

"My parents took me to see it last week. It's a peaceful place, surrounded by bougainvillea."

"What's *bougainvilly*?" Lydia asked, mispronouncing the word.

"It's a climbing vine with flowers that can be red or purple or even orange. My mother loves them."

Ava whispered "Thank you" to Wallace. She knew he was trying to distract Lydia and it was working. He started telling them about the local

Kumeyaay Indians. As he started to delve into their customs, the coach pulled to a stop. "We're already here. How about I tell you all about the Kumeyaay on the way home?" Wallace suggested.

"Don't forget!" Lydia said.

"I won't. Boy, the Hennessey girls are all fractious!"

Ava shook her head, not amused.

All four passengers thanked Gus for the ride, and he promised to wait for them. They walked down Calhoun Street, a main thoroughfare, which was oddly empty. Wallace suggested they head to the center of town.

Ava observed that Old Town was like a frontier town. A town square, a jailhouse, a courthouse, a saddlery, and a blacksmith were present. An American flag whipped high on a pole, waffling and sagging between gusts of wind. Beneath the flagpole sat a row of fixed, polished cannons. Soap, candles, oil lamps, tobacco, painted pottery, and brightly colored tapestries lined the shop windows. Striped blankets made of a thick woolen fabric woven in vibrant hues of red, orange, and blue were common among the goods for sale. Tall cone-shaped straw hats with wide round brims lay stacked on shelves. Suspended from the ceiling were a small wooden guitars and woven baskets.

They passed a two-story building, the Cosmopolitan Hotel, with a long porch hat wrapped around both floors of the building. The hotel, shops, and street appeared vacant.

"Where is everyone?" Ava said. But they kept walking and passed an old woman with dark braided hair who was seated on the ground. She pounded husks of corn. Behind her a bright fire burned in a domed, clay oven. Whatever she was cooking smelled wonderful. Ava stopped to ask the old woman where all the townspeople had gone. The woman smiled a toothless grin and continued threshing the corn. "She doesn't speak English," Wallace said. "And I don't speak a word of Spanish. Let's keep moving. I know where everyone is—they're up ahead."

They passed a clay house with a sign that read: Casa de Estudillo. Doors and windows were ajar. They kept walking. Another sign read Seeley Stable, and a tall weathervane spun slowly around on the building's rooftop.

Beyond the stable, they could hear music and singing. Men harmonized, and occasionally one would holler and yelp repeatedly. There was infectious sound from the rapid strumming of guitars, and horns blared. Ava had never heard such thrilling music before.

"Follow the mariachis," Wallace suggested, guiding them behind the stables. "What are mariachis?" Lydia asked, gathering her long, dress so she could traipse after Wallace. "They're musicians," he replied. They turned a corner and came upon a large crowd gathered around an arena. Men stood, pressed along a wooden-beam fence, while children sat on the highest rung, dangling their legs inside. Nearby was a grandstand, where women sat, observing the arena from beneath their parasols.

"Those are mariachis." Wallace pointed to the center of the arena. Six mustached men in straw hats stood playing to the crowd. They wore black shirts and pants, with ornate silver stitching and shiny buttons that ran down the pant legs. One man strummed a full-sized guitar, three others played tiny ones, and two blew brass horns. A seventh man shook small rattles, making a sound like dry seeds in hollow gourds. An eighth man plucked the thick strings of a large instrument that was planted firmly in the ground in front of him. The men silenced their instruments, harmonized in song, cried out, then resumed the music. Ava loved the music—it was loud, energetic, and joyful.

A dark-haired woman emerged in a tiered ruffled skirt and billowing blouse. She mesmerized the crowd, twirling while clapping her hands to the beat. One of the mariachis threw down his hat, and she twirled around it, stomping her feet in time with the music and swishing her skirt from side to side. The crowd cheered, and a few men whistled their approval. Ava was captivated by the dancing. She had never seen anything like it. Lydia watched with fascination, her mouth agape. "I want to be a mariachi dancer!" she exclaimed. Laughing, Wallace guided them around the arena to an opening along the fence that afforded them a closer look. "Only the musicians are mariachis," he explained to Lydia.

Lydia and Owen climbed the fence, perching on top, while Ava and Wallace peered through the beams. The mariachis played on and the woman danced. A red carnation tucked in her dark hair matched the bright red of her smiling lips. When the song ended, she bowed amid the flurry of red roses that were tossed into the arena. She picked them up, waving and blowing kisses to her admirers.

The mariachis and the woman departed, and a man entered the arena. He was dressed in boots, brown britches, and a straw hat, with a striped blanketlike vest draped over his shoulders. He made an announcement in Spanish, yelling "*Rodrigo!*"—and the crowd went wild. He removed his hat, bowed, then hurriedly ran from the arena. Ava thought he looked frightened.

A boy walked into the arena and stood alone, shielding his eyes from the sun with one hand, and holding a red cape with the other. It was Nathan. Ava caught her breath, overcome with sudden dread. She climbed onto the fence, pushing Owen aside and calling Nathan's name. Nathan turned his head from side to side, squinting against the bright sun. Ava waved frantically until he spotted her. He waved but quickly lowered his hand and looked around nervously. "Oh, Nathan, what have you gotten yourself into?" Ava said.

A gate from the barn opened, and a large brown bull charged into the arena. The crowd erupted into cheers of "*Rodrigo!*" and whistles. Nathan stood very still. The bull stopped abruptly, surveyed the arena, then charged toward the noisy spectators, ramming his thick horns into the wooden fence with a loud *thud*. Spectators nearby scrambled away in fear, and applause erupted in the grandstand. "*Rodrigo! Rodrigo!*" the hordes chanted. With some effort, the bull pulled his horns free from the beam. The tip of one horn was splintered, but Rodrigo was unfazed. He trotted around the arena.

Nate stood motionless in the center of the ring, gripping the red cape in his hand. Rodrigo paused, breathing heavily through his nostrils, then he charged at him. Ava screamed as the bull lowered his head, racing toward Nathan. He held out the cape to his side and wiggled it. The bull went for the cape, catching it on his horns and tossing it into the air. It fluttered to the far side of the arena. Nathan seized the opportunity and started racing toward Ava.

"Nathan, hurry! Get out of there!" Ava screamed. The bull trotted near the fence, causing skittish spectators to raise their dangling feet. Some began to laugh as the bull rushed toward them, stopping short. Turning, Rodrigo focused on Nathan again. The bull's nostrils flared, the muscles in his hind legs flexed, and he lunged forward.

"Give me your hat!" Nathan yelled to Ava, racing toward her. "Quick! Throw it!"

"What? My hat?" Ava yelled back, confused.

"Just do it!" he screamed.

Ava fumbled to loosen the ribbons of her hat, then tossed it into the arena. Nathan scooped it up and turned to face the bull, waving the hat to his right side. The bull ran at him, chasing the hat, which Nathan tossed in the air at the last possible second. The bull hooked the hat and kept running with it fluttering from his horn. The crowd cheered "*Olé!*" When the bull finally stopped, the hat dropped to the ground. Turning again, Rodrigo targeted Nathan once more. Lydia covered her eyes and squealed as the bull charged again. "Run, Nathan, run! Get out of there!" Ava screamed.

"Just another minute!" he hollered as he sprinted along the perimeter of the fence.

"No! Get out *now!*" Ava screamed even louder. *Does he think he is going to outrun this beast? He is out of his mind!* The crowd roared as Nathan ran by, with the bull gaining on him. Desperate to slow down the situation, Ava did the only thing she could think of. She lifted her violin case and threw it into the arena, just before the bull. He went for it, digging his horns into the case and smashing it into the dirt. The crowd roared and Lydia cried out, "Oh no, Ava! Your violin!" There was a loud crunching sound.

"What'd you do that for?" Nathan yelled, looking back at Ava incredulously. He dared to approach the bull, concerned about the violin. The crowd's roar was deafening. The bull's horn was stuck in the case. Rodrigo thrashed his head from side to side, lowering his horns to the ground. Stomping on the case, he finally pulled free, again taking notice of Nathan nearby. The bull lunged at him with a powerful kick of his hind legs in the air. Nathan twisted his body away, touching the bull's back as Rodrigo passed by. "*Olé!*" the crowd shouted. Before the bull could turn around, Nathan was running again—it was time to get out of the arena. Suddenly, another voice cried out, "Over here!"

Ava thought she would surely faint. Wallace had jumped into the arena and was waving his arms wildly. The bull stood still, confused over whom to pursue, Nathan or Wallace. Owen, Lydia, and Ava started screaming, but their voices were lost in the cheers of crowd. The bull looked back and forth between the two boys, decided, then charged toward Wallace, who was closer. Wallace darted back toward the fence, placing his right foot on the first beam. He pulled himself up to the third beam, but his shoe slipped and he dropped back to the ground. He tried two more times to gain a foothold and made it to the fourth beam. Ava leaned in, reaching for him with outstretched arms. The thundering on the ground grew louder as the bull approached. Rodrigo lowered his head to strike, just as two large hands grabbed Wallace under the arms and yanked him up to safety. The bull stabbed his horns into the fence with frustration, causing it to tremble violently.

"Father?" Ava said, shocked to see him lowering Wallace to the ground.

A whistle blew, the gate opened, and two cowboys on padded horses entered the arena, circling the bull and ushering him back into the barn.

"Thank you, Mr. Hennessey. You saved my life," Wallace said. Father nodded, then turned to his attention to his children. He looked very cross. Ava, Lydia, and Owen fixed their eyes on the ground as he scolded them. "What on earth are you doing here? If I hadn't gotten here in time, your friend here could've been killed!"

"I'm so sorry, Father, it's my fault. I'm to blame," Ava replied somberly.

"But we came to save Nathan's life!" Lydia protested.

"Mr. Hennessey—actually, it's my fault!" Nathan said, climbing over the fence. "If I hadn't needed the money, I wouldn't have taken such a chance."

"And running from a raging bull was your best plan?" Ava said, her temper flaring.

"I had it under control. A friend of mine from Mexico taught me how to read a bull. All I had to do was last two minutes in the ring to get paid." He shook the dirt from Ava's tattered hat, handing it to her. It had a large hole through its center.

"You call that '*under control*'? Did you *read* that the bull was about to gore you to death?" Ava replied, yanking her hat from him. "I can't believe they allowed a boy to do something so dangerous!"

"I told them I was older—and signed a waiver. A lot of people wanted to earn back the money they lost betting against me yesterday. We need a work permit for the farm, and we didn't have enough money. I'm really sorry about your violin, it's damaged beyond repair. Here, take my winnings and buy yourself a new one."

"I don't want your dirty gambling money! That was foolish of you to do!"

"I know. I just wanted to see you again—and to help my pop," he added quickly.

"Where is your father? Does he know you did this?" Ava asked.

"No." Nathan's expression turned dark. "He's been in the bar all week."

"No wonder you don't have the money." Ava's anger softened a bit. "Oh, Nathan, I'm just so happy to see you." She gave him a hug, feeling badly for him.

"Thanks to you and your brave friend here for helping me."

"I couldn't stand there and watch you get killed. I'm Wallace." Wallace extended his hand.

"I'm Nathan. I owe you one." The boys shook hands.

"I don't know if you boys are brave, foolish, or both," Father interrupted. "Let's be thankful nobody got hurt today. Boys, next time I expect a proper introduction."

"Yes, sir Mr. Hennessey," they each replied.

"It's time we get going. Your mother's waiting back at the saddlery, probably worried. Young lady, I'll talk with you at home."

"Yes, Father," Ava said.

Owen and Lydia followed their father as he walked away. Ava lingered for a moment longer.

"So, since I raised enough money, we'll be on the island by the end of the week," Nathan offered brightly. "That's something to celebrate, isn't it?"

"I'm still cross with you, Nathan!" Ava warned.

"Come on, Ava, don't be. I knew what I was doing all along."

"I saw you in there, running for your life. You did *not* know what you were doing! Wallace, thank you for getting us here and for saving Nathan. It looks like we'll be heading back with our folks after all. Tell Gus thank you for the ride."

"Anytime, Fractious," Wallace replied, stuffing his hands in his pockets and grinning.

"And my name is not *Fractious*!" Ava protested, throwing her hands up with frustration. The boys started laughing at the tattered hat that dangled pitifully in her hand.

I'll get my revenge, she thought as she stormed away, *as soon as I'm allowed to see the light of day again.* She knew her punishment would be severe.

Chapter 13

Ava shoveled the corral every morning and every afternoon for the next two weeks. She bore her punishment with dignity, knowing she deserved it. *Why didn't I just tell my parents the truth?* she asked herself repeatedly. The answer was obvious: they probably wouldn't have let her go to Old Town, a risk she wasn't willing to take. She brushed the horses, filled the water troughs, and pitched hay. It was backbreaking work. She had to keep an eye on the donkey all the while.

"You aren't going to eat my shirt today, Penelope," Ava said. The animal's long, gray ears drew back and she stared blankly. "I know you aren't dumb, so don't try acting like it!" For the past few days, Penelope had snuck up on Ava and either bit her or chewed on her apron strings. Each time Ava pulled her apron from Penelope's teeth, the donkey brayed and bared her gums. "We need to muzzle you, that's what we need to do," Ava scolded. Penelope's ears flattened, and she turned to face in a different direction.

While Ava raked hay, she thought about the book she was reading *Twenty Thousand Leagues Under the Sea*, written by a Frenchman, Jules Verne, a few years before she was born. She was captivated by the futuristic story that was unlike any other she had read. Each night after dinner, she couldn't wait to read further, but all too soon her mother would come along and blow out the candle to signal bedtime.

Ava imagined the mysterious Captain Nemo in the *Nautilus*, propelling through the ocean's depths, undetected by the world above. Everything in

Captain Nemo's world was so orderly and efficient. She imagined what it would be like to breathe underwater and walk on the ocean floor. It could never happen, she knew, but how creative Jules Verne was to write such a tale. She decided when she finished the book, she would turn it over and read it again. Very few books held her attention enough to get a second read, but this was one of them. Unless of course, Jules Verne had ruined the ending by writing something absurd into the plot. She couldn't wait to determine that for herself. *It has to be a good ending since the book is still in print*, Ava thought.

By late morning, Ava finished up her work and was hanging her apron when Father and Owen approached in the carriage. "We're picking up someone important at the ferry landing and giving him a tour of the island. We could use your help," Father said.

Ava smiled, knowing he was letting her out of her punishment for the day. "Be right there—let me wash up."

At the landing, a ferry called the *Coronado* docked after making a slow, wide turn. A tall man descended along the gangway with a cane, round spectacles perched at the end of his long nose. He wore a blue coat and hat, with a white shirt and gray tie tightly knotted around his neck. Although he limped, he moved fairly quickly and with purpose.

"Good morning!" the man said brightly as he approached the carriage. Father introduced himself, as well as Ava, Owen, and Lydia, who sat watching from the driver's bench. "Colonel Holabird is my name. Pleasure to make your acquaintances."

Father offered to help him into the coach but he refused. "Not to worry, small injury from the war. It's rather an old friend to me these days. Reminds me to keep perspective."

"You were in the war, Colonel Holabird?" Owen blurted.

"Owen, don't be rude!" Ava snapped, jabbing him with her elbow.

"It's no trouble at all. Yes, I was. First Vermont Infantry Regiment."

"Where you in battle, Colonel Holabird?" Owen asked.

"Gettysburg."

Owen gaped. He had never met anyone who had fought there.

"After Gettysburg, I served as a fireman aboard the *USS Monadnock*. I can hardly believe it's been twenty years already."

"We thank you for your service," Father offered.

"It was an honor to serve, particularly in our fine navy." His keen blue eyes gleamed behind the rim of his spectacles, and Ava guessed he was very bright.

"Colonel, what brings you to the island today?" Father said. "How can we be of service?"

"Land and advertisements. I'll be heading up the land auction for Mr. Babcock and Mr. Story, as well as drumming up interest around the country for your island here. Would you be so kind as to show me all that the island has to offer so that I might properly promote it?"

"We'd be delighted," Father replied, urging the coach forward.

"And I welcome the children's endorsements as well. It's always good to hear a young mind's perspective. Children lack a clutter of the mind, they say, or did I make that up?" He laughed. "I can't recall!" Ava liked him right away.

Colonel Holabird scribbled in his notebook as they toured the island. Ava and Owen offered phrases to help him describe the scenery, making him scribble wildly to keep up.

Owen said, "Coronado, the dream island with quail the size of jack-o-lanterns!"

"We don't want to frighten people, Owen. How about this?" Ava said, using a formal tone: "'You are going to travel through a wonderland. Astonishment and stupefaction will probably be your normal state of mind.'"

Colonel Holabird burst into laughter. "Is that Captain Nemo? I believe it is! How profoundly fitting! I wish I could use the inspired words of Jules Verne. *Stupefaction* is the perfect word for the emotion one feels when seeing this stunning island." Colonel Holabird added another quote from Captain Nemo, "'You will not easily become blasé about the sights continually offered to your eyes.'" He laughed heartily. "I've read *Twenty Thousand Leagues Under the Sea* countless times. Great book! What delightful children you have here, Mr. Hennessey."

Father was pleased by the compliment. Over the next hour, they showed Colonel Holabird every prospect on the island. He filled three pages of notes and promised to credit the children for his finest work. "I'll have people flocking to Coronado like sea gulls, or should I say giant quail?" Ava and Owen giggled.

When they returned Colonel Holabird to the ferry, a barge filled with ostriches was arriving. "Oh, look! Nathan's come at last!" Ava exclaimed. The birds looked anxious, and their small heads shifted in every direction.

"I daresay astonishment, stupefaction, and ostriches may very well be my normal state of mind!" joked Colonel Holabird, making Ava, Owen, and Lydia laugh again. "Right! Good day to all, and I hope our paths cross again soon."

"Goodbye, Colonel Holabird," they replied in a chorus. When he was aboard the *Coronado*, he waved a final farewell before the ferry departed.

"Father, is it possible for Owen and me to help Nathan get the ostriches settled?" Ava pleaded. "I don't see his father with him, and I'm not sure how he'll get them over to the farm."

"I thought you were cross with him?"

"I am. Those birds have a bigger brain than he does."

Father couldn't help but laugh. "This doesn't mean your punishment is over."

"I know. I have another week, but I want you to know that I have learned my lesson clear, Father. Truly!"

"Be home before supper, and don't let me find you in Old Town."

"Thank you," Ava replied, hugging him. "I won't make you regret this, I promise!" He gave her a wary look.

Ava and Owen found Nathan counting all twelve ostriches in a temporary holding pen. "You finally made it over," Ava announced.

"I told you I would." Nathan smiled. "Just had to take care of some administrative chores." The birds flapped their wings and stomped their feet, pressing their two-toed footprints into the earth.

"Where's your father?"

Nathan shrugged. "He was supposed to meet me here. I couldn't wait any longer."

Ava felt a surge of pity for him. "Can we help you get the birds to the farm, then?"

"I thought you'd never ask." He smiled meekly. "We have a place ready over on Seventh and A. If we can just herd the birds over there, we won't have to wait for my father to turn up. They're getting antsy."

"We're going to herd them over?" Ava asked, incredulous.

"Do you have a better idea?"

"I suppose not."

"I think we need horses," Owen suggested. "I'll run home and fetch them."

"Good, smart boy!" Nathan replied.

Owen returned riding Tina, with Ambrose tethered beside him.

Nathan shared his plan: "If I can get Twilah to chase me, the others may follow. So I'll run ahead of the birds, while you two keep them rounded up from behind. If one strays, chase after it and turn it around. Just pretend they're really tall sheep."

"Got it!" Ava and Owen replied in unison.

"And one more thing . . . When Twilah's on my tail, only chase her off if she has her wings out wide. That means she's balanced and she can kick me. An ostrich can kill a lion with one kick."

"Holy smokes!" Owen exclaimed.

"Oh, I'm nervous!" Ava confessed.

"Don't be. We can do this! We ready, then?" Nathan asked. Ava and Owen nodded. Nathan removed his brown bowler, opened the gate, and waved his hat, shouting loudly. The birds scattered in all directions, making odd clucking sounds. Their long necks moved upward and downward in constant motion, while their round bodies bounced over their long, scaly legs. Ava and Owen tried to flank the birds, but they darted like startled mice in a barn. Nathan chased after them, but they kept changing direction, and he ended up running in circles. Ava and Owen started laughing uncontrollably. Nathan hollered at the birds like a wild man, and soon

Twilah was chasing after him, just like he predicted she would. Her wings were folded in tight, so Ava and Owen left her alone. Nathan screamed as he ran, waving his hat. The ostriches squawked and flapped their wings. Owen and Ava spun their horses to round up the birds, which soon began chasing after Twilah, fast on Nathan's heels. They raced down Orange Avenue, turning left on Seventh Street.

When they got to A Avenue, Ava and Owen herded the birds through the corral gates. Nathan slammed the gate closed, red-faced and sweaty. He bent over with his hands on his knees, panting.

"That was really funny!" Owen said. Ava was wiping tears of laughter from her eyes.

"Next time," Nathan said, squinting up at them on their horses, "maybe less laughing and more herding?" He rubbed his shoulder where Twilah had nipped at him.

"We couldn't help it!" Ava said. "That was the funniest thing I've ever seen!" Fresh waves of laughter had her gripping her stomach.

"It worked, didn't it? All right, get your laughs in. I was eaten alive and you're laughing."

"I would say I'm sorry, but I just can't!" Ava doubled over her saddle, hysterical.

Owen pointed to the corral. "Hey, what's that ostrich doing anyhow?" They turned to find Twilah sitting on the ground, dusting up dirt with her wings. Her head swung from side to side as she tossed the dirt onto her back, flapping her wings.

"She's taking a bath," Nathan replied.

"A dirt bath?" Ava said, her laughter fading.

"They can't swim, and chasing them around with a water bucket is not an option."

"I'd love to see you giving them a bath. That would be funnier than you herding them with your hat." She started laughing again.

"Is that so? Nathan approached her. "You'd like to see that, would you?" She nodded until he slapped Ambrose on the flank, startling him into a run. Ava shrieked, taken off guard. She almost fell from of the saddle as

Ambrose bolted. "Nathan, I'll get you for this!" she yelled over her shoulder.

"So long, Ava!" he yelled back. "Who's laughing now?"

"That was a good one," Owen said, watching his sister go.

"Yep," Nathan replied.

"So, we'll see you around?"

"More than you want to, kid."

Chapter 14

July 4, 1886

Ten canons blasted from United States Navy steamships. They anchored offshore in front of the beach pavilion, because the San Diego bay was too shallow for their metal hulls. Brightly colored signal flags and large American flags waved from the tallest mast on each ship. All hands were on deck for each vessel. Sailors stood from bow to stern on the decks, rigidly saluting. The crowd cheered from bandstands along Ocean Boulevard and from picnics revelers had spread on the beach. In the pavilion, the orchestra played "The Star-Spangled Banner" and a soloist sang, holding every high note.

Colonel Holabird took the stage next, standing on an elevated platform in the pavilion. He addressed the crowd, speaking loudly into a megaphone "And there you have it, folks—the finest navy in the world! Let's hear it for the red, white, and blue!" He waited for the applause to settle. "And also for the lovely Miss Julia Christine, our soloist. That was a beautiful rendition of our national anthem. And now, without further ado, let our first Independence Day Parade begin!" Confetti fluttered through the air, the orchestra struck up a marching tune, and a procession of young military soldiers paraded down Ocean Boulevard, which ran parallel to the beach.

Ava looked over her sister's head to Nathan during the anthem. He held his bowler to his chest; his dark brown hair unruly. When the song ended, he noticed Ava stifling a laugh, and he quickly ran his fingers through his hair before putting his hat back on. He put two fingers in his mouth and whistled loudly. Ava returned to waving a red-white-and-blue streamer.

In the bleachers across the way, she spotted Wallace sitting with his family. He was fixated on the navy ships. His sister stood beside him, coughing into a handkerchief. Mrs. Gregory's face was hidden under a wide hat, which was piled high with patriotic-colored ribbons. Mr. Gregory, a tall, stern-looking man in a striped gray suit and top hat, looked preoccupied. He didn't smile.

Ava focused on the parade again. A comical group of young men sporting bowlers and suits rode by on penny-farthings. Ava was amazed that men's long coattails didn't get tangled in the bicycles' large front wheels. They rode in circles around each other, making the crowd laugh by their near collisions. When Ava looked back at the Gregory family, Wallace was gazing right at her. She waved excitedly and he grinned. Then his mother leaned over and whispered into his ear. Her hat blocked their faces from Ava's view, and when Mrs. Gregory moved away from her son, Wallace was looking down unhappily. Frowning, Ava turned her attention back to the parade. Nathan caught her eye, then winked at her, and she continued waving her streamer, wondering what Mrs. Gregory had said to Wallace.

Military officers marched by with glimmering medals on their jackets and swords at their hips. Dignitaries from San Diego followed. Colonel Holabird announced each of them: the mayor, county clerk, district attorney, judge, police chief, and dozens of others, all of whom waved as they passed, grinning at the crowd. Ava recognized Mr. Alonzo Horton from photographs she had seen. He had a long white beard and leaned on a cane as he ambled along, nodding to the crowd every few steps.

After the local dignitaries, the Babcocks and the Storys were announced. They rode by in a coach, driven by Gus. The two ladies wore hats festooned with patriotic-hued feathers and waved with their lace-gloved hands. The two gentlemen tossed candies to the children, and a frenzy ensued as they scrambled to collect the sweets from the ground.

"Ladies and gentlemen, may I present to you two fine gentlemen and their lovely wives!" Colonel Holabird announced. "Citizens of San Diego, transplants I might add—but aren't we all?" Colonel Holabird chuckled into the megaphone. "For having seen its beauty, who could live elsewhere? These gentlemen are visionaries. Their plans for the future of this island are so grand, so spectacular, they defy wonder! I'm hoping we might get a word?" The crowd supported the notion with loud cheers. Gus stopped the coach and Mr. Babcock descended, removing his hat and bowing to the crowd. He took the stairs to the platform, where he shook Colonel Holabird's hand vigorously.

Taking the megaphone, Mr. Babcock addressed the crowd. "Thank you, Colonel Holabird, and thank all of you for coming to our first Fourth of July celebration!" he bellowed. "The first of *many* we hope!" He waited for the applause to die down before he continued. "Not long ago, my colleagues and I conceived the idea to make something truly wonderful happen on this very island. Now, I don't want to spoil the surprise, but I'm going to let you in on a big secret: we are going to build the biggest, finest world-class resort our country has ever seen, right here!" The crowd roared, with the denizens waving their streamers. "What does that mean?" he asked, looking into the faces of the spectators. "It means prosperity! Jobs! Opportunity! Growth for San Diego! Tourism! We'll all benefit!" The crowd roared even louder. "Now, we have much to do, but I promise you this: While we build up this resort, we are going to have a lot of fun along the way. There will be celebrations, parades, music, and dancing for all! Did you know thirty-five hundred people have come to celebrate with us today? What a tremendous turnout! So let's enjoy the rest of the festivities. God bless America, our courageous military—and happy Fourth of July!" He handed the megaphone back to Colonel Holabird, who waited patiently for the crowd to quiet so he could make a final announcement. "This concludes the parade segment of our festivities! Please join us for a picnic on the beach, some surf-bathing in the ocean or the bay, perhaps even a carriage ride. Everybody have a wonderful time, and explore the island. The ferries will be running all day and late tonight, so you need not worry about getting home. Thank you!" The orchestra struck up again and horns blared.

"Want to meet me over at the boathouse dock for a swim?" Ava asked Nathan.

"Sure! I just need to check on the birds to make sure they haven't gone mad from the cannons. I was afraid we'd see Twilah running through the parade."

Ava burst into laughter. "I wouldn't have been surprised if she had. See you soon."

കbirths

The boathouse was under construction on a pier in Glorietta Bay. Only the framing had been completed for a square-shaped structure with a crow's nest and a turret. Beyond the boathouse, a dock extended at the far end of the pier. When the ocean was too rough, Ava preferred to swim here, where the water was calm.

Ava, Owen, and Lydia made a running start and leaped from the dock into the water. Lydia shrieked from the chill when she surfaced, and she clung to Ava to stay afloat. Nathan arrived a short while later. He stood at the end of the dock in a blue-and-white striped swimming suit. He touched his toes, jumped, flipped, and landed with a big splash. Laughter and more splashing followed. The children leaped from the pier tirelessly, enjoying the warming sun in a cloudless sky.

A small sailboat, the *Duchess*, approached, gliding near them as they sat on the dock.

"Oh, look! Wallace is here!" Ava exclaimed brightly.

"I thought I'd find you here," Wallace said, letting the sail of the boat droop loosely.

"Where have you been all afternoon?" Ava asked.

"Tending to really tedious family obligations. I couldn't wait to sneak away."

105

"You've come to the right place," Nathan replied, grabbing hold of the side of the boat and rocking it.

"Hey, wait! Don't do that!" Wallace warned, but it was too late, Nathan, along with Ava and her siblings, pushed in unison—and Wallace was flipped off the boat and into the water. He surfaced laughing. When he climbed up on the dock he tackled Nathan and the boys fell into the water. They stayed submerged for several seconds, causing air bubbles to ripple on the water's surface.

"Can you take us for a sail?" Ava asked, breaking up their fight when they surfaced.

"We won't all fit, so Nathan has to drag in the water," Wallace said.

"Fine by me," Nathan replied.

All five of them spent the next hour sailing lazily in circles in front of the boathouse. Nathan clung to the side of the boat, dangling in the water like bait on a fishing line. Owen joined him, claiming that doing so was more fun than riding in the boat. When they returned to the dock an hour later, Wallace and Nathan competed to impress Ava with their jumps, flips, and dives.

"You boys are foolish!" Ava said, amused by their antics. She and Lydia sat at the end of the pier, drying their stockings and shoes in the sun. They held up their fingers to tally the score of each acrobatic feat. Nathan was winning.

Wallace was wading in the water when he suddenly panicked. "Quick! Do me a favor—cover for me!" he called out to Ava, sliding behind his sailboat, which was tied to the dock.

Ava noticed a handsome coach approaching onshore. It stopped at the end of the pier. In it sat a young lady and an older woman, possibly her governess. Ava watched the young lady step down from the coach and look around distastefully. She lifted the hem of her silk dress and made her way down the pier with determined steps that rattled the wooden planks. Her governess followed closely behind.

"Is she coming?" Wallace whispered from behind the boat.

Owen and Nathan treaded water. "She's coming all right," Nathan replied. The young lady reached the end of the pier in no time at all.

"Good day," the young lady said. "I'm wondering where I might find an acquaintance of mine, Wallace Gregory? I was told he might be here." The girl spoke with just the hint of an accent. She had black hair pulled back into a low bun beneath a hat, steel-gray eyes, a pointed nose, and an air of self-importance.

"We haven't seen him," Nathan answered as he treaded water.

The girl glanced at all four of them—Nate and Owen in the water, Ava and Lydia on the dock—and locked eyes on Ava. "I had heard Wallace befriended a pretty little stable girl. I presume that's you?"

"Could be," Ava replied, feeling an immediate dislike for the girl, though she held her hard stare.

"I suppose the limited population on the island makes it rather preclusive," the girl concluded.

"We'll be sure to let Wallace know you've called on him," Ava replied in a cool tone.

"Right, yes—tell him Beatrice Claypoole came round for him by chance."

Lydia's eyes were wide with guilt, knowing they kept a secret. Owen climbed out of the water and shot Lydia a firm look, making her cower.

"Would you care to join us for a swim?" Nathan suggested. "The water's really nice." Beatrice threw her head back with a grating laugh. "I have too little time for childlike frivolity," she said. With a wave to her governess, she turned and stomped away. Dirt had collected on the hem of her petticoat.

"Have a good day, Beatrice!" Nathan called after her. Ava put her hand to her mouth to stifle a giggle.

When Beatrice had gone, Wallace came out from hiding and climbed up on the pier. "Tell Wallace I came round for him by chance!" he said, mocking her accent. "Beatrice doesn't do *anything* by chance."

"Is she English?" Ava asked.

"No, her governess is, so she pretends to be. She's followed me all the way from New York." Wallace didn't look pleased. "Her mother has it in mind to arrange us marriage."

"*You?* Marry *her?*" Ava replied. Her expression fell. *Is that why Beatrice is so unfriendly? She can't possibly be threatened by me, a stable girl,* she thought.

"That would be a lifetime of punishment!" Nathan added.

"And I have no intention of being punished by the likes of her," Wallace said. "Besides, I'm marrying Ava." Ava's eyes shot to his with surprise.

"Oh no, you're *not!*" Nathan shrieked, pushing him backward off the pier. Ava burst into laughter as his scream was swallowed up by water. Nathan jumped in after him, and the two of them wrestled until Ava called on them to stop acting like common ruffians.

ɤɣ

That evening, the children watched fireworks over the bay. Lights exploded into fiery mushrooms in the sky, reflecting on the water. Cymbals rang and horns blared from the orchestra, in sync with the colorful spectacle. The spectators were dazzled as fiery trails drizzled down from the sky, sizzling when they were extinguished in the water. The smell of gunpowder and white smoke hung heavy in the air. Nathan stole a few peeks at Ava while she watched. Her face filled with awe, illuminated by the bright lights. He caught Wallace watching her, too.

After the last fireworks faded, thousands cheered from the banks of the ferry landing and across the bay on the San Diego wharf. "That was the best fireworks show I've ever seen!" Ava gushed. "Wasn't it, Nathan?" She turned to him, giving him a spontaneous hug.

"It was spectacular!" Nathan replied, surprised by her affectionate gesture. He smiled at Wallace over her shoulder. Wallace simply rolled his eyes. Ava hugged him next.

"If only every day was as fun as the Fourth of July!" she opined, oblivious to the rivalry that had begun between her two would-be suitors.

Chapter 15

September 1886

"See? All is going to plan, Adella," whispered Mrs. Babcock. "The full moon, pavilion on the beach, music, dancing. What more could we offer? I daresay our guests are enchanted."

"Even the wind is cooperating," Mrs. Story agreed. "Look, there's Mr. and Mrs. Stirewalt from Los Angeles. They are interested in purchasing property, and there on the veranda are the Hortons, the Crawfords, the Muirheads, the Hampshires, Captain Lesher, and Captain Hinde—all potential buyers."

"All look to be having an excellent time," Isabella said. "Mr. and Mrs. Priddy have scarcely stopped dancing all evening. They've informed Elisha they are highly interested in purchasing a lot as well." Mrs. Story clapped her hands excitedly.

"Oh, look, there's Miss Ava!" Mrs. Babcock beckoned for the girl to come over.

"Yes, Mrs. Babcock?" Ava said when she reached the ladies.

"You look splendid, dear. My niece's gown fits you perfectly!"

"I'm quite enamored with it. Thank you for lending it to me for this special occasion. I've never worn such a beautiful gown!" Ava touched the fine white lace on the gown's high-collared neckline. She twirled for them. The rose taffeta of the skirt shimmered in the light.

"Absolutely beautiful, dear! Since my daughter is grown, how I long for the days when I could dress her up for occasions such as this," Mrs. Story lamented.

"Ava, we think it's time for a waltz," Mrs. Babcock said. "Would you be so kind as to signal the maestro?"

"Yes, Mrs. Babcock. Right away."

The waltz began and couples filled the dance floor. Flowing dresses swirled across the polished shoes of the gentlemen in long-tailed tuxedos who guided the ladies across the floor. Music, chatter, and laughter melded into one sound that carried with the wind across the bay to dockhands at the wharf. San Diego residents could hear the festivities and observed the island from their balconies. Torches lit up the night sky, meeting the glow from the full moon.

Ava stood beside the orchestra, watching the dancers.

"May I have this dance, madam?" Wallace asked, suddenly appearing before her and holding out his hand.

"I, well, I really don't know how to dance."

"Don't worry, I'll teach you." He led her to the corner of the dance floor and spun her around. She laughed as her dress swirled and he pulled her closer. "You look beautiful this evening," he whispered in her ear.

Ava felt light-headed. She wasn't sure what to say. "Pretty fancy for a stable girl?"

"You're not just a stable girl to me." He moved her along with measured footsteps, holding her right hand in his, with his left around her waist. Her hand trembled slightly and he reassured her. "You're doing fine. Try not to think so much, and just listen to the music."

They danced by Beatrice Claypoole, who stood gaping as she watched with her mother and Mrs. Gregory. Mrs. Claypoole whispered in her daughter's ear and motioned her toward the staircase where Nathan sat. Beatrice walked over to him. Ava could see her urging Nathan. He raised his hands in protest, but Beatrice persisted. Reluctantly, Nathan led Beatrice to the dance floor. She moved him over to where Ava and Wallace were and prompted him. Nathan lowered his head, clearly embarrassed, and then tapped Wallace on the shoulder, asking to cut in. Wallace, looking annoyed, relented and the dance partners switched.

"I'm sorry! Beatrice made me do this!" Nathan confessed, looking very uncomfortable. "I had to be a gentleman."

"I know. I saw her."

"I can't dance and I'm underdressed. I don't even own a tuxedo," he rambled. Ava took his hand and placed it on her side, then held out her right hand for him to take. "I don't really know how to dance, either. I've only danced with Lydia before tonight. Just step in a square, and I'll follow you."

Nathan went rigid, his palm turning sweaty. "I don't want to trip you!"

"Wherever you go, I will follow. One step at a time."

"Will you follow me off the dance floor?" he said, making her laugh. They danced quietly, and Ava could tell he was counting in his head. "You smell nice," he said.

"Thank you."

"And you look real pretty."

Beatrice edged Wallace away so he couldn't watch Ava and Nathan dance. Mrs. Gregory and Mrs. Claypoole smiled approvingly from the edge of the dance floor. Wallace kept turning Beatrice so he could peek over her shoulder, but Ava and Nathan were moving farther away. He steered Beatrice in their direction, but she twirled, forcing them to go the opposite way. When the song ended, Wallace quickly lowered his hands to his sides. "Thank you for the dance," he managed to say, leading Beatrice from the floor with a wave of his hand.

"You're not a bad dancer," Ava said to Nathan.

"Bad dancing is still dancing, right?"

Mr. Story and Mr. Babcock took the stage to welcome their guests and propose a toast.

"Want to get some fresh air?" Nathan suggested. Ava followed him down the stairs to the beach. They took off their shoes walked near the waterline, just ahead of the froth that rolled up on the shore. The moon glimmered on the ocean's smooth surface beyond the waves. The lighthouse on Point Loma flashed every four seconds, it's lamp rotating with pinpoint accuracy.

"Can you meet me later tonight? Around midnight?" Nathan asked.

"Meet you out here?"

"Yes. There's something I want to show you."

"If my father says no, then I can't."

"Can you sneak out? It'll be worth it, I promise. Something rare is going to happen tonight and I don't want you to miss it."

"How do you know about it if it's so rare?"

"From my friend, Mr. Wen Lee. He's a Chinese fisherman who lives on a junk. He has a three-legged dog named Lucky. Have you seen them? They're kind of local celebrities."

Ava chuckled, "A three-legged dog named Lucky?"

"Why would I make that up?"

"Oh, I don't know—maybe, to trick me?"

"I would never trick you," he replied, becoming serious.

"All right, but if I don't show, it means I backed out. I don't want to get grounded again. Last time I had to clean the stables for three weeks by myself. Remember? Because of you?"

"What are you too talking about so secretively?" Wallace said, approaching them. "And Nathan, thank you for that wonderful opportunity to dance with Beatrice." He patted Nathan on the shoulder. "She was insufferable as usual."

"Hey, sorry, she forced my hand. She said a gentlemen's etiquette allows for a *cut in* while dancing. Believe me, I didn't want to go anywhere near that dance floor."

"She wouldn't stop asking me questions. It was maddening!"

"What did she want to know?" Ava asked, curious.

"When my family is going back to New York. We were only supposed to stay through spring, but we extended for the summer. With my sister's medical condition, we may extend again. Beatrice is upset I won't be able to attend her extravagant birthday ball."

"I'm sorry to hear that your sister is still not well," Ava replied. "And it's a pity you'll miss the ball."

"She's planned it to coincide with President Cleveland's unveiling of a copper statue gifted to America from France. Of course, she claims she has already seen the statue in a private viewing in Paris. She says it's a giant woman holding a torch, but she only saw it in pieces. It will be assembled once it arrives in New York."

"That sounds incredible," Nathan admitted.

"The statue, yes. The birthday ball for Beatrice, no."

"Well, I for one am happy you aren't moving back yet. I can't imagine you not being here," Ava said.

"I don't want to go back to New York—ever. My father is sending for my tutor. I hate to say it, but I hope my sister never recovers from her cough." He picked up a pebble and hurled it into the sea.

"My mother is going to open up a schoolhouse soon. Nathan, can you attend?" Ava asked.

"I won't have time for school. I started working extra hours at the brickyard to pay for the farm."

"So that's where you've been. I've called on you a few times to bring you a book, but you weren't home."

"I'm not much of a reader." Nathan quickly changed the subject. "Do you want to come out with us tonight?" he asked Wallace.

"What is there to see?" Wallace asked.

"Something special a Chinese fisherman told him about," Ava replied.

"Sounds intriguing."

"Meet right here at midnight," Nathan said.

❧

Nathan sat on the beach with an oil lantern. The night had cooled and the island was quiet again. He watched the lighthouse flash, imagining its thick glass lens spinning endlessly around a lamp. He wondered how far it's light could reach—a beacon of joy for those at sea.

"All right, I'm here. This better be good because my parents don't know I slipped out," Ave said, plopping down beside him. "I would have asked, but they were fast asleep."

"It'll be worth it. Trust me."

"I brought you that book I've been meaning to give you. Maybe a good story will turn you into a reader after all." She handed him *Twenty Thousand Leagues Under the Sea* and he put it in his satchel.

"Thanks." Eager to change the subject, he said, "Let's start walking, Wallace can catch up. We don't want to miss this."

They made their way south of the pavilion and continued along the Silver Strand, the name given to the narrow stretch of land beyond the hotel grounds. A dark figure sprang out at them from the shadows and Ava shrieked. "Wallace, you scared the wits out of me!"

He laughed. "Where are we going anyway?"

"Further down to the Strand," Nathan replied.

They walked for five minutes, the brightness of the moon reflecting on the churning ocean. Whitecaps appeared beyond the waves. Nathan stopped and searched the beach in both directions.

"What are we looking for?" Wallace said, growing impatient. "I had to row over to get here since the ferries quit for the night."

"Just wait and keep watch. Take your shoes off, too."

They sat on the beach, removing their shoes in silence. Minutes passed. Ava wiggled her toes in the cool sand.

"Look right there," Nathan said, pointing. The waves rolling in had become thick and heavy, like sludge. When they receded, thousands of silver fish lay wiggling on the sand. With each rolling wave, more were deposited until the beach was teeming with shimmering fish.

"What in the world?" Ava exclaimed, rising and running toward the water. She held her skirt, giggling as slithering fish tickled her feet.

"Grunions!" Nathan announced.

"I've read about this!" Wallace said, "This is a grunion run!" Ava started laughing as the fish wiggled around her ankles. She stepped back, not wanting to hurt any of them. "I've never seen anything like this!"

"You see the grunions standing up straight in the sand?" Nathan explained, "Those are the females and they're laying eggs."

"Do people eat grunions?" Ava asked. "They look big enough to eat."

"Sure—my friend Mr. Wen Lee says they're delicious! He caught dozens of them last night and says tonight is the last night for them to run."

"Well, I don't want to eat any," Ava replied. "They're kind of cute."

"Suit yourself." Nathan reached for a few, but they wiggled free from his hand and dropped back to the sand. Laughing, he tried again, catching one and putting it in his pocket.

"It only happens a few times a year and only with a high tide and full moon," Wallace explained. "Look at how many there are! Some of them are seven inches long!"

The entire stretch of beach was now teeming with life. Each new wave brought in thousands of writhing grunions, then taking thousands back out to the sea. They watched the activity for the next hour, marveling at the spectacle.

On their walk back, they passed Mr. Lee and his dog, Lucky, which skipped up to them, wagging his tail. Mr. Lee was carrying two wicker baskets attached to a pole that he balanced on his shoulder.

"Thank you for the tip, Mr. Lee," Nathan said. "Happy fishing!"

Mr. Lee nodded once with a subtle smile. He shuffled down the beach, his baskets bouncing lightly, and his dog followed.

The boys walked Ava home. Luckily, the family's tent was still dark and nobody was awake, waiting for her. She warmly hugged each boy and disappeared inside.

The boys continued walking to the ferry landing, where Wallace had his rowboat tethered. Before he rowed away he asked, "You can't read, can you?"

Nathan visibly tensed. "No."

"Are you going to tell her?"

"I might have to—she just gave me a book to read."

"She won't care that you can't."

"She should," he said flatly.

Wallace departed and Nathan walked home, kicking pebbles along the way. It was dark in his house. His father hadn't returned from the cantina, and he knew he wouldn't make it home that night. At least he'd have food to eat the next day. He pulled three grunions from his pocket and put them in a bucket of water. He wasn't tired, so he sat outside on the porch, staring at the stars in sky. He saw two shooting stars and made two wishes.

Chapter 16

November 13, 1886

Colonel Holabird stood on a platform overlooking the crowd that had come for the land auction. He smiled to himself. He had traveled up and down the East Coast, leaving colorful brochures about Coronado in every major city and railway station. He left property maps and literature describing Coronado, even mailing information to stations as far away as Canada and Europe. He had notified all the major newspapers that the finest resort, with the most equitable climate in the world, was about to be built in San Diego. They ran with the story, posting daily weather conditions for Coronado alongside cities paralyzed by cold snaps: Chicago, Boston, New York City, Philadelphia. All had been recently buried in early snow. Now the fruits of his labor were about to pay off. There was good reason he had been dubbed the Father of the Boom in California. Mr. Story estimated there were six thousand people in attendance for the land auction.

Mr. Babcock checked his timepiece and slipped it back into his coat pocket. One day earlier, he had filed an official map with the county recorder, giving the Coronado Beach Company exclusive rights to water, gas, sewer, electric, and telegraph services, as well as the go-ahead to operate streetcars in Coronado. With these conditions in place, Colonel Holabird could start the auction, and they could begin selling lots. A good day would help them recoup the money they used to purchase the island, setting them up with funds to build the hotel. Mr. Babcock motioned to Colonel Holabird to begin the bidding.

With a megaphone in hand, Colonel Holabird addressed the crowd: "Welcome, everyone! I'd like to thank all of you for your interest in the future of Coronado and for coming today—and I hope that all of you will have the opportunity to secure the plot of land of your dreams." The would-be dreamers laughed. "Before I announce the rules for the auction, I'd like to thank the island's founders: Mr. Elisha Babcock and Mr. Hampton Story, both of whom are in attendance today." He found them standing in the crowd and motioned toward them. "Thank you, gentlemen, for your steadfast determination to make this dream a reality." Mr. Babcock and Mr. Story waved, their wives looking anxious beside them.

"Doesn't Orange Avenue look fantastic?" Colonel Holabird asked, whipping up the crowd's enthusiasm. "I've never seen a finer street in any city! There are actually orange trees on Orange Avenue! And I could go on and on about the magnificent new fountain, but that's not why we're here today, is it?" He chuckled into the megaphone. "All right, let's get started. I'm going to go over the rules for the auction and then hand it over to the professionals at the Pacific Coast Land Bureau, Mr. Easton and Mr. Pennell, to handle the bidding." Colonel Holabird pointed to a large poster behind him that detailed the terms of the auction. "The rules are as follows: Bidding starts at five hundred dollars per lot. The lots offered will be sold, without reserve, to the highest bidder. For a little extra incentive, if the winning bidder builds a home within six months, they will receive a discount of twenty-five percent on the cost of their lot. How is that for favorable terms?" The crowd cheered, and many of the potential buyers began waving their bidding paddles.

"There is one caveat, however: each land deed, once prepared, is not transferable and also contains a clause forbidding the manufacture or selling of intoxicating liquor. We are to be a moral community. At least until we have a police force in place to keep the peace!" Colonel Holabird joked. "Do we have an understanding on this? Please raise your paddles if you

118

agree." Every paddle went up, and a sea of numbers anchored to the sticks bounced around. "Very well, then let us proceed. I hereby give the floor to Mr. Easton and Mr. Pennell—thank you and good luck!"

The auctioneers began at a feverish pace. Mr. Easton held up a lot number for a location on Ocean Boulevard. Mr. Pennell rapidly called out numbers and described it as an exceptional lot with a stunning ocean view. "Do we have six hundred dollars? Yes, seven? Eight? Yes, do we have one thousand dollars?" Paddles rose quickly. "Twelve hundred? Yes, number 336 for twelve hundred! Do we have thirteen? Yes again, to number 607!"

The bidding climbed higher. Major Levi Chase raised his paddle continually until the sum reached $1,600 and no paddle remained but his. "Sold to the gentlemen holding paddle 607!" Major Chase grinned, nodding to Mr. Babcock and Mr. Story. Ava and Nathan, who were standing in the crowd, looked at each other in disbelief, $1,600 was a fortune.

The bidding continued at a breathless pace. Mr. Horton bought a small lot along Ocean Boulevard. Both Mr. Babcock and Mr. Story bid on lots near the location of the future hotel. By day's end, 350 lots were sold for a staggering $110,000, the exact amount it cost to purchase the island. Mr. Babcock saw this coincidence as a good omen and was thrilled. They would need to continue selling lots in the future to sustain the cost of construction, but the pressure was alleviated—temporarily.

Major Chase hosted a party that evening at his San Diego home. He gave a toast: "I raise my glass to the two gentlemen who have had the presence of mind to see the value of Coronado, Elisha Babcock and Hampton Story, and also to the silent partners, who have remained just that, *silent.*" The partygoers laughed. "Today's auction was a great success!" Everyone raised a flute. "To the continued success of Coronado!" Glasses clinked and were emptied, then refilled.

Out on the patio, Mr. Story clapped Mr. Babcock on the shoulder. "It was all your idea, Babcock! Congratulations!"

Mr. Babcock shook his head. He still couldn't believe their good fortune. "We still need to raise more capital before we can have the groundbreaking ceremony."

"Let's have Colonel Holabird double his campaign efforts and get the remaining lots sold," Mr. Story suggested.

"I agree. In the meantime, we have the ability to finance our next set of goals. Let's get the remaining roads paved and trees planted. We need a post office, and perhaps a small hotel for guests to stay in for the interim. I'm thinking we must create a streetcar system to transport people across town from the ferry landing. The Hennessey family can scarcely keep up with the demand these days. My coachman Gus is running his own carriage company now, but we'll need more coaches. I'm expecting a lot more visitors and we need to be prepared. We must have infrastructure."

"Always thinking ahead, Babcock."

"We can't afford to rest on our laurels. Tomorrow is a new day, and with it brings new challenges. Have you seen the latest design sketch from the Reid brothers?"

"Yes, it's magnificent," Mr. Story acknowledged.

"I cannot wait for the world to see what we have in store. Our Hotel del Coronado will be spectacular!" Mr. Babcock drew in a deep breath of the cool evening air and thought of an Aristotle quote: "You will never do anything in this world without courage. It is the greatest quality of the mind next to honor." Courage was the least of the attributes they would need to implement the next stage of their plan. Their hotel was going up soon without the funds to pay for it. Creativity and resourcefulness were the more appropriate traits that came to mind.

Chapter 17

Ava, Owen, and Lydia, along with their parents, watched with hands over their hearts as an American flag was hoisted up a pole on the roof of the stables. The flag caught a wind and stretched taught. A sign above the door read: Coronado Beach Company Stables. Ava was thrilled to be out of the tent and in a building at last, especially before Christmas. The stables had taken longer than expected to complete because the workers were divided among the many projects on the island. Ava's dismay was quickly forgotten, though; she had her own room with a large bookcase, and she could see the San Diego skyline from her window. Now she could stay up, reading late into the night without bothering anyone. Their living quarters above the stables and office were quite large. Mother was thrilled to have a kitchen again, complete with fresh water, and Father had a private study. Lydia decorated her room with a collection of porcelain dolls, and Owen outfitted his with model trains.

The following mornings were spent cleaning the stables, feeding the horses, and polishing the carriages. They acquired a few single-horse buggies, as well as several smaller wagons that children could ride in behind a donkey or mule. As soon as the morning chores were completed, Father rang a bell. This meant a ferry was crossing the bay and passengers would be arriving. To accommodate the great numbers of visitors to the island, Ava and Owen each drove separate carriages. Gone were the days when Ava could sit beside her father, chatting idly with the passengers. All five

Hennesseys had to help carry the load. Mother saddled the horses if a guest chose to ride rather than sit in a carriage. Lydia carried a bucket of carrots, feeding the horses throughout the day.

The beach filled daily with riders and buggies taking afternoon jaunts. Father said as soon as the train tracks were finished along Orange Avenue, the workload would ease up since there would be streetcars to help transport the guests to the pavilion. Everybody went to the pavilion. They went for parties, picnics on the beach, and even church services. It also was the best place to watch the hotel's foundation progress, and tourists liked to watch.

It seemed as though houses on the island were built overnight, and soon blocks filled up with new residences complete with flower gardens. Everybody wanted to get the 25 percent discount for building a home within six months of the land auction. On one occasion, Ava and Nathan watched a house get uprooted, rolled on logs onto a barge, and floated from San Diego to Coronado. It took dozens of horses to pull the house along the street until it reached its final destination, where it was plopped down on the owner's new lot.

Olive trees were planted on Olive Street and palm trees along Palm Avenue. Ava had to tell Mr. Babcock the disturbing news that she'd seen jackrabbits eating the oranges on his trees along Orange Avenue. This caused him great vexation. Even putting chicken wire around the base of the trees did little to stop the jackrabbits.

By late January, a post office, a small inn called the Hotel Josephine, and a nursery were all conducting business, and streetcars were operating, too. Mother opened the first public schoolhouse at 6th Street and D Avenue—a large white tent with six students enrolled. Ava, Owen, and Lydia attended classes in the mornings and worked from lunch until dinnertime. Nathan worked too many hours at the brickyard to go to school. But on weekends, he let Ava teach him how to read. What he thought once embarrassing, happened to be the one thing that allowed them time together. He struggled to sound out the words, but he was determined to learn.

Ava was adamant that he practice reading every day, and she praised his progress. They had already finished *Moby Dick*. One warm afternoon, as Nathan read to her on the beach, she dozed off to sleep. He studied her peaceful expression, watching her even breathing. She looked angelic. When she awoke, she smiled, stretching. "And that's the end of *Little Women*," he announced, closing the book.

"Very funny. There's no way you read it that quickly."

"Can't we read a pirate story, or something else with some action?"

"The March sisters knit and sing. That's action."

"Even worse! I mean, why are they so little anyway?"

"It's figurative. Would you rather we read medieval prose?"

"No, little ladies singing and knitting sounds wonderful," he replied glumly, making her laugh.

Wallace crossed the bay to visit as often as he could. Mostly, he spent his days with tutors, learning Latin, literature, and arithmetic. On the weekends, he taught Ava, Owen, and Nathan how to sail. The four of them spent Sunday afternoons gliding on the bay without a care in the world. Ava liked to drag her fingertips in the water, trailing a small wake. Beatrice had gone back to New York but promised to return sometime this month. Her father purchased a lot on Ocean Boulevard, which would serve as one of their summer cottages should they find themselves on the West Coast. Ava had to admit, she was happy the pretentious girl was gone for now, and dreaded her inevitable return.

～～

March 19, 1887

The masses gathered for the official groundbreaking ceremony for the Hotel del Coronado. Ava helped the island's photographer, Mr. Hawthorne, arrange the Babcock, Story, and Gruendike families for a photograph.

"Should we remove our hats?" asked Mr. Babcock.

Ava relayed the question to Mr. Hawthorne, who was buried beneath his camera's cloak, and she also answered on his behalf. "No, the hats and parasols are fine—just squeeze in a little more, if you could."

Mr. Babcock insisted on including others, standing nearby, in the photograph. They crowded in, staring hard at the camera's lens, afraid to blink.

Mrs. Babcock pierced the ground with a shovel, pressing it into the earth with the weight of her boot. She paused and smiled while Ava held up a flash on a wooden pole. The bulb popped as the photo was taken, with a puff of smoke rising. Mrs. Babcock shoveled some earth and tossed it over her shoulder amid cheers from the crowd in the pavilion. Another photo was taken, followed by another. Mr. Babcock then addressed the crowd that had gathered for the occasion: "Dear residents and guests of Coronado, thank you for taking part in this momentous groundbreaking ceremony, one we've all been waiting for." He paused for effect. "To date, we have raised over four hundred thousand dollars to build this hotel." The crowd hushed. Nobody had ever heard of such a large sum being put toward building a hotel. "And starting today, our resort goes up!" The crowd roared. "I welcome all visitors to come and watch the progress. Thank you."

A celebration ensued with an afternoon picnic on the beach, followed by music and dancing in the pavilion. Nathan arrived in a bowler and suit, twirling proudly for Ava. "May I have the first dance?" he asked, feeling bold. Ava grinned, accepting his request. He led her to the dance floor.

"You look handsome in your new suit," Ava said. You haven't been gambling, have you?"

"Me? I'd never do anything that irresponsible."

She laughed. "I meant you haven't been running from any bulls lately, or doing anything else foolish."

"I'm a changed man, I don't do that anymore. So, do I look dapper?"

She nodded. "Dapper indeed."

"Pardon me," Wallace interrupted, tapping Nathan on the shoulder with a devilish grin.

"I loathe etiquette," Nathan lamented. "That's my new favorite word, *loathe*. I read it in a book."

"Good. Look up *rivalry*," Wallace replied, taking Ava away from him. She giggled, waving goodbye to Nathan.

Wallace looked deep into her eyes, and she felt her heart race. He smelled of heady cologne, and he looked dashing in a dark suit. His hair was parted to the side and waxed perfectly into place, like it always was.

"I heard Beatrice is back in town. Where is she tonight?" Ava asked, scanning the room.

"Luckily, she had a previous engagement. We've been spared."

Ava concentrated on her footwork as they danced.

"Do you miss playing your violin?" he asked.

"I do, actually. It's been a long while." Ava vividly remembered the bull smashing her violin case into pieces.

I have a little surprise for you, then."

She looked away. Holding his stare made her feel light-headed. "I'm not very fond of surprises."

"There's someone I want you to meet. Someone you may find fascinating."

"I can't imagine who, and what it has to do with my violin?"

"You'll see. He's new to town from Europe. He's a bit of an eccentric but extremely charming."

"What makes him eccentric?"

"He calls himself a spiritualist. He's been known to dabble a little in the spirit world. Does that scare you?"

"If he's going to have ghouls chasing us, then yes."

Wallace threw his head back with laughter. "No, he won't send ghouls after us—just you." She looked horrified.

"You're so funny, Ava." He twirled her around. "He's a musician, too. His name is Jesse Shepard. He channels composers of old, like Mozart and Beethoven. They say when he plays, it sounds like there is more than one musician playing. Have you ever met a virtuoso?"

"No. He sounds intriguing. Can Nathan come?"

"Does he have to? I'm a little jealous. He pretends he can't read, and he gets all of your free time."

Ava gave him a sour look. "Are you serious?"

"Fine, he can tag along."

"Then I'll go. How can I pass up a chance to meet my first virtuoso?"

"Take the noon ferry tomorrow, I'll have a carriage waiting."

Chapter 18

Nathan and Ava took the ferry across the bay and spotted Gus sitting on the driver's bench of his coach. A baby boy with dark eyes and round, full cheeks sat beside him in a modified pram. Its wheels were removed, and the basket was anchored to the bench with saddle straps.

"Gus, is this your son?" Ava asked, grinning at the infant.

"Yes, this is. This is my new assistant coachman, Willard."

"He's precious!"

Nathan made funny faces for Willard, and the baby giggled, exposing two, tiny bottom teeth.

"We're very blessed. Isn't that right, son?" Gus laughed heartily and the baby grinned.

"Did you design the baby's seat yourself, Gus?" Nathan asked, leaning over to inspect it.

"I sure did."

"It's a very clever design. I bet you could make more and sell them, easy."

"You think so? I'm not so sure it'll work when he's toddlin' around, but it'll do for now." Gus burst into laughter. "Isn't that right, son?" he said again. The baby looked at his father with wonder lighting his eyes.

"Sorry I'm late!" Wallace huffed, climbing into the carriage. "Got held up with lunch at the Claypooles', where I succumbed to a sudden cough." He winked at Ava. "Gus, would you be so kind as to take us to the Jesse

Shepard home on K Street?"

"You're the boss."

Gus urged the horses forward, taking them south of town. They halted in front of a deep red two-story home with mossy-green trim. Red shingles on the exterior were both diamond-shaped and fishhooked, giving Ava the impression the house was meant to appear as if it were covered in scales, which was both eerie and intriguing. Two gargoyles—dragons with bared teeth—protruded from the rooftop ledges, confirming her impression. A pole extended from a cone-shaped tower, where another menacing dragon spiraled upward.

"Mr. Shepard must be a very interesting person," Ava stated. Nathan and Gus gaped.

"He most certainly is," agreed Wallace, "This is the Villa Montezuma. He designed it himself."

"Is it haunted?" Nathan blurted, gazing at the unusual bulbous tower with a pointed top. "It's kind of creepy."

Wallace laughed. "It's brand-new. How can it be haunted?"

"Does it have to be old to be haunted?" Nathan replied.

Ava, Nathan, and Wallace said farewell to Willard and climbed down from the carriage.

"You sure you want to be going in there?" Gus called after them, squinting up at the gargoyles suspiciously.

"We'll be fine. Mr. Shepard is a family friend," Wallace assured him. Gus shook his head as the carriage pulled away. "The youth these days," he muttered to his son. "I aim to raise you up with common sense."

ॐঔ

"Jesse is an avid traveler, as well as an accomplished pianist, vocalist, poet, and author. His house is filled with collectibles and gifts from his excursions," Wallace explained. He led them up a few steps to the front door and rang the bell. When nobody answered, he turned the knob and the door swung open.

"We aren't going in, are we?" Ava said nervously. "I mean, if Mr. Shepard isn't home, maybe we should come back another time."

Wallace stepped inside, looking back at his friends. "We're already here, aren't we?" Ava and Nathan hesitated after he disappeared inside.

"What should we do? Should we go in?" Ava asked.

Nathan shrugged. "If he says it's all right, it must be."

They entered the house, closing the door softly behind them. In the entry hall Nathan whistled. The floors and walls were richly paneled with dark polished wood. The ceiling was embossed with the same dark wood, in alternating patterns of circles and squares. The heavy scent of cologne hung in the air. Ava's eyes were drawn to oil paintings of people, flowers, and landscapes hanging in golden frames on the walls. An oil lamp dangled on a chain from the ceiling.

"This house is incredible!" Ava gushed, peering into the dining room. A silver tea set gleamed on a serving table.

"It's too rich for my taste," Nathan admitted. "I'm afraid I'll break something worth more than my head!"

Curious, Ava entered the room. Reluctantly, Nathan followed her.

"What's the matter?" she asked. "Are you afraid to be left alone?"

"In truth? Yes."

"I'm not afraid," she murmured as she ran a finger along the dining table. There wasn't a speck of dust. A wooden cupboard that extended from floor to ceiling displayed fine blue china. A fireplace stacked with logs had a hearth inlaid with deep blue tiles and painted lions on its base. Ava was drawn to a stained-glass window. Two girls gathered seasonal fruits and flowers with the words *Summer* and *Autumn* written beneath them. Ava imagined the girls in the windows at dawn, dull and darkened until the sun brought them glowingly to life each day. "These windows are fantastic!"

"I thought they only had art glass in churches?" Nathan said, puzzled.

"I think this house is his church."

They found Wallace in the drawing room, looking at an oval portrait of a young, fair man with dark curly hair, warm brown eyes, and a thick mustache. "Is this Mr. Shepard?" Ava asked, studying his earnest features.

129

"The very one," Wallace confirmed.

"He looks regal, like a picture I saw of the Prince of Wales," Ava said.

"They happen to be good friends," Wallace replied.

"They are?" Nathan said, dumbfounded.

Ava turned her attention to three round stained-glass windows—all of them depicting men—high on one wall. Each image had its own label written below: *Shakespeare, Goethe,* and *Corneille.* Ava recognized only Shakespeare. Mr. Shepard was clearly an inspired man.

"Let's go upstairs," Wallace suggested. "I want to show you the gallery."

"How do you know Mr. Shepard?" Ava asked as they climbed the stairs.

"We met him on a train in Belgium. My parents have shared a correspondence with him ever since, and were delighted to hear of his arrival in town."

At the landing at the top of the staircase loomed another set of stained-glass windows. Wallace offered an explanation: "This one is Montezuma, the Aztec king. The other is Saint George, the patron Saint of England." Montezuma stood fearsome; he was bare chested and muscular, wearing a headdress of colorful feathers. Saint George wore full body armor.

"Two warriors from very different ages," Ava noted. "Apart from that, I cannot imagine what they have in common. Did Montezuma slay a dragon, too?"

"He tried to slay the Spaniards when they captured his city. So, maybe in a figurative sense, he at least tried."

The gallery was like a museum, showcasing an impressive collection of memorabilia, letters, and art pieces. "Most of these items are gifts from European rulers and even the czar of Russia," Wallace explained. "Mr. Shepard played music for them at court and remained as their guest for quite some time."

Ava and Nathan were awestruck.

"Does he have an actual job?" Nathan asked.

"No. He has patrons," Wallace explained.

"That's what I need, a patron," Nathan replied. Ava giggled at this.

"Nothing in here is replaceable," Wallace added.

"Lovely." Nathan shoved his hands in his pockets. "Now I'm afraid to even *look* at anything, let alone touch it!"

The wall was papered in a floral pattern. Framed photographs of lovely ladies hung suspended by wire from the crown molding. Plant stands with clawed feet held sprawling ferns, which together with several chaise lounges, a bronze statue, and a marble bust filled the room to the brim. Ava was drawn to a framed letter, written in cursive. The language was foreign. She moved from one fascinating item to the next, piecing together her notion of the character of Mr. Shepard through the treasures he valued. He seemed adventurous to her, and not at all confined by the norms and routine of daily life. Ava imagined him drifting freely through the highest social circles of the world, collecting gifts and accolades wherever he went. She felt she would have to study his home for weeks before she could adequately account for all its flourishes. She approached a photograph of him wearing a polka-dotted bow tie, fur coat, checkered suit, and knit cap. She smiled at his outrageous attire. This man marched to his own beat. Papers sprawled on top of a bureau caught her attention next. "Who is Francis Grierson?"

"That's his nom de plume," Wallace answered.

"In English, that means what?" Nathan asked.

"It's his pen name. He writes under the name *Francis Grierson*— Grierson was his mother's maiden name. His uncle was General Benjamin Grierson in the Civil War."

"Why wouldn't he just write under his real name?" Nathan asked.

"A pen name is so mysterious," Ava remarked.

"If I called myself something else, would *I* be mysterious?"

"*No*," both Ava and Wallace replied.

"You two are cruel!" Nathan muttered sulkily.

Ava and Wallace burst into laughter.

"He does most of his writing in the tower," Wallace said, "but we won't go in there. It's time for the best room in the house." They followed Wallace downstairs and through a hallway to a room taking up the entire eastern wing. The scent of cigar lingered heavily. On the floor, a white polar bear hide sprawled before a fireplace, complete with head and bared fangs. Its glassy marble stare forever marked the moment of its unfortunate encounter with a hunter. Ava walked around the bear to study another stained-glass window that dominated the wall. *Sappho* was written beneath a woman playing a lyre.

"Sappho is a Greek poet, although I've never read any of her works," Wallace confessed.

"Mr. Shepard certainly holds her in high regard." Ava's eyes wandered the room, her gaze falling on oriental rugs, ferns, and paintings that hung from the mahogany-paneled walls. Sunlight streamed in through windows.

"So this is the music room if you haven't already guessed," Wallace announced.

Nathan spun around, taking it all in. A tufted sofa and reclining chairs faced a grand piano. Above the piano were stained-glass windows of two more men. Luckily for Ava, they were titled: *Rubens* and *Raphael*. Otherwise, she would never have guessed who they were. Beneath them, two long oval windows, also images of men, were titled *Occident* and *Orient*. The man depicting the Occident wore a knight's suit of armor. Ava took a closer look at the man depicting the Orient. A familiar pair of brown eyes gleamed brightly at her. "Hey, this looks like Mr. Shepard."

"I've heard it is meant to. He had his likeness painted into it," Wallace confirmed, striding over to her. "A tribute to his love of Eastern philosophy."

"Incredible." Ava pressed down a piano key. It rang out, echoing through the house.

"Here, sit down. I'll play for you," Wallace said. Ava didn't hesitate. He placed his fingers on the keys and began to play.

Ava became lost in the haunting beauty of the *Moonlight Sonata*, paired with the fluid movement of his fingers. The stern image of Beethoven, with his unruly hair and high collar, peered at her from the stained-glass window across the room. Nathan sat down in a nearby chair, looking anguished. He watched Ava's eyes become glassy as Wallace played. Despite his fingers racing up and down the keys, Wallace looked completely relaxed. He let the last note hang in the air. "A little melancholy, but it's one of my favorites," he said at last.

"You play it beautifully!" Ava gushed.

"I admit to years of practice. Are you ready for your surprise?"

"What surprise?"

"It's your birthday soon, isn't it?"

"Not until next Sunday."

"Close enough." Wallace got up and walked to a nearby cabinet. He opened the cabinet and pulled out a leather case, removing a violin from it. "Play it." He handed the violin to Ava.

"Oh, I can't! I'm sure it's much too valuable!"

"I insist. Play."

Reluctantly, she took the instrument, holding it up to a stream of sunlight to admire its smooth curves. It was worn in several places from obvious use. Turning it over, she could see a label in the F-hole of the body. She angled the violin, so the light would shine on the label, and read aloud: "*Antonius Stradivarius Cremonensis.*" She froze. "Wallace, this a Stradivarius!"

"So?"

"So? It says it was made in 1730! I can't play this!"

"What happened to Fractious? Come on, play it," Wallace urged. "I'll accompany you." He sat back down at the piano.

"This is a very expensive instrument, that's what happened to *Fractious*," she mumbled. Nathan gave them a puzzled look. Going against her better judgment, Ava placed the instrument against her shoulder, breathing in its cedar scent. Her fingers trembled.

"What key?" Wallace asked.

"I don't know. How about B flat?" He nodded.

Ava began to play a soft, soulful melody. The instrument sprang to life, filling the room in warm, rich tones worthy of a concert hall. She smiled, repeating the measure with more conviction. Wallace nodded, signaling her to continue. Nathan sat up in his chair, riveted as he watched Ava play with rays of light streaming around her. Sappho glowed behind her in the window, strumming a lyre. Ava moved the bow with long, even slides punctuated by short, sudden bursts. Wallace grinned, watching her play. He didn't need to focus on his hands; they knew where to find the keys. When Ava returned to the refrain, Wallace danced around her melody with piano chords.

Ava brought her bow to a full stop after Wallace rolled his fingers along the piano, ending on the highest key.

Applause erupted from the doorway, where Mr. Shepard stood clapping. Ava gasped, lowering the violin, and Nathan jumped up from his chair. "Bravo!" bellowed Mr. Shepard, entering the room with long, elegant strides. He wore a tan suit, crisp white shirt, and a straw boater hat.

"Good afternoon, Mr. Shepard," Wallace replied coolly, standing up from the piano bench. "I hope you don't mind we called on you today, only to find you weren't home. Until now that is."

"Not all! Wallace Gregory, good to see you, my friend. You are welcome in my home anytime. What's mine is yours!" He hugged Wallace affectionately. "Please, call me Jesse. I had heard your family was in town. How lovely to see you again! Introduce me to your friends." He turned, extending his hand. His brown eyes shined brightly, just as those depicted in *Occident*.

"This is Ava Hennessey and . . . Nathan." Wallace frowned, realizing he didn't know Nathan's surname.

"Beckman," Nathan added, shaking Mr. Shepard's hand firmly.

"Delighted to make your acquaintances. I see you play the violin, Miss Ava."

"Not very well at all, Mr. Shep—um, Jesse," she said. "I've failed to practice."

"Only because she threw her violin in front of a bull that was trying to kill me," Nathan explained. Jesse threw his head back and roared with an infectious laugh. "That sounds like a wonderful tale! How I love a great story! Say, my boating party is on their way over at the moment. Would you care to join our party and share your story with us? It's more of a literary gathering, if you will."

Ava, Nathan, and Wallace looked at one another. "I can stay for another hour or so," Ava said, unable to say no to the fascinating gentleman who treated them with such respect. Nathan nodded and Wallace agreed.

"Fantastic!" said Jesse. "Ah, here they come now."

The clatter of footsteps, lively conversation, and laughter filled the hallway. A stream of well-dressed, slightly tipsy guests spilled into the room—along with overly enthusiastic greetings. They all found seats. Several ladies stretched out on chaise lounges, sipping wine through lips freshly applied with color. Ava, Nathan, and Wallace found a sofa to share in the corner.

A gentleman, introducing himself as Mr. Seigenthaler, stood up before the assembled party. "Shall I read Dickinson's "Because I could not stop for death"? Or something less morose, like Longfellow's "Becalmed"? Which is fittingly nautical, as our day has been." The revelers laughed and unanimously voted for Longfellow. Mr. Seigenthaler cleared his throat, standing tall to project:

> Becalmed upon the sea of thought,
> Still unattained the land it sought,
> My mind, with loosely-hanging sails,
> Lies waiting the auspicious gales.

> On either side, behind, before,
> The ocean stretches like a floor,
> A level floor of amethyst,
> Crowned by a golden dome of mist.

> Blow, breath of inspiration, blow!
> Shake and uplift this golden glow!
> And fill the canvas of the mind,
> With wafts of thy celestial wind.

Blow, breath of song! Until I feel,

The straining sail, the lifting keel,

The life of the awakening sea,

Its motion and its mystery.

The audience applauded when he finished. A gentleman, leaning casually against a wall, called for Jesse to play. At everyone's insistence, he finally obliged, sitting down at the piano. "My transcendentalist friends, today I will channel the great Mozart." The room completely quieted. Before he played, Jesse closed his eyes and began to sing a melody. His silky voice rose high, holding a note, and then sank low. Ava was amazed by the range and clarity of his voice. Jesse opened his eyes and began to play furiously. His fingers moved so rapidly across the keys, it looked as if he had an extra pair of hands. The audience was captivated. When Jesse finished, he closed his eyes again, breathing heavily. A strand of his curly dark hair fell out of place and hung loosely over his eyes. With a flip of his head, he tossed it back into place, then smiled. Ava jumped up and clapped. She now understood why Jesse enjoyed the patronage of European royal courts. He was charismatic, charming, flamboyant—and his talent was utterly astounding.

"Thank you," he said humbly. "And now, I invite our young guests and new friends to play for us, and perhaps tell us a story."

Wallace played the piano and Ava followed him on violin. She was nervous, but her fear soon faded. Their song, a Celtic melody, compelled a redheaded woman to rise and sing in Gaelic. When their song ended, some of the men and women dabbed at their eyes with handkerchiefs. Ava bowed and Wallace grinned. Nathan was called next to stand in the middle of the room. He looked terrified. He swallowed hard, fixing his gaze on Ava across the room. She nodded to encourage him.

"So, this is a tale I call, er . . . 'The Fair Maiden and the Raging Bull,'" he stammered. Applause from the audience strengthened his resolve. Nathan projected in a deep, dramatic tone. "There he was, Rodrigo, breathing fire from his nostrils. Hatred raging in his black-coal eyes! I meant eyes as black as coals, my apologies." The crowd erupted into laughter. "He struck his hoof to the earth, kicking up dust, and charged at me—a young, handsome matador—intent on goring me to my youthful death!" More laughter. Nathan paused for dramatic effect, looking up to the ceiling and raising his hand, its fingers pinched together like he held a precious stone. "But then I saw her . . . the fair maiden in a blue hat." He motioned toward Ava, who giggled. Jesse started clapping, wildly amused.

"And what did this maiden do, you ask? I'll tell you . . . She tossed her hat into the hands of this brave matador, who hurled it fearlessly at the raging bull." Nathan paused to address the crowd more directly, speaking in his regular voice. "Truth be told, the matador threw the maiden's hat at the bull, and Rodrigo pierced it through, buying the matador precious moments in which to run." The crowd roared. "But the bull would spare him not! Rodrigo charged again," Nathan continued, focusing intently on the audience. "And upon his final approach, with the matador's death all but certain, the bull trips on a violin case that has also been thrown into the arena by the aforementioned fair maiden." More laughter. "He smashes it to pieces! And what, pray tell, did the bull do next? He charged at the matador once again, only to be distracted by a second matador, who jumped into the ring!" Nathan pointed to Wallace, who nodded back. "Which matador would be crushed under the hooves of the beast?" Nathan asked. "And who would win the maiden's heart?"

"Matador number one would win her heart!" a woman called out.

"Thank you, madam, I appreciate the vote of confidence, but the answer is . . . *neither*. The fair maiden's father yanked the second matador from the arena by his bootstraps, while the first matador escaped to freedom, his destiny forever changed. But it was not in vain! The fair maiden thought the first matador to be the bravest, most handsome young man on the planet. The end." Nathan bowed and returned to the sofa amid a roar of applause.

"That was an impressive oration," said Jesse.

"I'll say," Ava said, jabbing Nathan in the ribs with her elbow. "*Fair maiden?*"

"You got fairer by the minute, did you notice that?"

"*Aforementioned?*" she repeated, incredulous that he would use such a word.

"I read it in a book."

"Where was the part about how foolish the first matador was to be in the arena in the first place?" Wallace said.

"It's my tale, Wallace. If you want to make changes, you can tell your own tale. But the first matador is always better looking than the second matador."

"It's a tall tale, then."

The crowd laughed at their banter, not knowing the rivalry between the boys increased with each passing day.

"Will you boys, please!" Ava urged.

Wallace then nodded to Jesse, who stood to address the room, "With great sadness, I must announce the departure of our young friends. My home is a haven for literature, music, poetry, and song, and I hope you will join us again soon. You are most certainly welcome among us."

"Thank you," each of them replied, waving farewell to the guests.

Jesse offered the use of his coach to take them back to the ferry, and they departed the room to a final round of applause.

❧

"Let's get you home, Ava, before you get in trouble again!" Wallace said as they hurried out of the house.

"If I get in trouble, it was worth it." She held her hand over her heart. "Jesse is so obliging!"

They climbed into a coach. Once they were seated, Ava asked, "Why did Jesse move here? I mean, if he's famous in Europe, why would he move here when San Diego is so small?"

"He was recruited to bring culture and art to San Diego," Wallace explained. "Two local builders offered to build him a house, with his design, to lure him here and put San Diego on the map as a cosmopolitan city."

"Why didn't they just ask me?" Nathan teased. "I can sing a jig or two. Maybe I can get somebody to build me a house, too, because living with Twilah is gettin' real tough." Wallace and Ava burst into laughter.

"Can you really sing?" Ava looked at him with surprise.

"Maybe one day you'll be lucky enough to find out. Until then, I'm holding back until I get a few offers. I don't care if it's in the Stingaree district."

Ava giggled, shaking her head. "With the stories you tell, you *belong* in the Stingaree!"

Wallace had the carriage drop them off at the ferry landing. "Will you be around Sunday?" he asked Ava. "I have a little something for you. Can I bring it by?"

"Me too," Nathan added.

"If it's for my birthday, I don't need any presents."

Wallace rolled his eyes. "Just tell me. Will you be home?"

"I should be," she conceded.

"So will we, then. Won't we, Nathan?"

"If you're there, I'll be there first."

Chapter 19

April 13, 1887

"Ava, your gentlemen friends are waiting for you downstairs—with gifts," Mother said, standing in the doorway.

Ava looked up from her book, sighing. "I told them I didn't need any."

Her mother shrugged.

"Tell them I'll be right down." Ava marked her place in the book she was reading and headed downstairs.

Nathan and Wallace shared a bench in the front office of the stables. Wallace had a long, beautifully wrapped box in his lap, complete with a yellow bow on top. Nathan wouldn't look at it directly, and he appeared to be anxious, uncomfortable, or both. His gift was in a round box with a wilting daisy on top.

Father stood behind the desk, organizing invoices to submit to Mr. Babcock. He offered the boys a beverage, but both politely declined. Owen and Lydia pretended to busy themselves by stacking papers with Father.

Ava entered the room and both boys stood up. "Happy birthday!" Nathan blurted.

Wallace gave him a sidelong look, "Yes, happy birthday."

Both boys were dressed nicely, and Nathan had parted his hair and waxed it down the way Wallace often did. The smell of shoe polish hung in the air.

"Well, thank you for your thoughtfulness," Ava said. "You really didn't need to bring me gifts." The boys stood awkwardly to greet her.

"Here!" Nathan said, shoving his gift toward her. "And I brought you some apples, too." He removed a sack of apples that hung from his shoulder and handed it to her. "They're from Julian. Did you know they grow apples there?"

"No, I didn't know that. I love apples!"

He seemed pleased by her response. "I brought you thirteen, for your age."

Ava sat on the bench with the bag of apples at her side and the gift on her lap. "The daisy is lovely, too." She lifted the lid from the box, revealing a blue hat similar to the one the bull destroyed.

"Oh my goodness! My hat! Nathan, how did you do this?"

"I have a friend," he said with a grin. "I know, another friend, right?" he added, with a nervous laugh. "Anyway, I took your battered hat in and had her make another one like it. I feel real bad about your old one. Owen and Lydia gave it to me if you're wondering how I got it." Ava glanced at her siblings, who looked wide-eyed and guilty.

Ava placed the hat on her head. "It's beautiful—I really love it! Thank you." Her smile quickly faded, "But it must have cost you a fortune in wages, and you shouldn't have . . ."

"Don't worry. I got some extra hours at the brickyard. It was nothing, really," he lied, staring down at his scuffed shoes.

Nathan looked relieved when Ava said, "That's very sweet of you."

"I've brought you something, too," Wallace said eagerly.

"Sorry," Nathan stepped aside to let Wallace present his gift.

"Now, what did you do, Wallace? This feels heavy." Ava loosened the ribbon and peeled open the wrapping paper to reveal a leather case.

"Go on, open it," Wallace urged, his blue eyes gleaming.

Hesitating, she opened the case to find a red violin inside. "Wallace! What in the world!"

"It's an extra one that Jesse had, so I bought it. I hope you like it."

141

"Like it? It's more beautiful than my old one—even when it was new. It's too nice!" Her eyes lit up as she scrutinized the violin.

"Please, take it. It would hurt my feelings if you didn't. You only turn thirteen once."

"I have to go," Nathan abruptly announced, his face flushed. Ava started to protest, but Nathan turned and hurried out the door.

Ava and Wallace watched him go from the doorway.

"I wonder what's the matter?" Ava said, concerned. She had noticed Nathan wiping his eyes while departing so quickly.

"Don't worry, he's a scrapper. He'll be fine," Wallace said.

"I sure hope so. It's not like him to behave this way."

Wallace changed the subject. "I know you might want to play your new violin, but it's a fine day for sailing. Are you up for a lesson? There's room for Owen and Lydia, too. We could use the extra weight since you have a tendency to flip us over."

"It's not my fault we flip over! If you would be so kind as to just *tell* me the color of the rope you'd like me to pull, I would happily pull it. Instead, you confuse me by using three different names for the same thing."

"You're even *more* fractious on your birthday," Wallace replied, rolling his eyes. "There are no ropes in sailing—they are properly called sheets or halyards, of which *none* are called the blue one, the green one, or the red-striped one."

"It certainly makes more sense to me to call a rope by its color. It's hard enough to determine which way the wind is blowing."

"And that . . . is why we flip."

❧

Nathan ran all the way to the ferry landing and up the ramp. He leaped onto a ferry that was pulling away from the dock.

"You made that one in the nick of time, boy," an old man muttered, lighting a pipe with a stem that disappeared into his long white beard.

"Lucky break. Not too much of that going around," Nathan replied sourly. The old man nodded, puffing until the bowl of his pipe cast a fiery glow.

Nathan went to the deserted bow, where nobody would see his tear-streaked face. He looked across the water. It sparkled like a carpet of broken glass, each sliver reflecting light. He inhaled deeply, and his clenched grip on the railing loosened.

The horn blew and the ferry slowed to a stop in the middle of the bay. Passengers peered over the port side to see what was causing the delay. Nathan spotted a tugboat pulling a massive raft of thick logs tied together. The ferry captain made an announcement: "Folks, it looks as though the timber for the Hotel del Coronado has just arrived from up north. We'll be on our way shortly—sorry for the delay."

Nathan felt relief as he watched the raft float by, realizing he wouldn't need to move again in search of work. He and his father could stay put on Coronado forever—and he could be close to Ava. He wanted to impress her, but how? He couldn't compete with Wallace. Charm, looks, education, and wealth were all in Wallace's favor, and he was a better dancer. Nathan was tortured by the thought that he couldn't match him, not even in a million years. As the ferry pulled up to the wharf, Nathan got a wild idea. Maybe he *could* compete for Ava's good opinion and affection after all. Time was on his side, and implementing his idea would take some time. When Nathan disembarked from the ferry, he went to the only place that could help him with his plan: Old Town.

Chapter 20

Nathan walked down the dusty road to Old Town. Before long, a carriage came along, stopped, and picked him up. "I owe you one, Gus," Nathan said. "You're always there when I need you."

"We're square," Gus said, nodding as he drove on. He whistled a lullaby to baby Willard, who napped beside him in his modified pram.

In Old Town, Nathan entered the saddlery. "Excuse me, *Señora*, do you know where I can find Mr. Delafuente?"

An old woman with weathered skin used an oiled cloth to buff a saddle. "*Cantina. Siesta,*" she said.

"What's a *siesta?*"

"Sleep." She went back to buffing. *You get to take a nap and name it?* Nathan thought as he made his way to the cantina. *What a great culture!* He stopped to smile at a shoeless toddler playing with pebbles in the dirt. He passed a candlemaker and watched him dip string into buckets of melted wax, then cold water. Each time he lifted the string, a larger clump of wax clung to it, which he quickly shaped with his hands. On a nearby table, dozens of candles were cooling to a solid form.

A maze of carriages, horses, and people cluttered Calhoun Street. Nathan found the cantina and entered. Mr. Delafuente and a few of his friends were leaning back in chairs with their boots crossed at the ankles and their hats pulled over their eyes. *Now what?* Nathan thought. He found an empty chair and waited. Then he dozed off.

"*Guillermo, mira*, it's the kid that ran from the bull," a man said with a heavy accent, a silver tooth gleaming from his mouth when he spoke.

Nathan startled awake to find that the men were now surrounding him.

"What are you doing here, *amigo*? You know, I almost got fined by the sheriff for letting you run from that bull. If you're here for another wager, I can't do it." Mr. Delafuente's dark, penetrating eyes bore into Nathan.

"Hey, I signed a waiver with the county clerk," Nathan protested. "And I'm not here for another bet anyway I got myself a real job now. And besides, I made you money, didn't I? You said you owed me, remember?"

A smile revealed a gap between Mr. Delafuente's front teeth, and his hard stare softened. "Okay, *bueno*." He shrugged. "So what can I do for you?"

Nathan hesitated, feeling a little foolish. He was hoping he could talk to Mr. Delafuente alone, but it turned out, the whole band was there in the cantina—and everyone was staring at *him*. "Well . . . I want to be a mariachi," Nathan said. The men erupted into laughter. "No, I'm serious! I want you to teach me to play the guitar. Okay, maybe I can't be in your mariachi band, but I want to learn to play a guitar like a true mariachi." The men laughed again. "And I can pay you for the lessons."

One of the men produced a tiny guitar and handed it to Nathan, laughing hysterically. Nathan took it, reluctantly. "What is this? A ukulele?" The men continued to cackle with laughter.

Mr. Delafuente sobered. "*Amigo, why* do you want to play the *guitarra*? There is only one reason I will accept. If you have the right reason, *maybe* I will take you as a student."

The other men became silent, their laughter silenced.

Nathan's shoulders slumped and he gazed at the ground. *One acceptable reason? What can it be?* he wondered, his forehead wrinkling with tension when nothing came to mind. He decided he'd just tell the truth and let them laugh. "For a girl," he admitted quietly.

"Bravo!" shouted Mr. Delafuente, clapping his hands. The other men cackled again.

"*Really?*" Nathan brightened.

"That, *amigo*, is the *only* good reason to play the *guitarra*."

"So you'll teach me, then?"

"Maybe. *Pepe, traigame mi guitarra*," Mr. Delafuente ordered. Pepe ran from the room, returning quickly with a guitar.

Mr. Delafuente pulled up a chair across from Nathan and began to tune his instrument. "I'm available on Fridays, after *siesta*. In the beginning, you can learn to play on a little *guitarra*, and later a bigger one." He fanned the fingers of his right hand over the strings, unleashing an explosive, beautiful sound.

"When can I learn to do *that?*" Nathan said, impressed.

"The *rasqueado?* First, you need to learn the names of the strings, then I'll teach you chords and, later, techniques for the Spanish guitar. It's the only style that can win a woman's heart." Mr. Delafuente fanned his fingers across the strings again. He then plucked the strings so rapidly; the sound was like the cascade of a waterfall. "Tremolos." He strummed the guitar and simultaneously tapped it with his ring finger. "*Golpeadores* are 'strikes,' but only *later* will I teach you the *golpe*. Because if you don't know what you're doing, you'll make a hole in my *guitarra*—and then I will be very *enojado*, okay? And just in case you don't know, that means 'angry'!"

"All right, we'll wait on the *golpe*," Nathan agreed.

"Can you sing, *amigo?*" His fingers played up and down the fretboard with little effort.

"I've never actually tried. I mean, singing is not something we do at my house."

Mr. Delafuente's hands ceased playing. "*Amigo*, if you want to win the heart of a woman, singing is the only way."

"I thought you said the Spanish *guitarra* was the only way?"

"Singing *with guitarra*—even faster. Come on, sing something."

Nathan stared at his feet. "I really don't know any songs. What should I sing?"

"Okay, repeat after me: '*Estas son, las mañanitas!*'" Mr. Delafuente snapped his fingers and his men lined up dutifully. "It's a birthday song,

146

everybody knows it." He sang it again. *"'Estas son, las mañanitas!'"*

Nathan inhaled and tried to mimic Mr. Delafuente, singing the song in the same soulful manner. His voice cracked a few times, but he pushed through by singing louder. The men looked at him with surprise.

"You know, for a little guy, you have some power, *amigo*," Mr. Delafuente said. "When your voice finishes changing, you may sound pretty good."

Then men cackled again. Nathan was willing to take the criticism if it meant he could learn to play. Mr. Delafuente called everyone back to order. "Okay, again." Nathan repeated the line more confidently this time, and the mariachis chimed in with an explosion of harmony. Mr. Delafuente clapped slowly after the room fell silent. "See you next week, *amigo*," he said.

"Oh, thank you, Mr. Delafuente! I won't be late. How do you say *thank you* in Spanish?"

"Gracias."

"Gracias so much!"

Nathan could still hear them laughing as he departed, but he didn't care. He was going to learn to play the little guitar in his hands so well, they wouldn't laugh anymore. And then, one day, he would play it for Ava.

&⚬⚬

On board the *Duchess*, Wallace gave instructions. "This red sail is the spinnaker. It's the largest sail we have, and we only raise it when we're going downwind. I'm going to rig it up on the bow, and I'll tell you when we're ready to hoist it," he said. "We'll need to head into the wind, but don't tack without my word—or without letting your crew know—because the boom will swing across the deck, and it can hit us in the head."

"Aye! Spinnaker. Don't tack yet. Got it, Captain!" Ava replied smartly.

Wallace shook his head wearily. "Owen, I'm going to show you how to tie a bowline onto the spinnaker with this halyard. The halyard is the line, or green rope, as your sister likes to call it."

"I heard that!" Ava called out. She took note of which side of her face the wind was touching first. The right side first meant they were on a starboard tack.

"We aren't ready yet, so just stay the course," Wallace called over his shoulder.

"I know, I know, you told me already," Ava replied. "By the way, I think that boat over there is following us. Every time we turn, they turn."

"It's called jibing or tacking, not *turning*." Wallace looked up to study the boat Ava had pointed out. Shielding his eyes from the sun, he focused and confirmed, "That's the *Andromeda*."

"You know it?" Ava asked.

"It belongs to the Claypoole family. Beatrice must be on it. Let's tack now and see if they follow."

Ava pushed the tiller, and the boat responded quickly, tilting them at a sharp angle. Shortly after they tacked, the *Andromeda* did the same, gaining on them.

"Let's head into the wind," Wallace ordered. The boat lost momentum and slowed, allowing the *Andromeda* to catch up and cross below their stern. They were close enough now to see the sour look on Beatrice's face as she recognized them. She quickly shouted orders at the skipper, and a flurry of movement followed by the crew.

"I think she wants to race us," Wallace said.

"Even though they have a bigger boat and they're ahead of us now?" Ava asked, incredulous at the thought.

"*Bigger* doesn't always mean 'faster.' We're lighter than they are. You see that buoy they are about to round? We'll go around it, too, and if they want to race us, we'll give them a race."

"A race to *where*? I don't know how to race!"

"Back to the boathouse. Don't worry, I'll tell you what to do. Lydia, you help your sister with the tiller. Don't let her yank too fast to one side or the other."

Lydia nodded. "Okay, Wallace. I won't let her do it."

"Thanks a lot, Lydia!" Ava said. Lydia shrugged. "Captain's orders, sorry."

"When we round the mark, I'll give you word to throw the spinnaker, Owen, and I'll hoist it. Understand?" Wallace said. Owen nodded.

The *Duchess* rounded the mark, and Ava squealed as the wind filled their sail, tilting them at an angle so sharp she could easily touch the water.

"Now!" Wallace yelled.

Owen tossed the spinnaker up in the air while Wallace hauled it up, pulling in the halyard hand over fist as fast as he could. The spinnaker shimmied upward, flapped open, filled, then rounded out. Lydia started cheering. "It's like a big red balloon! It's so pretty!" Wallace pulled down the jib and left it in a pile on the bow.

The *Andromeda* crew hoisted their spinnaker, too, a large blue sail with a cursive *A* emblazoned on it. The breeze picked up, and both sailboats raced down the bay, passing anchored tall ships and waving to the vessels' crews.

"How do we beat a bigger boat?" Owen asked.

"Strategy. We outmaneuver them and get a jump on the good wind. See that ripple on the water coming our way? That's a puff of wind, and we're in a good position to gain from it. The wind pushes us upward and forward, and we ride it until we get the next puff. If we're lucky."

Wallace ordered tacks and jibes until they pulled up just below the stern of the *Andromeda*. "Wallace, don't bring us any closer to them—it's making me nervous!" Ava cried out. Beatrice was glaring back at them. She urged the skipper on. "Faster, Captain! Don't let them overtake us!"

"We need to get out of their bad wind, it's slowing us down," Wallace said. "Let's jibe. Owen, get your sheet wrapped around the winch and use the handle to trim it in."

Owen did as he was told, wrapping three loops of line around a winch drum.

"Okay, helms away!" Wallace called out.

"Helms away? What is that? I've never even heard that before," Ava protested. "Stop using new words!"

They went around another buoy and were heading upwind. "It's time to take down the spinnaker and put up the jib again," Wallace instructed.

"Ava, once Owen and I get it pulled back in, you're going to turn to the right, okay? It's a starboard tack. That's turning into the wind."

"Right!"

A wind gust filled their sails and they moved ahead of the *Andromeda*; its crew had pulled down the spinnaker but was having difficulty raising the jib. It had gotten twisted. Wallace called for a jibe and Ava pushed the tiller. The boom swung across the boat, and the jib was pulled across to the other side of the bow.

The *Andromeda* set a course perpendicular to theirs. "We're running out of room, Wallace!" Ava yelled in a panic. "They're coming right at us!"

The bow of the *Andromeda* was two boat lengths away and closing in.

"They have to give us room—we have the right of way," Wallace replied confidently. He cupped his mouth with his hands and shouted a warning to their skipper. "We have starboard tack!"

"What? Starboard tack? All right," Ava replied, pushing the tiller hard. Their boat spun in a rapid circle, causing the boom to swing violently. Lydia and Ava ducked as the boom swept across the deck, knocking Wallace overboard. He landed in the water with a big splash.

"Oh no!" Ava shrieked, letting go of the tiller and holding her hands to her mouth. Lydia grabbed hold of it and steered the boat as it rocked. The *Andromeda* swerved away, with Beatrice grinning triumphantly back at them.

Wallace was treading water when the *Duchess* drifted by him. "I don't think I tacked!" Ava called out to him.

"No, you didn't." He spat a stream of water high into the air. "In fact . . . you jibed."

"I did?" Ava cringed. "Oh. And I think we lost the race."

"I can see that."

Owen dropped the jib, then helped Lydia circle the *Duchess* slowly around Wallace to pick him up.

"Well, are you going to climb back in?" Ava asked, holding a rope to throw to him.

"I think I'd be better off swimming in. You're trying to kill me."

"I did *not* just try to kill you!" she huffed.

"You kind of did," Lydia admitted. Ava shot her a dour look.

"Owen, did I?" Ava asked, seeking his opinion on the matter. He winced and nodded.

"Well, if I had clearer directions, perhaps I wouldn't have panicked. I probably spared us a collision anyhow, so we are the better for it." Ava tossed Wallace the rope.

Wallace pulled himself in and climbed up, lying on his stomach across the bow in a soggy heap.

"Why don't you just tell me left or right next time?" Ava continued, her arms crossed over her chest defensively.

Wallace rolled over onto his back and chuckled softly. "I agree. For you, left or right next time."

"That will do just fine. That is if I ever decide to sail with you again, Wallace. It is clearly a dangerous sport!"

Chapter 21

The arrival of the timber rafts marked the beginning of the building frenzy. Spectators flocked to the island to watch the framing of the hotel from the safety of the pavilion. The clanking of hammers and wheezing of saws could be heard across the island. By dark, electric lights lit up the sky so the night crew could pick up where the day crew left off. Around the clock they worked, coming and going from the newly built boardinghouse for laborers. At the stables, the Hennessey family could scarcely keep up with the daily demand. Luckily, Gus was running his carriage company on the island, and his business was flourishing. Ava transported tourists in her carriage from sunup to sundown, going between the ferry landing and the pavilion in an endless loop. She had become well versed in providing tours along the way for her customers.

"On the right, we have our new post office, the *Coronado Mercury* news office, and the hotels Josephine and Oxford. Also, the offices of the Coronado Beach Company, Water Company, Ferry Company, Electric Company, Brick Company, and the Coronado Railroad Company." The tourists were greatly impressed with the rapid development as Ava transported them down Orange Avenue.

"Miss Ava, do you happen to know how many varieties of trees there are?" one lady inquired.

"Mr. Koeppen is the island's gardener. He has planted over two dozen varieties of palm trees as well as oak pine, pepper, jacaranda, olive, magnolia, eucalyptus, and citrus trees. Not to mention the flowers. It seems everything is happy to grow here."

"And why wouldn't it be?" the lady marveled. "Every prospect pleases! It really is quite lovely! Howard, we should purchase a home here and settle."

"Now, now, Rita, let's not get too ahead of ourselves, dear," the lady's husband protested weakly, chuckling.

Ava had heard this argument many times before, and she knew just what diversion was needed. "And over here on the left, we have Mathewson's Grocery, with the schoolhouse on our right, although it's still in a tent. And up ahead is our town garden and ostrich farm." Ava tried to catch a glimpse of Nathan, but she couldn't spot him anywhere on the grounds. He'd become so busy working extra hours at the brickyard, she rarely saw him. He wasn't available on Friday afternoons for a swim in the bay anymore, nor on Sundays to read on the beach. She sighed when they passed the farm with no sight of him. She missed him. The ostriches watched them pass warily. "They've also begun building Christ Church," Ava pointed out. "And if you're Catholic, there's a priest named Father Ubach, who rows over every Sunday morning to say Mass. There are also plans to build a Presbyterian church across the street."

A young boy on the sidewalk waved his hat. "Hello, Harry!" Ava called out to him. "That's my friend Harry West. He wants to be the first bellhop at the Hotel del Coronado when it opens."

They rode past a white tent with a lager banner written in bold letters:

CORONADO BEACH RESTAURANT, D. C. FOX - PROPRIETOR. MEALS AT ALL HOURS. A GOOD SQUARE MEAL 25 CENTS, AND DON'T YOU FORGET IT!

Tourists laughed at this sign every time, as if on cue. Ava smiled and continued her commentary. "The boathouse is to our left, and the jobsite for the hotel is there on our right." The men always whistled when they first saw the wooden framing and scaffolding for the enormous structure. At a glance, one could see dozens of workers hammering, sawing, and carrying in more planks. Like ants in a dirt mound, they worked with a common purpose and a sense of urgency. Stacks of planks lined the beach, ready to be utilized.

The carriage bumped across the road. "I do apologize for the bumps. They've recently put down rail tracks," Ava said. "Before long, we'll be able to take a train all the way around the bay and straight down the center of Orange Avenue. They'll be able to bring in supplies by train as well as by ferry." Ava halted the carriage before the pavilion. "And here we are."

"You are a wealth of knowledge, Miss Ava," one gentleman said by way of a compliment. "You have done a splendid job showing us the island. This certainly is a unique corner of the world!"

His lovely wife added, "You're doing a fine job, young lady. Your mother must be very proud."

"Indeed she is—thank you, ma'am. I hope you enjoy your visit and come back to stay when our new hotel opens."

"My wife will dream of nothing less, I assure you," the gentleman replied, "And speak of nothing less, either." His wife swatted at him with her closed parasol, making him laugh.

∂∾∽

Colonel Holabird was the next to board Ava's carriage, right on schedule. He immediately pulled out his notepad and pen. "What have you heard lately, Miss Ava?"

"A few new ones from today that you may like. There's: 'Every prospect pleases' and 'My wife will dream of nothing less' and 'This certainly is a unique corner of the world.' I've also heard the title: 'Unrivaled queen of resorts.'"

Colonel Holabird scribbled on his notepad. "Excellent! I think I'll use all of them." Ava returned the latest book she had borrowed, and Colonel

Holabird loaned her a tattered magazine called *Godey's Lady's Book*. "There's a short story in here from a man named Edgar Allan Poe. A little macabre, but riveting prose nonetheless, which is why I've kept it all these years. You may enjoy it. Is Mr. Babcock in today?"

"Yes, sir. He's in a meeting with the Reid brothers. They're poring over the building plans."

"As they do every day. I don't think they're even following them." He laughed. "You certainly are the eyes and ears of this island, Ava. Keep up the good work, and I'll check back with you soon for more quotes."

"Good day, Colonel Holabird," Ava replied, dropping him off at a tent facing the construction site. "Thanks for the new book."

"Read it during the daytime. I don't want you losing sleep."

"I like scary stories, don't worry. I won't be frightened. Remember, I read Mary Shelley's *Frankenstein?*"

"Of course! I couldn't sleep for a week after I read *Frankenstein*. Her monster still haunts me! In any event, I do hope Poe is to your liking."

Colonel Holabird left Ava and entered the tent to find Mr. Babcock, Mr. Story, and the Reid brothers comparing blueprints.

"It doesn't matter that they aren't following the plans to the letter per se, what matters is that she's going up at a fast rate," Mr. Babcock assured the others.

"They're building ahead of our blueprints," countered James Reid.

"Are you concerned?"

"I suppose not, so long as you aren't. They keep building additional rooms that are not indicated on our plans."

"As long as the corners meet and we ultimately have a square hotel with a courtyard in the center, what does it matter?"

Mr. Reid chuckled. "I must say I enjoy your spontaneity on this project, Elisha. It's a wonderful departure from what I'm accustomed to, I assure you, but I *am* providing a service and I intend to live up to your expectations."

"James, we haven't the time to rewrite the plans to perfection. I admire your integrity and most certainly your wisdom and experience on such matters as these. But I give you my word, I will not hold you accountable for departures we take from your brilliant design."

"Very well."

"I see progress is being made," interrupted Colonel Holabird, joining the conversation.

"Ah, Holabird, welcome to our planning committee!" bellowed Mr. Story.

Colonel Holabird looked at the design sprawled on the table and compared it to the structure going up outside the tent. "Looks nothing like it."

"Precisely! It's whimsical, just as I imagined it!" replied Mr. Babcock with a laugh. "We're starting on the simple side first so the builders can gain the skills necessary to tackle the more elaborate design features. In the end, it will more or less look like the plans you see before you."

"I have all the faith in the world," replied Colonel Holabird.

"And how goes our national advertising campaign?"

"Exceedingly well. I have brought for you the latest brochure that will hit Chicago and New York train stations on Monday." Colonel Holabird removed a stack of pamphlets from his attaché case and distributed them. They read as follows:

The Hotel del Coronado
America's Grandest All-Year-Round Seaside Resort—Opening Soon!
With its fine situation and lovely surroundings, everything is provided for which the heart can desire. Coronado Natural Mineral Water
To be used for all purposes at the hotel.
THE CLAIMS OF THIS EXCELLENT WATER
Are based on the results of its curative action upon hundreds who have been effectually relieved from Kidney and Bladder Ailments from which they had suffered for years. The most eminent physicians will tell you that the first principle of any cure to be arrived at is the formation of healthy, rich blood. The body is thus enabled to effect its own restoration. No Medicine known to man can produce this much-desired result so effectually as pure, wholesome water, such as that which flows

from the Coronado Natural Springs.

"Nicely done, Holabird, I particularly enjoy the medical benefits of our spring water," said Mr. Babcock. "Perhaps expand upon this. Maybe anecdotal ailments that could see a curative response?"

"I'll check with my physician. I'll update the brochure upon the completion of the hotel, and distribute copies across the country at once."

"Europe, too," suggested Mr. Story. All five gentlemen broke into wide grins.

Mr. Babcock beamed. "Our resort is going to be stupendous, gentlemen, simply stupendous!" he announced. He had no inkling they would run out of money—or that a land bust would send the investors fleeing Southern California.

Chapter 22

After school, Ava went to Nathan's house. Once again, he wasn't home, so she decided to wait for him on the front steps. The day had been mostly gray, with the same heavy cloud cover that had lingered since the start of June. She looked forward to August when the gloomy clouds would dissipate early and the sun would shine again. She had asked Colonel Holabird if he'd be mentioning the notorious "June gloom" in his brochures. He had replied that cool, cloudy days were preferable to the heated terms of New York, complete with insects that rivaled the plagues in the time of Moses. He always said the most interesting things, and Ava thought him to be one of the funniest men she had ever met.

Ava sat thinking about Poe's short story "The Cask of Amontillado," which Colonel Holabird had loaned her. She had brought the magazine for Nathan to read. When he rode up on his horse, he didn't see her. She watched in silence as he dismounted and tied his horse to a fence post. Just as he was about to remove a wrapped item from the saddlebag, Ava said hello, causing Nathan to startle and quickly shut the flap of the saddlebag. He spun around and backed up against his horse.

"Are you hiding something there?"

"Ava, hello, like what? What would I be hiding?" he laughed nervously.

"Oh, I don't know. I don't know anything about you anymore because I never see you. We used to be friends, remember?"

He forced a smile. "It's such a surprise that you are here," he countered. "It's nice to see you. Actually, I was going to call on you tomorrow in fact."

"Really? You haven't been to my house since my birthday, when you ran away. That was months ago. Now I'm supposed to believe you planned to come over tomorrow to call on me?"

"Look, I'm sorry about your birthday. I just . . . Well, I just wish I could have gotten you that violin since it was because of me that you lost your first one."

"Oh, it wasn't lost."

"I know, I mean . . . it got destroyed because of me. Foolish me." He looked down at his dirty boots and kicked at a clump of dirt.

Her voice softened and she stepped closer. "I don't fault you anymore, you know that. I just miss seeing you."

He looked into her hazel eyes and quickly looked away. An awkward silence fell between them.

"So, why were you going to call on me?" she asked, still thinking he was acting suspicious.

"To tell you about a surprise. Do you want to see it?"

"Are you kidding? Of course I do!"

"Follow me, then." He led her around the back of the house to the ostrich corral. "Be real quiet, we have to sneak up on it."

"I can be quiet," Ava whispered loudly.

Nathan rolled his eyes.

"All right, fine, I can't *ever* be quiet. Just show me!" she whispered, annoyed.

He got on his hand and knees and motioned for her to follow him through a patch of tall grass that ran along the corral. When they reached the fence, Nathan parted the grass so they could peek through the beams. She spotted Twilah, sitting in the dirt, snapping at bugs that flew around her head. Near her stood a tall, alert male, keeping his eye out for anything untoward. Nathan reached into his pocket and pulled out a piece of bread. He rolled it in his hands and, staying low, tossed it into the corral, away from the birds. Twilah rose quickly and charged after it, followed by the male.

"Do you see it now?" Nathan whispered, pointing to a nest with three large eggs in it. Ava stifled a giggle, her eyes lighting up. Twilah gobbled up the bread, sharing none with the male, and returned to her eggs. Ava giggled again, then clasped her fingers over her mouth to silence her noise. The male ostrich heard her and walked over to the fence to investigate. Nathan nudged Ava's head down into the grass and held his finger over his lips. The male surveyed the area, ruffled his feathers, then returned to protect the nest. Nathan yanked on Ava's foot to motion for them to retreat.

"When will they hatch, do you think?" she asked when they were a safe distance away.

"I don't know for sure, but I'll run and come get you when I think it's going to happen."

"Mean old Twilah is going to be a mother, what a laugh that is!"

"She's likely to get even meaner with little ones to protect."

"You're right about that. Be careful not to take your eyes off her if you know what's good for you."

"I'll try to remember that," Nathan said, laughing.

"Have you been practicing your reading?"

"Yes, ma'am. I don't have a lot of free time lately, but I do my best."

"Good, I brought you a new book."

"You said I didn't have to read *Pride and Prejudice*," he protested.

Ava smirked. "I did, but you're missing out. I think you'd like it a great deal more than *Little Women*."

"I'll take my chances."

"This one is a haunting tale about a man getting trapped in a room by bricks. I just thought you'd like it," she said. "Since you make bricks," she added awkwardly.

Nathan kept looking away from her. He was guilty of something, Ava was sure of it. "Say, are you going to the wedding?" she asked. "It's the first one to take place on the hotel grounds, you know?"

"They're going to have a wedding before it's even completed?"

"May Barnes told me she is besotted with Harold Scott, and she isn't going to wait another day to be his wife. I stopped by to make sure you were going."

"*Besotted.* Good word. Am I invited?

"The whole town is invited—of course you're invited! And your father, too."

"Then I'll be there."

"Good." She pulled the magazine rom her satchel and handed it to him. "The author, Poe, is a bit of a madman, but brilliant nonetheless. I couldn't put it down."

"Poe the madman. I can't wait."

Ava wasn't impressed with his cynicism. "See you at the wedding." She turned on her heels.

"Do you need a ride home?" he called after her.

"I prefer to walk. Thanks."

❧

As soon as Ava was out of sight, Nathan opened the saddlebag on his horse and removed the little guitar Mr. Delafuente had loaned him. He was learning quickly, and soon he'd be moving up to a full-sized guitar. He'd been saving a penny every day to buy one. His singing wasn't going as smoothly as he had hoped, but his playing was improving dramatically. He found he really loved the sound of the stringed instrument. At night, while lying in bed, he practiced the few chords he'd learned, memorizing every note along each string. He didn't know the names of each note, but he could find their equivalent tones in different places along the fretboard. The guitar was starting to make sense to him, and he was grasping the patterns in each scale. He wanted to surprise Ava. That day wouldn't be anytime soon, but one day he would play for her. If he showed her now, he'd look like a fool. While working at the brickyard, he often daydreamed of playing guitar and singing her a song. He'd confess that she was his muse and always would be. In the dream, she was awestruck by his talent. She also marveled at the shiny buttons on his mariachi pants and was enamored with his wide sombrero. But the dream always ended abruptly, with the foreman shouting orders for him to get back to work. Bricks needed to be made, posthaste. Nathan set a lofty goal: to perform for Ava on opening night at the Hotel del Coronado. He had less than a year to learn the guitar, practice, and make an excellent impression on her.

Chapter 23

June 9, 1887

Harold Scott waited expectantly beneath a canopy of evergreens dotted with white flowers. Nervous, he straightened the white rose on his lapel and adjusted his bow tie, craning his neck as if his collar were becoming too tight. His mother glanced worriedly over her shoulder, as did the mother of the bride, May Barnes. Ava subtly peeked down the aisle, too. A sinking feeling fluttered in her stomach. Earlier that day, she helped set up chairs on the beach, decorate the wedding canopy, and center the wreath above the space where the bride and groom would exchange their vows. A sign that read Harold and May hung on a temporary wooden wall covered by a white curtain; it had been fashioned to distract from the scaffolding, ladders, and framed turrets of the hotel in the background. Stacks of wood still lay on the beach, drying in the sun.

Ava wasn't well acquainted with either Harold or May, but she thought it was very kind of them to invite the whole town to their wedding. Theirs would be the first wedding on the hotel grounds, an honor May was reportedly thrilled about. *So where is she?*

Nathan and his father sat near Ava's family on the bride's side, while Wallace and his family sat on the groom's. Ava fidgeted with the pleats of her peach-colored dress. She wore white gloves and had her hair tucked beneath a white flowerpot hat.

Several awkward minutes passed. Wallace got up and walked to the rear of the assembly. He spoke with Mrs. Forbey, the wedding coordinator, who appeared distraught. Moments later, Wallace returned and discreetly motioned for Ava and Nathan to join him. Ava excused herself, apologizing as she made her way down the aisle, trying not to kick up sand.

"Ava, the violinist hasn't arrived yet. They can't start the wedding without music. Do you think you could play?" Wallace whispered to her.

"Me? Play right now?" she whispered back, looking stricken.

"Of course *you!*"

"I can't play for a wedding!"

"Yes you can!" he insisted. "They need you!"

"I can run and fetch your violin," Nathan offered.

"Take my horse—she's the Appaloosa tied to the last post. I'll buy some time," Wallace said.

"It's in your room, right?" Nathan asked.

"Yes, beside my bed. Oh, I'm nervous! What if I ruin their wedding?"

"You won't. They need you. Hurry, Nathan!" Wallace urged.

Beatrice discreetly listened to Wallace converse with Ava and Nathan. She rose, excused herself from her row, and went to locate the family's coachman. She found him sitting on a stool under the shade of a tree, smoking a pipe. "Hemsworth, go and fetch my violin. At once!" she ordered.

"Yes, Miss Claypoole!" Jumping up, he dumped the fiery contents of his pipe on the ground, stamped on the ashes, and departed.

Nathan returned ten minutes later, red-faced, with the violin case in hand. Ava removed the instrument and walked to the front of the assembly. She began to play a simple melody, her fingers trembling. The mother of the bride, flooded with relief, dabbed at her eyes with a handkerchief. Ava noticed Jesse Shepherd in the first row, nodding with encouragement, urging her to fight through her nerves. Ava bit her bottom lip and pushed the doubt from her mind. Soon, several flower girls tossed rose petals as they made their way down the center aisle. A chubby toddler escaped from his mother's arms and ran after them. "No, brother, you can't be a fairy, too!" one of the flower girls cried, causing him to squeal in protest. The guests laughed when the boy's frantic mother chased after him and scooped him up.

Beatrice suddenly appeared next to Ava, holding a red violin. Ava never thought she'd be so relieved to see her. She wore a purple silk dress with matching flowers piled on her hat. "Can you read music?" Beatrice asked, opening a book on a music stand. Ava shook her head no as she continued to play. "Can you play Schubert?" Ava shrugged, still bowing.

Beatrice pursed her lips. "But of course you can't—just try to stay with me, then. Pachelbel's Canon in D Major." Beatrice took the lead and Ava followed. May Barnes finally appeared at the end of the aisle, wearing an exquisite white gown in the current Victorian fashion. She carried a simple bouquet of white roses, and her dark hair was swept up in a romantic chignon. Mrs. Forbey clapped merrily. All eyes followed May as her father paraded her down the aisle. Her mother sobbed into a kerchief. Ava synchronized with Beatrice, both falling silent when the bride reached the groom.

Harold Scott and May Barnes exchanged wedding vows in the flow of a setting sun and pastel clouds. Ava looked at the well-wishers smiling in the audience. Wallace winked when he caught her eye. Thinking it was for her, Beatrice beamed before realizing she was mistaken. Wallace was grinning at Ava.

When the newlyweds walked down the aisle together, Beatrice snapped, "Now we play Schubert!" Rice hailed upon Harold and May, and Beatrice challenged Ava to keep up with her. She enjoyed Ava's struggle, until at last Ava stopped playing. "Beatrice, I'm not as well trained as you are. You are very talented." Beatrice smiled with satisfaction.

The wayward violinist arrived, looking flustered as he apologized for having missed the ferry. Ava relinquished her role, happy to be relieved of her musical duties.

By the punch bowl, Ava spotted Mr. Hawthorne, who was preparing to take a picture of the bride and groom. She quickly stepped up to assist him. He directed her to arrange the newlyweds on a bench beneath the greenery. She seated the couple and held up the flash while Mr. Hawthorne disappeared under the camera's curtain. The bulb popped, light flashed, and smoke rose. The couple sat very still for another photograph. Taking in their somber expressions, Ava could hardly imagine they were blissful newlyweds from moments ago. She decided that if she were a photographer, she would prefer to capture her subjects looking delighted for a change. After the last photo was taken, the couple departed for the dance floor, looking cheerier. A few flowers had fallen from the wreath, so Ava gathered them up and climbed on the bench to replace them. She heard someone approach from behind.

"I've heard better music from an alley cat," Beatrice said.

"I'm not very good, I know, but practice makes perfect." Ava stepped down from the bench and straightened the pleats of her dress.

"You can't practice your way into talent. You either have it—or you don't."

Ava felt her cheeks flush. "Any more than you can practice being *pleasant*."

Beatrice laughed but she didn't look amused. "You know, your friendship with Wallace will never amount to anything more than that."

"You said so yourself, it's just a *friendship*." Ava's cheeks were getting warmer.

"Have you ever wondered why Wallace hasn't introduced you to his parents?"

"What does any of this have to do with friendship or music?" Ava retorted defensively, standing tall and looking at Beatrice squarely.

"He never will. Mark my words. Go back to the stables, Ava. It's where you belong."

"That sounds splendid. I'd rather be in the company of an ass than the likes of you, Beatrice," Ava retorted, surprised by the words that flew out of her mouth. *Wallace is right, I am fractious,* she thought.

Beatrice's eyes hardened and her lips pressed into grim lines.

"What is this all about?" Nathan interrupted, approaching the girls.

"I was merely encouraging your dear friend to pursue a career in animal husbandry," Beatrice replied in a cool tone.

Nathan gave her a disapproving look and turned to Ava. "Jesse is asking for you to play music with him."

"I'd love to play with Jesse again," Ava replied, looping her arm through Nathan's.

"Mr. Shepard?" Beatrice clarified, unable to hide her surprise.

"Yes, Jesse," Ava answered, proud to show they were acquainted. Nathan gently pulled her away by the arm.

"You'll see that I'm right!" Beatrice called out as Ava walked away.

"Right about what?" Nathan asked when they were a safe distance away.

"Nothing. She's just a dreadful girl. Don't mind her—I don't."

The dancing and merriment carried on late into the evening. Ava played her violin so vigorously that strings on her bow began to fray. Jesse was a fantastic violinist, and he was much easier to follow than Beatrice. He taught Ava new scores, including festive melodies from the frontier, which Ava found a delightful departure from the classics. Soon, all thoughts of Beatrice faded from her mind, as did the stinging realization that Wallace hadn't introduced her to his parents, even when the opportunity arose during the reception.

Wallace and Nathan watched with admiration as Ava played. Her long brown hair had slipped from its clip and fell loosely past her shoulders. When the last song ended, Nathan whistled loudly through his fingers as the crowd cheered. Wallace offered to escort Ava home, but she declined, telling him she'd rather not tarnish his family name by exiting with him. Ava let Nathan walk her home. Wallace was left to wonder alone what Beatrice had done, aware that only she could be responsible for the riff.

Chapter 24

"I know you're avoiding me. You're not a very good actress." Wallace said, sitting on a bale of hay in the barn.

Ava didn't look up at him. She pressed her shoulder against Ambrose's muscular torso, leaning into him. The horse shifted his weight, allowing Ava to bend his knee and lift his hoof. She used a curved pick to clean out the mud and rocks packed into his shoe. "Can't you see I'm working?" She released the hoof, lifted a second hoof and cleaned another horseshoe.

Wallace watched her work, amused by her stubbornness. "I've come over three times and you've been working every time," he complained.

"Haven't you read the papers? There are ninety ferries a day coming to the island. That's one every twenty minutes." She finished cleaning the last shoe and began brushing Ambrose vigorously. "Prospective land buyers get free carriage rides—that makes me a very busy girl."

"I can't imagine you don't get some respite. I know Gus has a company working on the island, too. No, I'm guessing it's something Beatrice said to you, which God knows could be anything."

Ava continued brushing.

"I wish you wouldn't listen to anything she says. You know she's disagreeable."

Ava stopped brushing and looked at him for the first time. "That I know. I also know what she says has a thread of truth to it." She resumed brushing.

"And what might that be?"

"Oh, that you will never introduce me to your parents—which you haven't."

Wallace closed his eyes and exhaled.

"If you're embarrassed to be my friend because I'm a stable girl, you don't have to be."

Wallace got up and walked to her side. He looked her in the eyes, studying her fixed expression. "Look, I can see that you're hurt . . ."

"I am *not* hurt!" she snapped.

"Just hear me out. Please. I haven't introduced you to my parents, that much is true. But it's not because I'm ashamed to be your friend."

Ava's face was flushed. Wallace stepped closer to her. "I haven't introduced you to them, because I'm afraid they'll say something that will make me ashamed of *them*." Ava's eyes widened. "You're the most amazing girl I've ever met. There, I said it."

Ava didn't know how to respond. Her stomach fluttered—his troubled eyes were so blue and beautiful.

"My father is very demanding, as is my mother, and both are very proper. I'm not saying that you aren't!" he quickly added when Ava raised her eyebrows. "It's just that they value things I don't value. Money, stature, titles, appearances. They want me to be like them and I'm not. I'm afraid my parents will say something condescending and awful to you, and I couldn't bear to hear it. So I'm sparing you from them. You have to believe me."

After some silence, Ava's expression softened. "But why would you have to spare me at all?"

"Because they don't know how much time I spend with you. I lie to them."

"You lie?"

"They think I'm fishing most of the time. If my mother knew I spent all my spare time with you, she'd have me arranged in marriage to a boring daughter of one of her friends. So I hide you from them."

"Fishing? You've caught one fish all year."

"I know. Until I met you. You were my good luck charm."

"You don't need to go overboard. That fish wasn't even edible." She looked away. He was standing too close. "So, you plan to hide me from your parents forever?"

"No. I've been meaning to tell you that once my sister regains her health, we will be heading back to New York."

Ava's couldn't hide her disappointment. "I see."

"I was hoping my father would purchase a lot and we could live here permanently. But it appears he has pressing business matters. I don't know how much time I have. Which is why I no longer care what my parents think. I want them to know you are my best friend—you and Nathan."

Silence fell between them. Ava felt heavy and wanted to cry.

"So, if I invite you to go yachting with my family, will you come? I'll invite Nathan, too."

Ava pondered this, then brightened. "Do you want me to skipper?"

"Absolutely not."

Laughing, he hugged her. Ava stiffened, taken off guard. "Sorry! I know you're working," Wallace added, quickly withdrawing. He changed the subject. "Speaking of Nathan, his ostrich farm was in the paper this morning. Did you happen to see the article?" He pulled a rolled-up copy of the *Coronado Mercury* from his back pocket.

"No, I haven't had time. While I finish up, why don't you read it to me."

"Would you rather I help you?"

"No, just read."

Wallace sat down on a bale of hay and opened the paper. "Let's see, it's right here next to an editorial titled "The Curse of Curses." Ava burst out laughing. "No, it's true, it says so right here: 'Dram drinking has for all time had in its wake misery, wretchedness and woe.'"

"Well, that much is true, drinking too much is a curse," Ava replied.

"Moving along, ah here we are. It says: 'Ostriches, now on exhibition on block 40. A rare opportunity to see birds of various sizes and ages. The birds are completely rested from their journey and are as frisky as colts.'"

Ava laughed at this, and Wallace continued: 'The old ones are somewhat vicious, and have broken fence boards with a single kick. The brain of the ostrich is very small, weighing only about an ounce in a bird of 1,000 pounds.'"

"Now, that's an interesting fact, isn't it?" Wallace asked, looking up. "Doesn't it make you want to see them?"

"How much for a tour?" Ava asked, shaking out a saddle blanket and placing it on Ambrose.

"Forty cents." Wallace flipped the page. "This is an interesting advertisement. It says: 'Lower California, the Italy of America! The Florida of the Pacific! The tropics without malaria!'" Wallace turned the paper around so Ava could see the advertisement.

She chuckled. "Maybe you should show that to your father and he'd choose to stay," Ava suggested.

"I think I will. Why on earth would he want to leave the Italy of America for New York?" They both laughed.

Ava began raking up hay strewn around the floor while Wallace resumed reading. "You know the Oxford Hotel?" he said.

"It just opened, yes—I ride past it every day."

"The very one. This story is called 'Had His Boots On.' It says: 'A boarder at the Oxford Hotel was in such an absentminded state the other night that he went to bed with his work boots on.'"

Ava stopped raking, "Are you making this up? Don't make up silly stories Wallace!"

"No! I swear! It says so right here!" He pointed to the article. "Just listen to the rest of it. You can't judge a story unless you've read it all." Wallace continued: "'The fact being reported to Captain Peters, he went up to investigate. "What are you doing in there with your boots on?" asked the Captain in no very gentle tone.'"

Ava dropped the rake. "Scoot over, let me see." He moved and 'she took a seat beside him. Wallace continued: "'Who in the _____ _____ _____ (unfit for publication) are you?' was the man's reply.'"

Ava and Wallace started laughing. "It's the parentheses and blank

171

lines that are the funniest part!" Wallace said. "Here, you finish it, I can't!"

Ava took over reading the article: "'There was no light in the room and without saying a word, the Captain lit a match and stuck it under the fellow's nose. The result was profuse apologies. The boots were pulled off and all was serene again.'"

"Oh dear," Ava said when she finished the article.

"That was the funniest story I've ever heard," Wallace replied, gripping his stomach from the strain of laughing so hard. "Maybe they could use a little help down there at the *Coronado Mercury*. You can write well, Ava. Why don't you submit a few articles for the paper? Maybe you can earn a little money. Nobody knows more about what's happening on the island than you do."

"I've never thought to do that. Do you really think I could?"

"Anything would be better than what we've just read. It looks like they need stories to fill the pages. So far, it's all advertisements, the ferry schedule, and land auctions for Del Mar and La Jolla. Speaking of which, have you been up there yet? We should go sometime—the coastline is magnificent."

"No, I haven't been. I'm always too busy."

"How about this, then, on your next day off, I'll invite you to go yachting and we'll cruise up the coast. Sound good?"

"I'd love to!"

"Good, then we have a deal."

Just then, Nathan barreled through the stable door. "The eggs are hatching! Come quickly!"

Ava squealed with delight, and she and Wallace jumped up to follow Nathan. He hopped on his horse, bareback. Ava and Wallace climbed into a buggy tethered to a hitching post and followed him.

At the ostrich farm, the three of them waded through the tall grass until they reached the fence, where they settled in for a view of the pen. Twilah and her mate stood flapping their wings, watching the eggs wiggle. Twilah's small head bobbed up and down nervously. She scratched the earth and inspected her nest. A crack appeared in one egg and a small beak pecked a hole through the shell. Pecking followed from within the other two eggs. After their heads were exposed, the baby birds stopped moving. They panted listlessly. "They're getting tired," whispered Nathan.

"Won't she help them?" Ava asked, distressed.

"Nah."

Ava looked horrified.

"It makes them stronger to do this on their own. Their mother won't help them."

"It's nature's way," offered Wallace.

"Well, I don't like nature's way!" Ava blurted. "They're just babies!"

"Shh!" Nathan hissed as Twilah lifted her head, looking around warily. Her mate took a few long steps toward the fence. Nathan sank low into the grass and the others followed.

"Sorry!" Ava mouthed silently.

An hour later, the wet chicks broke free of their shells and stood up. Blinking and chirping, they ran toward Twilah and stood close to her long legs for protection. Their feathers dried quickly, and soon they were fluffy like newborn chicks in a henhouse. Before long, the chicks were brave enough to leave their mother, running around the corral to snap at hovering gnats and investigate their new world.

Ava giggled into her hands. "They're so adorable!"

Nathan motioned Ava and Wallace to retreat with him.

"I'm so happy we got to see that. That was amazing!" Ava exclaimed.

"Should be good for business," Wallace added.

"That's all I need!" Nathan lamented. "Forty cents for admission is not enough. Yesterday, I had three kids hanging from my neck!"

"Do they call you Uncle Nathan?" Ava asked, amused.

"By the end of the day, they do! I'm supposed to give tours, not be a walking scarecrow for kids to climb on," Nathan groused. "All right, they are cute, I'll admit it."

"Say, do you think you could get a day off and go sailing with my family?" Wallace asked.

Chapter 25

"It's beautiful, Mother!" Ava gushed, twirling in a white dress with a lilac sash tied around her waist. "And just in time for boating day! Thank you for sewing this for me." She hugged her mother and observed her own tall reflection in the mirror. Her features were no longer rounded and childish.

"You're growing into a lovely young lady, Ava," her mother said. "And keep your hat on,—you're getting too much sun," she warned as Ava raced down the stairs.

Ava grabbed a straw hat on her way out the door. Father and Owen escorted her on the ferry to the dock where the elegant *Lurline* was moored. It was the finest yacht they had ever seen. It was steel hulled, with two large masts and a steam funnel centered between them. The cabin had two levels, and Owen counted twenty-one portholes beneath the deck. "I bet you could sail all around the world in no time in that boat," he said.

"She's certainly seaworthy," Father agreed.

Chatting ladies in fine dresses and elaborate hats made their way up the ramp to board the vessel. Among them were Mrs. Babcock and Mrs. Story, who waved when they saw Ava arrive in the coach.

"Have a wonderful time," Father said as Ava descended from the carriage.

"How could I not?" Ava gushed. She straightened the folds of her dress and opened a white lace parasol. Nathan snuck up behind her, sporting a pin-striped blue suit, new shoes, and a straw hat. He twirled with his hands in his pockets. "Guess who's a handsome gentleman?" he said, grinning.

"You do look positively handsome this afternoon, Nathan," Ava agreed, looking him over.

"I even put wax in my hair again, but I can't show you because I'd have to remove my fine hat."

Ava giggled.

A whistle from above called their attention. Wallace stood on the bow, waving for them to come up.

"May I escort you, my lady?" Nathan held out his arm and Ava looped hers through it. "Boat ramps can be very treacherous for a young lady such as yourself. Might I add that you look lovely, and your dress captures the essence of a summer's day."

"Oh dear!" Ava replied. "Are you going to be in character all day?"

"I might."

They said farewell to her father and Owen, then Ava let Nathan guide her up the ramp. Wallace waited at the top, wearing a tan and white striped suit. He led them to a receiving line, and introduced them to the crew, the captain, and Mr. Spreckels himself.

Mr. Spreckels was a burly man, with lively blue eyes, as well as a thick mustache and ready laugh. "Welcome aboard the *Lurline*!" he bellowed. "You'll have to meet my children—they'll be delighted you are here. Where did they run off to?" he said, scanning the deck. "At any rate, there are several Spreckels children running about the place, who are likely playing a good game of hide-and-seek. They'll be thrilled you're aboard."

Ava liked Mr. Spreckels right away. He had a warm, friendly, fatherly way about him. "It is very nice to meet you, Mr. Spreckels, and we thank you for the invitation to join your party today," Ava said as she curtsied.

"A pleasure! Any friend of the young Mr. Gregory here is a welcome friend of ours," he said, shaking Wallace's hand.

"Your yacht is spectacular, sir," Nathan added.

"She is, isn't she? My daughter Grace can give you a tour. We set sail momentarily. I believe we are headed to a fine cove up the coast, where we will stop for lunch. Glorious day! In the meantime, enjoy yourselves and see if you can find my children," he said, chuckling. "Mind you, they are very good at hiding."

On deck, Ava recognized others in the boating party: The Holabirds, the Hortons, the Storys, the Babcocks, and Mr. Gruendike, who had recently returned from his cattle ranch in Oregon. Even Jesse Shepard was on board, dressed in a fine white suit and straw hat. He was having an animated conversation with two gentlemen, who laughed heartily. As Ava scanned the bow, she spied the scowling face of Beatrice Claypoole. She sat at a round table, holding a parasol in one hand and a teacup in the other. She looked away as soon as Ava spotted her, acting as if she hadn't seen her.

"Look, it's your dear friend Beatrice, Ava," Wallace teased. "How delightful she's among our party."

"I'm afraid I'm her least favorite," Ava admitted.

"Let's go find the Spreckels children," Nathan suggested, "I love a good game of hide-and-seek."

"First, let me introduce you to my parents," Wallace said. "We may as well get on with it. And at least have an escape plan in place."

Mr. and Mrs. Gregory stood on the port side on the bow, not speaking to each other. "Mother, Father, I'd like you to meet my friends, Ava Hennessey and Nathan Beckman."

Mr. Gregory shook hands with Nathan while Mrs. Gregory looked Ava over with narrowed eyes. The lace on the bodice of Mrs. Gregory's dress was one Ava had seen in a French magazine. Mrs. Gregory extended her gloved hand but barely touched the tips of Ava's fingers.

"So pleased to meet you, Mrs. Gregory," Ava said, politely.

"Likewise, a pleasure, Miss Hennessey," said, her lips tight. She smelled heavily of floral perfume.

The sails were hoisted and the yacht jolted away from the dock.

"Ah, look, we're underway all ready," Wallace interrupted, eager to cut the introduction short. "Mother, Mr. Spreckels has put us to the challenge of finding his children. Do you mind if we oblige him?"

"Certainly not." Her eyes were emotionless. Everything about her dripped of society, finery, manners—and unhappiness. Ava couldn't imagine having a mother so distant and cold. Wallace urged his friends to move along quickly before his mother changed her mind. Mrs. Gregory watched them walk away and round the captain's wheelhouse. She couldn't have seen the three of them break into a run once they disappeared from view—and Ava doubted she would have approved.

Wallace, Nathan, and Ava raced the length of the yacht, laughing as they went. They passed a galley, a library, a smoking room, a study with a guitar mounted on one wall, a pantry, and an elegant dining room. Nathan seemed to take an interest in the study and wanted to go in, but Ava called him into the dining room first.

A long, wooden table draped with a floor-length linen tablecloth stood in the center of the room. Ava noticed a pair of small shoes slip quickly behind the long cloth. She motioned silently to the boys, pointing beneath the table.

"I wonder if there are any Spreckels children in here?" Wallace said, walking along one side of the table. A muffled giggle seeped out from under the table. "Hmmm. Now, if I were a boy, where would I hide? Maybe under here!" Wallace yanked up the tablecloth, revealing a blond-haired boy eating a cookie. "Aha! I found one!"

The boy giggled.

"Is that a good cookie?" Ava asked him, lowering herself to his level. The boy nodded. "What's your name?"

The boy chewed and then gulped. "John Spreckels Junior," he said in a raspy voice.

"I see, John Spreckels Junior, and how old are you? Let me guess . . . five?"

He nodded again.

"Well, I'm Ava, and this is Wallace and Nathan. Do you want to help us find your brothers and sisters?" He grinned, his teeth smeared with chocolate.

"How many siblings do you have?"

He held up two fingers. "Two sisters!"

"Why don't you lead the way, John," Wallace suggested when the boy came out from under the table. They followed him into the kitchen. When they opened cabinets, a shriek rang out as they uncovered ten-year-old Grace and Lillie, who was nine.

They were beautiful children, all three with golden hair and lively blue eyes like their father. The girls wore big white bows in their hair and sky-blue dresses, and John Junior sported a coat, knickers, and a bow tie.

"Can we play another round of hide-and-seek?" begged Lillie.

"Sure we can. Who wants to be *it*?" Wallace asked.

"I will!" Lillie announced. "Since I know all of the best hiding spots, I'll be sure to find you quickly."

Lillie counted to thirty while her brother and sister, along with the three older guests, scattered in all directions. John ducked back under the dining table, clutching another cookie from the panty. Grace led Ava, Nathan, and Wallace through several staterooms, passing the study and music room along the way.

"Do you have a piano forte?" Wallace asked.

"We do, but it's off the ship being serviced." Grace said, leading them from room to room until they entered the master suite. The walls were lined with inlaid mahogany panels like the ones in Jesse Shepard's house. The floor was lushly carpeted in green hues, and etched-glass sconces covered the lights on the walls.

"Is it all right that we are in here?" Ava whispered, feeling intrusive. Grace nodded emphatically, assuring them it was fine. Wallace hid behind a heavy damask curtain, and the girls darted under the massive wooden bed.

They all stifled giggles of anticipation. Any minute now, Lillie could enter, looking for them. "Do you want to be my best friend?" Grace whispered to Ava, her eyes imploring.

"Yes, I'd like that very much," Ava answered, smiling at the girl.

"I can write you letters from San Francisco, and you can write to me." Ava nodded in agreement.

A moment later, Ava and Grace could see a pair of bare feet tiptoeing into the room. Wallace screamed when Lillie grabbed him behind the curtain. "How could you see me? This is the greatest hiding spot ever!" he exclaimed.

"Your feet, silly!" Lillie replied. "I could see your shoes sticking out." It didn't take her long to find the girls under the bed, both of whom squealed with laughter upon being discovered.

"I found John, too," Lillie said. "He was under the dining room table again, where he always hides. But I *can't* find Nathan." She looked puzzled.

"Let's look for him together," suggested Ava.

᠔᠊᠊ᢀᠶ

Nathan closed the door to the music room, locked the door and drew the curtains. He turned and stared at the guitar hanging on the wall. *Do I dare?* He approached the instrument and lifted it from its hook. He took a seat on a nearby stool and placed the guitar across his lap. It smelled of rich cedar. Inside the body of the instrument was a faded label that read: *Por D. Antonio de Torres, Sevilla. Calle de la Cartageria, numero 32. Año de 1867.* Nathan strummed all six strings, marveling at the beauty of sound that rang out. The clarity and depth of each note were possible only through the finest craftsmanship could make. He made an A minor chord and began to pluck the lower strings. He repeated the pattern, changing the chord to a G major. Was this an *arpeggio* or a *falsetta?* He couldn't remember. He fanned out the fingers of his right hand one by one over the strings, followed by an upstroke. One day, he wanted to own a guitar as fine as this one.

"Have you tried this room?" Ava asked, entering the cabin next to the music room. Nathan was so absorbed in the instrument, he didn't hear her approaching with the others.

"He's not in here," replied Grace, reaching for the door handle to the adjacent room. She turned the knob and it clicked. Locked. "We'll have to go around."

Nathan saw the handle turn and jumped up from the chair. He placed the guitar back on its hook and scurried to the door to unlock it. "Found

179

him!" said Grace when he opened it. "That wasn't a very clever hiding spot."

"You were taking so long to find me, I quit my hiding place and ducked in here instead," he admitted awkwardly.

"That was fun. We should play again later," Ava said, wondering why Nathan looked nervous. He wouldn't look her in the eye.

"Let's go to the bow and see where we are headed, shall we?" Wallace suggested.

"My father says we are going to anchor in a beautiful cove with caves. Have you seen them before?" Lillie asked.

"No, but I've heard of them. I think it's in a place called La Jolla, but you pronounce it with an *H*, like *holly*, not a *J*, like *jolly*. It's a Spanish name, but I don't know what it means."

"So, it's not La Joll-ah?" Nathan joked. "That's what I've been calling it."

"Not remotely close," Wallace replied.

They walked along the starboard side of the boat, looking out at the peach- colored cliffs along the coastline. Birds soared above and trees lined the cliffs' treacherous ledge. The children leaned over the railing, taking in the fresh air and watching the wake created by the yacht. As they continued on their way, they passed a window with curtains drawn. In it, they could see Mr. Spreckels signing papers at a large desk. Across from him were Mr. Babcock, Mr. Story, and Mr. Gruendike. All four gentlemen were smiling.

"I wonder what they're meeting about?" asked Ava once they had passed.

"Mr. Spreckels is buying a lot across from the hotel, where he plans to build a mansion," said a smug voice from above. Looking up, they spotted Beatrice sitting on a bench reading a book.

"How do you know?" Wallace asked.

"Let's just say I make it my business to know things. Don't doubt my sources."

"I believe you," Wallace replied. "We've just been playing hide-and-seek with the Spreckels children. Would you care to join us when we play later?" The children looked up at her, expectantly.

"I'm far too mature for childish games, and am surprised you would partake yourself. Your mother wouldn't approve."

"She doesn't approve of anything I do," he quipped. "Perhaps you should entertain some play."

"I'll pass." Beatrice turned the page of her book but kept glancing down on them. Clearly, she wasn't reading.

"My father says we can take a small boat into the caves once we've anchored. Would you care to join our party?" Grace called up to her.

"Don't expect me to row. My mother forbids me from manual labor."

"I'll row for you if you'll come," Nathan offered, being polite.

"Me too," added Ava. "I'm not forbidden from manual labor."

"We all know that to be true, don't we?" Beatrice sniped.

"Just come with us," Wallace urged.

"Fine. But I won't tolerate getting splashed."

Chapter 26

Two boats rowed toward the rocky shores of La Jolla Cove, leaving the *Lurline* anchored behind them. Jesse Shepherd boarded the boat with Colonel Holabird, Mr. Babcock, and most of the children—Beatrice opted for the other boat. "Perhaps I can teach you a song and we can sing," Jesse said.

"Oh, I love to sing," Grace replied eagerly.

"Very well, you have been appointed song leader. Now, *what* should we sing?" Grace giggled. Jesse looked to the blue sky for inspiration. "Not 'Row, Row, Row Your Boat'—I never was fond of it myself. I know . . . how about an old ballad, a legend about a horrible highwayman who terrified everyone in the English countryside?"

The children were instantly intrigued.

"Tell us about him first," suggested Colonel Holabird.

"His name was Dick Turpin, and until 1739, he lived in England, where he was ultimately hanged for his high crimes. He was a fearless, dashing, and daring robber who halted carriages along the king's highway shouting 'Stand and deliver!' That, of course, meant that you were to give him all of your money and valuable wares at once—or be put to the sword."

"Did they always give him what he wanted?" Ava asked.

"Of course! He was famous for his ruthlessness, and all of England was stricken with fear."

"I've read about him," admitted Mr. Babcock. "He rode on a mare he called Black Bess from London to York in less than twenty-four hours."

"So it is said," replied Jesse. "He was a horse stealer, too, but most often he rode his beloved Black Bess."

"So how does the song go?" Colonel Holabird asked. "We have to hear it now."

"I thought you'd never ask." Jesse rowed a few more strokes, then let the boat drift until it came to a slow stop in the middle of the cove. He stood up, rocking the boat as his weight shifted.

"How much ale has he had?" whispered Colonel Holabird to the children, who giggled. Jesse took a deep breath and began to sing with a dramatic English accent:

> *On Hounslow Heath as I rode o'er,*
> *I spied a lawyer riding before.*
> *"Kind sir," says I, "are not you afraid,*
> *Of Turpin, that mischievous blade?"*
> *O rare Turpin hero*
> *O rare Turpin O.*

Everyone in both boats clapped, and Jesse continued, projecting his strong voice to carry over the water.

> *As Turpin rode over Salisbury Plain,*
> *He met a judge with all his train.*
> *Then to the judge did he approach,*
> *And robbed him as he sat in his coach.*

Jesse pointed to Grace, who took the cue and sang the refrain. "O rare Turpin hero, O rare Turpin O!"

Jesse went on to the next stanza. His voice deepening in an air of doom as the song reached its climax:

For the shooting of a dunghill cock,
Turpin now at last is took,
And now he lingers in a jail
Where his ill-luck doth bewail.

Now Turpin is condemned to die,
And hang upon a gallows high.
His legacy is the hangman's rope,
For the shooting of a dunghill cock.

Both Grace and Jesse synchronized the closing refrain. She sang the soprano, he the alto: "O rare Turpin hero, O rare Turpin O!"

Applause erupted from both rowboats. "Bravo! Very impressive Mr. Shepard," said Colonel Holabird. "I do so love a good tale, although this one doesn't end well!"

Everyone laughed.

"Where did you learn that song?" Ava asked.

"When I was a guest at Buckingham Palace last year. It's nearly a hundred years old now. I would like to turn it into an opera sometime. It could be delightful if it's done artfully. A round of applause for young Miss Spreckels for her fine accompaniment!"

Grace bowed her head, acknowledging the applause.

Jesse took his seat and began rowing again, taking them into the caves. They were clay-colored stone, hewn by nature, with tall ceilings and enough room to paddle a rowboat in a wide circle. The sun shined through the crevices, lighting up the water to a sapphire blue. The noise from oars slapping the water echoed eerily around them.

They could hear Beatrice complain in the other boat. "This is nothing compared to the caves of Capri," she griped.

Wallace rolled his eyes.

"Shall we go ashore?" asked Jesse, rowing them from the caves toward a narrow beach. Their rowboat scraped over pebbles, eventually grinding to a stop on the sand. "Let's get a look around," Colonel Holabird suggested, limping along in the sunshine.

⚜

The ladies on the *Lurline* sat sipping tea under an awning on the upper deck. Mrs. Spreckels placed her hands on her swollen abdomen. "I'm due in October with our fourth child. Perhaps it's another boy, it feels just like little John did."

"You look very well," Mrs. Gregory said. "I looked positively ill during my pregnancies. Wherefore I stated two is quite enough." She waved a fan before her face, although she wasn't warm.

Mrs. Babcock and Mrs. Story stirred lumps of sugar into their tea, then deliberately placed their spoons beside the saucers. "It is a glorious day, is it not?" said Mrs. Babcock.

"It is indeed," replied Mrs. Spreckels. "San Francisco in summer is foggy and chilly. It's so nice to be warmed by the sun. San Diego suits my husband, I think. It's not quite as warm as Hawaii, but it's been some time since we have lived on the island."

"Do you plan to return? I hear the culture is quite exotic," commented Mrs. Story.

"It is. However, we are quite settled in San Francisco, where John can run his father's business interests on both the mainland and the islands."

Mrs. Babcock sipped her tea. "Mmm . . . the Spreckels sugar is fantastic!"

"I certainly hope so. They've built an empire upon it," Mrs. Gregory interjected with a hint of envy.

Mrs. Spreckels smiled wanly and changed the subject. "I understand you two will be making a voyage to Europe soon."

Mrs. Babcock and Mrs. Story lit up with enthusiasm. "Yes, we leave the day after tomorrow!" Mrs. Story replied. "My brother, Mr. Westlake, will accompany us. We sail from Boston to Paris, and we can hardly wait. Just in time for the autumn couture showcase! Paris is so fabulous in summer."

Mrs. Babcock chimed in, "Our husbands are sending us off on the most extravagant shopping experience of our lives. It seems a dream!"

"And you're purchasing for the hotel?" inquired Mrs. Gregory.

"Yes, for the interior items: linens, china, silverware, stemware, furniture, and tapestries."

"How will you go about purchasing such a massive amount? Who will assist you?"

"It turns out, Mrs. Spreckels has been kind enough to put us in contact with the Comtesse du Boulanger. She is currently in the employ of the Palace of Versailles, in the restoration of antiquities department. She also furnishes dozens of royal estates around Europe. Her taste is reputed to be impeccable."

"And very costly, I'm sure," added Mrs. Gregory, clearly impressed. "How did you go about securing her services?"

Mrs. Babcock and Mrs. Story broke into wide smiles. "It turns out, the comtesse has a love of canines. She collects them from all over the world. She was quite eager to obtain a new breed from Boston, some sort of terrier mix, soon to be an official breed. The comtesse said that if we were to bring her one, she would happily assist us in our purchases throughout Europe."

"You're bringing her a *dog*? Astonishing!" cried Mrs. Gregory. The ladies laughed in the restrained manner deemed acceptable for teatime.

"Yes, a female puppy. Cutest little thing! She's black-and-white, with a white stripe down the center of her face," Mrs. Story replied. "My brother has already secured her. The comtesse will be the first person in Paris to have a Boston terrier—America's first breed—and she will be all the rage!"

"She's already named the little pooch, too," Mrs. Babcock added.

The women sipped their tea, except for Mrs. Gregory, who found the conversation unnerving. "Pray tell me, what is to be her name? And what if the comtesse doesn't like the dog you bring her?"

"Her name is Monique, and I wondered the very thing," admitted Mrs. Babcock. "But the comtesse wrote saying her dog Clancy will decide if Monique is a good fit."

"I've never heard of anything so absurd in all my life!" retorted Mrs. Gregory.

The ladies burst into a fit of giggles.

"I quite like the name Monique," Mrs. Spreckels said, prompting all the other women to nod and then return to sipping their tea.

๑๛๏

The children climbed to the highest point overlooking La Jolla Cove. It was a breathtaking view of cliffs dropping into the calm, clear water of the bay. Long strands of seaweed swayed in the gentle current. John Spreckels Junior pulled out a telescoping ocular to survey the land. He looked to the beach across the bay, beyond where the *Lurline* was moored.

"See anything?" Nathan asked.

"There's something on the beach. Something large is moving, and several other large things are on the sand," John Junior replied. "Let me get into focus." He twisted the instrument and paused. "*Cows*. There are cows on the beach." Laughter followed.

"I thought cows preferred pasture," Grace said.

"Maybe they like to eat seaweed," John Junior replied. They each took turns looking through the ocular. Ava grinned when she saw the cows reclining lazily on the sand.

"Children, over here!" called Colonel Holabird. They crossed over several large flat stones, leaping over the gaps between them. A strange barking sound rang out, and Colonel Holabird pointed. "See there, near the water's edge?"

Several dozen sea lions dozed on the rocks near the water, absorbing the sun's warmth. Some sat still, with their noses raised up like those of dogs waiting for scraps. Others barked in random directions, and for no apparent reason. A few waddled to the water's edge and slipped into the water. Many were huddled together, sleeping as if they didn't hear the barking at all. John Junior pulled out his ocular to get a closer look, sharing it with the others. Ava focused on the whiskers of a large sleeping sea lion with two pups playing nearby her. The pups bit each other playfully. They barked, rammed into each other and into their mother, who awoke and became very annoyed. She barked at them, then lunged her large body away

187

from them in rolling movements like those of an undulating caterpillar. Only then did she settle back to sleep. Every now and again, a sea lion would jump up out of the sea and waddle along to find a resting place.

In a crag along the rocks, waves swelled and rolled in, shooting a spray of water high into the air. A large male seal lion observed the boating party with his head cocked to the side.

Nathan dared to hop down closer to him. "This guy looks like he's in charge around here," he said.

"Be careful, Nathan," Ava said, cringing as Nathan moved closer still. The sea lion erupted into a fit of barking, causing his neck to ripple and his sharp bottom teeth to protrude from his open mouth. He then shifted his weight onto his flippers and started to lunge toward Nathan.

"All right, all right!" Nathan said, backing up. "It's your rock." He was laughing when he rejoined the others at a safer distance.

Ava could have watched the sea lions for hours. Their antics were so amusing, but the *Lurline* needed to be underway before the sun began to set.

☙❧

"Mr. Spreckels, thank you for a such special day," said Ava.

"Yes, thank you, sir," Nathan and Wallace both chimed in.

"A pleasure to have you aboard," Mr. Spreckels replied. "Especially since my Grace has become so fond of you all." His blue eyes were illuminated by his warm smile. "Perhaps a game of polo next week?"

"The polo field is still under construction, Mr. Spreckels," Ava informed him.

"Right. Then we'll play on the beach."

Although neither Ava nor Nathan had ever played polo before, the plan was settled. The Spreckels children waved goodbye, standing along the railing of the upper deck of the *Lurline*.

"I'll write you my first letter tonight!" Grace called to Ava upon disembarking.

"All right!" Ava felt as if she'd known Grace for years rather than just an afternoon. She couldn't wait to tell her mother all about her new best friend.

"Would you write to me if I wrote to you, Ava?" Wallace teased Ava, mimicking Grace as they walked down the ramp to the pier.

"It depends. Some letters are worthy of a response, while others are not."

Wallace chuckled at her smart reply.

"What if I were to write you?" Nathan asked.

Ava took a deep breath before replying. "So long as I had the time, I would consider responding to you both, but I can't make any promises," she said.

Nathan grasped at his heart as if he were wounded.

"I told you Nathan . . . she's fractious," Wallace said, shaking his head.

Chapter 27

Crack! Ava liked the sound the mallet made when it struck the ball, sending it down the beach.

"Are you sure you've never played polo before?" Wallace said, striding by on his horse.

"Never." She smiled to herself, pleased. "Girls aren't usually allowed to play, remember?"

"She's a natural!" bellowed Mr. Spreckels. "And lucky for us, she's on our team."

Nathan chased after Wallace, blocking his ability to attempt a goal. Their horses kicked up sand as they stomped around the ball while the boys hooked mallets. Wallace got the better of Nathan, freed his mallet, and made a shot, sending the ball flying through the goal posts for a point. Nathan's face reddened as applause rang out from the audience in the bandstand.

"It's okay, Nathan," Ava said, circling her horse around him. "He's played before and you haven't."

"But I can ride better than he can," he muttered.

"It's not just about riding. It's about being in position to take the shot. Try playing in a dress!" He had to smile. She was perched sideways in a riding habit with a stiff coat buttoned up to her neck.

The ball bounced down the field. Ava and Nathan spurred their horses, swinging their mallets forward. They stopped quick, scuffling in tight circles around the ball. Nathan maneuvered it under his horse and away from Ava. He drew back his mallet to take a shot and froze.

"Take the shot!" Ava urged, but Nathan didn't move. His teammates began screaming for him to hurry, and the crowd in the bandstand went wild—but Nathan didn't move. Frustrated, Ava rounded him and swung, sending the ball down the field to Wallace, who passed it along to a Mr. Spreckels for another goal.

Ava circled Nathan again on her horse. "You know, just because I'm a girl, it doesn't mean you should let me take it!" she said getting angry. "Why didn't you fight for it?"

He didn't answer. "Nathan, you have to fight sometimes to win, or you never will! You can't just give up!"

"I didn't," he replied, but she was already racing down the field.

"It's only a game, right?" Wallace said when she trotted up next to him. "He isn't cross, is he?"

"I don't know, but I sure am."

The rest of the game, Nathan played more aggressively, scoring one goal and taking on Wallace at every turn. But Wallace had the greater skill. When the game ended, Nathan was quick to depart and didn't stay for the beach picnic.

"What's gotten into him?" Wallace asked Ava.

"I don't know. I've never seen him behave this way before."

❧❧

Ava went to Nathan's house twice in the following few weeks. Both times, Mr. Beckman said he was in Old Town with his Mexican friends.

"That's funny, Mr. Beckman, he's never mentioned them to me."

"You know Nathan—that boy doesn't know a stranger."

"That's for sure. Can you tell him I stopped by again? And these books are for him, too."

"Will do, Miss Ava."

Ava rode Ambrose home, wondering why Nathan was always in Old

Town. The puzzle nagged at her. What was she missing? It used to be just Fridays, but now he was there on Wednesdays, too. He wasn't acting like himself. Nathan was up to something, and Ava was determined to get to the bottom of it.

Chapter 28

The *SS La Bretagne* slowed as it approached the coast of France. After a nine-day transatlantic crossing from New York Harbor, its two funnels ceased spewing steam that had fueled its propellers. Two tugboats pulled the steamship safely into the port of Le Havre.

"Ladies, we have arrived. Paris awaits! Are we ready to disembark?" asked Mr. Westlake, taking a peek through the cabin door.

"Yes, brother, once we've captured little Miss Monique, we'll be ready," Mrs. Story said.

Giggling, both ladies looked down at the floor, lifting the hems of their dresses.

"Well, where is she off too now?" Mr. Westlake lamented. Out from under their seats raced the puppy, growling and shaking a knotted rope in her mouth. Mrs. Babcock scooped her up before she could get away. "I've just grown so attached to her, I'm saddened to part with her." Monique dropped the rope and licked Mrs. Babcock's face eagerly, eliciting a laugh.

"Do you think the comtesse will keep her?" wondered Mrs. Story. "Or should I say will *Clancy* approve of her?"

"I daresay they will keep her. This pup is healthy, very bright, and adorable! Isn't that right, Miss Monique?" Mrs. Babcock replied. The puppy continued to lick her in a frenzied manner.

"Remind me to never cross the Atlantic with a puppy again," grumbled Mr. Westlake.

"My dear brother, how difficult can a puppy be?" Mrs. Story asked.

"*Extraordinarily* difficult."

"Well, we are indebted to you, and very soon Miss Monique will no longer be in need of your services."

"Thank the good heavens above!"

They departed the steamship with Monique, walking down a ramp to a sea of waiting coaches. A gentleman held a sign that read Westlake, standing before a handsome black-and-gold coach with large red wheels. He introduced himself as Pierre and loaded their trunks as they climbed into the coach.

Mrs. Story, Mrs. Babcock and Monique peered from the window as the coach lunged forward, taking them from the harbor to the French countryside. It would take several hours to reach Paris.

An hour later, the ladies were still taking in the scenery. They passed endless fields separated by lines of tall trees, and tranquil villages with cobblestone streets and church steeples rising amid shops and cottages.

"I never tire of the French countryside," Mrs. Babcock said wistfully.

Mrs. Story agreed.

Miss Monique napped on Mr. Westlake's lap. "Why does she insist on sleeping on me? I, who cares the least about pets!"

"Oh, brother, nonsense. We know you're fond of her," Mrs. Story teased. "She's partial to you."

"She snores," he protested. The puppy wheezed away on his lap. When he tried to gently set her aside, she growled, so he was resigned to let her lie. Both were snoring when the Paris skyline came into view.

They reached Paris before noon, driving by a construction site with wooden scaffolding of massive proportions. "What on earth could that be? I've never seen anything like it," said Mr. Westlake. "It looks like four vertical bridges." Four iron pylons, set widely apart, arched upward in an unusual lattice configuration. "I'll have to inquire about it. I must know."

"Paris is a city of wonder, brother," commented Mrs. Story as they crossed a bridge over the Seine River. "Isabella, look at the gowns the women are wearing. They are absolutely glamorous! We must each have one!"

"High bustles and long trains must be the rage next season," Mrs. Babcock noted.

"Stripes, silks, taffeta, and every color of the rainbow. So elegant!" Mrs. Story gushed, waving a hand through the air. "And the gentlemen, what fine ensembles!" Men in gray-striped coats with long tails tapped canes along the sidewalk as they strolled.

"Perhaps new suits for our husbands?" suggested Mrs. Babcock. They crossed the wide Avenue des Champs-Élysées, turning onto the Rue de Rivoli, and again onto the Avenue de l'Opéra. "Look! It's the Opera house! Oh, how I adore the French opera! If only Elisha were here to take me!" Mrs. Babcock exclaimed.

Even Monique peered out the coach window, taking in the sights and sounds of Paris. The streets became a labyrinth of tall structures—all five stories high—that stretched the length of each city block. Bakeries shared common walls with residences, shops, and restaurants, making each block appear unified. Penthouse apartments had patina roofs that pitched at an angle over small windows with dormers. Chandeliers hanging from crown molding where walls met the ceiling were visible through the floor-length double door and wrought-iron balconies of some lower apartments. Ornate candelabra lampposts and trees lined the sidewalks.

Pierre brought the carriage to a halt in front of Le Grand-Hôtel de la Paix. "At last!" said Mr. Westlake, eager to escape the commentary on fashion and opera. They were escorted into a richly furnished lobby with flourishes including marble floors, decorative columns, frescoes, and luxurious red sofas. While their trunks were taken to their rooms, a service boy took Monique for a walk and they were directed to the Café de la Paix, on the ground floor of the hotel.

"The service here is quite exemplary!" whispered Mrs. Story in a low tone, stirring her tea. "We should recruit staff for the Hotel Del."

"Not whilst we are guests," replied Mr. Westlake. "Or we may find that the quality of our service changes considerably by the management, who are at present most accommodating." The ladies giggled.

"I'll take down their names anyway," said Mrs. Babcock, "just in case."

"It says here that Victor Hugo held parties in this very hotel," said Mr. Westlake, reading from a hotel brochure. "How interesting."

"When was his *The Hunchback of Notre Dame* published? I love gothic cathedrals and long to see it!"

"This brochure says 1831."

"We should bring back a copy of the book for Miss Ava. She'd be delighted."

"We should," Mrs. Story agreed. "She has the loveliest disposition. I simply adore her! And such a pretty little thing." Mrs. Story sipped her tea. "Brother, when do we meet the comtesse?"

"She left us this note with the concierge," Mr. Westlake said, producing the note from his coat pocket. "We are to meet at her château tomorrow, near Versailles, and we are instructed to bring *le pooch*." He folded the note and smiled. "As if I would delay my moment of liberation."

The ladies let their eyes wander from table to table, although they tried to be discreet about it. Coy French women chatted, laughed, and teased the gentlemen in their company. An air of open flirtation electrified the room.

"Isabella, we simply must acquire a hat like hers," whispered Mrs. Story, pointing her spoon to the left. A stunning young woman in a peacock-blue dress and a wide-brimmed, black hat sat alone. Her lips were ruby red against her pale, porcelain-like skin. She appeared anxious as she checked her timepiece.

Mrs. Babcock casually peeked at the lady. "It's magnificent! We must!"

"As soon as we've purchased linens for four hundred rooms, furnishings, stemware, china, paintings, and silverware, we can certainly find time to shop for the latest in women's hats," teased Mr. Westlake.

"Oh, Mr. Westlake," laughed Mrs. Babcock. "You're incorrigible!"

A handsome young gentleman rushed in, looking desperately around the café. The lady in the elegant black hat rose and kissed him passionately before they both sat and began staring deeply into each other's eyes. Mrs. Story and Mrs. Babcock blanched, looking quickly away from their open display of affection. The ladies sipped their tea, pretending not to notice the couple kissing again across the table.

Mr. Westlake broke into laughter. "Welcome to Paris! The uninhibited city of love!" he bellowed, causing the ladies to blush and drain their cups.

Chapter 29

Pierre opened the coach door and stepped aside. Mrs. Story and Mrs. Babcock pinched their cheeks and straightened their hats before stepping down into the front courtyard of a charming château. The imposing residence's stone walls, were covered with thick green ivy, which was trimmed neatly around its many windows. Mrs. Story held Monique, sound asleep in her arms. A butler, Monsieur Dubois, met them at the door and showed them to the parlor. The comtesse would join them soon. The ladies gaped as they looked around the room. A massive fireplace, complemented by a hearth made of dark, intricate woodwork, dominated one wall. Faces protruded from wooden pillars around the hearth, and tiles with brightly colored family crests were inlaid throughout it.

"This hearth is a masterpiece!" exclaimed Mr. Westlake. The women agreed, moving around the room. Chairs with lion-claw feet and burgundy upholstery were placed around an exotic Persian rug. A chandelier dazzled above, hanging from a high ceiling. The stained-glass windows depicted tall ships and the faces of distinguished-looking gentlemen with high-collared white shirts that ruffled around their necks. Their hair was brushed forward and unruly, in the common style of the last century. The ladies took in every detail. Paintings on another wall drew their attention. One was ballet themed, painted in vivid blue hues. *Degas* was scrawled in gold in the lower right corner. Beside it was a painting of a smiling girl with warm, dark eyes and a red hat. Another painting was a joyful depiction of couples dancing in the sunshine, while onlookers chatted amiably, seated around small tables. The gentlemen wore straw hats and the women black-and-white striped dresses. *Renoir* was written in cursive on both paintings.

"These are absolutely fantastic," Mrs. Babcock said.

Mrs. Story agreed. "Undoubtedly originals."

They heard the comtesse approaching, her high heels tapping on the marble floor. She spoke rapidly in a raspy, sultry voice, giving orders to various members of her staff who followed closely, jotting down notes.

When the comtesse entered the room, her commanding presence and floral perfume filled it immediately. An entourage of canines trailed behind her. Only a reddish-haired exotic-looking dog with large brown eyes held the prestige to walk in front of her.

"The Comtesse du Boulanger," announced Monsieur Dubois, standing in the doorway.

Mrs. Story and Mrs. Babcock curtsied, while Mr. Westlake bowed.

"Comtesse du Boulanger, what a pleasure it is to finally make your acquaintance!" Mr. Westlake said, approaching her. She wore a bustled champagne-hued gown covered with black Chantilly lace that was excessively elegant for daytime wear. Her blonde hair was swept up in an elegant twist that highlighted her high cheekbones and creamy skin. Her bright blue eyes were unmistakably keen, and she cut a fine figure. One could only guess at her true age.

Six dogs filed around her, obediently sitting at the hem of her gown. There was a poodle, a pug, a boxer, a Great Dane, a Pomeranian, and the odd orange-haired dog. Monique roused upon hearing them, and started to whimper and squirm in Adella's arms. The comtesse became immediately aware of her. "Monique!" she exclaimed in a thick French accent, stepping forward with arms outstretched. Wide, heavy rings with dark gemstones adorned her fingers.

Mrs. Story handed the puppy over, struggling to maintain a grip on her. Monique wiggled and cried excitedly. The comtesse lifted her toward her face and laughed heartily. "Oh, my little *peu d'amour*, I've been waiting for you, my darling!" Monique licked her immediately, loving the thrill in her voice. "Look, my darlings, we have a new *bébé!*" the comtesse announced, holding up Monique for the dogs to see. Monique kicked wildly. All the dogs wagged their tails except for one—the orange-haired dog.

"But of course! How could I forget?" the comtesse assured him. She lowered Monique to the ground, and the orange-haired dog cautiously approached her. Monique cowered low and rolled onto her back when he sniffed her. For one tense moment, the orange-haired dog sternly looked her over. Monique held still but she couldn't resist sneaking a quick lick to his face. The orange-haired dog took a step back, alarmed and wide-eyed. He sat, then wagged his tail.

"Monsieur Clancy approves!" the comtesse declared, clapping wildly. Mrs. Story and Mrs. Babcock clapped, too.

"We're so delighted!" exclaimed Mr. Westlake, looking gleeful. "This is wonderful news! Isn't it wonderful, sister?" Mrs. Story gave him a sidelong look.

"Already, I adore her!" the comtesse confessed. The other dogs moved in to inspect the newest family member. Monique licked each one and scampered around their feet playfully.

"Clearly, Monsieur Clancy is the alpha canine," Mr. Westlake said with amusement.

"*Oui!* He runs the show as they say in America."

Mr. Westlake threw his head back with a laugh. "And what breed of dog is Clancy? I've never seen a dog like him before."

"Nobody has. He is a shih tzu. The Empress Tzu Hai of China gifted him to me after my tour of Indochine. She's very fond of the breed, and only the royal family has them there."

This impressed Mr. Westlake. "May I ask how he got a name like *Clancy*? It doesn't sound French, nor does it sound Chinese."

"It is neither. I named him after an American who once visited Paris. He was a cowboy from Texas," the comtesse said wistfully, staring up at the ceiling and holding her hand over her heart. Mr. Westlake coughed into his hand, shocked by her brazen response.

"Oh dear, my apologies," Mr. Westlake said, changing the subject. "Allow me to introduce Mrs. Isabella Babcock and my sister, Mrs. Adella Story. Both of whom I believe you shared a correspondence with."

"Delighted to meet you, Comtesse," the two ladies said in unison, curtsying again.

"Please, call me Lorraine—and excuse my lack of formality!" she kissed each lady on both cheeks twice. "I was so excited to see my Monique at last!"

"French customs are so lovely!" raved Mrs. Story leaning in to receive the comtesse's warm pecks.

Lorraine flashed a brilliant smile. She liked these ladies already. "Please, sit with me. Is this your first time to Paris?"

"A second time for Isabella and me, but it has been many years," admitted Mrs. Story. "Mr. Westlake has been here many times before. We did study French in primary school, but we speak it very poorly."

"May I interest you in tea? A cigar perhaps, Mr. Westlake?" the comtesse said. But before anyone could answer, she beckoned for Monsieur Dubois. The butler nodded in response to her order, bowed, and departed. Monique chased the dogs in circles around the parlor before following them out of the room. The comtesse and her guests could hear her playful bark echoing down the hallway.

"I daresay the city gets more beautiful with each visit," said Mr. Westlake. "We came upon a new structure that has me intrigued. The iron pylons going up in the center of town? Do you know of it?"

"Ah, you mean the tower?" Lorraine replied, her eyes lighting up. "In two years, France will be celebrating the anniversary of the storming of the Bastille."

"The centennial is in 1889? Has it been a hundred years already? Yes, I suppose it has."

"To commemorate the event, Paris will be hosting the Exposition Universelle, an international exposition that is to be the largest in the world. There was a contest to design a structure that would define the exposition. One hundred architects submitted designs, and my dear friend Gustave

Eiffel won the bid. What you see going up is his tower. It will be the tallest structure in the world."

"How extraordinary!" Mr. Westlake said. "Is he the same Eiffel who built our Statue of Liberty, America's wonderful gift from France?"

"He is a true innovator. Perhaps I can introduce you to him during your stay in Paris. No?"

"It would be an honor!" Mr. Westlake could scarcely conceal his enthusiasm.

"I'll have a soirée, and you can meet all of my Parisian friends. Now, tell me all about your project."

Mrs. Babcock spoke first, "Well, our husbands are building a rather large hotel resort in Southern California called the Hotel del Coronado. The plan for completion is late this year, and our expected grand opening will be in the spring. We need to purchase all of the interior furnishings."

"Sparing no expense of course," added Mrs. Story with an encouraging smile.

Monsieur Dubois brought in a rolling cart with a polished silver tea set on a white linen tablecloth embroidered with yellow French knots that formed flowers. A crystal bowl overflowed with grapes, pears, and figs.

"How many rooms?" Lorraine asked.

"Four hundred, I believe," answered Mrs. Babcock. "It will be the largest hotel in America."

Lorraine raised her eyebrows at this, nodding her approval. The dogs returned to the parlor, having free rein of the space. Monique and the pug gnawed at each other playfully, causing Lorraine to laugh though the Great Dane watched warily. "Don't be afraid, Aldrich!" she said to him, then turned back to her guests and giggled. "You see the largest dog is most afraid? Ah, but back to your hotel! You will need linens, stemware, flatware, silver, etcetera?"

"Yes, everything—and china with small crowns upon them because our hotel has a crown theme," Mrs. Babcock replied. "Preferably red crowns. We are willing to travel throughout Europe to find the best of everything that is available."

"There may not be a need. The finest vendors in Europe bring their wares directly to me. In my boutique, you could do all of the purchasing for your hotel at once if you prefer."

"What a relief!" bellowed Mr. Westlake. "I must admit, I am reluctant to shop across continental Europe with two indecisive ladies." His sister shot him a dour look.

Lorraine laughed heartily. "And your expected, how do you say, budget?" She didn't pronounce the *t*, making the word sound more like bud*jay*.

Mr. Westlake retrieved a folded piece of paper from his coat pocket, unfolded it, and placed his spectacles on his nose. "Ah yes, the budget. It appears we have four hundred thousand American dollars allotted to spend on all interior furnishings."

Lorraine's eyes flashed and she broke into a wide grin. "We are going to have a *fantastique* time together! Monsieur Dubois pour the champagne!"

"To the Hotel del Coronado, the most exquisite hotel in America," Lorraine declared, raising her champagne flute.

"Let the shopping begin!" Mrs. Babcock added, taking a sip.

Mrs. Story giggled, sipped, then giggled some more. Mr. Westlake mopped his brow with a handkerchief.

Chapter 30

Old Town, San Diego

Nathan yanked up on his pants, which had shiny silver stitching running the length of each leg. "Mr. Delafuente, I think these pants might be too tight," he called out from behind the curtain.

"*Hermanito*, mariachis all wear *pantalones* that are too tight," replied Mr. Delafuente. "It's from my mother's sister's cooking." Nathan could hear the men cackling.

Shaking his head, Nathan yanked up on the pants again, hopping as he pulled them over his hips. *Why did I sign up for this*, he thought. "I think I've got it!" He buttoned the pants, slipped on an embroidered shirt, a short-waisted black jacket, and worn black boots that were too large. A feeling of pride surged through him as he placed a sombrero on his head.

"*Silencio hombres!*" ordered Mr. Delafuente as they waited for Nathan's grand entrance. They could hear his spurs scraping along the tile floor. Nathan walked slowly from behind the curtain and stood before the men. "Well?" he asked with uncertainty, spinning around. The men burst into laughter when they saw his pants stretched tightly across his backside. "If these *pantalones* rip while I'm onstage, I'm going to be real cross with you hombres," Nathan stated. They laughed uncontrollably. "I know it's funny, but really—how do I look?"

"Like a mariachi, Nito!" Mr. Delafuente exclaimed. "Quick, bring him his *guitarra* so he can get the full affect."

Pablo, the trumpet player, brought it to him at once. Nathan placed the strap over his shoulder, slapped the body of the guitar for percussion, and started strumming a rapid tune. Pablo joined in with his horn, and the bass player caught up with them, setting the pace.

"*Viva hermanito!*" the others yelled, raising their mugs of beer and howling like coyotes. Mr. Delafuente started singing the popular song "Cielito Lindo" with his rich baritone voice:

> *De la Sierra Morena,*
> *Cielito lindo,*
> *vienen bajando,*
> *Un par de ojitos negros,*
> *Cielito lindo, de contrabando.*

Nathan and the men chimed in for the chorus:

> *Ay, ay, ay ay!*
> *Canta y no llores,*
> *Porque cantando se alegran*
> *Cielito lindo, los corazones.*

❧✦

"What does '*Canta y no Llores* mean,' Mr. Delafuente?" Nathan asked at the end of their rehearsal after the others had gone home.

"It means 'Sing and don't cry,' because singing makes you happy."

"That makes sense. I like it. Who wrote it?"

"Two guys, Mendoza and Cortés, about five years ago."

"That wasn't very long ago. I thought these folk songs were supposed to be old?"

"Most of them are, but 'Cielito Lindo' is new."

"So, do you think I'm ready?"

"Yes, Nito, you are almost ready. When is the big concert you want us to play at?"

"The hotel doesn't open officially until spring next year, but they'll start taking guests earlier and having parties. There'll be looking for musicians. Will I be ready by then?"

"Keep practicing."

"I will. You know that song you want me to sing, 'Rosita'? Can I change the name a little?"

"To what?"

"Something similar—like *Avalita*."

Mr. Delafaunte started teasing him right away. "Avalita, eh? Is she the girl that has stolen your heart?"

"Her real name is Ava."

"And you want to sing for this girl?"

"Yes, as a surprise. She doesn't know I'm a mariachi yet."

"I promise you, Nito, if you sing 'Avalita' to her, she will fall in love. There is nothing more magical than a mariachi singing a *seranata* to his woman. It's like casting a spell on her."

"You think so?"

"*Claro que sí!*" Mr. Delafuente sank back in his seat, raising his boots on a nearby chair and tilting his hat over his eyes. He was getting ready for a siesta.

"What if she likes someone else?"

"How do you know she likes someone else?"

"She hasn't ever said anything, but just smiles at him a lot."

"Does she smile at you?"

"I guess she does, but she smiles more at him."

"If you don't have to fight for it, it's not love."

Nathan smiled at this. "As long as I don't have to sit down or anything while we perform, I won't split my britches. How would that work for casting a spell?"

Mr. Delafuente's shoulders started shaking. He lifted his hat, sat up, and turned to Nathan. "I'll teach you a special mariachi trick if that happens—walk backward then run off the stage," he suggested laughing.

"Very funny. And you've been calling me *Nito* for a while. What does it mean? It doesn't mean rat or something awful, does it?"

"*Nito* is short for *Hermanito*, which means 'little brother.'"

"Good. I like that much better."

"And you can stop calling me Mr. Delafuente."

Nathan brightened at this. "Really? What can I call you?"

"Guillermo."

Nathan repeated the name. "*Guillermo*. Nice name."

"*Oye, Nito*, before I forget, do you like to fish?"

"I love fishing. I never catch much, but when I do, I really love it."

"I want to talk to you about a little proposition."

"I am open to all propositions."

"My cousins are starting a fishing company in Mexico. We're looking for strong deckhands to work on the boats. Big fish. Five times bigger than you. This time you'll catch them."

"What kind of fish?"

"Everything. Tuna, mackerel, dorado, everything."

"But I'd have to leave here?"

"Yes, most of the time we would be away. Just think about it, Nito. You could make a lot more money than staying here, feeding birds that try to kill you."

"I make bricks, too, and I don't just feed birds, I secure fashionable feathers for ladies."

Guillermo started to laugh again.

"What about my career as a mariachi?" Nathan asked.

"You can do both. We can sing while we fish. I know Avalita is here, but maybe you can make some money fishing and win her heart later. Money works even faster than music." He rubbed his fingers together.

Nathan smirked. "So much for the magic of the *serenata* you told me about. Let me think about it."

Guillermo put his hat over his face and sank back again, raising his boots to the nearby chair.

"Special mariachi trick," Nathan muttered as he walked to the door.

Guillermo started laughing again, causing his hat to wiggle.

✂❧

Ava and the Spreckels family sat on the beach, enjoying a picnic. Mrs. Spreckels reclined under an umbrella, rubbing her growing abdomen as she elevated her swollen ankles. Ava and the Spreckels children watched the builders carry planks from a woodpile stacked high in front of the hotel. One by one, they carried them inside to be used for framing the guest rooms.

"It's going up so quickly now," Ava commented. Bright red shingles nearly covered the great turret and bay windows had been installed around the ballroom. Near the top of the turret was a narrow, balustraded platform that circled it entirely. From there, it was possible to see everything of interest: the bay, the ocean, the city, and even the courtyard at the center of the hotel. Ava wondered if she'd ever get to look around from up there. "What's the difference between a crow's nest and a widow's walk anyway?" she asked.

Young John Spreckels answered, "A crow's nest is a lookout on the mast of a ship."

"And a widow's walk is on a rooftop, where a lady can watch for the return of her husband from sea," Grace added. "I've never seen one around a ballroom turret. I can't wait to dance there when it's finished. Won't that be glorious, Ava?"

"I can hardly wait! Watching it go up has built such anticipation!"

"Who likes surprises?" Mr. Spreckels asked, his blue eyes twinkling.

"I do!" cried John Junior and Lillie.

"Ava and I love surprises, Father!" Grace chimed in. "Don't we?" Ava nodded.

"How would you like to tour the inside of the hotel today?"

The girls looked at each other, wide-eyed. "Can we?" Grace replied.

"Absolutely! Mr. Babcock has offered to take us in now that it's relatively safe."

"Father, that would be fantastic!" Grace gushed.

"As long as we are careful. There are likely a lot of tools lying about the place."

"We won't touch a thing, Father," Lillie promised.

"I'll stay behind." Mrs. Spreckels smiled feebly. "My ankles are giving me grief. You'll have to tell me all about it."

"Certainly, dearest. Is there anything I can do to ease your discomfort?" Mr. Spreckels asked.

"There's nothing one can do so late in term but bear it out. Thank you, love." He smiled at her adoringly.

"Look, there's Mr. Babcock, and he's speaking with the foreman now," Ava pointed out.

"Then let us go and have a look, shall we?" Mr. Spreckels said.

Ava and the children jumped up and followed him to the stairs that led to the hotel. Ava felt butterflies swirling in her stomach. She couldn't believe she was going to see the inside. She had dreamed of this moment for more than a year, and suddenly it was upon her. She closed her eyes, promising to commit everything to memory and write about it in her diary when she got home.

"Are you coming, Ava?" Grace called excitedly, seeing that she had fallen behind.

"I'll be right there!" Ava raced up the stairs and together, they walked inside the perimeter of the hotel, where nobody was allowed.

❧❧

"Good afternoon, Mr. Spreckels, Miss Ava, children," said Mr. Babcock cheerfully. "Shall we proceed?" Ava and the children nodded eagerly. "I'll bring you around to the front entrance so we can enter just as our guests will. You'll get to see our new elevator! I'm thrilled with its construction— it's the Otis number sixty-one, one of America's first fully electric elevators."

Signs around the jobsite read: No Smoking Anywhere. They followed Mr. Babcock up a flight of stairs to the main entrance, where a gentleman held open a pair of wooden doors with oval etched-glass centers. "Good afternoon, Manfred," Mr. Babcock said.

"Good day to you, Mr. Babcock. Having another tour, are we?"

"My daily tour, yes." Mr. Babcock chuckled. Ava felt time slow as she walked through the front doors. She could no longer hear the men's jovial conversation. Her heart pounded in her chest. *I finally get to see inside*, she thought. The smell of new paint and wood stain immediately overwhelmed her. Her shoes clattered with those of her companions on the tile floor. The lobby was dark. It took a moment for her eyes to adjust from the brightness outside. Mr. Manfred flipped a light switch, and a great chandelier with daffodil-shaped glass sconces illuminated the room.

"Wow!" cried John Junior.

Lillie clapped her hands. "It's so pretty!"

Ava spun in a slow circle, awestruck. The square rotunda was massive and lofty. Dark redwood paneled the walls. Every dozen feet or so, rectangular wooden pillars supported a ceiling sixty feet high, inlaid with crossbeams that made a waffle pattern on the ceiling.

"I feel like I'm inside of a big, beautiful tree house!" Lilly exclaimed.

Above them, a second-floor balcony lined the perimeter of the enormous space. A golden cage flanked a wide, carpeted staircase at the far end of the room beside. Mr. Babcock led them straight to the cage. "Here it is!" he said, beaming. "Our new elevator." He pulled the gate open from left to right, then opened an interior gate, revealing a small carpeted room.

"I've never been in an elevator before," Ava confessed.

"Let's take it up!" Mr. Babcock ushered everyone inside, then pulled the gates closed, locking them in. He pushed a button that lit, and a rumble began. The cage lifted from the floor. The children reached for the handrail, giggling nervously. The elevator came to a gentle stop at the second floor. "And here we are!" Mr. Babcock opened both gates. "Otis makes the finest elevators in the world. They've recently been contracted in Paris, where Mrs. Babcock is at present, to make an elevator that will go straight up a tower proposed to be the tallest in the world."

"Fascinating! Yes, Eiffel's Tower, I've read of it," said Mr. Spreckels. "It's said it may reach a thousand feet."

"We will have to place Mr. Eiffel on our guest invitation list," joked Mr. Babcock. "I'm quite certain Mrs. Babcock has already extended invitations throughout all of Europe. I do hope she's been very clear that we haven't yet opened."

Ava and Grace approached the balcony railing, peering cautiously over the spacious rotunda. From this prospect, curious guests could observe new arrivals as they registered at the front desk, or merely observe the happenings below. Ava couldn't believe the scale of the room. She imagined the look of wonder on the face of every guest entering the hotel for the first time.

"Shall we continue our tour?" Mr. Babcock led them down the stairs and paused to point out the various stages of planting in the courtyard garden. "Mrs. Kate Sessions, the horticulturalist, is already planting exotics. She's requested permission to plant a dragon tree near the main entrance. I had to ask her if her dragon tree would devour my guests." The children giggled. "She has since reminded me that horticulture is not in my area of expertise, a fact I readily admit to."

Mr. Babcock pointed to two sets of closed doors. "In there, we have the Crown Room and adjacent Coronet Room, both of which I believe we can sneak a peek of. He opened the doors to the Crown Room first. "This is where all of the dining will take place." The oval-shaped room was long, with dark, wood-paneled walls that continued up to a great arched-ceiling. The far side of the room was made entirely of windows that let in natural light. Ava and the children were amazed, which pleased Mr. Babcock. "This room is a spectacular feat of architectural ingenuity," he said spinning around. "It's one hundred and sixty feet long, sixty feet wide and thirty-three feet tall—made entirely of longleaf sugar pine, so the flawless wood is without knots. It's assembled in a tongue-and-groove fashion that doesn't require a single nail to hold it all together." He looped his fingers together to demonstrate the idea. "If you notice, there's not a single pillar to hold up the ceiling."

"It's spectacular!" Mr. Spreckels declared. "I tell you, Babcock, what you've done here is pure genius. Bravo!"

"Mr. Babcock, what is that up there?" Grace asked, pointing to a narrow second- floor balcony with built-in alcoves.

"That's the orchestra loft, where musicians will play during dinner. I thought if they were up higher, the acoustics would resonate equally throughout the room. Perhaps one evening you can play violin up there, Miss Ava. What do you say?"

"Oh, I'd love to!"

"Then we shall plan for it. We are installing chandeliers and dining furniture next, then this room will be completed." The Coronet Room was much smaller, though it, too, had a vaulted ceiling and large windows. "Now, allow me to show you the greatest room of all, the Grand Ballroom." Mr. Babcock was giddy as he led them down a long hallway, then through a set of tall doors. Ava caught her breath as she entered the room.

"This is incredible!" Ava exclaimed. She, Grace, Lillie, and John Junior walked to the center of the room and stared up into the great cone that was the turret.

"Indeed it is," replied Mr. Babcock, beaming from in response to their awed reaction.

A narrow second-floor balcony went around the entire ballroom. Above it, sunlight streamed in through a dozen tiny windows.

"Maybe one day we can watch a grand ball from that balcony," Grace said.

"How do you get to the widow's walk?" asked young John.

Mr. Babcock replied, "There will be a spiral staircase. It isn't completed yet, but soon."

Elegant chandeliers shimmered from the ceiling before a raised stage, complete with a proscenium arch and drawn curtains. Ava could almost hear the clanging of cymbals and blaring of horns as she imagined an orchestra playing.

Mr. Babcock led them to the bay windows that overlooked the ocean.

"This will be a fine prospect for a sunset, to be certain!" said Mr. Spreckels.

"In the winter months, we will have an unobstructed view of every sunset. During summer, however, the sun drops behind Point Loma."

"How many lots did I purchase, Babcock? Perhaps I need to purchase a few more," teased Mr. Spreckels.

"I would be happy to provide you with a multi-property discount and the most favorable terms," replied Mr. Babcock with a laugh.

"You already have, good man! "This resort—and this island for that matter—will be all that you claimed: the finest destination in all of America. Well done, Babcock, well done! Investing in your vision has been a very wise decision on my part."

"I pray for more businessmen like yourself to come along and invest. She will be magnificent, undoubtedly, but very, very costly."

"And your ledger balance?"

"Dwindling, which calls to mind a Chinese proverb: Pearls don't lie on the seashore. If you want one, you must dive for it."

Through the bay windows that curved around the ballroom, Ava watched waves silently crash along the beach. This was one of the views she longed to see, from this very spot. She couldn't believe it was real.

"Ava, soon we will be dancing right here!" Grace announced, twirling with an imaginary partner in the center of the dance floor. "I'm going to dance with a prince! Who will *you* dance with?"

Ava smiled at the younger girl, who had become like a sister to her. She imagined the room on opening night. It was easy to see herself being led around the ballroom, with her gown sweeping across her sparkling shoes. "I'm going to dance with Wallace," she replied, surprised she had said it out loud.

&

Across the bay, Wallace stared over the water from the balcony of the Claypooles' house.

"Are you longing for Coronado already?" Beatrice asked, feigning sweetness. "Or are you longing for a certain young lady who is likely sweeping out stalls at this very moment."

Wallace gave her a cursory glance as she took a place standing next to him. He remained quiet. "Is she getting an education? I wonder if she has the time with all that work she does."

"Yes, Ava is getting an education. She's exceedingly bright," he finally said with open annoyance.

"I didn't realize you know so much about her." Beatrice squinted, her cold eyes.

"It turns out that I do." He returned to gazing at the hotel across the bay. "She's an avid reader, a gifted writer, is hard working, has a creative mind, and is talented musically."

"That does seem a lengthy list of accomplishments," agreed Beatrice, but her expression showed her true feelings. It bothered her that Wallace seemed to find Ava so intriguing. "She is pretty in a plain sort of way, although she smiles too much and her laugh is rather unsettling."

"Pretty?" he guffawed. "She's beautiful, and one day, there won't be a man within miles who won't fight to win her hand."

"Girls in her unfortunate situation are neither sought nor fought for in marriage—not among our class. Her father will likely consent to the first suitor that comes along."

"Then I won't have any competitors, will I?" Wallace retorted. He didn't watch Beatrice storm into the house. She made her way through the guests chatting in the salon, looking for Mrs. Gregory. When she spotted her on the sofa with an empty space beside her, Beatrice smiled and made her way to her.

"Mrs. Gregory, I have something of grave importance to tell you . . ." she said, taking a seat.

Chapter 31

Isabella Babcock sat at a bureau, ink pen in hand. She could scarcely sleep from the lingering excitement of the day. She decided to write her husband and dated the letter:

August 30, 1887

My dearest Elisha,
I write to tell you of the great progress we are making. Thus far, the comtesse has seen to all of our needs, and I daresay we are moving along faster than expected. We could very well make all of the necessary purchases by week's end, and could be returning home sooner than planned.

Isabella paused and stifled a giggle as the memories of the day in Lorraine's boutique flooded her thoughts. She relived it moment by moment. The champagne, the caviar, the vendors streaming in, one after another, displaying their wares while a stringed quartet played festive music. China patterns were chosen, linens swished between her fingers, and crystal stemware was held up to the light. Lorraine coordinated everything— waving in each vendor for a presentation—all the while holding Monique in her arms with Clancy at her feet. Isabella and Adella pointed, sampled, touched, decided upon, and signed dozens of invoices for billing. "Oh, this is such fun!" Adella babbled on more than one occasion.

One vendor brought in a peculiar grandfather clock with spiderwebs carved into the wooden frame of its pediments, on either side of the timepiece. Isabella wasn't sure whether the thrill of the moment or the champagne caused her to make the decision to purchase it, for at that very moment, she decided they *had* to have it. Adella eagerly agreed, insisting it was a "unique masterpiece and sensible necessity. After all, spiders are good luck and there is a small, carved spider." When Isabella signed the invoice, the vendor grinned and the ladies broke into a fit of light-headed giggles.

Isabella smiled and continued writing:

I thought perhaps a clock would be a prudent purchase, as our guests will likely be in need of the time. It wasn't on our wish list, but not to worry, Adella and I have secured one nonetheless. I only wish you could be here with me to share in the experience. Paris has been nothing less than enchanting! We met an artist today that has had the privilege of showing his work in the Paris Salon.

She remembered the young artist, Pierre Auguste Renoir, who had called on Lorraine to unveil his latest work. Tall and handsome, he wore his dark hair parted to the side and his beard trimmed. After several kisses on both cheeks were exchanged with Lorraine, he clapped his hands and boys he called *garçons* brought in paintings covered in cloth.

"Auguste, these are my guests from America, Mrs. Babcock and Mrs. Story," Lorraine said, introducing them. The ladies curtsied while he bowed, seductively kissing each woman on the hand. "*Bonjour!* It is my great pleasure," he purred. His thick accent and lingering gaze made the ladies feel flattered. His were eyes that could capture moments, faces, and places and then splash them onto canvas for all eternity.

Monsieur Dubois filled their flutes with more champagne.

"Auguste, it is always a joy to see you and unveil your latest collection." Lorraine said.

"Today I bring you something special." He raised one eyebrow flirtatiously.

"You know I sold your *Luncheon at the Boating Party* in less than two days?"

"But of course I remember, *madame*! This is why you are the first person I unveil my pieces to. A starving artist needs a willing patron. Although, my new collection may be perhaps more for the, let us say, less inhibited collector."

"I'm intrigued already, *monsieur*!" Lorraine teased with a laugh. She placed the sleeping Monique in a velvet bed, where Clancy was already fast asleep.

The ladies sat and Auguste grabbed hold of the linen cover, stripping it away dramatically. Isabella and Adella gaped, and Lorraine gasped. Before them stood naked, full-bodied women without a stitch of modesty—or, apparently, a care in the world.

"I call them *The Large Bathers*, and they are part of a new collection on the sunbathing theme," he explained. *Renoir* was scrawled in the bottom right corner of the painting.

"*Très jolie, Auguste!*" Lorraine acclaimed, moving closer to observe the painting. "You've captured the light so perfectly, the colors are vibrant, and as always, your models are like angels! Perhaps for a boudoir?"

"A boudoir, yes, or a gentleman's study," Auguste suggested. "It would go nicely with cognac and cigars, don't you think?"

"The perfect pairing. Let me contact a few buyers. I can think of two already that would love to add this to their collection. I'll start a bidding war."

"*Oui! Oui!* I will leave it with you to share. A private screening perhaps, *madame*?"

"I'll place it here, in my parlor, where it will be seen by all of my clients. It's a masterpiece! You have grown tired of landscapes, no?"

"Portraits, dancing parties, and landscapes have had their time," he said, smiling. "Now I celebrate beautiful women!" Isabella and Adella blushed. The French were certainly very open about their passions.

"What do you think, ladies? Would your husbands prefer *The Large Sunbathers* next to the spider clock in your hotel?" Lorraine asked. The ladies became flustered, and before they could answer, Lorraine burst into laughter. "I'm only teasing you!"

"Oh, Lorraine, you truly are wonderful!" said Adella, and they all laughed.

Isabella thought to write to Elisha about the incident but decided she would instead tell him in person. He'd have such a laugh over it. She wrote more of her and Adella's events in fluid cursive strokes:

I have had the chance to meet many interesting people whilst staying in Paris. We've become quite fond of Lorraine and hope she can journey to America and stay as our guest sometime. She is impressively connected in Parisian society, and she revels in the opportunity to introduce us to her friends. We've met so many local artists of the Impressionist style: Manet, Monet, Caillebotte, Cézanne, and Degas. All incredibly gifted and most obliging. There's a fascinating woman, Berthe Morisot, whose works I'm particularly fond of. Perhaps one day we can collect a few of her pieces. Remind me to tell you of an interesting story about her and the Manet brothers, Édouard and Eugène. Needless to say, she dated both and married one. The jilted brother now morbidly paints her wearing all black in a public display of his contempt for her.

We also happened upon Mr. Gustave Eiffel at our café. He is building the large tower for the exposition that I wrote to you about earlier. He's an interesting character. Extremely bright and driven—he reminds me of you. I have invited him to be our guest when our hotel opens, which pleased him greatly. I daresay he is a very busy man, and it could be years before he can leave Paris.

We've also met some gentlemen who are well acquainted with the musical talents of our friend Jesse Shepard. They long for his return to Europe and hold him in the highest regard. I only hope we can keep Jesse in San Diego for as long as possible. We will have to keep him happy and very, very busy, or he will be lured away, I'm afraid.

Well, my love, I am thinking of you. With our purchases nearly complete, we should be returning home within a fortnight. Promise me we will return to romantic Paris soon. I long to walk along the river while holding your hand.

Forever yours, Isabella

Isabella folded the letter into thirds. She took a crystal atomizer with a bulb at the top and pumped it once, spraying just a whiff of French perfume onto her letter. She fanned it, letting the letter dry before placing it in an envelope, which she promptly addressed. Ready for bed, she blew out her candle, and the room went dark.

Chapter 32

Ava watched an endless parade of furniture and goods from Europe arrive with the train cars. There were chairs, bed frames, chaise lounges, sofas, a grandfather clock, light fixtures, paintings, rugs, as well as crates of silverware, flatware, china, and linens. The exterior of the hotel was now complete, and furnishing the interior was the only work that remained. The hotel buzzed with activity as workers added final touches to the rotunda. A steady stream of foliage arrived, too, ordered by Mrs. Sessions. There were palm trees, flowering trees, citrus trees, roses, hedges, perennials, annuals, climbing vines, and an exotic dragon tree.

Nathan delivered bricks made at the kiln to be used in the fireplaces. Every guest room had a private bathroom, a luxury unheard of in any hotel. Exemplary staffers from the finest hotels in the country were recruited, persuaded, hired, and trained to ensure all the Hotel Del guests would be treated like royalty. Sunshine and great pay had been enough to lure experienced East Coast workers to California. Young Harry West quit school so he could begin working as a bellhop his dream come true. A Mr. Seghers from Chicago was hired to be the general manager, and a Mr. Rossier as his assistant. Mr. Gomer for clerk, Mr. Fosdick for pharmacy, and Mr. Keoppen continued as gardener. Serving staff arrived daily, boarding at the newly built Oxford or Hotel Josephine, on Orange Avenue at Fourth Street. There were cleaning ladies, nannies, bellhops, chimney sweeps, and a gourmet chef from France, a Monsieur Campagnon, who constantly sniffed herbs he crushed with his fingertips. Opening day was a mere month or so away, and the excitement on the island was palpable.

Ava took notes on all activities so she could submit an article to the *Coronado Mercury*. She had been submitting articles under the alias, J. A. Paul, knowing they would never publish a thirteen-year-old girl's work. After several months of submissions, she finally saw her first article in print. It had been about the new church being built on C Avenue, Christ Church, and the plans for a new Presbyterian church nearby, which was to be named after the parents of Mrs. Babcock née Graham. Down the same street, Sacred Heart Catholic Church was in its proposal stage and had been approved to move ahead with development. Father Ubach, the parish priest, would no longer have to row his boat across the bay to hold Mass services.

Thrilled by seeing her first published article, Ava had clutched the paper to her chest. She knew the editor of the paper suspected she was the author since she dropped off articles each week; but because she didn't expect payment, no questions were asked. Ava decided she'd share her secret only with Grace.

Ava was always on alert, looking for newsworthy stories to write about. One morning, she saw Mr. Hawthorne taking photographs of wagons filled haphazardly with furniture. The wagons looked as if they had been packed in haste. People with long faces held up a sign that read for the picture that read: Busted. Mr. Hawthorne didn't smile after the photograph was taken, and neither had his subjects. Ava had the feeling something awful had happened to them, but she didn't want to ask.

At dinner that evening, her parents talked about the land bust. They looked worried.

"Will people be moving away?" she asked her father.

"Undoubtedly. They've already begun."

"But San Diego has a population of forty thousand people," Owen said.

"Not for long. A land bust happens quicker than a land boom. Without hope for a brighter future, people will leave."

"But what about the Del?" Ava cried. "Who will come and stay when it opens?"

"This isn't good news for the Del. The timing couldn't be worse. I've also heard they've run out of money to complete the interior. Captain Charles Hinde loaned a large sum, but it's not enough, I'm afraid."

Ava felt a sharp pain in her stomach. *What can be done?*

The following day, she drove a very preoccupied Mr. Spreckels to the Coronado Beach Company offices of Mr. Babcock and Mr. Story. The two men looked bleary-eyed when they welcomed Mr. Spreckels in, quickly closing the door behind him. Ava started an investigation. She needed to understand what caused the land bust and report on it right away. She hunted down the only person she knew could help explain it all to her. She found Mr. Holabird in his office.

"You see, Ava," Colonel Holabird said, "Southern California is experiencing a land value correction after growing so quickly. I expect the population in San Diego will decrease dramatically in the next few weeks. People need work and opportunities. With a land bust, speculators will panic and investors will be scared away. We've just been dealt a tough blow, and all of us will suffer for it, I'm afraid."

"What about the Del? Will it still open?"

"I'll let you in on a little secret. It won't be a secret for long, but for now, just keep it to yourself. We've run out of money to complete the hotel. With the land bust, it's going to be impossible to secure the funding for it."

"That's awful!" Ava cried. "What will Mr. Babcock and Mr. Story do? They've worked so hard for this." On the verge of tears, Ava felt her chest tighten. "So it will never open?"

"Don't distress, my dear. I haven't told you the secret yet. It turns out that our good friend Mr. Spreckels has a great fondness for our island resort. He has an entrepreneurial spirit, backed by great affluence. I suspect the urgent meeting he's having right now is about this very issue."

"But what can be done? All of their dreams will be ruined!"

"Wait and watch, my dear. These men are problem solvers. I have all the confidence in the world that a solution is at hand."

Feeling glum, Ava waited in her carriage outside the offices of the Coronado Beach Company. Traffic to the island had come to a halt. Nobody waited for her to give them a tour of the island or asked her questions about lots for sale. The streets were eerily empty.

After several hours, Mr. Spreckels and Mr. Babcock emerged from the building. Mr. Babcock looked weary. "It's at times such as these that I'm reminded of the wisdom of Aristotle, who said: 'It is during our darkest moments that we must focus to see the light.'"

Mr. Spreckels replied, "He also said: 'The beauty of the soul shines out when a man bears with composure one heavy mischance after another, not because he does not feel them, but because he is a man of high and heroic temper.'"

"Thank you for saving our dream," Mr. Babcock said, looking grateful.

"We will finish your project Babcock, and everyone will have you to thank for it. This hotel is and will always be yours."

Mr. Babcock smiled wanly.

Ava gave Mr. Spreckels a ride to the ferry landing and pulled the carriage to a stop. "Is everything going to be all right, Mr. Spreckels?"

"Absolutely, my dear. It appears I've come along to the right place at the right time. Say, you write for the paper, don't you?"

"You know about that?" Ava's eyes widened.

"Grace has taken a sudden interest in the Sunday paper. She never has before. She showed me a fantastic article by a local author named J. A. Paul. I inquired about him, but nobody knows who he is."

Ava suppressed a smile.

"Will you convey a message to J. A. Paul for me?"

"Sure."

"Tell him, or *her*, to run a story in three days that John D. Spreckels has purchased holdings for the Hotel del Coronado and the Coronado Beach Company. The hotel will open as planned, the island will continue to prosper, and all will be untouched by the unfortunate turn of events in the land market."

Ava broke into a wide grin. "I'll be sure to pass that along."

Mr. Spreckels winked at her as he stepped down from the carriage. "Very well and good day, Miss Ava. I look forward to reading your work."

That Saturday, Ava submitted an article for the Sunday paper:

Announcing major changes to the ownership and future of the Hotel del Coronado. With the misfortunate downward spiral of the market, Mr. John D. Spreckels, of San Francisco, has kindly stepped in to fund the remainder of the Hotel del Coronado, loaning $100,000 for its completion. He has also become a partner, buying out the shares of Mr. Hampton Story. Mr. Elisha Babcock, however, will remain as a shareholder and manager of the project. The Hotel del Coronado is expected to open as planned in February of 1888.

Ava sat reading her article on the front porch when Nathan walked up, carrying a bouquet of wildflowers.

"Nathan, what a pleasant surprise. I'd almost forgotten we were friends."

"Yeah, I've been real busy," he said awkwardly.

His demeanor puzzled Ava. It wasn't like him to act so bashful. "What lovely flowers. Did you bring them for me?"

"Actually, they're for your mother. I remembered it was her birthday. Could you give them to her?" He finally looked up and held Ava's gaze. She could see a tinge of sadness in his eyes. "That's so sweet of you to remember."

"I remembered it from last year. My mother liked flowers. Lilies especially, but I couldn't find any, except for what's in the hotel's garden, and it would be a crime to take them."

"My mother will love them. Thank you. Can I ask what happened to your mother?"

"She died of a fever when I was young, but I still remember what she looked like and the way she laughed. She had a funny laugh."

"I'm really sorry. I'm sure she was lovely."

"She was." He looked away for a moment.

" Would you like to stay for dinner and cake?"

"I can't. I have to get back to the kiln. We're making forty thousand bricks a day, so they can't do without me. I've been working overtime."

"Maybe next time, then. Are you keeping up on your reading?"

"Yes, teacher, I finally finished *Sense and Sensibility*. Do you know how hard that was to hide from the boys at the kiln? Next book, give me something about Hercules or Samson."

"I'm sorry, it's all I had!" Ava said, laughing. "The good news is Mr. Spreckels is opening a library soon."

"That is good news. Then I can pick out my own books."

Ava laughed.

"I really have to get back to work." Nathan rubbed his neck, wincing.

"Good to see you and thanks again for the flowers."

As Nathan walked away, he stopped and turned back to her. "Say, are you going to be at the grand opening?" he asked

"Of course, isn't everybody?"

"Just making sure you'll be there."

Ava wondered what Nathan was up to. He was so mysterious these days. She delivered the flowers to her mother, then went back to reading the paper on the front porch. Colonel Holabird was running a new advertisement that read:

The Largest and Most Elegant All-Year-Round Seaside Hotel in the World
Will be open to receive guests about February 1, 1888.
Rates by the month, $2.00 per day and upwards according to location of room. Rates by the week, $2.50 per day and upwards according to location of room. Transient rates, $3.00 per day and upwards according to location of room. In no case, however, will a higher rate be charged than at other first-class hotels. Special inducements will be made for families and permanent guests.
The hotel is supplied with elevators and every modern convenience, including incandescent electric lights, etc., etc. Every room has open grates for wood or coal, and public rooms are also supplied with steam heaters. The ballroom can comfortably accommodate 2,500 visitors. The seating capacity of the dining room, 1,000."

J. B. SEGHERS JR., of Chicago, and T. Thompson, of New York City
Manager and Chief Clerk

Another brochure Ava read boasted the following:

Darkness soon bids fair to become unknown in Coronado. Biggest building to be
electrified."

And finally, one of Colonel Holabird's finest pieces:

The hotel will be perfect in all its appointments. The grand front will be immediately on
the seaside, the side fronts, both east and west, giving sunshine to every room. Beautifully
adorned grounds will adjoin the house, planted with the rarest tropical flowers. There are
spacious verandas, a grand ballroom, guest rooms en suite and single, with every luxury
known to the modern ingenuity. Of the cuisine, there shall be nothing to complain, the
intent of the managers being to cater to a class of patrons who are accustomed to and who
appreciate luxury.

Ava laughed to herself, saying the line: "Of the cuisine, there shall be nothing to complain." She hoped they were right, but from what she had learned driving guests around the island, the very wealthy always had *some* trifling thing to complain about.

Chapter 33

Mr. Babcock opened the Hotel del Coronado early, on the nineteenth of February 1888. The official opening was set for March, but he thought it prudent to be operational beforehand. Train cars with furnishings still arrived daily, and finishing touches were needed, but by and large, the hotel was ready. The newspapers heralded the staggering accomplishment for a hotel so grand to have been built in only one year's time.

Guests anxious to be the first to stay flocked to Coronado by ferry, train, and steamship. Ava delivered them endlessly in her carriage from the ferry landing to the white staircase of the porte cochere leading to the hotel's main entrance. Nearby was a second entrance, parallel to the first and separated by a covered porch. It was designated for those returning from sport, like hunting and fishing, and in a less presentable state.

Guests and spectators milled about on both staircases of the porte cocheres and in between them, sharing the excitement of opening day. Ava watched glamorous ladies wrapped in fur stoles peer up from under their wide-brimmed hats, extending their gloved hands to gentlemen who helped them down from her carriage Their exotic perfumes lingered in the air. Trunks studded with copper rivets were hauled away by fast-moving bellhops in crisp uniforms and caps shaped like small drums. Young Harry West was among the bellhops. "Well done, Harry!" Ava said. The boy saluted her, proud to be in his uniform. He rushed to the next carriage, eager to be of assistance.

Ava especially enjoyed delivering guests with children. Most of her young passengers clapped their hands excitedly when Ava pulled the carriage to a stop in front of the hotel. One young boy marveled at the grand turret over the ballroom. "I want to go in there!" he exclaimed with wonder in his eyes. During all the activity of checking in at the front desk, he was accidentally left behind and stood staring up at the turret until his father came back to retrieve him. "Come along, Alfred, we're all inside now. Be a good boy—you mustn't fall behind." His father had to pull him along to break him out of the trance inspired by the turret.

A short while later, Ava witnessed a disappointed Alfred outside the hotel again. "I thought there would be a carousel in there!" he wailed.

The boy's anxious mother tried to console him, embarrassed by his public tantrum. "Alfred, dear, it is a ballroom, *not* an amusement park. We will find you a carousel, Alfie, Father has promised that whatever you want, you shall have it."

"But I want a carousel *now!*"

Ava hid her giggle. Mother had warned her to expect some overindulged children, and little Alfred was her first example. "And I want a great, *big* carousel!" he demanded sourly. "Bigger than the one in London."

"But of course, Alfie! We will find you a bigger carousel."

Somewhat appeased, Alfred followed his mother back inside.

On her next delivery, Ava had to swerve around a black-and-gold Pullman car as it pulled to a stop. An older woman exited, dressed in a hat perched at an angle and striped silk dress with a long train. Ava guessed she was European and someone of importance. The woman clutched seven leashes for seven barking dogs that pulled her forward. She paused, eyed the hotel, smiled broadly, and then climbed the white staircase to the main entrance. Everyone on the porch watched her ascent, riveted by her regal manner.

Ava wanted to know her name. The *Coronado Mercury* and San Diego papers planned to publish the names of those who registered weekly. There would be great interest in a European woman, arriving by herself with numerous canines in tow. Especially an elegant woman who appeared so perfectly prepossessing.

Inside the rotunda, Mr. Spreckels, Mr. Babcock, and Colonel Holabird greeted guests. "Welcome to the largest hotel in the world! So good of you to come, Mr. and Mrs. Beatty. I do hope the long journey wasn't too taxing for you," Mr. Babcock said. "I can assure you rest and recuperation are imminent here at our establishment!"

"Not at all, Babcock," Mr. Beatty replied. "Fine place you have here. My wife insisted we be among the first guests, ever since she read a brochure for the Hotel del Coronado. She has become tired of European destinations, and quite frankly, so am I. A train ride from New York is far more pleasant than a transatlantic voyage. I thank you for providing us an opportunity to stay in our country, and I hear you have every sort of amenity here, is that so?"

"Everything one can imagine: swimming, bowling, tennis, billiards, croquet, tennis, golf, boating, archery, fishing, hunting, and polo. We also have tranquility rooms for more passive indulgences such as reading, writing, playing cards, and chess. Not to mention a cigar and music room."

"Capital, Babcock! Your resort is just as it claims to be, perfect in all its appointments!"

Some guests sat reading newspapers in wicker rocking chairs or milled about the rotunda, chatting amiably. On the balcony upstairs, ladies waving fans peered over the banister, curious to see who arrived. The wealthier the couple, as revealed by their attire, the faster the ladies fanned themselves to mute their whispered conversations about the registered guests. They tried to catch a glimpse inside the private lobby reserved for ladies who were not accompanied by gentlemen. Unfortunately, the many pillars and ferns around the lobby obscured their view, denying them the ability to speculate as to the women who dared to show such strident independence.

A boisterous woman, dripping in sparkling gems, entered the rotunda with her arms stretched wide. "*Ciao! Signore Jesse!*" she cried in a booming voice. Jesse Shepard, who was there to celebrate on opening day, rushed to embrace her. "*Bella Signora Celestina!* So good of you to come all the way from Sicily! I long to hear you sing again!" They exchanged kisses on both cheeks. "You are my favorite coloratura! In fact, I refuse to play Bellini without you there to sing!"

Signora Celestina belted a line from the opera, and her voice carried above the chatter of guests. The room fell silent as she held a high trill, raising her hands dramatically. Applause erupted, and both Signora Celestina and Jesse broke into laughter. "Just like old times!" she said. "And I will cook for you Jesse, no? I'll make your favorite, *carbonara*!"

"I thought you'd never ask. Please come to my home—my kitchen is yours. We'll have a dinner party in your honor." Signora Celestina squealed with delight at the prospect.

The ladies on the balcony fanned themselves feverishly. "I suppose that's how those *I-talians* are," one woman said.

Another nodded in agreement. "A bit boisterous for my taste," she sniped behind her fan.

Mr. Spreckels mingled with guests, offering personal invitations and suggestions. "Yes, I believe cigars are in order. Would you care to join me after supper, perhaps for a round of billiards? Splendid. Enjoy your stay with us." Alfred ran through the crowd, chased by his frantic mother, which caused Mr. Spreckels to laugh. "Let the boy run—he's on vacation!"

"The Comtesse du Boulanger!" announced a butler in a heavy French accent. The rotunda quieted in an instant, and all eyes were fixed on the front entrance. Lorraine stood expectantly in the doorway with her chin raised, bathed in glorious sunlight. Her dogs stood protectively at her feet. The guests were wide-eyed as they beheld her, looking like royalty. Applause erupted and she smiled appreciatively. She was now permitted to enter the rotunda after having been properly announced. Mrs. Babcock and Mrs. Story rushed to greet her.

"Lorraine, you made it! You look fabulous and what a grand entrance! It's so wonderful to see you again!" Mrs. Story gushed. Double kisses were exchanged and Monique yelped. Adella swept her up, letting the dog lick her on the cheek. "I've missed you, Monique!"

"The hotel is *magnifique*!" exclaimed Lorraine. "I would not miss the opening for all the world."

"Come, let us give you a tour." Mrs. Babcock waved to Harry West, directing him to take the dogs.

"Yes, ma'am!" he replied, springing into action. He quickly became tangled in dog leashes as he made his way out the door, causing guests to laugh.

The ladies walked into the courtyard, chatting about Lorraine's journey from Paris. A deep male voice interrupted their conversation, saying, "Hello, Lorraine."

Lorraine stiffened. Alarmed by her reaction, Adella and Isabella followed the voice to a man sitting in a chair with his long legs extended and his boots crossed at the ankles. He was smiling a crooked, confident smile that echoed the twinkle in his blue eyes. He wore a black hat and fringed leather vest. He stood up slowly, removed his hat, and held it to his chest. Lorraine turned to him, looking dazed. The man looked at her longingly, and Lorraine caught her breath. Isabella and Adella realized at once they were standing in the middle of a couple with a long history.

Lorraine quickly regained her composure. "I'm surprised to see you, Monsieur Clancy. It's been a very long time." Her lips pouted in a show of sophistication.

Clancy strode over to her, taking her hand in his. He bowed and kissed it slowly, all the while locking his eyes with hers. "It has been a long time," he said. "I was hoping I'd see you here." His Southern drawl was thick and charming. He stood tall, placed his hat on his head, and winked. "Ladies," he said, tipping his hat to the three of them. He strolled away with a confident smile on his face.

Isabella and Adella rushed to Lorraine's side. "Are you all right? Do you feel faint?" Isabella said.

Lorraine clasped both hands to her face.

"Oh dear!" cried Adella as Lorraine's shoulders began to shake.

"She's discombobulated!" cried Isabella. "How can we help? Shall I fetch you sniffing salts?"

Lorraine lowered her hands, and it became clear she was stifling a fit of laughter. "How did I look?" she asked.

"Well, I'd say calm, collected, and . . . *fantastique*," suggested Isabella. Adella agreed.

"*Très bien!* I'm so happy I packed extra perfume."

Adella and Isabella gaped, then all three women began to giggle.

～∙⌒

Most of the hotel guests planned to stay from several weeks to several months. The registration ledger listed their names and cities of origin, all handwritten with the remarkable penmanship that typified the educated class: Nelson Morris, Don A. Sweet, Miss L. White, Samuel E. Berry, Joseph Davis and family, Mrs. Van Immagen, C. J. Sterling, James L. Mason, Miss Mollie Saint Julian, Chester Snider. Every line of the first three pages in the ledger was completely filled in, and the hotel was alive with activity. Opening a door was like lifting the lid on a music box: a joyful chorus of laughter played in each room.

Ava, Owen, and Lydia spent the afternoon running children up and down the beach in horse-drawn buggies or on horseback. Even the donkey was put to use to pull a wagon filled with toddlers.

"Would you mind if I took a photograph?" Mr. Hawthorne asked the children. "If you could just place yourselves in front of the hotel and pause for a moment for me, that would do just fine." Ava orchestrated the buggies and horses, instructing the children to face the camera.

After two flashes of light, Mr. Hawthorne reappeared from under his curtain and waved. "Perfect! Thank you, children. Carry on."

The buggies returned to the beach, joining the dozens of coaches that trotted up and down the stretch of golden sand in front of the hotel. Gentlemen and ladies sat with perfect posture in each coach, enjoying the California sunshine and fresh air. Only the sea gulls were dissatisfied, having to circle in the sky because there was no safe place to land that wasn't overrun by coaches.

On the beach in front of the ballroom turret, ladies sat under parasols, watching the coaches go by. Toddlers dug holes in the sand while their governesses tried in vain to keep them tidy. In the ocean, just beyond the waves, a man still wearing his top hat floated contentedly on his back, smoking a cigar.

"Would you like to see the ostrich farm?" Ava asked the children. They nodded eagerly. "Very well, I'll take you for a tour."

ॐॐ

Nathan pulled the bowler from his head when he saw four carriages and one donkey-drawn wagon filled with children pull up at the farm. "I guess you all want to see some ostriches. Who wants to see mean old Twilah?" he asked. A dozen hands went up. "Come on, then."

The children and Ava followed him to the corral. "Now, she's had a few babies and they're adorable. See them over there?" Nathan asked.

The children giggled, watching the awkward young ostriches race around the pen in crazed circles. "Do they really have small brains?" one child asked. "Why are they always flapping their wings in the air if they can't fly?" another said.

A chorus of more questions followed: "Why can't they fly?" "Have you ever ridden on one?" "Can you make an omelet from their eggs?"

"Let me answer one question at a time," Nathan replied. "Yes, they have small brains. I don't know why they flap their wings since they can't fly. And yes, I've ridden one and lived to tell the tale. No, I've never had an ostrich omelet."

The children broke into giggles. Ava picked up the youngest girl and held her on her hip so that she had a better view. The children pointed and laughed as they watched the young ostriches chase their mother, huddling for protection around her long legs.

After an hour, it was time to return to the hotel for dinner. "Thank you, Nathan, for giving the kids such a wonderful tour," Ava said, smiling at him.

"Giving tours is in my new job description. Mr. Spreckels asked me to do it himself."

"You work hard enough as it is. I can't imagine you taking on one more thing."

"Oh, I can take on *many* things," he replied, winking. "You'd be surprised. See you tonight?"

"Of course. I'm playing violin with a string quartet during dinner. The orchestra is playing in the ballroom, and I heard there's a band from Old Town performing there. Maybe Jesse will play piano, too, if we're lucky."

"Promise me you won't miss the ballroom concerts."

"Why?" She eyed him suspiciously.

"To save me a dance, of course."

"I think you're hiding something."

"I'm deeply offended by such a notion."

Ava smirked at him. "See you tonight."

Chapter 34

As the double doors to the Crown Room swept open, members of the stringed quartet began to play their violins. They stood in the orchestra loft overlooking the extravagantly decorated room. Chandeliers illuminated long tables set with white linens, red-rose centerpieces, and sparkling stemware. Bone china inlaid with small red crowns were set between shining silver flatware. Every gleaming detail was fairy-tale perfect. The music from the violins rose pleasantly up the walls and curled along the arched ceiling, reaching the far corners of the vast space. Stealing glances at the guests filing in, Ava kept an eye out for Wallace.

Tuxedo-clad waiters in long tailcoats and white gloves escorted guests to their tables. The guests appeared to be amazed as they took in the room. The quartet played a simple melody, and soon the level of chatter in the room rose to them. Ava noticed Signora Celestina cackle with laughter at something Jesse whispered to her. He threw his head back when she responded, matching her robust laughter with his own. Ava could tell they were old friends.

The Babcocks, the Storys, the Holabirds, and the Spreckels shared a table with Lorraine, the Comtesse du Boulanger. The elegant woman from Paris was greatly admired by the ladies in the room, in no small part because she wore a glamorous gold evening gown. Across the room, a tall man from Texas couldn't take his eyes off her, either. He wore a tuxedo topped with a cowboy hat, which he politely removed for dinner. The French woman glanced his way only once, smiled coyly, then returned her attention to dinner-table conversation, ignoring him completely for the remainder of the meal.

Ava saw the Gregory family was seated with the Claypoole family. This didn't surprise her. Beatrice placed herself next to Wallace and kept glancing up at Ava, looking away as if she hadn't. She whispered into Wallace's ear, but he seemed to ignore her. Instead, he tilted his chair away from her so he could watch Ava play. Ava thought he looked handsome in his striped tuxedo. He smiled up at her. Ava had to make a concerted effort not to spy on him during dinner. Lately, Wallace had been making her feel unsteady. He was always standing too close and looking too deeply into her eyes. Her stomach fluttered with every encounter. She would say something opinionated, and he would call her Fractious, laughing away the tense, awkward moment that had just passed between them.

When the guests had taken their seats in the Crown Room, Mr. Babcock climbed the steps to the orchestra loft to make a speech. He raised a flute of champagne and said; "Looking over this room, filled with guests at last, is a dream come true. It's hard to believe the time is finally at hand. Our vision for this island and for this hotel has been realized because you are all here. It is truly an honor to have you as our first guests." His voice cracked with emotion, and his eyes welled up. "I would like to welcome all of you to the largest, most elegant hotel in the world, the Hotel del Coronado." Enormous applause erupted.

"I'd like to thank a few people before we share our first dinner," Mr. Babcock said. "Firstly, Mr. Hampton Story, would you please stand up?" Mr. Story did so, waving to those around him. "Hampton, our vision has come true—and without you, none of this dream would have been possible. I thank you sincerely, from the bottom of my heart." Everyone clapped.

Mr. Babcock had more key players to acknowledge. "Silent partners for this venture, please stand up," he said. Mr. Gruendike and two other gentlemen stood up. "Thank you for believing in the shared vision for the hotel, for not finding us insane and for funding us!" Mr. Babcock joked. "Lastly, I'd like to thank Mr. John D. Spreckels for helping us reach the finish line and for saving our hotel. The value of your support and friendship cannot be measured, and I thank you, sir. What a blessing and honor it is for all of us that you came to visit Coronado and fell in love with its charm." The applause continued. People began to stand to acclaim Mr. Spreckels, who waved and grinned at the well-wishers.

"Finally," Mr. Babcock continued, "I've invited Father Ubach to bless our meal this evening. Some of you may have seen him rowing the bay every Sunday morning to hold services in the pavilion."

Father Ubach, a bearded priest in a black cassock and white collar, appeared in the orchestra loft. He extended his arms to embrace the room, bowed his head, and began to pray in a booming voice: "Bless us, Oh Lord, and these thy gifts, which we are about to receive, from thy Heavenly bounty, through Christ, Our Lord. Amen." He made the sign of the cross and kissed his closed fist. A chorus of "Amen!" rose from the crowd.

Mr. Babcock addressed the room again. "We have a great lineup of celebrations, not only for tonight but throughout the week. We hope you will enjoy our fantastic meal, prepared by our chef, Monsieur Frederic Pierre Campagnon, the finest chef from Paris. Where is he?"

Mr. Babcock surveyed the room, spotting the chef dressed in a white double-breasted buttoned jacket and with a bulbous toque blanche on his head. "Ah, there he is!" The chef bowed, nodding repeatedly.

Mr. Babcock continued, "And if there is anything you may need whilst staying with us, don't hesitate to ask our staff so that we may promptly accommodate you. After dinner, join us in the ballroom for music, dancing, and libations. We hope that you enjoy your stay—and that you stay for as long as you wish. We welcome you. Cheers to good health and prosperity!" Mr. Babcock raised his champagne flute, and the guests followed suit. After the toast, the chatter in the room began to escalate. Mr. Babcock winked at Ava, prompting her to play again. She smiled a little when she placed her bow across the strings. She was grateful for the small part she got to play on this historic evening.

Wine was poured, champagne bubbled, and silver platters made their rounds through the Crown Room, delivering caviar, exotic cheeses, and oysters to each table. Subsequent course after course was whisked in by fast-moving waiters—fish, lamb, beef with fragrant herbs on a bed of steamed, locally grown vegetables, followed by delicate chocolate and cream confections. No detail was missed, no expense spared, and all diners were impressed by the attentive service and quality of the meal.

When dinner concluded, a bell rang and the doors to the Crown Room were opened again. It was time to move the celebration into the ballroom. Ava quickly packed up her violin, left it at the registration desk, and followed the crowd across the rotunda and down a long hallway to the opposite side of the hotel. The double door to the ballroom was closed, and it was guarded by two male staff members. Guests would have to wait momentarily for the room to open. The chatter and excitement rose to a dizzying level along the length of the hallway as the anticipation built.

Ava found Grace in line, and they passed the time discreetly by commenting on the many lovely ladies and their elegant attire. The women wore bustled gowns draped in tiers to the floor, diamond brooches, lace petticoats, stoles, fur muffs, and butterfly hair clasps. Their laughter was songlike, and their perfumes were an intoxicating mix of gardenia, jasmine, and rose water. Gentlemen wore crisp tuxedos and white gloves. Some tapped fashionable walking canes or extended an elbow for a lady to cling to.

When the doors to the ballroom were at last opened, the waiting crowd gasped. Crystal chandeliers cast an enchanting glow over the room as the guests filed in. Jesse Shepard sat at the piano on the main stage, playing feverishly. A curly strand of his hair fell into his eyes as his fingers pounded and rolled along the length of the keyboard. He threw his head back to dislodge wayward the strand and continued to play. Ava watched with amazement from the foot of the stage.

"He is fantastic, isn't he?" Wallace whispered in her ear after sneaking up on her. Smiling, she nodded. "Save me a dance later?" he asked, then disappeared.

The room filled and couples began to twirl around the dance floor. Outside, fireworks erupted, and people rushed to the bay windows to see the flickering light display. Jesse continued to play a concerto that seemed to synchronize with the bursting fireworks. When the pyrotechnic show ended, he blew a kiss to the crowd and exited the stage. The curtains promptly closed, and the hotel manager, Mr. Seghers, announced the orchestra would commence playing shortly. Brisk waiters balanced trays filled with flutes of champagne and glasses of wine, passing them out liberally as they circled the room.

Ava noticed Nathan standing near the wall, watching the festivities unfold. She walked over to him. "I was wondering where you were tonight, and here you are, hiding in the corner." She thought he looked nervous. "Are you all right?"

"Yes, I'm fine. I'm just waiting for a friend." He quickly changed the subject. "I heard you play earlier—I snuck into the Crown Room. You were really great!"

"Thank you. I've been rehearsing for weeks now. I was really nervous to play for the grand opening."

"You couldn't tell, and I like your dress."

"Do you? My mother made it for me. That's really nice of you to say."

"You look beautiful in anything," he said, looking away as he said it.

The orchestra began to play.

"There you are, you promised me a dance," Wallace said, interrupting Ava and Nathan as he approached them.

Nathan's expression darkened slightly. "Promise me you won't go anywhere," he whispered to Ava, his eyes burning intently. She agreed, not knowing what he meant or why he seemed so adamant about her presence. Wallace took her hand, but she kept looking back at Nathan as they walked to the dance floor.

"He'll be fine," Wallace said.

Beatrice was watching, so Wallace moved Ava to the center of the dance floor, where other couples surrounded them.

"I'm worried about Nathan," Ava said. "He seems really anxious about something."

❧❦

Pushing Ava from his mind, Nathan scanned the room for Guillermo. He found him on the opposite side of the ballroom. Guillermo gave him a hand signal and Nathan nodded, slipping behind the curtain of the stage. It was time to get ready.

"Hey, do you mind if I take you somewhere where we can talk?" Wallace asked Ava. "I want to show you something."

Ava looked up, surprised. "Nathan doesn't want me to go anywhere." She was still thinking about how nervous he had seemed. The anxiety was unlike him.

"*Please!* It's important, and it has to be right now, not later," Wallace insisted.

"Why? Where are you taking me?"

Wallace pointed up, toward the cone of the turret. "Will you just trust me and not fight me for once? There's something you have to see. You're not afraid of heights, are you?"

"I don't think I am."

"Good. We may have to sneak a little. I don't want us to be followed." He motioned to Beatrice, who was watching them like an alley cat.

"I guess I can go, but we have to be back soon. I promised Nathan."

Wallace led Ava through the dancing crowd, peeking back at Beatrice, who was trying to spot them again. They hid behind a waiter, walking closely behind him until they had circled around Beatrice. Wallace led Ava past a rope flanked by a Closed sign. They proceeded up a narrow, spiral staircase to the second-floor balcony. All the music and conversation funneled loudly into the cone of the turret. Wallace led Ava by the hand around the perimeter of the space to a small door and hidden ladder. "You may have to leave your shoes behind so you don't slip."

"All right." Ava took her shoes off, not caring that she would ruin her stockings. She followed Wallace up the ladder.

⤳⬳

In a room backstage, Nathan yanked up his pants. They fit even tighter than the last time he'd tried them on. "Guillermo, I think they got smaller!" he said frantically.

Guillermo burst out laughing, "Maybe you grew some more, Nito! Don't worry— just remember what I told you: walk backward off the stage!" Amused members of the band grinned, some with teeth darkened from chewing tobacco. They all wore their finest white shirts, pants with silver stitching, and wide sombreros. Some held guitars, while others carried brass horns or violins.

"Hey, Guillermo, why didn't we wear our spurs?" Nathan said. "If I was wearing my spurs, Ava would *definitely* fall in love with me."

"The floor of the stage is too nice. *No spurs*. We go on in fifteen minutes, amigos," Guillermo announced. The button on Nathan's pants popped open, causing the men to cackle. Guillermo gave him a belt and cinched it up tight. "There, that should hold for a little while."

"I can't even breathe, let alone sing!" Nathan protested.

"Your part is high anyway."

"That's not funny, Guillermo!"

"*Oye*, where is Fernando?" Guillermo said, looking among the men.

"*Está enfermo*," replied one of them, shrugging.

"Sick? He *can't* be sick!"

"*No puede cantar*," the man added.

Guillermo ran his hand over his beard. "Okay, Nito, you have to sing Fernando's part."

"What?" Nathan's voice cracked. "I can't sing his part— my voice is still changing."

"You can sing it, I've heard you." Guillermo patted Nathan on the back. "You want Avalita to fall in love with you or not?"

"What did I get myself into?" Nathan said in a panic. "This is going to be a disaster."

Guillermo looked him straight in the eye, grasping him by the shoulders. "Who are you, Nito?" he asked firmly, shaking him once. "*Who are you?*"

Nathan tried to regulate his breathing. Finding his resolve, he replied, "I'm a mariachi."

"That's right. And tonight, you show everybody who you are."

Nathan nodded, gulping. "Thanks, Guillermo. I really mean that."

Nathan went to the corner of the stage and peeked through the curtain, hoping to find Ava on the dance floor. But she was gone.

☙❧

"*Ma-dem-oi-selle*, may I have this dance?" Clancy's slow Texas drawl was like a cello to her ears. Lorraine was hoping he would find her in the crowded ballroom. With her heart pounding in her chest, she turned to him. He bowed, holding his hat to his chest. After a deliberate pause, she held her hand out to him.

A waltz began, and Clancy led her to a cleared space on the floor. He spun her around slowly, and she kept her eyes averted, watching his boots rather than meeting his eyes. She couldn't look into them. The silence between them was heavy as he waited for her to speak.

"How did you know I would be here?" she asked. Her voice cracked slightly, and her accent was heavy.

"A brochure said this hotel is furnished with the finest Paris has to offer," Clancy explained. "I knew you were behind all of it. I also knew you couldn't pass up a grand opening."

Lorraine chuckled. He moved her around the ballroom floor with ease. They passed the Babcocks and the Storys on the dance floor. Isabella nudged Adella, and both ladies watched, wide-eyed.

"I never stopped thinking about you." Her ear was an inch away from his measured words. She closed her eyes, remembering his familiar scent—beeswax and cedar from the pomade he used on his mustache.

"You never came back. I waited."

"I wanted to. I got injured by a bull."

Lorraine caught her breath, and her grip tightened in his hand.

"I'm not the young, foolish woman I was then."

"No, you're not. You're better."

She became tense in his arms. "Would you liken me to a fine wine, monsieur? Improving with age?" she said, challenging him and feeling her resolve slip away.

"Improving like a Tennessee whiskey."

They danced in silence.

"Why didn't you send for me?" she finally demanded to know, her eyes searching his. This question had haunted her for years. She had spent many nights wondering what the outcome might have been if she had been more direct with him. Instead, she had been as noncommittal as a flirtatious dancer, kicking up her heels in front of a rowdy crowd.

"I did. *Twice.* You never replied."

She caught her breath. "You did?" She lowered her head, but he lifted her chin.

"We belong together, you with me," he said. "I don't want to spend the rest of my life without you."

"But what about your ranch? The cattle?"

"I can sell it all."

"And what? Return to Paris with me?"

"If that's what you want. I don't care if we are here or there. I want to marry you, Lorraine."

Lorraine never thought she could find love and happiness again at her age. Her eyes brimmed with tears as she nodded yes.

"But there is one thing you might want to know first," he added.

"What is this *thing?*"

"You ever heard of a bloodhound? I have four of them, and I just can't part with them. They're hunting dogs, and truth be told, they're *really* loud. They're always hollerin' at something or another."

"There's something you need to know, too. I have seven dogs, and I can't part with them, either. One is named Clancy. Don't be offended."

"Does he have to sleep outside?" Clancy joked.

"On the contrary, he stays closest to me."

They both started to laugh and continued to dance.

Chapter 35

Ava reached the last rung on the ladder and followed Wallace through a door that led outside. The widow's walk was three-feet wide and circled below the top of turret. "I've always wanted to come up here," Ava confessed, daring to look out over the handrail. The steep slope of the red-tiled roof gave her pause. Light shined through the dormers, glimmering like little candles along the turret. "How high up are we, do you think?"

"A hundred and fifty feet. We're almost ten stories high," Wallace said.

Ava backed away from the handrail. "It feels even higher!" She looked upward, observing the tip of the turret with a flagpole extending from its center.

"This is the best place in the house to see this . . ." Wallace said, pointing east. A pale moon ascended like a sand dollar, creeping over the jagged ridgeline of the distant mountains.

"It's magnificent!" Ava exclaimed.

"Isn't it?" Wallace enjoyed her reaction. They watched the moon rise for a few minutes, taken in by its beauty. Music wafted up through the rafters with perfect clarity. "Why does the orchestra sound better up here?" Ava asked.

"I suppose the turret acts like an ear trumpet, condensing the sound."

"We should come up here for every concert, then!"

"We should."

The moon cleared the mountains and slowly climbed the sky, joined by a few bright stars.

"What else can we see from up here?" Ava made her way around the widow's walk.

"Everything. There's downtown San Diego, and those lights in the distance are Old Town." Wallace followed her around the turret. A bright light flashed every three seconds on the precipice of Point Loma, overlooking a sea of black ink. White waves crashed and rumbled along the shore. "And there's Tijuana." Lights twinkled on a far hillside.

Ava looked over the railing into the courtyard below. The hotel sprawled beneath their feet like a hollow square, with its central courtyard hidden in shadow. Along the roofline, the moon's light outlined the other towers like those of an enchanted castle. "This view is spectacular," Ava commented. "You really have to see the hotel from up here to appreciate how massive it is." The music from the orchestra below silenced, and they could hear the hum of lively conversation. An occasional hearty laugh escaped above the fray and rose, echoing in the cone of the turret. "Can we get in trouble for being up here?"

"No. My family and I are registered guests this week."

"Only this week?" Her heart sank a little. "Then you're returning to the Horton House, right?"

Wallace became serious. "Just this week. That's what I wanted to talk to you about. We're leaving."

"*Leaving?* But you said your departure could be months away, and there was a chance you might stay."

"That's what I was hoping, but something has come up and my father needs to return to New York."

"Oh." Ava turned away from him, looking over the hotel grounds. "When will you be coming back?"

"I don't know." He sounded troubled. "Ava, I want you to know that whatever happens, I'm coming back for you. No matter how long it takes."

She turned back to him, realizing he was serious. He took a step closer and her heart started racing.

"And I really like you," he said, looking deep into her eyes.

"You do?" Ava said simply, not able to think clearly. *Where was Fractious when she needed a smart reply?* She focused on his lips as he spoke.

"I always have."

Ava caught her breath.

"And there's something I really want to do. May I?"

Ava felt light-headed as he stepped closer, his lips only inches from hers. Her heart beat so wildly, she could almost hear it thudding in her chest. Instinctively, she closed her eyes. Wallace leaned in and kissed her softly on the lips. Ava felt her knees might buckle. She reached for the railing, gripping it. She could smell the soap in his laundered shirt, the wax in his hair, the spice in his cologne. She could feel his cool breath. Her mind spun in circles. Her body felt heavy, powerless to move, like she was trying to run through water. Slow. Impossible. She felt his arms wrap around her and he kissed her again.

In the dark courtyard below, Nathan's sombrero tilted as he lowered his head. Searing pain squeezed his chest like a vice grip. Winded, he exhaled, clutching his hand to his chest. He had come outside to look for Ava, and he saw Wallace kiss her up on the turret. Saw she hadn't resisted. He saw them kiss again with the moon shining down on them, and he knew his heart had broken in two. As he turned to walk away, he noticed Beatrice standing nearby in the shadows. Her hands were clenched in fists by her sides. With nothing to say to her, Nathan went inside. He had a song to sing.

☞☜

"We welcome the Delafuente mariachis. Among them is our very own Coronado resident, Nathan Beckman!" The crowd applauded as the curtains opened, revealing men in glittery costumes on the stage. They began to play.

"Did you hear that?" Ava said. "I think they said Nathan's name. I have to go!" She raced down the stairs, leaving Wallace on the widow's walk. From the second-floor balcony inside the turret, Ava could see Nathan strumming a guitar onstage. He sang in Spanish. Incredulous, Ava descended to the dance floor and pushed her way through the crowd to the center of the stage. Nathan advanced alone with his guitar and sang a sorrowful ballad, looking directly at her with a lone tear streaming down his cheek. Ava thought her heart would break. The curtains closed when the song ended, and the crowd cheered.

Ava pushed her way backstage, looking for Nathan. With everyone dressed alike, she couldn't pick him out.

"Nathan left already," a man in a sombrero said to her.

Chapter 36

Ambrose gnawed on the bit in his mouth as Ava led him out of the stables. The sun was just peeking over the mountains, quivering like a sliver of fire. Ambrose snorted through his nose. He seemed to sense they were going for a long ride, and he was eager for it.

Ava grabbed hold of his mane and jumped up, swinging one leg over his broad back. She hadn't put a saddle on him, and she wore her brother's riding pants. Mother wouldn't approve, she knew, but she didn't care. She had a lot on her mind. Turning Ambrose sharply, she squeezed her ankles against his belly. He tossed his nose up. then lunged into a gallop. The clatter of his metal shoes on the street gave way to thuds on the soft sand.

Ava welcomed the wind in her face; it dried the tears that were flowing freely again. It tore her apart that she had hurt Nathan, but how could she deny her feelings for Wallace? How had the perfect night ended with her crying herself to sleep? When she reached the hotel, she slowed Ambrose to a canter. No lights shined from the guest room windows. The curtains in the ballroom windows were drawn. Ava stopped Ambrose and stared up at the great turret. Butterflies fluttered in her stomach at the sight of it. Wallace's lips had been so soft against hers. Then she remembered the announcement of the mariachis below. She recalled hearing someone say Nathan's name.

Ambrose stomped in place, throwing his head from side to side. She loosened the reins and he bolted. His torso stretched out over his powerful legs, which pumped, extended, and curled again as he gained speed. Ava's mind scrambled thoughts and feelings and images. She could see Wallace smiling at her after their kiss. Her face flushed at the memory. Then she could see Nathan looking so distraught on the stage. He had to have seen them. Had to *know*. She saw the hurt in his eyes and his tear-streaked face. Missing pieces of the puzzle started falling into place. Every time she had called on Nathan, he was in Old Town. Now she knew that he had been rehearsing. But why hadn't he shared this with her? It suddenly occurred to her with a pang of guilt—*He wanted to surprise me*. Poor Nathan! He had probably been preparing for months so he could sing her a song. He even learned it in Spanish. The night would have gone just as he planned had Wallace not stepped in with a plan of his own. What would she say to each of them? What would they say to her?

Ava was so lost in thought, she didn't realize she had ridden all the way to Imperial Beach. At the hog farm, a young girl named Sarah was throwing out slop for the pigs. Sarah hoped she could go to school in the fall if her folks didn't need her help on the farm. Ava promised to help her learn to read, whether she got to go to school or not. Sarah waved. Ava should have stopped to talk with her but didn't, knowing she must look frightful. Maybe Sarah would understand a girl crying as she rode her horse in her brother's clothing. Maybe not.

Ava turned Ambrose around. The horse was tireless and he pressed onward. Foam began to build along his thick neck. Ava ran him through the shallow water and let it spray them both. Down the beach near the hotel, she spotted a figure walking alone in their direction. Butterflies fluttered in her stomach. Was it Wallace? *I can't let him see me looking this way! Should I turn around?* Ava decided against it, racing toward the lone figure. If it was Wallace, she needed to talk to him, even if she looked dreadful.

As she got closer, she realized with a stab of disappointment that the figure was wearing a dress. Worse yet, it was Beatrice. Ava was forced to stop and exchange a greeting. "Good day, Beatrice. You're up awfully early this morning."

Beatrice looked her over disapprovingly. "Do you often ride in *pants*?"

she asked incredulously.

"Sometimes." Ava felt her cheeks flush.

Beatrice chuckled with disbelief.

"Are out without your governess? How independent of you."

Beatrice smirked dismissively. "I was up early to see a dear friend off."

"Somebody's left already? The festivities have just begun."

"It was a sudden departure."

Ava didn't want to play into her hand, so she kept her interest in check. "Well, I hope nothing untoward has happened and your dear friend can join us again soon."

Beatrice's steel-gray eyes hardened. "I would say 'untoward' is a fine choice of words to describe the situation."

"I'm not very good at your riddles," Ava finally said. Ambrose was breathing heavily through his nostrils. "What is it that you want to tell me? Just say it."

"Wallace is gone. And he isn't coming back," she blurted.

Ava caught her breath. The corners of Beatrice's mouth curled up in a smile. She had delivered a blow and gotten the reaction she wanted to see—pain.

"Well, that was rather sudden." Ava gulped, trying to sound indifferent. "Did he have a reason? He expected to stay for another week at the very least."

"Mrs. Gregory confided in my mother that she longed to return to New York society. She feared Wallace was, what was the word she used? *Regressing*. Wallace agreed that being here was hindering the advancement of his studies."

"He said that?"

Beatrice nodded. "On several occasions, yes."

Ava looked distraught. "I guess I didn't realize he felt that way. Aren't you disappointed he's gone?"

"I don't fret his departure, no. The Gregory family will be joining my family at the world exposition in Paris next year. We share common interests. Lucky for Wallace, I'm fluent in French, so I'll be able to show him around."

Ava blanched.

"Oh dear, are you not feeling well, Ava? Perhaps you should rest and not work today." Beatrice's eyes flickered with amusement.

"Perhaps you're right. I need to go home and lie down. My best to your family." Ava spurred Ambrose onward.

"Good to see you!" Beatrice called out from behind her. It was the first time Ava had ever heard a cheerful note in her icy voice.

ॐ∽

Ava reached home looking ashen. Her mother rushed to her side, helping her down from the horse. "You look positively ill! Come in the house straightaway. I'll draw you a bath."

Ava sat in the steaming tub with her arms wrapped tightly around her knees, "Did I get any mail this morning?" she asked sullenly.

Mother looked at her worriedly, pouring a bucket of warm water over her hair and shoulders. "It's Sunday," she said gently, "but Nathan stopped by and dropped off a note for you."

"He did? Where is it? What does it say?"

Ava moved to rise from the tub, but her mother insisted she soak longer. "The steam will help," she insisted. She pulled the note from her apron pocket. *Ava* was scrawled across it in sloppy cursive.

"Can you read it to me, please, Mother?"

Mother frowned but relented. She opened the note. It was short and folded in half. She read it slowly:

Dear Ava,

I left town. Went to start a fishing company in Mexico with some friends. There isn't enough work for my pop to keep me and the farm going, and we all know my singing in Spanish won't pay the bills.

I'll write to you and I'll miss you.

Your friend, Nathan

Tears welled from Ava's eyes and she burst into sobs.

She stayed in bed all day, and that night, she cried in her mother's arms. "My friends have all gone! They just left me without even saying goodbye!" she wailed. "And Grace is going back to San Francisco!"

Mother comforted her, stroking her hair softly. "It will be all right. I know it feels like the world is ending, but I promise you it isn't." When Ava fell asleep, she put an extra blanket over her then blew out the candle in her room.

Chapter 37

Ava cried regularly for the next month, and almost anything could make her emotional: a puppy, a sweet baby in a pram, accidentally dropping a dish and seeing it shatter on the floor. Mother said her emotional swings were because of her tender age. Whatever the explanation, Ava's emotions waxed and waned like a tide not even the moon could predict.

By the fifth week, her hurt feelings began turning into disdain. How could both Nathan and Wallace have abandoned her without at least saying goodbye? She was distraught about Nathan, her oldest friend, and her anger spiked regarding Wallace. *Did he know he was leaving the next morning but didn't tell me? Is that why he kissed me? Am I to blame for causing his "regression"?*

Ava threw herself into work to keep both boys off her mind, and during her free time, she read book after book. She decided she would improve upon her mind so that nobody could ever claim she was a simple stable hand's daughter, or the cause of *regression*.

Colonel Holabird gave her an English translation of Victor Hugo's *Les Misérables*, which at first she was reluctant to read. Firstly, for the title, which to her meant admitting she was the miserable one, and secondly, because she wasn't inclined to read about Paris. It would make her think of Wallace and Beatrice, an unsettling thought.

Despite her resistance to plunging into the novel, Colonel Holabird convinced her otherwise. "This is the unabridged translation—a bit lengthy but a must-read. Particularly since the great Victor Hugo recently passed away. I know you'll find it the story compelling if you give it a chance."

Ava relented, taking the book in her hands and thanking him. "I owe you a debt of gratitude, Colonel Holabird. You've always been so kind to share your book collection with me."

"I am simply sharing my love of literature with a fellow enthusiast. My wife and I are both avid readers, as you know, and we look to foster the pleasure of reading in others. Incidentally, I've heard a wonderful rumor . . . The library will open in two weeks." Ava smiled at this news.

"Might be worth mentioning in the local paper," Colonel Holabird added with a wink.

"Thanks for the lead. I'll pass it along."

࿐

The summer of 1888 passed in a stream of parades and glittery galas. The Hotel del Coronado was heralded in newspapers across the country as the premier destination for rest, relaxation, and rejuvenation. Colonel Holabird continued to advertise the amazing benefits of sunshine, clean air, and pure water in restoring one's spirit and being. "Every breeze is laden with health and every prospect pleases," he wrote in his most recent brochure.

Ava attended all the hotel's events with Grace. She was careful to avoid Beatrice. Ava listened in on conversations and tried to glean knowledge from learned circles. She studied the ladies who visited the Hotel Del—the way they moved, what they wore, how they behaved. She wrote about their goings-on and listed their names from the Hotel Del's guest register in the paper. Each week, she also delivered editorials about current events to the *Coronado Mercury*, still writing under the name J. A. Paul.

By the end of summer, Ava had to remove the Spreckels family name from the weekly listing. Sadly, Grace had to return to San Francisco to begin school, but she promised to write regularly. Another noteworthy departure was that of the Claypoole family.

"I'm moving onward," Beatrice stated, cornering Ava at the

registration desk as she copied names from the ledger into her notebook.

"Well, I wish your family a safe journey back to New York," Ava replied politely, not wanting to engage the girl.

But Beatrice would not relent. "And just in time! There's a party for my dear friend Consuelo Vanderbilt, she's like a little sister to me."

Ava had read about Mrs. Alva Vanderbilt and her daughter, Consuelo, in the newspapers over the years. It appeared there was every intention of having Conseulo entrenched in society circles well before her debut. "I'm certain it's an event not to be missed," Ava replied.

"Wallace will be there, and all of New York society fortunate enough to be invited." Beatrice looked for Ava's reaction. Ava kept her expression unreadable.

"And this is simply an autumn celebration. You should see Consuelo's birthday parties every March."

"I cannot imagine." Ava went back to copying down names from the ledger.

"I'll be sure to tell Wallace you are well and working as hard as ever."

"No need—we aren't friends anymore. Safe journey to you are your family." Ava closed her notebook and left Beatrice looking very satisfied in the lobby.

☙❧

The remaining summer guests departed and classes began in the schoolhouse. Ava attended school three times a week. On Sunday afternoons, she tutored Sarah from the hog farm in both reading and writing. Sarah was a dear girl and an eager pupil. She offered to pay Ava what little she could afford, but Ava declined. It was worth the effort to see Sarah's eyes light up when she sounded out a difficult word or wrote a complete sentence. It reminded Ava of when she taught Nathan how to read. He had been so proud. Why hadn't he written again? She hoped he was safe and tried not to worry about him.

Ava took notes on her school lessons and shared them with Harry West, the bellhop at the hotel. As with Sarah, there wasn't any way he could attend school, so he was greatly appreciative.

When Ava wasn't studying, reading, working, writing, or tutoring, she practiced the violin. She played sorrowful songs at first, but as time went on, she moved on to melodies that were feverish in pace and pitch. She longed for stormy weather to fit her mood, but storms never came. Every day in Coronado was as sunny and bright as the day before. She thought less and less about the boys until one day in late October, when she received a postcard from Nathan with a one-line greeting on the front: *Having a whale of a time in Cabo San Lucas! Wish you were here!* The accompanying cartoon illustration showed a whale breaching from a bright blue ocean.

Turning the card over, she smiled as she read Nathan's familiar sloppy scrawl:

Hello, Ava.

I hope my card finds you well. I'm real busy these days—fishing is hard work! I caught my first swordfish the other day and it was bigger than me. We start out most days real early and stay out at sea for days at a time. I'll write when I can.
I miss you.
Your amigo,
Nathan

The postmark showed the card was mailed a month earlier. She realized her anger toward Nathan for leaving her was starting to subside. She missed him terribly. He didn't include a return address. When she got home, she tucked his postcard into the mirror frame of her vanity.

Several weeks later, the editor at the *Coronado Mercury* handed Ava a letter addressed to J. A. Paul. "I guess it's not a secret anymore that J. A. Paul is me, is it?" she said sheepishly, taking the letter from him.

"No, ma'am. Knew it was you from the very first article," he teased.

"Thanks for keeping my secret."

"You've got a good eye for journalism. Keep up the good work, young lady."

"I will, sir. Thank you." Ava walked to the ferry landing and found an empty bench. She looked out over the water as she pulled the letter from her pocket. It was probably an accusatory letter to the editor in response to one of her recent articles. Had she gotten something wrong? Her sources were usually accurate, giving her a firsthand accounting of events. She opened the envelope and pulled out a single folded page, noting its weight. It was written on quality stationery. Inside, the flowing penmanship of a skilled hand wrote:

Dear Ava,

I know you must be cross with me because I know you, but please hear me out. I didn't know we were leaving right away. It appears my mother had an informant—and she didn't approve of my activities. I'm so sorry I didn't get to say goodbye. I stay up late thinking of our last night together. I relive every moment like it was yesterday.

I'm in New York, going to preparatory school again. It's getting cold already. I sure miss you and our lazy days sailing in the California sunshine. I hope you can forgive me. Please write me.

Yours truly,

Wallace

Ava's hands were trembling as she held the letter. *Yours truly* he had written. Her temper flared, but her traitorous stomach fluttered. She read the letter once more and smelled it. A stale scent—from an envelope that had changed hands dozens of times across the country before reaching her. She sat for a long time watching ships navigate the bay. *Should I write him back?* she wondered. *Not yet.*

Ava waited three weeks to write Wallace a return letter. Grace suggested two weeks was an appropriate amount of time to wait, so she wouldn't appear too eager. Ava added another week just to be sure. It took her that long just to figure out what to write:

Dear Wallace,

I'm happy you are settled and well. I am well also and busy these days, too. I continue to write articles for the local paper and I'm going to school. Tourists arrive daily, although we are in the off-season. Mrs. Babcock has hired me to work for the Del directly, in the capacity of a children's activity coordinator, so I will no longer be working at the stables. I've been practicing a lot on the violin you gave me. I can finally play that piece you helped me with.

If you must know, I am resolved to put your sudden departure and the events preceding it in the past. There is no need to apologize or make mention of them ever again.

Be well,

Ava

After three versions of the same, purposefully indifferent letter, Ava placed it in the mail.

Chapter 38

Ava didn't hear from Nathan or Wallace for a long time. If she had angered Wallace by her curt letter, so be it. She didn't believe his claim that he didn't know he was leaving the next day. When she thought of Nathan, doing so always brought a smile to her face along with a searing pang of guilt. She couldn't erase the image of him in his tight mariachi clothing strumming his guitar onstage. She would rather have been kicked by a horse than cause him pain, but nothing could be done to change that night.

As time went by, Ava pushed both boys from her mind again. By December she no longer checked the mail, hoping to find a letter or postcard, she was far too busy observing the interesting guests who checked in at the hotel. She may not have been able to see the world, but the world came to her, one guest at a time.

When Ava wasn't writing about guests and posting the guest list in the *Coronado Mercury*, she scoured newspapers from larger cities, looking for world events to mention. In the Whitechapel district of London, a madman had committed another murder. They called him Jack the Ripper, and the city was gripped with fear over when he would strike again. A Dutch painter, Vincent van Gogh, had cut off his ear and mailed it to a woman for safekeeping. *Hardly pleasant topics*, Ava thought, *but intriguing nonetheless.*

The year ended with holiday events and a New Year's party. Guests arrived in droves to escape the New England winter, staying for the winter months. Ava's job coordinating children's activities gave her little respite.

259

She taught children to swim, ride horses, sing songs, play games, and paint week after week. Before she knew it, spring arrived, then summer—and half of 1889 had passed.

That autumn, a postcard from Wallace came from Paris. It was properly addressed to Ava this time, not J. A. Paul in care of the *Coronado Mercury*. *What does this mean?* she wondered. *Is he no longer hiding their rare correspondence?* On the front of the card, *L'Exposition Universelle de Paris 1889* was printed in an elegant white font against a red background. An image of an enormous iron tower rising from four legs dominated the Paris skyline. Ava flipped it over, her heart racing as she read;

> *Dear Ava,*
> *I went up to the top of the Eiffel Tower, the tallest structure in the world, and thought of you. Wish you were here.*
> *Yours truly,*
> *Wallace*

Ava slid his postcard into the mirror frame of her vanity, next to Nathan's tattered one from Mexico. She should have thrown it in the garbage, but something made her keep it. The thought of Wallace and Beatrice gallivanting around Paris didn't even upset her. Perhaps she was over Wallace. Yes, she should keep the postcard as evidence she had grown past her heartbreak.

Two weeks later, another card arrived from Nathan. The front panel had the bright colors of sunset and the words *Greetings from Cabo San Lucas!* On the back, he wrote:

> *Dear Ava,*
> *I've been out to sea for months, moving from town to town. I'm learning everything there is to learn about fishing. Learning Spanish too. A tourist gave me a copy of <u>Pride and Prejudice</u>. Can you believe that? I'm reading it slowly. I like it better than <u>Little Women</u>. You were right. One day I'm going to come back to Coronado and start my own fishing company. I hope you will still be there.*

Wait for me.
Your amigo,
Nathan

Ava glanced at their postcards every time she sat at her vanity, brushing her long hair and pinning it into a loose chignon. She was a young woman now, and no longer a silly girl in hair bows. Even her style of dress reflected her blossoming maturity. Ruffles were replaced by lace and floral prints with stripes; collars now buttoned up high on her neck. She gazed at the postcards again, their edges worn and wrinkled from the number of times she pulled them from the mirror to read them again. She hadn't replied to Nathan or Wallace because neither had included a return address. A fact that bothered her—not that she would write to either of them anyway. She was far too busy becoming *prepossessing* to write anyone but Grace.

∂∼⌐

By the summer of 1890, Ava earned her own column in the *Coronado Mercury*, which she wrote under her own name. Her secret had gotten out, and everybody knew she was the author using the name J. A. Paul. She was thrilled to be accepted as a junior member of the staff, and she was even paid a small stipend for her contributions. In her column, she wrote about current events along the lines of:

"The Coronado Lyceum will be meeting to discuss prohibition Monday nights at 5:00. Coronado's ferryboat, the Silver Gate, has crashed into the docks again, knocking all of her passengers down. People are beginning to think the vessel is cursed, having been commissioned on April Fools' Day."

"Mr. Spreckels plans to create an official polo field as well as a Japanese tea garden have begun. The Boating Club, Tennis Club, Fishing Club, Hunting Club and Billiards Club have all been established with meetings at the library. Please see the schedule for upcoming Yacht Club races, and Moonlight Rowing parties. For those not invited to join

the by-invitation-only Glorietta Club, a rebuttal group called the Good Time Club has been established for anyone wanting to just have fun."

"A gambling dispute erupted into a fight out at the lumberyard near First Street, where a Mr. Ah Gow was felled by a shovel after getting knocked out by Mr. Tom Wing. Mr. Wing has since apologized and paid Mr. Gow money that was owed to him."

On a lighter note, Ava posted a wedding announcement. It was outdated, but she posted it anyway, knowing there would be public interest:

"The Comtesse Lorraine du Boulanger wed Mr. Clancy Monroe of Tyler, Texas, in a large ceremony followed by a weeklong celebration in Paris, France. Eleven dogs were in attendance."

By September of 1890, Ava wrote about the US military's intention to purchase land on North Island, finding Coronado an ideal location on the Pacific for a naval station. In October, she wrote of Coronado residents becoming disenchanted with the taxes and assessments they paid to the city of San Diego without reciprocal support from their neighboring city. Coronado lacked a police and fire department, which meant the Coronado Beach Company had to maintain all the island's grounds, parks, and schools, as well as paying for sundry additional expenses. Residents that worried if a fire broke out, nothing could be done other than to watch the island burn to the ground. Coronadans, as they were now called, felt they owed San Diego nothing, and the body of water that separated the peninsula from San Diego was a more than adequate reason to consider Coronado independent.

As the issues went unresolved, Coronado residents, led by Mr. Babcock and Mr. Spreckels, ultimately sought to become segregated from San Diego. Major Levi Chase, arguing on behalf of segregation, took the case all the way to the California Supreme Court. Terse letters for and against segregation poured into both the *Coronado Mercury* and *San Diego*

Union newspapers.

Ava read every argument and subsequent rebuttal as tension mounted between the two cities. One rebuttal was particularly harsh, but Ava found it terribly amusing. The article described a gentleman by the name of S. P. Duzan, of Coronado, and his response to one Joseph Falkenhan of San Diego. In it, Mr. Duzan argued that Mr. Falkenhan had: "Written an article of about 2,000 words, more or less, of concentrated idiotic nonsense, wherein not a single word expressed a sensible idea or gave an expression of truth."

Ava laughed aloud and continued reading:

"It is a laborious effort to assail, misrepresent, and insult the people of Coronado, done because they, the people of Coronado, are indisposed to quietly submit to what every honest man knows is a shameless attempt to steal from a community both their property and rights of self-government . . . I will mince no words, hunt no polite phrases. The attempt to hold Coronado against her consents as part of a municipality of San Diego is an attempt to steal, and if successful will be a theft accomplished."

In these times of political strife, Ava was grateful for the Wit and Humor section of the *Coronado Mercury*. There were always pearls of wisdom to be had that helped distract one from the vitriol that flew back and forth across the bay. One day, she cut out a wise quote from the Wit and Humor section, attributed to the *Richmond Recorder*, to share with Mr. Babcock: "You may not have noticed, but you will find that the man who shakes hands the hardest is the hardest to shake."

❧

The California Supreme Court upheld the decision for Coronado to have a vote of segregation from San Diego. The vote was held on October 10 1890, and Coronado won handily. By December, articles of incorporation were filed, and Mr. Babcock threw a party to celebrate the island's independence. Streetcars rang their bells, ferries blared their horns, gunpowder was ignited in the street, and a parade marched down Orange Avenue. Mr. Thompson and his son, Willard, tossed candy from their coach to elated children in the streets. Coronadans promised San Diegans that Coronado's continued draw of tourists would benefit both cities financially and the hatchets were eventually buried.

The tumultuous year 1890 ended with an endless agenda of holiday parties that united Coronado and San Diego high-society circles. King Kalakaua of Hawaii came to stay at the hotel and visit his good friend Mr. Spreckels. In articles for the *Coronado Mercury*, Ava wrote of the king's great kindness, and of his entourage of hypnotic dancers who twirled fiery torches to the rhythm of beating drums.

The Hotel del Coronado's events were so spectacular, they garnered rave reviews from guests that spread across the country by letter, post card, and word of mouth. As a result, a steady stream of influential people flocked to Coronado the following year. Even the president of the United States, Benjamin Harrison, visited, making a stop for breakfast at the Hotel Del. He was greeted by a sea of waving flags and smiling faces along Orange Avenue. Young boys tossed their hats high into the air and chased after his train car. President Harrison gave an inspiring speech about innovation in America, and attended a dinner gala held in his honor. Mr. Hawthorne, the island's photographer, elicited Ava's assistance to hold the flash as he captured the historical event on film. Ava heard so many flashbulbs pop and fizzle the week of the president's visit, she imagined hearing more in her sleep.

Colonel Holabird continued to advertise Coronado, hailing it as "The Land of the Lily and the Rose" in brochures that circulated throughout the United States. Mr. Babcock ran weekly advertisements in local papers, headlining the island as "The Ideal Summer Resort," and boasting of its "magnificent structure" and the values of Coronado Mineral Water. Below one week's Hotel Del advertisement appeared another advertisement with the headline: "PIMPLES." A guarantee claimed the vegetable balm could remedy: "tan, freckles, pimples, blotches and blackheads, leaving the skin soft, clear and beautiful."

Ava laughed, knowing Mr. Babcock would not be pleased to see his beloved hotel's advertisement placed just above notice for a pimple remedy.

She went to her vanity and sat, staring back at her reflection. The postcards from Wallace and Nathan were still tucked into the mirror's frame, their edges starting to curl. She was sixteen years old now, and although she was told she was a beauty, she saw nothing exceptional in her reflection. *Mothers are supposed to say such things aren't they?* She leaned in closer to the mirror to inspect her skin. To her displeasure, she found a few blemishes and winced. She went back to the newspaper on her bed and circled the pimple remedy ad.

Ava returned to her task of typing guest names from the hotel's register to post in the *Coronado Mercury*. The weeks turned to months and another year slipped by. She didn't know that one November day in 1892, she would post a name that would change the history of the hotel forever: Miss Lottie A. Bernard, from Detroit.

Ava would never forget the moment she laid eyes on the unfortunate woman. Nor the moment, under the horrible circumstances of death, she would type a correction to her name in the paper. As it turned out, her name wasn't Lottie Bernard after all, it was Kate Morgan.

Chapter 39

A petite, attractive young woman in her early twenties exited the Coronado Railroad Company trolley in front of the hotel. She had thick black hair with bangs that complemented her dark, troubled eyes and flattered her round face. She was finely dressed in a full-length black gown with a high lace collar and a black sealskin stole over her shoulders. She peered up at the hotel from under her lace-brimmed black hat. She had no luggage, instead holding only a small clutch and a black parasol. She took a few steps and winced, gripping her stomach. She breathed in deeply, swaying a little.

"Ma'am, are you all right?" Ava rushed to her side. "Do you have a companion, or are you traveling alone?"

"I'm quite fine. I just need to get to my room and take my rest. Yes, I am alone at present."

"Can I have your luggage retrieved for you, then?"

"I have no luggage—my brother took my baggage check. He had to depart our train in Orange unexpectedly. But not to worry, he's coming soon with my trunk."

The lady blanched and swayed again, still clutching her abdomen.

"Please, let me assist you! Perhaps I can register for you? There is a private entrance for ladies."

The woman nodded, looking slightly relieved. Ava took her parasol and held her trembling hand as they walked toward the hotel's front entrance. The woman took slow steps, then stopped, gripped again by pain.

"May I call the doctor for you, ma'am? You are not well!" Ava declared, fearful for the pretty woman with those suffering brown eyes.

"Indeed, I am not." The woman studied Ava quickly, deciding what she should or should not divulge. "I am afflicted with stomach cancer, but please do not tell anyone. I hate for people to worry, and there isn't anything that can be done."

Ava gasped. "I am so sorry! Please let me help you get settled in straightaway so you can take your rest."

Ava walked slowly with the woman to the ladies' entrance of the hotel and had her take a seat in a lobby chair.

"Wait here. I'll get your room number and key. Can I have your name and place of origin?"

"Detroit. My name is Lottie. Lottie Bernard." Her voice was barely a whisper now, and her eyes had become dull from pain.

"Very well, Miss Bernard, I won't take but a moment."

Ava signed her in, writing the woman's name in cursive in the hotel's registry. She was given a key to room 302 and quickly returned to the woman's side.

"Bless you, dear girl!" the woman said, managing a thin smile.

"There is a bellhop coming named Harry West. He will escort you to your room. If you are in need of anything, please don't hesitate to call upon him or me. We will gladly oblige you during your stay."

Miss Bernard smiled weakly. "I thank you. What is your name, young lady?"

"My name is Ava Hennessey. I work here at the hotel, coordinating activities for children, but I am at your service as well should you need any further assistance. I hope the ocean air brings great improvement to your health, Miss Bernard."

"I have but little hope."

Ava squeezed the frail woman's hand reassuringly. Harry West arrived, and escorted Miss Bernard with great care to her room.

⋐⋙

Ava didn't see Miss Bernard for several days. She spotted Harry on a lunch break and inquired about her.

"Miss Bernard has called on me on several occasions. To retrieve things mainly—things she needed, like drinks from the bar and medicine from the apothecary," he confided. "She once had me light the fire in her fireplace to burn some letters, and even called me up to dry her hair with a towel after she accidentally submerged in her tub."

"She did?" Ava looked at him, puzzled.

"I thought the request was a bit odd, too, but I obliged her nonetheless. If drying her hair is part of my job description, then I'll do it. She wanted to tip me, but I didn't feel good taking money from a sick lady. She groans a great deal."

"Did she tell you of her affliction?" Ava asked.

"She did. Says she has neuralgia."

Ava looked at him with surprise. "*Neuralgia?*"

"Yeah, it's some sort of nerve pain. Mr. Gomer, the clerk, told me what it was. But Miss Bernard told him she has stomach cancer. He suggested she see Mr. Fosdick, the pharmacy manager for something to alleviate her suffering. When Mr. Fosdick suggested she see a physician in town, she said her brother is a doctor, so there was no need because he was expected at any time."

Ava became suddenly confused. *Why is this woman telling different stories of her affliction? She clearly is ill, but why the contradictions? And why hasn't her brother arrived yet when she is clearly expecting him?*

"She said her brother is a doctor?" Ava asked.

"Yes, a Dr. Anderson."

"How do you know she burned letters in the fireplace?"

"She called me up to bring matches. I saw her burn them." Harry looked around, suddenly nervous. "She takes walks on the beach some evenings, real slow, always looking sad. I probably shouldn't be telling you this."

"Don't worry, Harry. I won't write about it in the paper. She is a bit of a mystery, though, and I am worried for her well-being. There is something in her story that doesn't make sense."

☙❧

Miss Bernard checked daily for correspondence from her brother, but to no avail. It had been five days, and neither letter, nor brother, nor trunk arrived. Left with no alternative, she wore the same black dress every day. Oddly, she declined an offer from Ava to help her purchase another dress. Her appearance markedly deteriorated, becoming more disheveled and gaunt with each passing day. Her dark eyes looked sunken in their sockets, encased by shadowy circles. She looked as if she hadn't slept or eaten adequately, and she refrained from socializing in the common areas. Miss Bernard kept to herself, charged everything to her room, and refused to have her fireplace lit again for warmth, even though a storm had moved in and the November nights had turned cool.

That afternoon, she announced to the registrar she was going into town to claim her luggage. Mr. Fisher, the real estate agent who lived at the hotel, overheard her. "Ma'am, it seems too bad out there for you to go over in town—with you suffering from neuralgia—in this stormy weather."

Miss Bernard smiled wanly. "I am compelled to go. I forgot my checks, and I have to go over and identify my trunks personally." She walked slowly down the stairs of the hotel's porte cochere and made her way to a waiting trolley. She climbed the trolley stairs one deliberate, painful step at a time, clutching the handrail so tightly her white knuckles looked like those of a skeleton.

From the trolley, she boarded a ferry that took her across the bay to San Diego. Miss Bernard was the last person to disembark from the ferry, her progress slow but steady as she made her way down the ramp. Worried the ferry would fall behind schedule, the captain urged his first mate to assist the poor woman down the ramp. She accepted his hand, and he guided her to a row of waiting coaches.

"Can you take me to a department store that sells cartridges?" she asked the coachman."

The coachman gave her a curious look and took her to the Ship Chandlery store on 5th Street. Once inside, Miss Bernard requested cartridges from a sales clerk, who wore a name badge stamped with his last name: *Heath*.

"I'm sorry, ma'am, we don't keep cartridges here. You'll have to go to Chick's, it's just across the street."

A look of disappointment flashed across her face. She managed a weak smile, thanked Mr. Heath, and walked out of the store as slowly as she had walked in. She crossed the street, located the gun store called Chick's, and walked toward it. From the corner of her eye, she could see a man on a bench outside the store. He was staring at her. She pretended not to see him and entered the store.

Mr. Chick stood behind a wooden counter with his back turned, facing the guns and ammunition in a showcase on a wall. Hearing a bell chime on the door, he turned to find a young woman, dressed in all black, at his counter.

"May I see some pistols?" the woman asked calmly.

"Certainly."

"I want to buy a gift for a friend," she added. "I don't need an expensive one."

Mr. Chick grabbed an American Bulldog, an inexpensive revolver, from the showcase and placed it on the counter before her.

Miss Bernard ran a trembling finger over its short nose and handle. "I'll take this one," she said quickly, hiding her shaking hand behind the counter. "I need cartridges, too," she added. Mr. Chick rang her up, and she gave him cash for the gun and a box of .44 caliber cartridges.

"How do you load it?" she asked casually.

Mr. Chick showed her. He removed a cartridge from the box, turned the gun over in his hand, loaded it, and then unloaded it. Miss Bernard's dark eyes widened as she watched. Mr. Chick placed the unloaded gun on the counter. Miss Bernard picked it up, aimed it away from them, and asked, "Is this thing hard to pull?"

"Not at all." Mr. Chick carefully took the gun from her, pointed it at the wall, and easily pulled the trigger three times. The pistol clicked loudly as the hammer pulled back and struck the primer.

He placed the gun back on the counter, and Miss Bernard picked it up again, pulling the trigger once. After the empty pistol clicked, she set it back down. "This will do."

Mr. Chick wrapped the pistol and cartridges, and Miss Bernard departed, thanking him for his assistance.

On the ferry ride back to Coronado, she cried softly, trying to conceal her face from the other passengers.

Chapter 40

November 29, 1892

"Ava! Ava!" Harry West called as he ran into the stables.

Ava was grooming Ambrose and froze, startled by Harry's appearance. His eyes were wild, and he was sweating from exertion.

"What is it?" she said, rushing to him.

Harry was heaving, trying to catch his breath. "It's Miss Lottie! She's dead!"

Ava gasped, dropping the brush in her hand and clasping her hand over her mouth. "No! This cannot be true!" she said, catching her breath.

"It is! Mr. Koeppen, the gardener, told me they found her by the steps near the tennis courts with a bullet wound to her head!"

Ava felt suddenly ill.

"They've taken her to the coroner's."

"Oh, this is awful! That poor woman!"

"They want me to testify at an inquiry," Harry said, bursting into tears. "I'm terrified of sitting in front of a courtroom and talking about this."

"You can do this, Harry. You *must*. I'll be there to support you." Ava gave the shaken boy a firm hug and let him weep against her shoulder.

"When is the inquiry?"

"Tomorrow."

᪥᪥

Coronado Island and the city of San Diego were in an uproar over the death of Miss Lottie Bernard. Efforts to contact her next of kin resulted in failure. Nobody would claim the poor woman. It was thought that perhaps she had been using a false name. A pencil sketch of her was circulated in newspapers across the country in hopes that somebody would come forward. The drawing of her stared blankly from the page. Many people visited the mortuary in San Diego, Johnson & Company, curious to see the deceased mystery woman. Mr. Story and Mr. Babcock were beside themselves with grief over the incident. Ava was asked to write an article about Miss Bernard in the *Coronado Mercury*, and as a journalist, she was allowed to attend a public inquiry into her death.

Ava's headline for the story commanded attention: "Who Was This Beautiful Stranger?" Soon, other newspapers picked up on the phrase, and many referred to the mystery lady as the "Beautiful Stranger."

The inquiry was led by the coroner, Mr. W. A. Sloane, to a room filled with concerned citizens and a jury of ten gentlemen. Ava learned many details as to what had transpired on the last day of Miss Bernard's life. Sitting in the back of the courtroom with a press pass around her neck, she took notes as a panel of jurors took their seats. The coroner first asked Mr. Cone, the electrician, to the witness stand.

"Mr. Cone, where you at the Hotel del Coronado the night before last?"

"Yes, sir."

"Do you know any of the facts in relation to the finding of the dead body at the hotel?

"I believe I was the first to find it."

"State the facts in reference to the discovery of the body."

"Yes, sir. Every morning I commence at seven o'clock to trim the electric lights around the hotel." Mr. Cone continued to provide details about his daily duties. "And when I was just going to climb the pole, I saw the body lying on the stone steps right close to the pole."

"Who was it?" the coroner asked. "Do you know?"

"I have no idea."

"Man or woman?"

"Woman."

"What was the condition of it?"

Ava scribbled notes, noting the coroner called Miss Bernard's body *it*, which seemed unfair.

"It was lying on the steps, with its feet towards the ocean, head on the steps, almost on the top step. The clothes were all wet, and the body seemed to have been lying there for a quite a while, to have been dead quite a while."

"The person was *dead?*"

"Yes, sir."

"Did you find any weapons there?"

Mr. Cone nodded. "There was a large pistol lying at the right-hand side of the body." The bystanders in the courtroom gasped audibly.

"Did you discover any wounds on the person?"

"No, sir."

"You say there was blood?" the coroner summarized, looking over his papers.

"Yes, sir, on the steps, on the right-hand side."

"Have you seen the remains that are at the undertaking establishment Johnson and Company in the city at this present time?"

"I have—yes, sir."

The coroner leaned forward, looking over his glasses. "Was it the same person whose body you found?"

"It is, to the best of my knowledge."

Mr. Cone then described fleeing the scene to find Mr. Koeppen, the gardener. "I showed him the body, then I went to the office and informed the chief clerk. Then I went back and trimmed the light at the corner and went on about my work. That is all I know of it."

After a series of confirming questions, the coroner held up the gun to the witness.

"Yes, that is the pistol," Mr. Cone confirmed.

"You did not touch it at all?"

"No, sir."

The court reporter read the testimony, Mr. Cone was sworn in and agreed under oath that his testimony was true. Ava looked around the courtroom. In the first few rows sat Colonel Holabird, Mr. Story, Mr. Babcock, and Mr. Seghers. All looked weary and grief stricken. Harry West sat behind them. He kept glancing back at Ava, seeking encouragement.

Mr. Koeppen was called to the stand next.

"Where were you the morning of the twenty-ninth?" the coroner inquired.

"Well, in making my rounds, going around the hotel, I met this electrician, Mr. Cone. He said there was a body lying on the steps. Both together, we went down and looked at the body. I said I was going to report it to the management. I met Mr. Rossier, the assistant manager, and both him and I went and looked at the body." Mr. Koeppen went on to describe how he went to his tool house and took a canvas and covered up the body until the coroner came and examined it, then took it away.

"Have you seen the remains since her death, since she was brought over here?" the coroner asked.

"Yes, sir."

"Is it the same person?"

"Yes, sir.

Ava jotted down more notes, detailing again the alternating references from *her* to *it* and back to *her* again. Everybody was clearly uncomfortable and uncertain about what to call the remains of Miss Bernard. Many had gone down to view her body, mainly out of vulgar curiosity, but Ava had refrained. She felt Miss Bernard deserved to rest in peace after her troubling last days on Earth.

Mr. Heath was sworn in next, the clerk from the Ship Chandlery store in San Diego.

"Have you seen the remains of the person whose body was viewed by the coroner's jury at Johnson's parlors?" the coroner asked.

275

"Yes, I have," Mr. Heath responded.

"Did you see that person in her lifetime?'

"Yes, sir."

"When and where?" the coroner inquired.

"Day before yesterday. In the store where I am employed."

"What transactions did you have with her?"

Mr. Heath squirmed in his chair beside the coroner. "She asked me if I kept cartridges. I told her we did not, and directed her where she could get them."

"Did she say anything as to what number she wanted?"

"No, sir, she did not."

"Where did you direct her to?"

"To Mr. Chick."

The spectators looked around at each other, wide-eyed. Mr. Chick owned a gun store.

Mr. Mertzman, a surgeon, was interrogated next. He wore a white lab coat and tie.

"Were you called to view the remains of the lady who was said to have been found dead at the Hotel del Coronado?"

"Yes, sir, I was."

"When was that?" the coroner asked.

"About a half hour ago."

"Just recently?" the coroner looked up, surprised.

"Yes, sir."

"You made an examination of the remains there?"

"I made an examination of the remains and found a gun-shot wound in the right temple, just between the ear and the outer edge of the eyebrow." Mr. Mertzman continued, detailing the exact location of the wound. "The ball entered into the brain, and that is the only opening I could find—no exit at all."

"Are you able to judge the size of the ball?"

"From the looks of it, I should say about .38 or .40."

Mr. Fisher, the real estate agent was sworn in next. He testified as to the last conversation he had with Miss L. A. Bernard, as he called her, and how she had insisted on going to town to claim her baggage.

"And the next time you saw her was when she was lying dead on the steps?"

"On the steps, dead," Mr. Fisher confirmed.

"Nobody heard a pistol shot?" the coroner asked.

"No, sir."

"It was near the ocean side, the surge would have a tendency to prevent people from hearing?" the coroner clarified.

"Yes, sir . . . the surf probably would deaden the noise."

A juror asked Mr. Fisher a question. "You say you knew what her name was?"

"Yes, sir."

"How did you come to know it?"

"I was told since, and I've seen it in the newspaper."

Harry West took the stand next. He trembled, looking small in the leather chair. He shot Ava a desperate look and she nodded at him reassuringly.

"Where do you live?" the coroner asked him.

"With my folks, between Sixteenth and Seventeenth on I, in San Diego."

"Where are you employed?"

"I work at the Hotel del Coronado, bellhop" His voice was weak.

"Have you seen the remains of the woman whose body is at the undertaking establishment of Johnson and Company?"

"Yes, sir."

"Did you ever see her before, alive or dead?"

"Yes, sir, I saw her alive." Harry kept his eyes fixed on Ava in the back of the room. She settled his nerves and his voice grew stronger.

"Saw her in her lifetime, when?"

Harry leaned forward, "In her room, where she was sick."

"When was that, when did you see her?"

"I seen her all the time. The last time I seen her was half past six in the evening, that was night before last. I seen her on the veranda."

"Which veranda?"

"Second floor."

"Do you know where she was found dead?"

"Yes, sir, I know where she was found dead. But I didn't see her."

"Was her room anywhere near there?"

"No, sir, it was on the opposite side."

The coroner asked a series of questions in relation to Harry serving Miss Bernard.

"So you attended to her constantly?"

"Yes, sir."

"Did you have any conversation with her, in reference to her sickness?"

"No, just that she had the neuralgia. That is all."

"Did she send you for any medicines or anything?"

"She sent me down to the drugstore for an empty pint bottle and a sponge. She sent me to the bar twice."

"What for?"

"Liquors. Sent me once for a glass of wine and once for a whiskey cocktail. That was day before yesterday."

"That was day before yesterday?" the coroner repeated for the record.

"Yes, sir. I fixed her a bath in the morning and got her a pitcher of ice water, and she told me she was going to stay in an hour and a half to two hours. About twelve o'clock she rang, and I went up there. Her hair was all wet and she wanted me to rub it, and I did so. She told me she was so weak, she was standing on the side of the tub and fell into the tub and got her hair wet. And I rubbed it and got it dry."

"That was half past six, Sunday evening?"

"Yes, sir."

The coroner frowned, flipping through his stack of papers.

A juror interjected, "Excuse me—I think the young man means *Monday* evening."

"When did the shooting occur?" the coroner asked.

"Tuesday," Harry replied, realizing he had gotten his days mixed up.

"Then that would be Monday evening," the coroner confirmed, scribbling a note. "What was her appearance and conduct—did she appear to be suffering from pain?"

"Yes, sir, she appeared to be suffering a great deal. She groaned a great deal, and slept most of the day. She would sleep a little while, and then wake up and be groaning. She looked pale in the face."

"What time was it when she sent you for the liquor?"

"For the liquor?" Harry said. "In the morning, about twelve o'clock, somewhere just about twelve o'clock."

"Did you take money for it?"

"No, sir, I did not—charged it to the room."

Harry West was excused. A look of relief washed over his face as he took his seat again.

Following Harry's interrogation Mr. Gomer, the hotel clerk, testified. He told the story of when the "peculiar person," as she was called, arrived without luggage and with the explanation that her brother had mistakenly taken her baggage ticket. She did not know where her brother was at the time but was expecting him. She thought he could be in Orange, Los Angeles, or Frisco.

"When Harry West, the bellhop asked for a whiskey for the lady, I thought it necessary for someone to see her. The housekeeper had been trying to induce her to call the house physician to see just what her condition was, and the housekeeper was unsuccessful—she kept telling the housekeeper she knew what her trouble was, and her brother was a physician, and this it was not necessary to call a physician. But after this boy who has just testified asked for a whiskey, and said the lady fell in the bathtub and had wet her hair, I went up to the room myself and suggested, first, that we call the house physician. She was in bed then, covered up, and she was totally opposed to calling the physician."

Mr. Gomer went on to say it was a gloomy day, and she refused to let him make a fire for her. "She further told me that the doctors had given her up, that she had cancer of the stomach, and that her case was hopeless."

Mr. Gomer looked at each of the jurors, then at the coroner. "I endeavored to find out something about her identity. On the table in her room were some letters. I could not find the content of them without picking them up, and of course that was out of order. The only thing I saw on the table were some envelopes addressed to herself. I did ask her if she was supplied with funds—thinking that in her condition she must necessarily need some fund—and she said yes. She suggested the name G. L. Allen, in Hamburg, Iowa. At her suggestion I wrote a telegram and sent it to Hamburg, and left her then in the room."

The room was quiet as Mr. Gomer continued his testimony. "The last time I saw her was that evening about somewhere between seven and eight o'clock. She called at the office . . ."

"Now, what day was that?" the coroner asked.

"This was on Monday. She called at the office and inquired if there were any letters or telegrams for her. I said, 'Nothing' and went about doing something, and that was the last time I saw her until yesterday morning. This man came to me," he said, pointing at Mr. Koeppen, "and reported that there was a corpse out on the ocean side of the hotel. And I immediately went out there, and of course discovered that it was this woman."

"You say you noticed letters addressed to her on the table?"

"Just letters, two or three possibly."

"Did you notice the address?"

"This same address."

"Lottie A.?

Mr. Gomer nodded. "Bernard, Detroit."

"And has there been any reply, subsequently, to the telegram?"

"Yes, yesterday morning, a telegram came from Hamburg, Iowa, signed by some bank—but I neglected to bring the telegram with me, and forget the name of the bank—saying that they would honor her draft for $25, show this to the bank. Then I immediately telegraphed to this same party that this person had suicided on the hotel grounds."

Murmurs erupted in the room, then silence was restored.

The coroner shifted in his chair. "Have you received any reply to that?"

"No, we have received no reply."

Mr. Chick testified next.

"What is your business?" the coroner inquired.

"Gunsmith, gun dealer."

"Have you seen the remains of the woman whose body is at the undertaking parlors of Johnson and Company?"

"I have," Mr. Chick said.

"Did you ever see her before?"

"I think I did."

"If so, under what circumstances and where?" the coroner asked.

"Well, it is a woman dressed a great deal like the one who came into my store about three o'clock Monday afternoon and wanted to look at some pistols. Said she wanted to get one to make a Christmas present to a friend of hers."

Ava noticed a discrepancy in the time line of her notes, but the coroner made no mention of it. Mr. Heath, from the Ship Chandlery store had testified that Miss Bernard was there between four and five, which wasn't in sync with her being at the gun store at three o'clock.

Mr. Chick continued, "I showed her the pistols, and she selected one and bought it."

"What kind of pistol was it?"

"It was a .44 caliber American Bulldog."

"Examine the pistol, will you, Mr. Chick?" A young clerk brought the pistol forward.

"It was one just like that."

"You would not be able to identify it positively?"

"No."

"Did you sell her any cartridges?"

"I sold her two bits' worth of cartridges."

"Did you have any conversation with her?"

"None whatever."

"Was there anything in her appearance that attracted your attention particularly, or in her manner?"

"No. Not at all."

"That is all the conversation you had upon it?"

"Yes, sir."

A juror asked Mr. Chick a question: "Did you load the pistol for her?"

"No, sir, she asked me how to load it, how it was loaded. I turned the cover back and showed her. I put it in a box and she took it away."

The coroner asked a follow-up question, "You, I understand, identified her positively?"

"No, sir, not positively. It looks a great deal like the woman, and the like clothes she wore—but I would not swear it was the same woman."

Ava jotted down a note. Mr. Mertzman, the surgeon claimed the bullet lodged in Miss Lottie's brain was a .38 or .40 caliber. Mr. Chick says he sold Miss Lottie a .44 caliber Bulldog. *Why isn't anybody mentioning this discrepancy?* Ava wondered.

A man by the name of W. P. Walters was sworn in to testify to Mr. Chick's testimony as a witness. He claimed the woman passed him, walking right by him very slowly, dressed in black, and walked into the showcase, and asked for a pistol.

"Mr. Chick showed her one," Mr. Walters said. "She said she did not want a very high-priced one, and she bought the pistol. She asked for some cartridges and asked Mr. Chick to show her how to load it. Mr. Chick opened the thing, shoved a cartridge in, and pulled it and took it out again. Then she took hold of the pistol, and pulled it and says, 'Isn't this hard to pull?' He said, 'No,' and he took hold of it and pulled *click-click-click*. She took hold of it again and pulled, and it clicked, and then she asked to have it put in a box and wrapped up."

"Did you notice anything peculiar about her?"

"Why yes, she came in just as slow, and walked out straight, slow, again, and I remarked, "I think, that woman—she is going to hurt herself with that pistol. I spoke to a man who was sitting on a bench outside the store, and he thought the same thing."

"That is all you know in relation to the matter?" the coroner said.

"That is all I know. I did not speak to the lady, and with the way she walked past me, I did not see her face."

The coroner addressed the jurors. "I believe, gentlemen, we have all of the testimony we can get. Unless there is some further inquiry you can suggest, I will submit the case to you. You can take the case and prepare your verdict."

After a short deliberation, the jury voted unanimously that that Miss Lottie A. Bernard, of Detroit, had suicided on the property of the Hotel del Coronado. Newspapers around the country carried the story of Lottie A. Bernard, often accompanied by the sketch of her, and readers everywhere speculated on who the mysterious young woman was and why she took her own life. The *San Diego Union* featured articles daily on possible clues and theories, calling her "attractive, prepossessing and highly educated." She was also described as "reserved and ladylike," with "fine clothing." Handkerchiefs found after her death were embroidered *Lottie Anderson* and were reported to be "of the finest linen."

Stories trickled in that the lady had quarreled with a man on a train in Orange, prior to her arrival in San Diego, and her companion had left her. There was speculation, too, that perhaps the man was her lover, not her brother. Why wouldn't a brother have come forward?

For several weeks, her body lay unclaimed. It became widely accepted that perhaps her name wasn't Lottie Bernard after all. Other possible names surfaced, including Josie Brown and Lizzie Wyllie. But all were eventually debunked.

By mid-December, it became known that Lottie A. Bernard was in fact Kate Morgan née Farmer, a domestic who had disappeared from Los Angeles. She had been married to a gambler from Hamburg, Iowa, whom she was not happy with. Doctors speculated perhaps she had been *enceinte* (the French word for "pregnant") rather than deathly ill with cancer. At the time, it was said, stomach cancer rarely developed in women under the age of forty and was almost unheard of in women younger than thirty-five.

Kate Morgan's trunk was eventually found, though it was emblazoned with the name *Louisa Anderson*. The contents included a lock of hair and a photograph of Kate Morgan, as well as handkerchiefs and a tin box also marked *Louisa Anderson*. There was also a wedding certificate for Thomas E. Morgan and Kate Farmer, married in Hamburg, Iowa was. The names, dates, and addresses on all the documents in the trunk had been obliterated, except for the details on the wedding certificate.

A relative came forward at last, J. W. Chandler, Kate's grandfather, asking that she be properly buried in a local cemetery and that he be sent the statement. The funeral took place at the parlor of Johnson & Company, attended by many San Diego and Coronado residents. Floral bouquets were gifted by prominent families, but nobody followed the body of Kate Morgan to her interment at Mount Hope Cemetery.

Chapter 41

With the mystery of beautiful stranger laid to rest, Coronado returned to an island of relaxation, parties, music, laughter, and dancing late into the night. The orchestra always played at the Hotel del Coronado and the cymbals struck, night after night.

Guests came and went, bringing their enthusiasm and leaving their hearts, taking with them their fond memories and promises to return to the Hotel Del. Although the population in San Diego began to climb again, the city did lose one of its most celebrated residents: Jesse Shepard decided, with a heavy heart, to return to Europe.

"I have been away for far too long," he explained at a celebratory dinner party in the Crown Room. "A large part of my heart will always remain in this beautiful city—thank you, San Diego, for having me. I will forever cherish my years here," He later dazzled the guests with a final piano concert.

The next time Ava heard from Wallace was in October 1893, by way of postcard sent from the World's Colombian Exposition in Chicago. The photo on the front of the card featured tall white buildings with pillars surrounding a long, rectangular lake with a massive Greek statue in the center. On the back, Wallace wrote:

Ava,

The White City in Chicago is amazing! The Chicago World's Fair is just as impressive e as the one in Paris. I wish you could see the world's first Ferris Wheel—it's a huge wheel that spins you around in sky!

I just enlisted in the navy. I'm not sure when I will get back to Coronado, but I will one day just to see you. I promise.

Yours truly,

Wallace

Joined the navy? Ava wondered how his parents allowed him that decision. Did he join against their wishes? His mother had certainly wanted him to follow in his father's footsteps and go into business. It didn't make any sense. Wallace never mentioned a desire to join the navy, although she remembered how riveted he was by the warships at the first Fourth of July parade. She read the card and studied the image again. She realized he still had an effect on her, and it bothered her that her heart raced at the sight of his handwriting. She placed his postcard into the mirror frame of her vanity, next to the others.

When Nathan last wrote, he sent a photograph. It showed him standing next to immense fish hanging in a row. His hair was disheveled and he was grinning. He looked bigger, and less boyish, but she'd recognize his eyes anywhere. On the back he scribbled:

Dear Ava,

Catching lots of fish. Doing well. I miss you. I'll come back someday, I just don't know when. There's so much work for me in Mexico.

You're still my best friend though.

Nathan

❧

Several years passed without another word from either of them. Eventually, Ava put their postcards in a box she kept under her bed. Sometimes, she would take them out and look at them. The ink was beginning to fade, and their edges were now curled and frayed. Both

Nathan and Wallace had forgotten her. All their promises to return hadn't been true. If she were to ever see either of them again, she was resolved to be perfectly disinterested and positively prepossessing.

In 1898, war broke out between the United States and Spain. The *San Diego Union* announced that the Battleship *USS Maine* had been sunk under mysterious circumstances in the harbor of Havana, causing US retaliation and support for Cuba in its fight for independence from Spanish rule. The war was waged in Spain's occupied colonies in the Caribbean and the Pacific. Every day, newspapers reported updates from the field. In Cuba, a US cavalry volunteer regiment called the Rough Riders, led by the former mayor of New York and assistant secretary of the navy, Colonel Theodore Roosevelt, stormed up San Juan Hill to victory with swords drawn. Cartoons depicted the Rough Riders' attack on horseback, but in reality, members of the regiment had been on foot because their horses couldn't get past a barbed wire fence. The Rough Riders were aided by the 10th Cavalry, a regiment made entirely of Negro soldiers they called Buffalo Soldiers since their time fighting in the Indian Wars.

Ava wrote articles giving updates on the war for the *San Diego Union*, since the *Coronado Mercury* was no longer in print. The most recent developments for the war were the focus of all dinner conversations at the Hotel Del. After ten weeks, the war ended in a crushing blow to the Spanish, who were ill prepared to defend their distant colonies. Concessions included a liberated Cuba, with the United States gaining the Philippines, Guam, and Puerto Rico. Ava worried about Wallace, certain he was involved in one of these theaters. She often thought of their time together: laughing and leaping from the dock at the boathouse, warmed by the sun after a cool swim, or sailing lazily in the bay. She tried not to, but she always pictured them on the top of the turret, sharing their first kiss. When an ostrich egg was discovered on the beach among the grass, she thought of Nathan, knowing he would be amused to hear that one of the females was escaping from the pen.

Both of them had abandoned her, and their written promises to return were unfulfilled. Ava had come to doubt she would ever see either of them again.

Chapter 42

June 28,1900
Twelve Years Later

Ava looked herself over, standing before a full-length mirror in her bedroom. She had been living in the Hotel Del since she was offered a full-time position managing events. She turned sideways, tying a black sash around her small waist. The floor-length burgundy dress that was her uniform had a fitted embroidered bodice, bell-shaped skirt, and long sleeves that puffed above each shoulder. Ava was grateful shorter collars were in fashion. The older styles had often made her feel like gagging from a bed of ruffles and lace below her chin. She twisted her long hair into a low bun and placed a straw hat with a burgundy ribbon on her head, tilting it slightly forward. Looking left to right for any defects in her attire, she grabbed a file of documents from the table nearby, along with her key, and left the room.

The elevator operator, Mr. Reddington, greeted her cheerfully, as he did every morning. "Good day, Miss Hennessey! Getting a little work done before the ceremony, I see?"

"Good day, Mr. Reddington. You know me too well!"

"This hotel couldn't operate a single day without you!" he added.

Ava laughed. "Certainly it could! I'm merely a spoke in the wheel!"

Ava walked across the lobby, along the hall, and down a flight of stairs to her office on the lower level. Sarah, her assistant, was already there, preparing notes for Ava.

"Here they are," she said, handing Ava a sheet of paper. "Need me to send that to the newspaper for you?" Ava handed her the file she was carrying along with a recent article she had written. "Yes, thank you." She traded with Sarah, and looked over her notes. A few corrections had been made in a red pen.

"I took the liberty to correct a few errors. I hope you don't mind. Aren't you glad you taught me to read?" Sarah teased.

"With every passing day." Ava smiled at the young woman who had become her highly valued secretary. "Managing hotel events used to require a team of coordinators. Look what we've been able to accomplish with just the two of us?"

"Because all you do is work, Ava. You haven't taken a holiday all year."

"I love what I do. So few women are able to work outside of teaching, or nursing, or running a household. We're lucky Mr. Spreckels allowed us to take on different responsibilities. What would I do with time off anyway? "

"Perhaps acknowledge one of your many gentlemen callers? Letters arrive daily, all from suitors begging for your hand."

"You sound like my mother. She would have had me married off ages ago. It's a new century, Sarah. We are modern women in a modern age. We no longer have to marry before we're one and twenty."

The spider grandfather clock chimed in the hallway upstairs.

"You'd better get going. Don't forget Mr. Baum is reading again this afternoon at two," Sarah reminded her.

"Right. I'll see you then. South lawn?"

Sarah nodded. "Parasol?"

"Not today. My hat will do."

Ava walked down a long hallway, turning several corners as it snaked its way through the underbelly of the hotel. She passed the apothecary, the land sales office, a confectionary store, and more upper management offices. On the south side of the hotel, she took a flight of stairs up and out into the bright sunshine. It was a beautiful, crisp day for a grand-opening ceremony. A coach was waiting under the hotel's porte cochere.

"Can I give you a ride, Miss Ava?" A coachman in a striped suit and top hat smiled down to her.

"I welcome a coach these days—the island has been overrun by trolleys! How are you, Willard, and how is your father?"

"Old Gus? Ornery as ever."

Ava chuckled. Rather than climbing into the coach, she took a seat beside Willard on the driver's bench. "Your father is a good man," Ava said. "How is business? My parents tell me demand for coaches has slowed down."

"It has. Just wait until automobiles take over. Have you seen Mr. Spreckels's new Winton touring car? She's a real beauty!"

"I have. He's quite smitten with it. It may be time for you to learn how to drive an automobile. There'll be a need for chauffeurs in the future."

"If you think so, Miss Ava." Willard led them a short distance across Orange Avenue and down the Silver Strand, stopping the coach behind a raised stage. They could hear the commotion of a large expectant crowd on the other side. "There must be five thousand people here for the grand opening," Willard marveled.

"You know Mr. Spreckels—nothing less than grandiose! Thanks for the ride. Take care of yourself, and give my best to your parents."

༄༅

Ava ascended the stairs to the stage, where Mr. Babcock greeted her. "Ah, and here she is, right on time."

"A stitch in time saves nine," she quipped.

"And haste makes waste!" Laughing, he handed her a megaphone She quickly glanced at her notes, folding the paper and placing it in her skirt pocket. She turned to address the crowd, stepping out to the center of the stage.

"Good morning! My name is Ava Hennessey, I'm the events coordinator at the Hotel del Coronado. We welcome all of you today to share in this momentous occasion."

The crowd cheered wildly. Ava recognized many of the children, their smiling faces pressed against the railing. They waved excitedly at her, making her laugh and wave in return. Beyond the sea of faces, hats, and parasols in the crowd, Ava could see rows of red-and-white-striped canvas tents with thatched roofs—a tent city.

"I want to introduce you to a very special man. Someone who has done wonderful things for the City of Coronado, namely to create an opportunity for all working Americans to come and enjoy what this island has to offer. Please join me in welcoming Mr. John D. Spreckels and his lovely family."

The Spreckels family strode up the stairs and onto the wooden stage, waving to the crowd. The boys, John Junior and Claus, his younger brother, carried an oversized red ribbon. Ava handed Mr. Spreckels the megaphone. "Thank you, Miss Hennessey," he said into the cone, his condensed voice projecting loud and clear. "It is a great honor to welcome all of you to our very own Camp Coronado! A tent city of amusement for all to enjoy throughout the summer. We have a saltwater plunge, bathhouse, carousel, sea lion exhibit, confectionery, an ice-cream parlor, a soda fountain, and later this week, the largest dance pavilion on the West Coast will be opened!" The crowd roared. Ava motioned to the boys to get into position and hold the ribbon taut across the stage. The Spreckels girls, Grace and Lillie, handed their father a pair of oversized scissors. Behind them, the elegant Hotel del Coronado loomed on their left, with the boathouse on their right. Mr. Hawthorne seized the opportunity, positioning his camera to commemorate the special occasion with a perfect background. He signaled the grinning family to hold still. They froze in place and waited for the bulb to flash.

"So, without further ado," Mr. Spreckels continued, "I officially declare Tent City open to the public!"

Ava took the megaphone so he could cut the ribbon, sending its loose ends floating to the stage floor. A balloon overhead burst open and confetti swirled down over the cheering crowd.

Ava followed Grace and Lillie down the stairs and into the backseat of their father's automobile. Several boys stood around it, gaping at its white rubber wheels, black spokes, and shiny black paint. It was the first automobile the boys had ever seen. A cloth top folded back behind a tufted-leather bench-seat like an accordion. Mr. Spreckels took his seat behind the wheel, and allowed the boys to step closer; he then he startled them by squeezing a bulbous horn that honked loudly. The boys leaped backward, causing Mr. Spreckels to burst into laughter.

Mrs. Spreckels, beside him on the front seat, swatted him playfully on the arm. "Don't frighten the boys, dear."

"What? It was funny!" he protested. "Sorry, boys!"

"That's all right, Mr. Spreckels! We really like your automobile!" the eldest boy replied.

"I'll take you lot for a ride sometime!" Mr. Spreckels promised. The boys looked at one another in disbelief. Mr. Spreckels started up the engine and it roared to life, then sputtered as it idled.

Snare drums were struck, cymbals clanged, and tubas blared, commencing the start of the celebration parade. John Junior and Claus held a banner in front of the marching band and followed the automobile down Main Street, Tent City's new thoroughfare. Ava, Grace, and Lillie waved tirelessly at spectators, tossing candies to eager children who scrambled to collect them on the ground.

After the parade, Ava and Grace walked from attraction to attraction. They passed an arcade, a bowling alley, a merry-go-round, a children's pool, and a sandbox with a springboard where brave little ones could practice diving. Anchored in the bay was the ill-fated *Silver Gate* ferry, converted now to a floating casino that doubled as a Sunday school. The young ladies crossed Main Street, stepping over railway tracks for the Blue Belt line. A double-decker trolley designated car #41 halted on the tracks, ready to transport guests. The conductor rang a bell, calling out, "All aboard! Step right up!"

Two young men stopped Ava and Grace, offering to buy them ice cream, but they declined politely.

"We're trying to keep our girlish figures," Grace said flirtatiously. Ava squeezed her arm.

"Maybe next time, ladies. We hope to see you around," one of the men replied hopefully, flashing a smooth, white smile.

"Grace, don't talk to strangers. Hasn't your mother warned you about that?," Ava said as they walked away.

"They don't look so strange to me!" Grace retorted with a giggle.

They passed a sign on the boardwalk that read: Tents $4.50 per week. Bathing suits 25¢ per day.

A father and son emerged from a changing tent, wearing matching striped one- piece swimsuits and wide grins. They raced each other down to the beach, eager to go for a swim. Farther down the boardwalk, a crowd gathered around the shooting gallery. Ava and Grace went to see what the commotion was about.

"Some of you may know me from my younger years as a deputy sheriff," an older man said, standing inside the shooting gallery. He was graying at the temples but had youthful, lively blue eyes. He looked at everyone squarely, holding each stare. "For those of you that don't know, my name's Wyatt Earp." Applause erupted and he broke into a dazzling grin. "And I'm going to teach you a few shootin' tricks today. Luckily, we're just shootin' rubber ducks and not outlaws." The crowd laughed. He held up a Colt pistol with a long barrel and spun it around effortlessly.

Behind him, a row of rubber ducks moved slowly across a painted backdrop of tall reeds. Young boys in the audience pressed in closer to get a better look. Mr. Earp spun around, shooting every duck in less than five seconds. Smoke rose from the end of his pistol, and he bowed to roaring applause. "Thank you!" he said. "I'll be here all week!"

Ava nudged Grace. "I need to get back to the Del. It's story time with Mr. Baum."

"Sure, we can go, I wanted to be there for that, too. Is he reading from his new book, *The Wonderful Wizard of Oz*?"

"Yes, the second half of it. The first half was yesterday."

"I've read it twice already. It's an instant classic!"

Ava agreed. "There's a theme today—everyone wears white. Mr. Hawthorne wants to take a photograph."

"I love themes!"

Ava and Grace walked back to Main Street and hopped aboard streetcar #41. They made several stops on their ride through Tent City, picking up more passengers along the way back to the hotel.

Out in the ocean, five white ships puffed smoke from their stacks as they coasted toward the shore. American flags waved from their masts. "Say, aren't those navy ships?" Grace asked.

"Yes, some of the navy's Great White Fleet line are coming to town. They're here to start preparing North Island as a military installation," Ava replied.

"It sure is helpful that you work for the paper," Grace said. "You know everything that's happening in this town."

"Both the good and the bad," Ava admitted. "Of that I assure you."

❧❧

Commander Wallace Gregory, dressed in a high-collared, long blue coat with a row of gold buttons down the center stood at attention. Beside him, his fellow officers and sailors lined up along the deck of their ship as they steamed toward the California coast. Wallace had dreamed of returning to Coronado for years, but unforeseen obstacles and war had prevented him. He knew somehow he'd find a way back. He also knew that Ava Hennessey was still writing articles for the newspaper, no longer in the guise of J. A. Paul. He had a recent *San Diego Union* newspaper in his stateroom, her byline circled: *Ava Hennessey.* She hadn't married.

The Hotel del Coronado dominated the skyline, causing awe among the sailors. They had earned two weeks of liberty, and once in port, they intended to enjoy every minute of it. Excitement was in the air as the fleet slowed to a stop and anchors were dropped. Because of the ships' deep draft, the bay was too shallow for their hulls, so the vessels had to remain out in the ocean, several hundred yards from shore.

Wallace looked through his ocular, spotting dozens of red-and-white-striped tents along the Strand. He smiled. He had read about Coronado's Tent City and had followed its development in the papers. The sky was a perfect blue and the air crisp, just as he had remembered it. Seagulls hovered above, observing the sailors curiously. When the birds determined the navy ships weren't fishing vessels, they veered away with loud cries, flying back to shore. Wallace inhaled deeply, closing his eyes. *This is real*, he told himself. When his ship's horn blasted, his heart started racing. It was time to disembark.

⤳∽⤶

A fishing vessel, *El Canción del Mar*, coasted into the bay, after passing the navy's fleet from a safe distance. On deck, a net was rolled into a large heap with lines anchored to buoys made of cork. Upstairs in the captain's cabin, a tall, a tan young man with dark, unruly hair stood behind the wheel. On the chair behind him was a tattered *San Francisco Chronicle* newspaper, dated a month prior. An article headlined "Navy Comes to Coronado, California" had been circled three times with a heavy pen. Commander Wallace Gregory, assistant to the fleet's admiral, was quoted: "It makes all the sense in the world for the navy to have a Pacific base in Coronado. It's an ideal location. We are looking forward to establishing a long relationship between the United States Navy and the citizens of Coronado moving forward."

Nathan glanced again at the article that had prompted his sudden return. He had sold his shares in his fishing company, a highly profitable decision, and said farewell to Cabo San Lucas. After twelve years, it was time to return to Coronado at last. How had the years slipped by so quickly? He had dreamed of his return often, especially on those dark, early mornings when he was headed out to sea. It was then, when the calm water reflected the stars like a mirror that he thought of Ava. He always pictured her smiling at him.

Only his business successes had kept him from coming back sooner. Luckily, he had arrived in time, just ahead of the navy. With Wallace returning, he guessed Ava was still there, but were they too late? At twenty-

296

three, had she married by now? Most women had by her age. He prayed that she had not. Why would Wallace return if she had? It gave him hope. If Ava wasn't married, he couldn't let Wallace sweep her off her feet. Not without a fight. Only this time, he wasn't the awkward, impoverished, uneducated boy he'd once been. There was only one person he wanted to reel in: Ava Hennessey.

Chapter 43

Ava, Sarah, and Grace looked on as the children huddled around Mr. L. Frank Baum on a bench beneath a young tree. He read from his newly released book, *The Wonderful Wizard of Oz*, with great animation in his voice and excitement in his warm brown eyes. The girls wore all white from their bows down to their shoes. The boys sported white button-down shirts, white shorts, and long socks. Mr. Baum chuckled heartily as the children pressed closer to him, fearful of the Wicked Witch of the West. He was a middle-aged gentleman with a happy disposition and a hearty laugh. Dressed in a fine suit, he wore his dark hair neatly parted down the center, his thick mustache firmly waxed into place.

Two girls shrieked when Dorothy was captured and carried away by fearsome flying monkeys. Upon her rescue from the witch's castle by her loyal friends, the Lion, the Scarecrow and the Tin Man, the children sighed with relief. The wicked witch was dead; her magical broomstick was given to the wizard; and Dorothy discovered the magic of her ruby slippers, which transported her home to Kansas. The children listened with fascination as Mr. Baum turned the final pages of the book, reading Dorothy's last line: "'And here is Toto, too. And oh, Aunt Em! I'm so glad to be home again!'"

The children clapped as Mr. Baum closed the book. One of the youngest girls became serious. "What happens next, Mr. Baum? In the next book? You're not going to bring back those flying monkeys, are you?"

298

"They are really frightening!" another girl admitted.

"I quite liked them," said a bold boy. "I wish one would take my governess away."

Surprised laughter escaped from Mr. Baum, and the children giggled. Ava gave the troublesome boy a stern look. He crossed his arms over his chest, standing by his statement. "Well, she is excessively strict."

"Not to worry, children, there shall not be scary flying monkeys and mean governesses in the next story," Mr. Baum reassured them. "But there may be another wicked witch!"

The two skittish girls shrieked again, causing the others to laugh.

"Is she a munchkin witch?" a shy girl managed to ask in a small voice.

"Munchkins don't have witches," the troublesome boy insisted. "It would have to be a witch from the North or the South."

"Oh," replied the girl, forlorn for having missed the obvious. She fiddled with the sash on her dress.

"You are a very clever boy. Pray tell me, what is your name?" asked Mr. Baum.

"James," the boy replied.

"Very well, James, pleased to meet you. Now, children, I'll let you in on a little secret. I've already begun writing the sequel." This news sparked smiles of approval. "Would you like to know what happens next?"

The children nodded.

"Let's see, where were we . . . Yes, Dorothy has returned safely home to Kansas, and she now has a pet chicken named . . . Billina."

"A pet chicken?" James said, looking skeptical.

"Yes, James, she has a pet chicken named Billina," one of the older girls scolded, impatient for Mr. Baum to continue telling the story.

Mr. Baum tried to conceal his amusement. "Then one night, there is a thunderstorm, and Dorothy and Billina return to Oz only to find the great city is in shambles—and the Tin Man and the Cowardly Lion have been turned to stone."

The girls gasped. "Oh no!" cried the younger ones.

"And guess what? Billina can now talk."

"A talking chicken?" James said, incredulous.

Mr. Baum nodded. "Don't you remember that everything can talk in Oz? The trees, a scarecrow, even the Lion and the Tin Man."

Intrigued, James was kind enough to let Mr. Baum continue. "An evil Nome King has taken over Oz, and nothing is as Dorothy left it six months earlier."

Mr. Hawthorne arrived just in time to snap a candid photograph. The children were having a discussion with Mr. Baum, perched on the bench, before a bell rang, calling them for tea.

"That's all the time we have today, children," Mr. Baum concluded. "We will finish the story tomorrow, under this exact tree at the same time."

The children moaned in protest as their governesses herded them away. Ava thanked Mr. Baum for offering story time to the children. "They have really enjoyed it!" she said.

"I adore children, and if I had half of their imagination, I could write dozens of books far wilder than the Wizard of Oz," he admitted. "Their minds are so wonderfully uncluttered."

ॐ

In the Crown Room, Wallace smiled a little while he sat, sipping tea, and watched Ava through the windows. She had grown tall and had become quite beautiful, just as he imagined she would. She looked elegant in a white flowing dress and cloche. He placed his empty teacup on its saucer, both emblazoned with matching Hotel del Coronado red crowns.

"She's more beautiful than ever, isn't she?" asked a deep but familiar voice.

Wallace turned to find Nathan sitting at a table nearby. He had been watching Ava, too.

"Nathan? Is that you?" Wallace jumped up and moved to hug his old friend, regarding him with amazement. "You've gotten so—well, you're not a scrappy kid anymore, let me put it that way!"

"Neither are you," Nathan said with a hearty laugh. "Look at you, an officer with the navy. Who would have guessed?"

"Not my parents, I can assure you that."

"Well, navy life suits you. You are looking very well."

The two men looked each other over. Nathan was tall, with muscular arms and rough hands from years of manual labor. He was dressed in a brown suit and bowler. Wallace was also tall but lean, and he was dashing in his naval officer's uniform. Colorful medals lined the left chest pocket of his blue jacket, with shoulder boards that indicated the rank of commander: three gold-lace stripes and a star. His blond hair was cut short, parted, and tidy. Nathan and Wallace broke into wide grins.

"Are you here for her?" Wallace asked, peering back through the windows at Ava. She was still conversing with Mr. Baum.

"Are *you*?"

Wallace nodded. "Primarily, yes."

"Well, may the best man win, then," Nathan said jokingly.

Wallace laughed good-naturedly. "Fair enough. Are you staying with your father?"

"No. I'm a guest here." It was hard for Nathan to conceal his pride in saying this, and he held up his copper room key as proof.

"That's fantastic!" Wallace said, truly happy for Nathan's apparent success.

"I sold my fishing company. It was a lucrative decision."

"I'm glad to hear it. You always were determined. I admired that about you."

Nathan looked surprised. "Really?"

"Of course! I knew you had what it takes to succeed. Are you going to the dance tonight?"

"Absolutely. You?"

"Yes, but perhaps we can play a few games of billiards before we go," Wallace suggested. "And get caught up."

"Sure, but I wouldn't place any wagers if I were you," Nathan warned. "In full disclosure, I happen to be quite good at billiards these days."

"Is that so?"

"Don't say you weren't warned."

Wallace patted his old friend on the shoulder good-naturedly. His hand thudded against firm muscle. "From fishing?" he asked, impressed by Nathan's solid build.

"I've pulled in fish bigger than the both of us," Nathan admitted.

"We'll have to see if that helps you pull in the greatest catch of all."

"I'll need everything I have to combat your charms, Wallace. You're the one with the baby blues."

"Providing she'll even talk to us after all these years. Did you promise her you'd return?"

"With every postcard."

"So did I. There's a good chance she won't talk to either of us at all. She's grown up, but I doubt she's changed that much."

"You think she's still fractious?" Nathan joked.

"Undoubtedly."

Wallace and Nathan laughed about old times as they walked from the Crown Room to the rotunda. Rather than wait for the elevator, they took the stairs. Just as they were out of sight, Ava entered the lobby with Grace. They said their goodbyes, having made plans to meet in the rotunda after dinner and then go to the new dance pavilion together. With a small hug, they went their separate ways, excited about the evening ahead of them.

Chapter 44

Ava's mother pinned up her daughter's hair with pearl clasps, leaving loose tendrils around her face. She smiled lovingly at her daughter, who was seated at the vanity in front of them as they both peered into the mirror. "You look beautiful, dear."

Ava turned her head from side to side. "Do you think so?" She wrinkled her nose. Her skin had a healthy glow from the hours she spent in the sunshine.

Mother dabbed a little color with shine to her lips.

"Am I finished?" Ava asked. "You'll have me looking like a doll if I don't put an end to it." She stood up and smoothed the bodice of her rose-colored silk dress, again looking at her reflection in the mirror. Her mother smiled proudly. "Don't let your sister dance with any strangers."

"I *won't*," Lydia insisted, fidgeting impatiently on Ava's bed. Her thick blonde hair was swept up in a pompadour. "Are you ready yet? I can't bear waiting any longer!" She wore a peacock-blue dress with a modest neckline. "It's opening night at the dance hall, and Robert will be there. He's already promised to ask me for the first dance!"

"Lydia, your father will be picking you up at ten thirty," Mother reminded her.

"Please, can't I stay later, Mother? I'll be with Ava. She can watch over me, and Owen will be there, too. I'll have a chaperone every minute!"

"You know what your father has said. When you turn eighteen, we can discuss your curfew."

"That's not until after summer! Oh all right. Then let's hurry, Ava—the doors open at eight!"

Ava and Lydia hugged their mother goodbye and left Ava's room, taking the elevator down to the first floor. Grace was waiting for them in the rotunda, wearing a champagne-colored dress and pearls. The three of them exited the hotel's rotunda, eliciting great admiration from gentlemen who tipped their hats to them.

Outside, Father and Owen waited near a red coach. Owen, now twenty- one, was taller than his father, with sun-kissed freckles. He greeted his sisters and Grace and opened the coach door, holding the hand of each young woman as she navigated the steps in a long dress. Owen then joined his father on the driver's bench, and off they went.

The ladies chatted and laughed en route to the dance pavilion. "You are going to dance tonight, aren't you, Ava?" Grace asked. "Not just write for the paper about everybody else dancing?"

"Yes, Ava, please dance this time!" echoed Lydia.

Ava sighed. "I won't make any promises. After all, I haven't even been asked yet, have I?"

"Nor will you if you keep saying no!" Lydia teased.

"Don't you ever want to marry Ava?" Grace asked.

"I'm already a spinster, so why should I worry at this point?"

"Spinsters are old and mostly disagreeable, not young, beautiful, and intelligent like you," Grace replied.

"I believe twenty-three is considered old. Don't worry about me, I'm perfectly happy with my lot in life," Ava assured them. "I've just never met the right man."

The carriage halted before the dance pavilion, an enormous structure on the boardwalk along the bay at the far end of Tent City. Music spilled out from its wide-open doors, and a crowd of excited revelers filed inside.

๑๑๑

Wallace looked beyond the point of his cue stick as he aimed at the cue ball. His bright blue eyes squinted as he slowly withdrew the stick between his fingers, then slammed it forward, sending the cue ball across the table into a pyramid of striped and solid balls. The balls scattered, and two dropped into opposite pockets on the far end of the table. Wallace stood up, pleased with his first shot. He wore a crisp white uniform with a high collar, was cleanly shaven, and his hair—short on the sides and back, and longer on top—was perfectly in place.

"Not bad," Nathan admitted after Wallace dropped another ball into a side pocket, but then missing the next shot.

Nathan coolly targeted and sank ball after ball into various pockets.

"You weren't kidding about your skills with a cue. How'd you get so good at billiards?" Wallace asked, clearly impressed. "I thought you were fishing all this time."

"I was," Nathan said, measuring his next shot by walking around the table. "But sometimes . . . the fish aren't biting." He sank another ball into a pocket.

A gentleman at a nearby table whistled and commended him. "Good shot, young man!"

"Thank you," Nathan replied. He sank two more balls, then missed an impossible shot. He pulled at the tight collar of his tuxedo jacket, his dark, unruly hair flipping up at the ends. "Do I really have to go up against you in that navy uniform? It makes anybody look good," he complained.

Wallace laughed. "You worried?" He broke up a cluster of balls since there was no viable shot.

"I'm just going to have to make up for the disadvantage in other ways." Nathan dropped the winning ball in the pocket. "Maybe I'll recite some poetry about fishing."

Wallace chuckled. "You do that, and she'll be all mine."

Both men shook hands. "Good game," Wallace added. "Glad you didn't let me place a wager."

"Don't bet against me—and I mean that in every possible way."

A clock on the wall chimed, and eight gongs rang out. "Before we go, a toast," Wallace suggested, "To old friends reuniting."

They each raised a snifter of cognac.

"To forgiveness," Nathan said, throwing his drink back in one smooth motion.

"For a woman scorned, we'll need luck as well as forgiveness."

Nathan laughed. "And I'll need better looks."

They parted ways and headed to the dance pavilion separately.

Chapter 45

Ava and Grace looked down over the dance floor from the second-floor balcony of the dance pavilion. They enjoyed watching eager guests file in through the grand entry. The great room was electrified with energy as soon as the orchestra began to play. Lydia was already dancing with Robert, a boy who worked at the ferry landing. She waved to her sister.

"Look at all of the naval officers arriving! Aren't they handsome in their uniforms?" Grace said. Dozens of young men in white coats filed into the pavilion, removing their hats and tucking them into their arms. They talked among themselves, surveying the available young women waiting to be asked to dance. It didn't take long before they began to mingle, taking ladies by the hand and leading them to the dance floor.

Ava turned to face Grace. "Will Alexander be here tonight?" she asked.

"I certainly hope so. His parents have been visiting a great deal with mine lately."

"There's nothing to complain about there. He's handsome and from a wonderful family. Do you think he will ask you to marry him?"

"I'm not sure." Grace giggled.

"Surely, he will! Why would he not? You're what every fine gentleman seeks in a wife."

"Speak of yourself." Grace became suddenly serious. "Don't look, but there's someone staring at you. Yes, I'm certain he's staring at you."

"Up here? How can anyone even see me up here?" Ava replied with a laugh.

"He's in a navy uniform. He's coming up the stairs now, and he's still staring at you. He's walking toward us."

Grace stopped talking abruptly, while Ava stirred her soda with a straw, her eyes averted.

"Hello, Fractious," the man said, smiling down at Ava.

When she looked up, she froze. "Wallace?"

He laughed at her shocked expression.

Grace sat, wide-eyed by their awkward exchange

"Aren't you surprised?" Wallace asked.

"*Stunned* is more fitting." Ava was too flustered to stand up and properly greet him. She stared at him as if he were a ghost.

"Will you dance with me?"

As she began to stammer a decline, Grace interrupted. "She'd love to!"

Ava gave her friend a stern look, but Grace was unapologetic. Wallace held out his hand and, reluctantly, Ava took it. Her face flushed—she was short of breath and on the verge of perspiring.

Wallace led her down the stairs to the dance floor and turned toward her, placing his right hand on her lower back, his left hand in hers. "You're all grown up and beautiful," he said as he glided her around the floor.

He was tall, and more handsome than she remembered. She stared at the shiny brass buttons on his jacket. She couldn't think of anything smart to say; her mind was racing. He closed his eyes, smelling the sweet perfume of her hair.

"It's been twelve years!" she said at last. Fire burned in her eyes when she finally looked up at him.

"Don't be angry, Ava. I was deployed at sea—I couldn't get back until now."

She swooned from the musky scent of his cologne. "If you thought I was fractious before, you have no idea how fractious I am now."

"I expected no different." He chuckled, then became serious. He focused on her pouting mouth, so near his. "I came back to see you. I promised you I would."

He could feel her fingers tremble, and they returned to silence as they danced. When the song ended, she finally spoke. "Well, I haven't forgiven you," she said flatly.

"You haven't let me apologize yet, and I do apologize wholeheartedly. You have every reason to be cross with me."

"*Cross* is an understatement!"

Someone tapped Wallace on the shoulder, saying, "Do you mind if I take it from here?"

"Nathan?" Ava said, incredulous. Wallace's smile faded. "Just like old times," he muttered, letting go of Ava.

"At least I waited for the song to end," Nathan replied. "I didn't use to."

Ava couldn't believe her eyes. "I must be dreaming!"

Nathan laughed, lifting her up as he hugged her. "You're not dreaming!"

She squealed and beat him playfully on the chest as he twirled her around. "You're so big! And look at your hair!" she exclaimed as he set her down.

"I know. I look like a wild man! I haven't even had time to go to the barber. I only just arrived today. Pardon us, if you will, Wallace."

Reluctantly, Wallace moved away from Ava and Nathan so they could dance.

Nathan moved Ava skillfully across the floor, no longer the clumsy dancer that counted each nervous step.

"And don't think I'm not mad at you, too!" Ava hissed.

"Here comes the lashing. I know! I feel terrible! Did you get my postcards?"

"Of course I did. But you never sent a return address," she pointed out.

"I didn't have one, I swear! I was out at sea."

"That's the second time I've heard that excuse tonight, and don't think a weak apology is going to magically fix everything, either!"

"Oh, I have much more than an apology planned to win you back."

"I'll have you know I can't be won."

"We'll see about that."

Wallace returned, dancing with Grace nearby. He kept moving the two of them closer, trying to listen to Ava and Nathan's conversation. But Nathan twirled Ava away, out of earshot. When the song ended, Ava excused herself. She motioned to Grace, and the two of them headed for the powder room.

❧

"Ava, what is happening? I cannot believe they've both come back at once!" Grace said. Both ladies stood before a mirror, each dabbing at her face with a powder brush.

"I'm as surprised as you are," Ava said trying to regain her composure. *Was I too eager?* she thought critically. Eyeing her reflection, she wished she had worn a prettier dress. She tried to steady her breathing. "Stay calm," she said to herself. She had dreamed of Nathan and Wallace's return so many times. She had even rehearsed her cold reception to the two of them, and here she was, acting like an excitable schoolgirl, when the reunion actually happened.

"They're both so handsome, don't you think?" Grace asked, adjusting her hair clasp with her fingers.

"They aren't boys anymore, I'll admit to that."

"Ava! They were your closest friends. How can you be so indifferent?"

"I'm not indifferent," Ava replied, becoming aloof. "I'm *prepossessing*."

"Oh dear! I see now," Grace said, giggling. "Well, they only have eyes for you, so this should get very interesting if you've suddenly become *prepossessing!*"

"Very interesting indeed." Ava flashed Grace a wicked smile.

Back in the dance pavilion, Alexander arrived, whisking Grace away to dance. Not wanting to stand alone looking awkward, Ava returned to their table on the second-floor balcony. Gazing down at the floor below, she spotted Lydia dancing with Robert again. Owen danced with Ava's assistant, Sarah, which surprised and delighted her. *What a great couple they make!* she thought. How had she not thought of it sooner? Owen was educated, and his kindheartedness was a perfect complement to Sarah's gentle, loving disposition.

Near the powder room, Ava spotted Nathan and Wallace immersed in conversation. They appeared to be waiting for her and hadn't seen her slip out. Ava sipped her soda and tried not to watch them, but she couldn't help sneaking glances. She couldn't believe they had both returned on the same night. She realized that Grace was right—they were both handsome. She felt a pang of emotion surge through her. The little girl in her wanted to race down the stairs and hug them both tightly, but she suppressed the feeling. *They'll only hurt me again*, she reminded herself. *I'm not the same Ava. I'm prepossessing now.*

A male figure approached, looming over her. Ava looked up and recognized the persistent young man who had offered to buy Grace and her an ice cream the day before on the boardwalk. He grinned sheepishly, holding out his hand. "Would you care to dance with me, ma'am?" he asked.

Ava's eyes lit up, and she set her soda down on the table. "I'd love to."

His name was Antonio, and he walked her by Wallace and Nathan, who instantly dropped their conversation to watch her pass. Ava smiled back at them. *This is going to be fun!* she thought. Antonio was a fabulous dancer, and he twirled Ava expertly around the dance floor, making her laugh. Nathan threw one hand up in the air with frustration, and Wallace ran his fingers through his perfect hair. Winning back Ava wasn't going to be easy for either of them.

Chapter 46

The next day, Ava received two formal invitations. Wallace wanted to go for a sail on the bay, and Nathan wanted to go for a carriage ride on the beach. She declined both invitations, writing to each of them that she was far too busy with a deadline for the newspaper, work obligations, and a monthly meeting with the Coronado Good Time Club. *Perhaps tomorrow?* she added to each note. She smiled to herself as she handed her handwritten replies to Sarah, who went to deliver them. Each man would have a letter waiting for him in the key cabinet behind the front desk.

When the next day brought two new invitations, she declined them again.

That evening, out of luck, the men played billiards, betting on each game.

"Did she turn you down again today?" Nathan asked, guessing Wallace had gotten a note, too.

Wallace leaned over the pool table, aimed, and sent the cue ball slamming into a ball that sank into a side pocket. "Very quickly and with pleasure, I believe." They both smiled but neither of them looked happy.

They continued playing until both of them won two games each and ultimately broke even. They enjoyed a cigar, sitting in rocking chairs on the covered patio that overlooked the ocean. They could hear waves crashing, and they watched the moon shine, casting a quivering beam of light on the ocean's surface.

"She lives here now, doesn't she?" Wallace said. "I wonder what room number."

"She does and I'm not telling you," Nathan replied, blowing smoke high into the air.

"Money?"

"No good."

"How about I play you another game. If I win, you have to tell me."

"And if I win, I get to take her out first."

"Deal."

A lively crowd of gentlemen in tuxedos filed into the room as their game began. It was well after dinner, and the elegantly clad men were holding snifters of brandy. They watched the highly competitive match, cheering loudly after every good shot.

"What is the wager?" an old man slurred, his glassy eyes finding it difficult to focus.

"A fair maiden's heart," Nathan replied.

"Ex-HUT-cellent," he slurred, hiccupping. "Never was a worthier cause."

"There's a lot of green on the table," another man warned. "You've got a difficult shot, young man."

Undaunted, Nathan bent low over the cue stick, squinted, measured, adjusted his angle, took the shot, and sank the ball for the win.

Applause erupted from the gentlemen assembled. Nathan and Wallace shook hands. Nathan would get the first date . . . if Ava accepted his invitation.

……

The following morning, Nathan and Wallace each sent a third invitation to Ava for an outing. She accepted an afternoon carriage ride with Nathan at 3:00 p.m. and an early-evening sail with Wallace at 5:00 p.m.

Why would Nathan want to take me on a carriage ride? Doesn't he realize that's all I've ever done on this island? she wondered. *Maybe he wants me to give him a tour.* She put on a peach-colored frock with a white lace hat, tying a bow under her chin. As she exited the doors from the lobby, she could hear the rumbling of laughter outside. She soon found out why. Nathan had two ostriches harnessed to a small buggy with two large wheels.

"My lady," he said, removing his bowler and bowing deeply. Ava couldn't help but laugh. Nathan held her hand as she stepped up into the buggy.

"Where on earth did you get this idea?" she asked, amused. "It's absolutely ridiculous!" The ostriches raised and lowered their small heads excitably.

"It's Mr. Campbell's, the manager helping my father run the farm. He helped us get the business charter when we first moved here. You didn't think this was going to be just *any* carriage ride, did you?"

"I see I've underestimated you."

"I like to be underestimated. It gives me the element of surprise."

"Is that so?" Ava laughed.

"It is. Now, I can't make any promises—the birds are new at this," Nathan warned. "It's a bit of a miracle that I got them here at all." He shook the reins, but the birds didn't move an inch. Their dark eyes were shifty and anxious. Nathan shook the reins more vigorously and tried coaxing the ostriches to move. Still nothing. Ava burst into laughter again, holding both hands to her lips. Guests who gathered on the stairs and balconies laughed, too. Then, without warning, the birds lunged forward, flapping their wings wildly. Ava shrieked as she and Nathan were forced back into their seats.

"Whoa!" Nathan cried. "I should've known not to pick crazy Twilah's offspring!"

Ava was caught up in a fit of giggles. The birds pulled the buggy in tight circles in front of the hotel. "I guess I'll just let them go wherever they want." Nathan dropped the reins and crossed his arms over his chest. The onlookers clapped and whistled their approval.

Finally, the buggy stopped spinning, and the birds headed down a path away from the hotel.

"What if we go too fast?" Ava asked between giggles.

"Then we jump."

"Nathan, that's not an option!" she cried.

The birds ran down Orange Avenue, passing trolley car #41 and several glamorous coaches. Nathan saluted the passengers in the various vehicles, casually removing his bowler and tipping it to them. Each encounter sparked a new fit of laughter from Ava.

They trotted toward the beach. Ava stole a few sidelong glances at Nathan. "You've changed," she said to him at last.

"I had a lot to change."

"No, I didn't mean that in a bad way—I mean you've grown up a lot."

"Living in Mexico will do that."

"What was it like?"

"Wonderful. The fishing was hard work, but the people were friendly and very kind. They accepted me as one of their own after a while, and made me part of their family. I never had a family that cared for me the way they did. It was hard to leave."

"So why did you?" Ava asked, searching his eyes for the truth.

"For you." Nathan's tone suddenly turned serious. "But enough about me. Let me ask you the most important question of the day."

"And what is the most important question of the day?"

"Am I devastatingly handsome?"

She slapped him across the arm, and they burst into laughter again. "Yes, and I'm certain you aren't lacking admirers," she added.

"Admirers?" he looked shocked. "Who? Do I have a secret admirer? That should be a crime!"

"I'm sure you have many."

Nathan looked dumbfounded for a moment. "Oh, well, there was one, Ana Bautista. But she is like a sister to me."

"Really?" Ava gave him a wry smile. "Does *she* think she's like a sister?"

"All right, all right, I caught her a big fish one day, and she thinks I'm the strongest man on the planet. That must be why."

"Will you stop it?" They both laughed again.

"Actually, I was hoping you'd say you were one of my admirers," he said soberly, then looked away.

Ava became quiet, remembering that she wasn't the only one who had been hurt.

Nathan guided the ostriches onto the beach, and their unusual buggy moved among polished coaches that carried fancy people in fine clothing. Those people stared and laughed.

"How is your first stay at the Del?" Ava asked when the birds slowed to a walk.

"Horrible! Funny that you should ask—worst night of sleep I've ever had."

Ava looked astonished. "Is there something inadequate with your room?"

"I'll say. The light turns on by itself in the middle of the night, my wallet has been moved twice, and I swear someone yanks my blankets off me!"

Ava's face fell. "Oh no! Are you in room 302?"

"How did you know? Are you spying on me?" he teased. "Was it you turning on the light?"

"No, of course not! Why would I spy on you? What a ridiculous notion!"

"I don't know, maybe because you're my secret admirer? I thought we already figured this out?"

She shook her head. "No, you have Kate Morgan's room, the young woman who died on the hotel grounds."

"I do?" Nathan looked horrified. "Somebody told me her story the other night."

"It was terribly sad, and ever since she died, there have been strange occurrences in the room where she stayed."

"It's haunted?" Nathan asked, exasperated.

"So I've heard, but it's a bit of a secret. The management thought it would be best to keep the story quiet, so as not to frighten the guests. I didn't believe the rumor about it being haunted was true, but I believe it if you say so."

"I demand a refund, then!" Nathan declared. "That, or I'm just going to have to tell Kate Morgan to leave me alone. This is the first real bed I've slept on in twelve years, and I don't fancy her playing pranks on me."

"She's harmless, really. Although a maid and a bellhop claim they've seen her floating down the hallway. Nothing bad ever happens, though. Poor, dear woman, God rest her soul. I can't forget the last time I saw her, she was so melancholy."

"Well, tonight I'm going to recite fishing tales—that ought to keep her out of my room for good."

Ava giggled and looped her arm through his. "Oh, Nathan, you're absurd."

He smiled down at her, loving the touch of her hand on his forearm.

After the ride along the beach, Nathan managed to guide the birds to the boathouse. A white yacht was anchored there, with Wallace standing on the deck. Seeing the ostrich carriage and Ava, cheerful with her arm linked through Nathan's, he muttered, "Well done, Nathan."

When Ava saw Wallace and the yacht, she exclaimed, "Wow—what a boat that is!"

Nathan helped her down from the buggy, his heart sinking. It was an incredible yacht, and Wallace looked like a prince standing at the helm, perfectly groomed in khaki slacks and a white collared shirt with rolled-up sleeves. Nathan could tell Ava was impressed.

Wallace climbed down from the yacht as Nathan and Ava approached the dock. "Nice ostrich buggy," he said by way of a greeting.

"Thanks," Nathan said flatly. "Nice dingy." *My ostrich carriage will be forgotten once she climbs into that yacht,* he thought sadly. Nathan prayed there would be no wind. *But no wind means they'll have the stillness to sit and talk quietly—and the mood could turn romantic. Better that I pray for lots of wind so they can't talk at all.* He smiled to himself at the image he imagined: Ava clinging to the stanchions as the yacht keeled, perhaps losing her hat to the wind, while Wallace desperately tried to settle the boat. *Maybe the boom will swing across the deck and knock him in the water for old times' sake.*

"So, I'll see you tomorrow for our fishing date?" Nathan said loudly, turning to Ava.

"Yes. I'm looking forward to it."

"Good. We'll be gone all day, so don't accept any other offers for your time." He shot Wallace a warning look.

"I won't," Ava said. "Thank you for the carriage ride. It was truly memorable." She noticed the none-too-subtle posturing between the men and smiled with satisfaction.

"The wind is picking up, shall we?" Wallace said, extending his arm to Ava.

She looped her arm through his, and they walked together down the dock.

Nathan could hear Ava's laughter as she climbed aboard the yacht. He pulled some treats from his pocket and fed them to the ostriches. "Thanks, boys," he said glumly. "Strong work today." The birds poked his hand with their beaks, searching for more. "You want to hear a story about the biggest fish I ever caught?" he asked them. They stared at him with dark, glassy eyes. "I'll tell you all about it on the way home."

Chapter 47

"Whose boat is this anyway?" Ava asked, trying to sound casual. *Be prepossessing*, the voice in her head warned. The winch drums and cleats were polished steel, the deck a pristine light teak, the bench cushions white and new. The well-appointed yacht was very costly, of that she was certain.

"Friend of the family. Steer for me." Ava took the tiller while Wallace pushed the boat from the dock, then hoisted the mainsail, pulling in the halyard hand over fist. The sail waffled gently as it climbed the mast one foot at a time. It filled with wind, and they eased away from the slip. Wallace raised the jib next. Ava kept the boat pointed into the wind, where resistance was lower. Wallace wrapped a halyard around the winch drum, grinding in the sail with a handle. "Could you tail for me, too?" he asked, grinning as he handed her the end of the halyard.

Ava smirked at him. "Anything else, Captain?"

"Maybe."

She steered with one hand and tugged on the halyard with the other, keeping the tension by pulling in the slack while he grinded up the jib. She tried not to look at the muscles working in his arms, or his fine profile, or perfect hair. As he secured the halyard, she looked away, feigning a fascination with the city skyline. They immediately picked up speed.

"There, now we're in business." He took the tiller back from Ava. "Thanks. Please, have a seat." He motioned for her to sit on the cushioned bench. "I can't have you crewing the entire time, can I? You're meant to enjoy yourself."

"Who says that I'm not enjoying myself?" She replied. He looked like he belonged on the cover of a yachting magazine. "And you may still need me. We have to jibe soon—that schooner has the right of way." She pointed to a boat headed their way.

Wallace grinned. "Well, look who knows how to sail these days!"

"There's a lot that I've learned since you abandoned me," she quipped.

"Bearing away," he said with a laugh, jibing the boat to avoid the schooner. The boom and mainsail swung over their heads, while he pulled the jib around the mast to the opposite side of the boat.

They sailed upwind in the bay, jibing and tacking around tall ships in the harbor. Once they neared Point Loma, Wallace turned the boat around. "There, now that we'll be downwind, it will be much smoother. It's time for a drink. Would you like a glass of wine?" His blue eyes were bright from exertion, enhanced by his tanned skin.

"Sure," she said too quickly.

"Do you prefer a pinot noir or a pinot grigio?"

Ava scrambled to remember the difference between the two. "White, please." She felt tongue-tied when she looked at him—her wit seemed to vanish. He asked her to steer again while he went below in the cabin, returning with two glasses and a bottle of chilled white wine. He poured and handed her a crystal glass, and she sipped the crisp wine right away, hoping it would ease her nerves.

The wind died and their sails luffed loosely. They drifted with San Diego on their left and Coronado on their right.

"So, Coronado is officially the Crown City by the sea?" Wallace said. "I read about it seceding from San Diego. That must have been highly contentious." He kept one hand on the tiller, holding his wineglass with the other.

"It was. Lots of strongly worded letters back and forth in the paper." Ava started to feel light-headed. Was the wine already influencing her, or was it the effect of Wallace gazing at her? She looked out over the water, avoiding his eyes. The afternoon sun began to soften, and the city's buildings took on a golden hue. She hoped he couldn't hear her heart thudding in her chest.

"So tell me what you've been doing all of these years? Did you get my postcards?" he asked.

"I did. I still have them, but I put them away in a box because you never came back."

"There she is! There's the fractious girl I met right over there." He pointed to the rocks where he had been fishing that day she stumbled upon him. "You were playing your violin, horribly might I add, right there."

"I *was* horrible, but I'll have you know I've improved since then."

"I should hope so after all this time."

"And we argued on our first meeting," Ava remembered, shaking her head. "I guess I wasn't an agreeable girl."

"Now you're articulate in addition to being disagreeable, and that's a double barrel," he teased.

"Undoubtedly!"

They both laughed and then silence fell between them.

His expression turned serious. "I wanted to come back sooner."

"Then why didn't you?"

Wallace sipped his wine as he gazed, lost in thought, over the bay. "My parents. They forbid it. They had my life planned out for me: what I would study, where I would work . . . who I would marry." His eyes met hers.

"Is that why you joined the navy?" She wanted to steer the conversation away from marriage.

"I joined the navy for a lot of reasons. A few of them had to do with you."

"I don't understand." She felt herself being dazzled by his blue eyes.

"I joined the navy to get away from my parents. Once I signed my name on the line, there was nothing they could do to stop me. I belong to the US government now, or at least for the next few years, I've already served one tour, and I signed up for another. My parents are furious. I lost my inheritance."

Ava's eyes widened with surprise.

"And I don't care. I don't want to be controlled by them, and I don't want their money."

They drifted in silence. Ava was so overwhelmed by the magnitude of what he'd revealed, she couldn't think of anything to say.

"And I knew that the navy was setting up a base here in Coronado. I knew, eventually, I could come back to you."

Ava drained her glass. *Is he telling me he joined the navy and lost his inheritance for me? Who would do that for me? Nobody.*

"It just took me longer than I thought to get here. I had to sail all over Southeast Asia and fight in a war first." He chuckled. "So now I'm a penniless sailor."

His smile made her feel faint. "I don't know what to say. You gave up everything to join the navy. That's remarkable!"

"I didn't give up *everything.* There are still a few things I want." He winked at her and smiled.

Ava felt heat rise in her face and quickly looked out over the city skyline again. She dared not speak for fear she'd reveal the jumbled mass of turmoil she felt. Wallace sat down next to her on the bench, keeping one hand on the tiller extender. He poured more wine into her glass and his.

They leaned back against the cushions, looking up at the fluttering sails and the pastel pink clouds of sunset. Wallace pulled the tiller slightly, correcting their course. Across the bay, ripples formed on top of the water, and a dark line moved steadily in their direction. A wind gust was coming. He handed his glass to Ava, then loosened the sheet, trying to hide another smile. The sails suddenly filled with wind, and the boom swung violently across the boat. They keeled hard, causing Ava to slide over until she was pressed firmly against his side. He grinned down at her, wrapping his arm firmly around her.

"You knew that was coming, didn't you!" she cried, pushing away from him.

"Jibing," he announced, laughing.

Ava's cheeks reddened. "It's a bit late to make that call, and I almost spilled my wine and yours. I don't trust you, Wallace! I'll steer from now on, you trim," she said, taking the tiller from him. "And I'll make all the tactical calls, too. Ahead of time!"

"It was an honest mistake," he pleaded, still laughing. "Fine, you skipper."

"I may be a stable hand's daughter, but I wasn't born in that stable!"

"Most certainly not."

They coasted back to the boathouse pier. Wallace dropped the sails and tethered the boat to the dock.

"Thank you, that was a nice sail," Ava said, daring to look him in the eyes. "Even though you played tricks on me."

"I hope we can go again soon." He stepped closer, his gaze focused on her mouth.

Ava was afraid that if he stood so close a second longer, he would kiss her—and she would let him.

"So, I understand you're fishing tomorrow," he said. "Maybe you can save some time for me the following day, or has Nathan already staked his claim on that day as well?"

"Nathan? Oh, uh, yes," she stammered, "We are fishing tomorrow." She thought for a moment. "But I might be free the day after." Suddenly, she changed her mind. "Or I might not. I'm not sure. I have a meeting with the Good Time Club and a deadline for an article for the paper. It depends on how much I get accomplished."

Wallace nodded, fighting back a smile. "Sure. How about we wait and see?"

"Let's do that," Ava agreed.

"Can I give you a ride home, then?"

"Oh, no. I'm fine. The hotel isn't far. I prefer to walk."

"All right, Fractious," Wallace said coolly, he stepped closer and leaned in, kissing her on the cheek when she thought he was going for her lips. "I'll see you soon, hopefully—if you're not busy, that is." His eyes gleamed mischievously.

"Thanks for the sail." She cringed. "I said that already, didn't I? See you soon." Flustered, she turned and walked up the dock toward the boathouse.

Wallace watched her go, his smile fading. He was running out of time. He had to win Ava's heart before his ship set sail at the end of the week.

Chapter 48

It was still dark when Ava and Nathan reached the docks. The fishing pier was poorly lit by flickering gas lamps that hung from poles. Ava was grateful she wore her brother's yellow wind jacket against the morning chill. The air smelled heavily of wet nets and coiled ropes used too often to fully dry out in sun. Small waves lapped against the pier, and beams creaked under their footsteps. Men with weathered faces and gray beards cast long shadows as they dragged nets along the docks. All of them had a job to do before they headed out to sea. Each day brought new hope for a good catch.

"Is this your fishing boat?" Ava asked, clearly impressed as she followed Nathan onboard. "It's really big!"

"It's about seventy feet long—really big, for catching really big fish. It took me years to save up the money to buy it, but it's all mine."

"What does the name mean?"

"*El Canción del Mar*? Here we'd call it *The Song of the Sea*." Nathan took her up the stairs to the captain's wheelhouse. "This is where I steer the boat to wherever my spotter, who sits higher up, tells me the fish are. The rest is just pure luck, but I'm pretty lucky."

"What's the biggest fish you ever caught?"

"I pulled in a four-hundred-pound bluefin tuna once. I had an even bigger one on the line, but a shark came along and bit the bluefin in two. Sharks are the rats of the sea. I've lost many a great fish to those scavengers."

"I've never seen a shark and hope I never do," Ava admitted.

Two young Mexican men boarded the ship, both signaling him with a thumbs-up.

"That's my crew, Arturo and his brother Herman. Great guys. Also, I meant to tell you. I hope you don't mind a few friends will be joining us today."

"With a boat this large, I would hope it's not just us fishing."

"And here they are now, right on time. Good morning!" Nathan called out.

Mr. Babcock, Mr. Story, Mr. Spreckels and his son John, and Colonel Holabird boarded the boat. Owen came sprinting down the dock after them. "Oh, and I invited your brother, too," added Nathan.

"Thank you, Nathan, that's so sweet of you." Ava smiled at him, warmed by his thoughtfulness.

"Let's go catch some fish. You ready?" His eyes lit up and she could see the thrill that had kept him out to sea for the past twelve years. He whistled to Arturo and Herman, and they pushed the boat from the dock, coiling the lines and jumping aboard.

El Canción del Mar steamed out over calm waters, heading toward the Coronado Islands. A number of smaller fishing vessels followed in their wake, heading to the same fishing area. The sun peeked over the mountain range in the east, lighting up the sky in glowing shades of orange and pink. Ava sat in the captain's chair, smiling as she watched the sunrise. Nathan stole glances at her. Above them, crying sea gulls hovered, following closely behind.

"Shall we greet our guests?" Nathan said, letting Herman take the wheel.

Ava followed him down the steps to the back of the boat.

తసౌ

"I can't tell you how timely your invitation is, Nathan. I'm indebted to you for getting me off the island," Mr. Babcock said.

Colonel Holabird clarified Mr. Babcock's dilemma. "Old Babcock here is in such high demand these days, he has to literally hide from the crowds," he explained.

"It's the price you pay for being the life of the party," Mr. Spreckels added.

"Even my wife has stated she cannot attend one more party or luncheon or ladies' tea or any other social function. It's simply too much!" Mr. Babcock agreed.

"We live in a paradise of parties, parades and picnics," added Mr. Story. "Far be it from me to complain."

"And I thought Hawaii was a fantasy island," Mr. Spreckels agreed with a laugh.

"It is nice to see a young lady on a fishing expedition," Mr. Babcock said, "I might press you to encourage Mrs. Babcock to give it a go herself."

"This is my first time fishing," Ava said. "I hope you gentlemen don't mind my informal attire." In addition to Owen's jacket, she was wearing her brother's breeches and rubber boots, all of which were far too big for her.

"Any lady that's willing to fish with the boys is welcome to wear whatever she likes. Your secret is safe with us, Miss Ava," Mr. Babcock reassured her. "We are, after all, in a new century."

"And once you catch your first fish, you'll be hooked, as they say," joked Colonel Holabird.

Ava laughed. These kind men had been like beloved uncles to her.

"Where have Owen and John Junior gone?" Ava asked.

"Down below, preparing our bait. We're using poles today, not nets," Nathan replied. "I'm feeling lucky, lady and gentlemen! Let's catch some fish!"

As they neared the Coronado Islands, Nathan gave directions to his crew in perfect Spanish. He pointed for them to go south of the islands while the other fishing vessels went north. Ava took in the view. She had always wanted to see the islands up close after spending so many days on the beach staring at them from a distance. They were stark, dotted with dry vegetation and rocky cliffs with deep crags that dropped straight into the sea. The water around them was a deep, dark blue. No sandy beaches buffered the harsh land from the relentless force of the water crashing against it. Ava imagined all the life teaming below the islands, countless creatures of all colors, shapes, and sizes fighting to survive another day in their unforgiving habitat. She was grateful to be floating safely above their merciless cycle of life.

The crew brought out a number of fishing poles, already baited with live mackerel. Nathan slowed the boat to a crawl, and Ava and all the men threw their lines in the water, letting them unreel. Arturo climbed up the ladder to a chair above the captain's wheelhouse to scan the ocean and spot schools of fish. He watched the birds in the sky, the current, and the boat's distance from the jagged islands with his deep-set, dark, knowing eyes. Arturo gave orders to Nathan, who altered their course.

Nothing happened for an hour, but Ava enjoyed herself nonetheless. That something *could* bite had the party in good spirits. Suddenly, she felt a hard yank on her rod, and her reel begin to spin wildly.

"I've got one! I've got one!" she yelled. Mr. Spreckels's reel spun next, as did Mr. Story's. Both men started yelling "Fish on the line!" Nathan stopped the boat and raced down the stairs to be at Ava's side.

"What do I do?" she cried.

"Don't let go of the pole!" Nathan replied, grinning at her excitement. "Let him run—when he gets tired, we'll bring him in. Owen, would you mind steering the boat? We may need to back up at some point."

"*Me?*" Owen replied, thrilled, "Certainly, I will!" He placed his pole in a holder and ran up to the captain's wheelhouse.

Mr. Spreckels reeled in his catch with his rod bent like a horseshoe from the strain on it. He struggled to raise the rod high, then reeled rapidly, taking up the slack in the line.

"Okay, Ava, I want you to do exactly what Mr. Spreckels is doing," Nathan said. "We're going to set your reel, then raise your rod and start bringing it in."

Ava nodded. She raised her pole, arched backward, then reeled.

"That's it, just like that. Good job. Keep working at it," Nathan encouraged her.

"This is hard work," Ava said after a few minutes. "It must be a really huge fish!"

Nathan smiled at her. "Oh, it must be!"

"No, I mean the biggest fish ever!" Sweat was beading on her forehead.

Arturo started laughing. "Oh jes! Itsa big wan!" he said in broken English, making Nathan and Herman laugh.

"What's so funny?" Ava asked.

"Nothing, just reel," Nathan replied.

The boat weaved and bobbed in place, and more sea gulls arrived, hovering overhead and quarreling as they waited for scraps.

"Got one on!" called Mr. Babcock. Now everyone had a fish on the line, and all were working feverishly to bring them in. Ava's fish started to move, so Nathan guided her under Mr. Story's line and over Mr. Babcock's line along the side of the boat.

"This is so fun! I love this!" Ava said. "Where's my fish going now?"

"Anywhere but in this boat as far as it's concerned!"

Ava began to tire, but Nathan wouldn't let her give up. He wrapped his arms around her and helped her raise the rod. "You reel and I'll help you," he directed.

She liked the feeling of his strong arms around her. "Sorry," she said, realizing she had stopped reeling. He closed his eyes, discreetly reveling in her closeness. After twenty minutes, she had pulled in yards of line, and the fish was somewhere beneath the boat.

"I'm going to let you bring it in all by yourself," Nathan said.

"Okay," Ava said shakily.

Nathan looked over the railing into the dark blue water. "I see it—it's getting close. Just a little bit more."

Ava peered over the railing and saw nothing but shades of blue water. "How can you see anything? I can't see a thing!" The birds now swarmed over the back of the boat, screeching as they waited above.

"Practice. Lots of practice," Nathan replied. He positioned a net on a long pole and held it over the water. Suddenly, Ava's fish breached and began swimming sideways on the water's surface, struggling against the pull of the line. Its gills heaved against the open air.

Ava shrieked. "There it is! I see it!"

Her fish, exhausted from its long struggle, succumbed to the net, and Nathan scooped it up. Ava was confounded when he lowered it onto the deck. "That's it?" she said, incredulous. "I thought for sure it would be five hundred pounds!" The men burst into laughter.

"Itsa big wan!" Arturo said again, laughing heartily.

"It's a yellowtail," Nathan said. "They're big fighters. Don't sell yourself short—it's a nice size."

"I can't believe it! I caught my first fish!" Ava was beaming, no longer disappointed that her fish was only a foot long. "I don't mind if you all laugh at my expense, I caught a fish!"

"She's hooked now. Look out!" teased Colonel Holabird.

The others pulled in bluefin, grouper, and sea bass. When Owen picked up his line again, he got a bite. It took him two hours to bring in a shark. "Look at that. It's got teeth so sharp it could cut you just to look at them!"

"That's a mako. We let them go," Nathan told him, carefully using pliers to remove the hook. The shark thrashed about on the deck, causing everybody to move as far away as possible.

Owen was thrilled. "I've always wanted to catch a shark!"

"You caught a nice one. I think you're cut out to be a fisherman."

"I'd love to do this every day!"

"You can, then. You're hired."

"Really, Nathan? I can work for you?"

Nathan laughed. "Sure you can. Starting today."

Ava was moved by many things about Nathan: his kindness to her brother, his strength, his command of his boat, his knowledge of fishing, and the respect he earned from the men aboard *El Canción del Mar*. He had succeeded on his own terms, and she was proud of him. He had come a long way from being the insecure, awkward young boy she remembered.

When the fishing party returned to the docks, they hung their fish along a line from largest to smallest, and Mr. Hawthorne took a picture. Ava grinned, standing next to her fish. It was the smallest catch of the day, but her smile was the biggest. The only person who didn't catch a fish was Colonel Holabird. He shook his head, recalling when his line had snapped. "I will *not* be writing about this mishap in my next brochure."

"Be of good cheer, Holabird—it's the one that got away," said Mr. Spreckels. "There's always one." He patted him on the shoulder, and Colonel Holabird shrugged.

Pictures of their successful fishing trip made it into the newspaper that circulated in town. The headline read: "Coronado Local Returns, Starts Fishing Company." Wallace studied the photo and Ava's wide grin, then let the paper drop on the table. "Well done again, Nathan," he grumbled.

On his way to the Crown Room for lunch, Wallace glanced into the ladies' entrance to the hotel. At the registration desk, causing problems as usual, stood Beatrice. She was arguing with the reception clerk. "Yes, I understand the guest list is private in nature, but I'd like to see the ledger all the same." Her mother stood behind her, scowling. "Don't they print names in the paper anyhow?" Beatrice spat.

Wallace froze, his heart thumping in his chest. *Don't see me!* he willed silently, glad he had paid the clerk not to enter his name on the ledger. He stepped out of view and walked rapidly across the rotunda.

Chapter 49

"You're engaged? That's wonderful news!" Ava exclaimed.

Grace giggled. "I know! I can't believe it! Alexander met with my father and he consented. I'm getting married!" she squealed. The ladies hugged as they walked down the boardwalk. When they saw a vacant cage-like swing, they headed for it. The swing had two wooden bench-seats that faced each other and shared a common footrest. It was suspended in a frame that moved freely between support posts. Ava and Grace sat facing each other and rocked gently.

"So tell me what's been happening? How are the boys? Have they started jousting for your hand?" Grace teased.

"No jousting but civil competition. I'm really not sure why they're going through all this trouble."

"They've only been in love with you since they were fourteen. It's easy to see why they're both falling all over themselves to win you over now. It's cute, really, seeing them posturing like peacocks. So tell me, who are you in love with?"

"*In love with?*" Ava looked painfully conflicted. She pressed her forehead against the railing of the swing, closing her eyes.

"Well? Which young man has your heart?" Grace asked when Ava didn't answer.

"I don't know. Can I say both?" Ava gave her a helpless look.

Grace burst into laughter. "Yes, of course you can! There are no rules that say you cannot."

"It's just that I feel differently when I'm with one or the other."

"Differently how exactly?" Grace looked amused.

"Well, when I'm with Wallace, I'm tongue-tied and my hands start to sweat. I feel like I'm under a spell. I feel clumsy around him. He's so . . . I guess *eloquent* and *charming* are the words."

"You always were in love with Wallace."

"Remember I told you I was going to marry him when we were girls?"

"I remember."

"But I'm not that silly girl anymore," Ava quickly added.

Grace stifled a smile. "Of course not. Tell me about Nathan."

"Nathan's so easy to be around, and he makes me laugh. They both make me laugh. But with Wallace, I feel like I'm in a fairy tale, and with Nathan, I feel like, myself, only . . . better. Am I making any sense at all?"

Grace smiled. "You don't have to make sense when you're in love. Have they tried to kiss you yet?"

"*Kiss me?* No!" Ava cried. "What would I do if they did?"

"Oh, I don't know, kiss them back?"

"Grace!" Ava scolded.

"What? You're not getting any younger, Ava. Be open to love and marriage. A little kiss here and there is perfectly acceptable in courtship."

"I *am* open to marriage, I just never expected it would happen to me. I guess I gave up on it long ago. I love my work, Grace. It's all I've had time for. I'm so grateful your father allowed me my job when so few women can have a career. I do want a family someday—I just wish I could do both."

"My father does defy societal conventions. Did I tell you he's taught Lillie and me to drive?"

"Did he? How does your mother feel about it?"

"She's horrified." They both laughed at this.

Grace gave Ava a long look. "Maybe you *can* do both. Have you thought about the traits you seek in a husband?"

Ava looked at the clouds through the bars of the swing as it rocked gently back and forth. "Well, he has to be kind, honest, hardworking," she said, then paused. "Wealth isn't as important to me as a sense of self and a sense of humor. Oh, and he must be intelligent. I could never marry a fool."

"Heavens no!"

"Did I tell you Wallace gave up his inheritance to join the navy?"

Grace looked dumbfounded. "You should have told me that from the start! He gave up his inheritance for you?"

"Well, he didn't say that exactly. I'm more of a secondary cause I think."

"I think not. That may be the most romantic thing I've ever heard." Grace looked at the sky for a moment, thinking. "So, one gave up his inheritance to have you, the other earned his own wealth to prove himself for you . . . I don't know, Ava, this is a tough choice."

"Tell me about it. Mind you, nobody has asked me for my hand."

"Trust me—the question is imminent. Let's sort out what we know: Wallace is only here for another week before his fleet departs. That's a disadvantage. I'm guessing he's going to have to make his move rather soon, so be prepared."

Ava winced.

"As for Nathan, is he here to stay or is he moving back to Mexico?"

"Staying. He sold his business and he's here for good."

"That's an advantage. He built a business, sold it, and came back for you. I like that."

"Nathan isn't doing it for me. He's starting a new fishing company here. He says there's a lot of Sicilians and Portuguese in San Diego now, and they are really good fishermen, like the Mexicans. They're planning to go after tuna and see if they can create a market for it."

Grace rolled her eyes. "He can fish for tuna anywhere! Have you ever been to Monterey? There's a cannery up there. Trust me, he's here for you and nothing else. And he knows that Wallace has limited time, which limits him, too. They'll both be making their move soon. I'm guessing by the Fourth of July. I predict parade, fireworks, and proposals."

Ava pressed her forehead against the metal railing of the swing again.

"*If* either is going to make any move at all. Why can't they both just write me a letter? I'm so much better with written words."

Grace frowned. "Ava, it's supposed to be exciting! You're supposed to swoon."

"It is exciting, but it affects my nerves horribly! If this were a book, I'd skip right to the end to see how it ends."

"You wouldn't dare!"

"I would, too. And let us not forget they both abandoned me before. This could all be one big presumption on our part."

"They went away to grow up, and now they're both back to win your heart. I see no presumption whatsoever. With all the reading you do, Ava, surely you've come across a few romances that involve swooning."

"The stories I read usually end badly."

"Like what? Not Jane Austen? Tell me we're both still fans of Jane?" Grace shot Ava a worried look that made her laugh.

"Of course we're still fans of Jane. I meant Poe," Ava explained. "I read Poe."

"Oh dear! Why do you read such morbid tales?" Grace said, exasperated. "There isn't a pendulum swinging over you, threatening to cut you in half!"

"He lives actually, thanks to the rats," Ava said, referencing the protagonist in Poe's popular story "The Pit and the Pendulum."

"Poe looks like a madman, with his hollow eyes and square head."

Ava burst into laughter. "He is a bit haunting, I'll admit to that, but I'm sure his head isn't as square as it's depicted in drawings. At any rate, he may be disturbed, but he truly is a gifted writer and his stories are intriguing. Enough about me and Poe—let's talk about your wedding. Will it be here or in San Francisco, do you think?"

"San Francisco next spring, so save the date. You have to be there because you're my maid of honor."

"Are you serious?" Ava jumped up to hug her friend, and the lopsided swing lurched, the vacant side soaring high into the air. The young women erupted into giggles.

"Where would I be without my *bestest friend*!" Ava teased.

"You still remember that?"

"I still have your letter!"

"Let me guess, in a box under your bed?"

Ava nodded.

"Who taught me grammar, incidentally? What dreadful prose!"

"I have to head back," Ava said when their laughter faded. "There's a new family arriving this afternoon—twin boys and a girl. Their grandparents are asking for nanny services for the entire week. But there isn't one available, so I said I'd do it."

"Sounds like you're going above and beyond your job description again. Don't forget to make time to be swept off your feet and get engaged."

"I'm *not* getting engaged," Ava said flatly.

"We'll see about that."

Chapter 50

July 3, 1900

Ava stood checking the registry for guest arrivals when a clerk beckoned her aside. "Miss Hennessey," he whispered, "I'm not supposed to tell you this, but your friend Mr. Gregory has checked out."

Ava's eyes widened and she felt a ripple of panic surge through her. "Wallace checked out? He hasn't left town, has he?"

"No, ma'am. I believe he rented a tent in the city."

Ava frowned. "That's odd. I wonder why he didn't tell me. Thank you for keeping me informed."

He nodded. From behind them, a man called her name.

"Miss Hennessey? Are you Miss Hennessey?"

Ava turned to find a one-armed older man carrying a young girl on his back, with a young boy wound around each leg. Ava tried to conceal her surprise. She guessed the man was the children's grandfather.

"Keep walking, Pops!" one boy demanded with a heavy Southern accent. The man stepped forward despite the boys still clinging to his legs.

"We have to take this here bull down!" the other boy commanded, trying to trip his grandfather.

"Now, boys, what did your grandmother tell you? We aren't in the country anymore."

Ava couldn't help but laugh. "Are you Mr. Hawkins?

'Yes, ma'am," he replied. "We just got in from Wyoming." He wore a brown leather jacket festooned with tassels and a feather embroidered on the front pocket. Despite being an older man, he appeared to be strong—and Ava could tell by the look in his eye that he'd seen a thing or two on the frontier.

"It must have been a long trip," Ava said. "Why don't you let me take the children while you get settled in." He sighed with relief, and the tension eased from his face.

Ava turned her attention to the children. "Now, you must be Miss Clara Belle, and the two of you are Clarke and Simon?" she said.

"Proper manners," their grandfather said. Reluctantly, the boys released their grandfather and stood, side by side, each extending a hand. "Pleased to meet you, Miss Hennessey," they said in unison. Their identical smiles were mischievous.

"Clara's three and the twins are seven," Mr. Hawkins added. "This is our first vacation with the grandchildren, so we sure do appreciate your services. I will warn you, being honest, our grandchildren are wild as mustangs."

"Not to worry—I love lively children, Mr. Hawkins. I'm sure we're going to have a fine time together. Aren't we?" The children nodded sweetly, and Ava could see a twinkle in the boys' eyes. It was going to be a long day, Ava was sure of it. After Mr. Hawkins departed, she again turned her attention to the children. "How would you like to go on a carriage ride along the beach?"

Clara Belle nodded agreeably, but the boys were hesitant. "How fast?" one of them asked, looking skeptical.

"Can you handle a two-horse carriage?"

"Grandpa taught us everything he knows."

"Let's start with moderate speed." Ava winked at the boys.

They looked at each other, and a slow, wicked grin began to spread across their faces.

☙❧

Fine carriages moved along the beach at a leisurely pace. Ladies wearing riding habits sat beside gentlemen sporting suits and top hats, all taking in the fresh air and abundant sunshine. The genteel ladies and gentlemen smiled serenely until Ava's carriage careened between the others. Clarke held the reins and suddenly urged the horses into a gallop. Simon hollered like an Indian while Clara Belle and Ava screamed. As they flew past the hotel, sunbathers reclining under striped umbrellas watched with great amusement.

"Wait! Stop! Hold them up!" Ava cried. Her riding bonnet flew off her head, landing in the sand behind them. She looked back in time to see a sea gull pecking at it hungrily. "No! My favorite hat!" she wailed. Clara Belle clung to her side like a clam to a rock—then Clarke let go of the reins. Ava heard herself cry, "No!" But she was too late.

The reins dangled loosely between the horses' legs, bouncing along in the sand. Clara Belle started to scream again, the pitch even higher, and Ava joined her. The horses raced around more carriages, kicking up sand on everyone as they headed beyond the hotel toward Tent City.

"I can fix this, Miss Ava! Don't worry!" Simon said, jumping out of his seat. He darted across the yoke and, with a daring leap, hopped onto the back of one of the horses. Ava and Clara Belle shrieked as he flipped over to one side of the horse, hanging on with the strength of his legs. He grabbed hold of the reins and managed to right himself again, slowing the carriage to a full stop.

"Oh, thank you, Clarke!" Ava said, trying to catch her breath.

"I'm *Simon*."

"No, *I'm* Simon, he's Clarke!" the other boy insisted.

"Simon? Clarke? Whichever boy you are, thank you for stopping us. That was very brave! You had me scared to death! Who taught you how to ride like that?"

"Our grandpa was a Pony Express rider back when he was coming up small," the boy explained. "He taught us everything we know. He learned how to ride from the Paiutes."

"Well, that explains it."

The children started giggling when Ava tried to straighten her mass of tangled hair and wipe the sand from her dress.

"He was one of the youngest riders they had. He was fifteen, only they didn't know it," Simon clarified.

"Grandpa told a fib," Clara Belle explained. "He was sayin' he was older when he really wasn't."

"I see," Ava replied. "He must have really wanted the job. Is that how he lost his arm?"

"No, Papa lost his arm in the war after the Pony Express."

"He must have been very brave," Ava replied. "In the meantime, I'll remember not to give you boys the reins ever again."

Simon whacked his brother on the arm, and Clarke yelped.

"You won't rat us out will you, Miss Ava?" Clarke pleaded, rubbing his arm.

Ava looked at each boy, then shook her head no, managing a smile. She liked these children—they seemed happy, lively, and not overindulged. Children who had seen and done everything were harder to please these days.

"I promise I won't tell if you promise not to do that ever again."

"Chief's honor," the boys replied together, holding their hand to their hearts.

"They always say the same thing," Clara Belle said.

"That's good to know. Now, how would you children like to see a diving horse?"

"Horses don't dive," Clara Belle declared, troubled by the notion.

"This one does. Come on, I'll show you. The show starts in a few minutes."

∽⚬∾

"And now, ladies and gentlemen, boys and girls, what you are about to see is the most extraordinary horse in the world!" a man announced to the eager crowd. "Introducing . . . Cash, the diving horse!" The man pointed to a platform forty feet above them. Applause erupted, and the people in the

340

crowd shielded their eyes from the sun as they stared upward. A small black horse walked out to the edge of the platform and stopped, looking straight ahead. The horse stood perfectly still, except for its tail swishing from side to side. A drumroll started. Below the platform was a narrow pool of water that appeared to be shallow. Some adults in the crowd cried out in fear. Several children covered their eyes.

"Now, Cash is not your ordinary horse, folks," the announcer assured, raising a hand to silence the drummer. "He's actually a polo pony that refuses to take a bit. He dislikes saddles, and he doesn't like to be ridden. He does, however, like to dive and swim." Some adults in the crowd chuckled. The children were awestruck.

"Can I get a drumroll again please?" the announcer said. The crowd quieted, and a boy struck a snare drum hanging from his neck. "I give you Cash, the diving pony!" the announcer yelled. Cash backed up a few paces, then ran forward, leaping from the edge of the platform. Some girls shrieked, and Clara Belle used Ava's dress to cover her eyes. The horse seemed to hang suspended in air for a long moment, then dropped, diving headfirst into the shallow pool. After a big splash, he surfaced almost immediately, climbed out of the pool, and shook the water from his fur. The crowd cheered and clapped, amazed by the fearless horse.

"Wow!" said Simon.

"That was the greatest horse trick I've ever seen in my whole life!" Clarke replied.

"The best!" Clara Belle agreed, even though she hadn't watched Cash dive.

Ava then took the three of them for a ride on the carousel, followed by a stroll along the bay with ice-cream cones. They came upon a number of giggling young ladies who surrounded a young man. Ava couldn't make him out at first, but he was certainly causing a stir.

"I want to be first, Nathan! Oh, won't you let me try?" one girl pleaded, batting her lashes coyly.

"Sure, you can be first. Your name again is?"

"Moira."

"That's right, *Moira*. So, sit low on the front of the plank and once the boat gets moving, make your way back to me and stand up inside my arms."

"You won't let me fall, will you, Nathan?"

"No, ma'am."

"You must be really strong," she added, her lips curling into a flirtatious smile.

"And brave," Nathan replied.

All the ladies began to laugh.

"He's just so funny!" one young lady said to another.

"My mama would just *love* him if I brought him home," another added.

Realizing that the young man with the entourage of giddy young ladies was Nathan, Ava rolled her eyes.

"You're very popular, as usual," she said to him.

"Oh, Ava, hello! Are you or the kids interested in aquaplaning today?" He looked surprised to see her.

"I don't know what that is exactly. Perhaps another time," she said, trying to sound disinterested. She noticed his tan arms were strong, his shoulders broad in his rented striped bathing suit. The young ladies around Nathan gave Ava an appraising, dissatisfied look.

"We used to do this all the time in Mexico. It's great fun! Why don't you let the kids watch, and then maybe you'll want to try it sometime?" Nathan suggested.

"You said we were first, Nathaniel," one young lady said, shooting Ava a sidelong glance.

"You're right, I did. So, which one of you lovely ladies wants to be first?"

While two ladies jockeyed for position, another pretty lady advanced, pushing them out of the way.

"No need to squabble, everyone gets a turn. What's your name, darling?" Nathan asked.

"Eunice."

"That's a beautiful name. So, Eunice, you'll sit on the front of the

342

plank, and I'll be in the back holding on to the line. When we have enough speed, make your way back and stand up next to me. If you're feeling brave, you can climb up on my shoulders."

Eunice clapped like a schoolgirl. Nathan could see Ava smirk in the background.

"Can we watch, Miss Ava?" Clara Belle pleaded.

"Fine, but just for a few minutes," Ava said reluctantly. She took a seat on a bench with Clara Belle and her brothers, who were still eating their ice cream.

Nathan placed a long wooden plank, the size of an average door, in the water. Ropes extending from it were attached to a pole on a small boat. The skipper of the boat looked back expectantly. Nathan whistled, and the boat pulled forward. Eunice shrieked and Moira pouted.

The plank dragged along in the water with Nathan and Eunice crouched low upon it. Nathan held on to the rope and stood up slowly on the back of the plank. Eunice, on the front end, continued to shriek, causing onlookers along the bay to stop and watch with great interest. None of them had seen aquaplaning before.

The boat pulled Nathan and Eunice in a wide arch, then began to pick up speed, which moved the nose of the plank lower into the water. Eunice crawled back to Nathan, holding on to his leg before standing up shakily between his arms. Grinning, they sped along the bay, and Eunice began to wave from the safety of Nathan's arms. Ava rolled her eyes again, although she had to admit, aquaplaning *did* look fun.

"This is like the circus!" Clarke exclaimed, melted ice cream dripping down his chin and shirt. Simon was even messier.

"Oh dear, look at you boys. Let's get you cleaned up. If I bring you back looking like, this your grandmother will faint!"

The boys grinned happily.

"Miss Ava, will you still take us to the parade and the saltwater plunge tomorrow, please?" Clara Belle asked in her sweetest voice.

"But of course! Be ready after breakfast, and we'll go."

Clara Belle beamed. "You're my best friend, Miss Ava."

"And you are the sweetest girl, Miss Clara Belle!"

"What about the ice machine? You promised we could watch it make ice!" Clarke reminded her. "And see the tunnels under the hotel, too."

"There's time for all of it. Come along, let's get you back to the Del. I have a polo match to catch this afternoon."

"We've never had a nanny two times in a row," Clara Belle confessed. "Our last nanny ran off without even getting her pay."

Ava burst into laughter at this. "I don't even want to know what happened to the poor girl."

👁‍🗨

Nathan tried to spot Ava, but there were too many spectators along the bay to single her out. A few bumps in the water forced him to return his attention to aquaplaning. Eunice was still on his shoulders. When they crossed over the wake, she giggled and screamed.

As the boat returned to the dock, Nathan saw that Ava and her three young charges were gone. His heart sank. Meanwhile, Moira shoved Eunice aside. She was ready for her turn on the water with Nathan.

Chapter 51

Ava changed into a full-length burgundy skirt with and an ivory blouse. She pulled her hair up under a wide-brimmed white hat adorned with an ostrich feather. Pinching her cheeks for color, she left her room and departed the hotel. She took the trolley down to the polo field on K Street, getting there just as the polo match started.

The players on the field faced each other, ready to claim the ball as the umpire tossed it high in the air. Mallets hooked together and horses shuffled their feet. Somebody connected with a mallet and sent the ball flying down the field. All the players chased after it, leaning from their saddles and swinging their mallets wildly. The fans cheered their approval when the ball went spiraling in the opposite direction. It was going to be a good match.

Ava spotted Wallace right away. He was riding a shiny black pony with protective bandages around its lower legs. He and his team wore blue shirts, white trousers, white helmets, and black riding boots with kneepads. The number four was stitched on the back of Wallace's collared shirt, and Ava thought he looked terribly dashing. He smiled when he spotted Ava, and she felt a tingle along her spine. His horse shook its halter and sidestepped anxiously.

Ava climbed the stairs holding her skirt and took a seat in the grandstand. Across the field, she could see inside the tent where the Spreckelses, Babcocks, Storys, and Hortons were watching the match.

Waiters meandered among them, serving appetizers.

After three chukkers of the game were completed, women and children ran onto the field, stomping down divots of grass that had been kicked up by the horses' hooves. The women giggled at the silly task, and the feathers in their oversized hats billowed in the breeze.

The players took to the field again. The match was tied and the crowd became riveted. Hooves thundered down the field, and foam bubbled along the necks of the wild-eyed horses that seemed as eager to reach the ball as their riders did.

Ava noticed two newcomers join the Spreckelses and others in the tent across the field. The ladies—one older, one younger—were dressed in similar tiered gowns. The gentlemen in the tent stood up to formally welcome them to the party, and their ladies greeted them with hugs. Whoever they were, they were well known and well liked. With their backs turned, Ava couldn't make out who they were.

Wallace watched the newcomers, too. Distracted, he was suddenly knocked to the ground by a swinging mallet. The crowd gasped, and Ava jumped up from her seat, her hand over her mouth. She could see blood trickling from his brow. Wallace was rushed off the field and quickly replaced by another player; his horse was led away by a groom. Horrified, Ava gathered up her skirt and raced down the stairs and out of the bandstand to find him.

಄ೲ

Wallace sat holding a compress over his left eye in the players' tent. He was surrounded by concerned people, and someone had bandaged the cut above his eye. "Hey, can you get me out of here?" he whispered to Ava rather urgently.

"Yes, but you've got a bad gash, and you may need stitches. Shall I fetch Dr. Bates?"

"I'm fine, just get me out of here." He scanned the tent. "Quickly!"

"Who are you hiding from?" Ava asked, peering at him suspiciously.

"Just please?" he pleaded, avoiding the question.

"All right. Meet me out back in a minute."

Wallace slipped out of the tent and found Ava waiting in a coach driven by Willard. He climbed up and slumped low in the cabin beside her.

"Go ahead, Willard," Ava urged. They headed toward Ocean Boulevard.

"Shall I take you to the infirmary?" she asked Wallace.

"No. The Japanese Tea Garden," he suggested. The bandage on his brow was tinged with blood.

"The *tea garden*? Surely, you must have a head injury."

"I'm fine, I would just like some tea," he assured her.

"Willard, to the tea garden, please!" Ava called out.

"Yes, ma'am," he replied over his shoulder.

The carriage pulled to a stop outside a wooden building painted in shades of green. It had a slanted roof of dark green tiles, with wooden spikes protruding at each corner. A sign in front read: George T. Marsh's Japanese Tea Garden, Courtesy of John D. Spreckels.

"Thanks for the ride, Willard," Wallace said, looking more at ease as he and Ava stepped down from the coach.

"You take care now. It looks like you might be havin' a rough day, Wallace."

"You don't know the half of it. Say, where's your father these days?"

"Old Gus? He's out in Julian, picking apples at his orchard. He bakes pies now." Willard laughed heartily.

"Isn't that nice. Do tell him I said hello, and if he comes to town, I'll buy a few pies. I love apple pie!"

"That makes two of us! I'll pass it along." Willard tipped his hat to Ava and drove away, refusing payment.

Ava followed Wallace through a narrow doorway into the teahouse. Two Japanese women in bright silk kimonos with wide black sashes bowed gracefully to greet them. Their dark hair was swept up into a large bun on top of their heads and decorated with butterfly clasps. Wallace greeted them in Japanese, bowing his head. The women nodded as they bowed a second time, then motioned for them to be seated on cushions on the floor, instead of chairs, at a low table.

Ava and Wallace sipped jasmine tea from small porcelain cups with black matchstick letters painted on them. Ava glanced around the spacious room, noting the serene decor. On a nearby wall, a painting of a narrow tower with a three-tiered blue-tiled roof stood before a snowcapped volcano. She spotted a porcelain figurine of a cat, sitting with its left paw raised. "What is the meaning of the cat?" she asked, leaning over her teacup.

"It's a talisman for good luck. It's called a *maneki-neko*," Wallace explained.

"Why does it wave?"

"It's not waving, it's beckoning." Wallace smiled.

"Oh." Ava sipped from her cup feeling uninformed and impressed by his knowledge of the Far East. His face was still flushed from athletic exertion and his blue eyes shined brightly. He was so handsome, even in his disheveled state. She wanted to ask him how much time he'd spent in Japan, but she could barely look him in the eye. They fell into silence, except for the soothing sound of water trickling nearby. Wallace fixed his gaze on Ava, amused as she stirred her tea uncomfortably.

"You checked out of the hotel," she finally said, broaching the subject. "Why?"

"News gets around quickly."

"Not much gets past me, no," she admitted. "But really, why?"

Wallace became serious. "Ocean breezes. One of the brochures I read claimed 'Every breeze is laden with health in Coronado,' and I wanted to see for myself."

"That's your answer?" She gave him a doubtful look.

"Why don't you come over to my tent and I'll show you." He gave her a wicked smile.

Ava rolled her eyes. "I'll bring my chaperone."

He grinned, offering no further answer.

"You're not going to tell me, are you?"

"No." He drained his teacup. "Let's go outside."

Ava followed him out of the building into a lush garden of reeds, flowers, and boulders. A stone path crossed to a wooden bridge that arched over a pond. Colorful butterflies fluttered from flower to flower, bouncing lightly on the air as if leaping from invisible steps. Small stone statues peeked from the foliage, adding to the garden's tranquility.

"Over there, near the pagoda." Wallace pointed to a gazebo next to a tiered tower similar to the one in the painting on the wall.

"Is that what it's called?"

"A pagoda in Eastern culture is actually a temple," he clarified. "This bridge is called a *taiko bashi*. It's a drum bridge because when you see its reflection on the water, it looks like a drum."

They looked over the handrail, together seeing their reflection rippling on the water's surface. Ava noticed large spotted fish swimming slowly by.

"And those are koi. We don't eat koi," he added, guessing her next question.

"You know, I've never been in here before but always wanted to see it," Ava confessed. "How do you know so much about the culture?"

"We stopped in a Japanese port last year."

They watched a Japanese woman pass on the other side of the pond. She wore wooden sandals and socks, and she walked with dainty shuffling steps. She held a flat parasol made of colorful paper and bamboo slats. Ava marveled at her poise. *Perhaps Japanese women are the most prepossessing of all*, she thought.

They crossed the bridge and settled on a bench inside the gazebo. Wallace leaned back against the wall and closed his eyes, wincing slightly. His bandage was soaked through.

"I have another bandage," Ava said, reaching into her bag. "You need a new dressing. Let me see. May I?"

He nodded his approval. Ava moved closer, removing his soiled bandage, her eyes filled with concern. He watched her as she dabbed at his brow, so close he could see the curve of her neck through the collar of her blouse. She placed a clean bandage over his cut and pressed it firmly in place. "You don't need stitches after all. It's just a bad scrape. It's stopped bleeding."

Wallace closed his eyes. She smelled like clean linen and lavender. When he opened them again, she was looking into them, and he leaned forward and kissed her.

"You don't need stitches, but you should try to keep it clean," Ava added as she pulled away from him. Her heart thudded in her chest, and she was certain he could hear it.

"You said that already." His vivid blue eyes gleamed like they had a light source behind them. He leaned forward and kissed her again, this time, placing his hand gently along the side of her face. Her bottom lip trembled slightly, and she pulled away again.

"Marry me," he said.

She inhaled sharply, her face flushed. "I think you do need to have your head examined. You aren't thinking clearly."

"I'm serious. I came back here for you. I want you to marry me, Ava."

Ava slid farther away from him on the bench, but not too far. "Now I know you need your head examined." She clasped her hands in her lap. She could feel the weight of his eyes bearing down on her.

After a moment, she answered him flatly, "No."

Wallace broke into a wide grin. "I knew you would say that the first time."

Her eyes widened. *Am I that easy to read? Like an old, worn book?* she thought.

"It's Nathan, isn't it? Is he what's holding you back from me?"

"Nathan has nothing to do with it. I make my own decisions."

"Is that so?" he replied. "Are you certain?"

"Why yes, I'm certain!" She felt her temper rise. "You know, you think you can sail into town after all of these years and just sweep me off my feet in a few days and have me marry you?" She sounded steadier than she felt.

"That was my plan," he admitted, "and I am kind of pressed for time."

"Well aren't you something?" Her face was reddening. "It's a little presumptuous to think that I've been waiting here for you, knowing you're going to sail away again with the navy and leave me and . . ."

Before she could argue further, he moved closer and this time kissed her with such conviction she felt her spine tingle. Time slowed. She melted into his arms. Her protest floated away like the butterflies bouncing in the breeze. She smelled the sweetness of flowers mixed with his heady cologne.

Her eyes were still closed when he finally released her, letting her exhale.

"Now let's see if Nathan can change your mind." He smiled devilishly, seeing how affected she was.

"Stop doing that to me!" she protested weakly.

"I'll be waiting for you on *our* turret tomorrow night. You can answer me then. Be there before the fireworks end. My ship leaves the next morning."

Chapter 52

Ava went home to have supper with her family that evening. She was preoccupied, ate little, and pushed the food around her plate. Mother watched her with concern. "Nathan called on you today," she said.

"He did? When?" Ava perked up with sudden interest.

"This afternoon. He said you weren't at the hotel or the polo fields, so he came here. He helped your father mend a carriage, and he helped Owen feed the horses."

Ava turned tense. *Thoughtful Nathan*, she thought with a tinge of guilt.

"He knew you were coming home for dinner and was hoping to catch you. We invited him to join us, but he declined. He left a note for you."

"He did? Where is it?"

Lydia, Owen, and Father smiled at her eager reaction. Father pulled the note from his shirt pocket and passed it to her.

Ava immediately read it in silence.

"What does it say?" Lydia asked. Mother frowned, and Lydia lowered her head and stifled her urgent questions.

"He's asked if I could join him after supper. He wants me to bring my violin." Ava thought for a moment. "We were meant to have a family visit tonight. Do you mind if I go?"

"Not at all," Father replied. "We can have another family dinner next week."

"We can help Mother with the dishes," Owen said.

"Go ahead," Lydia agreed.

Ava looked surprised. "It seems everybody is eager for me to meet with Nathan."

"He's a fine young man," Father said, and they all nodded.

"I believe that settles it," Mother said. She watched knowingly as her eldest daughter rose from the table.

Ava could hear her parents and her brother and sister whispering as she headed out the door.

❧

Wallace showered quickly in the men's bathroom in Tent City, then he put on his navy-blue military uniform. He fumbled with the buttons on his coat, combed and parted his wet air, dabbed at the cut over his eyebrow, and stepped out through the canvas door of his tent. He took streetcar #41 to the Hotel Del, ascended the stairs at the entry two at a time, and crossed the rotunda. As he made his way down the hallway, he glanced at the spider clock—he was right on time. The clock started to gong just as he slipped into a private room where government business could be discussed. Admiral Boyle was conversing with Mr. Babcock, Mr. Spreckels, and several other naval officers, as well as an army general.

Wallace saluted his superiors and stood next to Admiral Boyle.

"You all know my aid, Commander Wallace Gregory?" Mr. Boyle said.

"Indeed, we've known him since he was a boy," boasted Mr. Babcock. "Haven't we, John?"

Mr. Spreckels agreed, and Wallace shook hands firmly with each man as he patted him on the shoulder.

"Excellent!" Admiral Boyd continued. "Which is why I asked him to be here. I trust we all know why I've called for this meeting." He motioned for the men to sit. "The United States government is concerned about national defense and the possibility of enemy invasion at our ports. Coronado needs fortification. San Diego has become an important harbor, and its proximity to an international border along with its long beach makes it an ideal target for invasion. What is our current artillery status in Point Loma, General Morgan?"

General Morgan cleared his throat, leaning forward as he spoke. "Currently, we have blueprints for stations at Ballast Point and Point Loma, each fitted with eight- and ten-foot guns. For Coronado, the plans include two eight-foot guns and four mortars to protect the channel, but it appears a lack of funding has prevented these plans from being activated."

Admiral Boyle responded. "I'm here to tell you that has since been rectified," he said. "The president has in mind is to purchase more land in North Island for future military development, providing, of course, that we have the continued cooperation and support of the Coronado Beach Company."

Mr. Spreckels and Mr. Babcock nodded in agreement. "A military presence would be good for Coronado's economic growth," Mr. Babcock said. "Previously, we sold several acres of land on North Island intended for the army to build a fortification, but it has since fallen into disrepair."

"Yes, Fort Pio Pico. Now that the protective jetty has been completed on the Zuñiga Shoal, we plan to rebuild the fort and supply it with long-range guns. This will be a joint navy–army operation."

"We can assure you agreeable terms for land purchase, and we welcome such a development," Mr. Spreckels said.

"Capital. Once these arrangements have been made, I'll get orders for some of my best officers to return, led by Commander Gregory."

Wallace looked up, surprised.

"Commander, you are to be promoted to commanding officer overseeing operations at Fort Pio Pico. I need someone familiar with the area that has existing relations with the community."

"Yes, sir," Wallace said, hiding his glee. He couldn't have dreamed of a better post. His thoughts went immediately to Ava. He wondered if returning as the commanding officer stationed at Fort Pio Pico would persuade her to marry him. He couldn't wait to tell her and could scarcely concentrate on anything else for the remainder of the meeting. When it finally adjourned, toasts were made to the future of a military presence on

Coronado and dinner was served.

Mr. Babcock smiled broadly at Wallace. Noticing the scrape over his eye, he said, "That was a good game of polo you played today, Commander Gregory."

"Until my abrupt dismount, I suppose it was."

The other men in the room burst into laughter.

❧✦

Another note had been left for Ava at the registration desk. Harry West, who had recently been promoted from bellhop to clerk, waved her over with the note in his hand.   "Oh good! You came after all," he said. "Nathan wasn't sure you would. I was given explicit directions to give you this." He handed the note to Ava.

"Thank you, Harry, and congratulations on your new position."

Harry was clearly pleased. "You like my new uniform?" he asked.

"I do. You look very dapper. I will miss your little bellhop cap, though."

Harry laughed, and Ava opened the note and read: *I'm up in the tower near my room. Meet me up there. Nathan*

Ava took the elevator to the top floor and walked down the long corridor flanked by doors until she reached the staircase that led to the tower. It was the second-tallest tower—the ballroom turret was the Hotel Del's tallest structure—and rather than having a round widow's walk, it had a square balcony that echoed the tower's structure.

Through the tower windows, Ava could see Nathan staring out over the lights of Tent City. He didn't hear Ava approach until she was standing by his side.

"You came? I wasn't sure you would!" He smiled, hugging her.

"Of course I did. And I brought my violin, too."

"Excellent!"

They stared out over Tent City as dark clouds scudded overhead. A sliver of a moon, surrounded by stars, shined brightly.

"It's really nice up here," Ava said.

"Best-kept secret," Nathan admitted. "I've been coming up here every night."

"Have you?"

"I *have*. It's where I can think. Everybody makes a fuss about the ballroom turret, but not me. I like this one. There's even room up here to dance."

"Don't tell me you dance up here while you're thinking," Ava replied.

"Sometimes."

She laughed. "And what do you think about when you're up here dancing?"

"You."

He looked at her for a moment, then gazed again at the city twinkling below them. "And how I can steal you from Wallace."

She laughed again, and then silence settled between them. "He asked me to marry him today." She could feel Nathan become tense.

"I figured he would. He's running out of time."

"He wants me to answer him tomorrow night at the big turret before the fireworks show. He says that's *our* turret."

"How melodramatic and unoriginal," Nathan remarked sourly. He thought for a moment before protesting further. "Well, this is *our* tower, and he's not allowed over here. Wallace is so *cliché*. You see, I know a French word or two." They both laughed. "You can't even dance over on that one," he added. "You ready to go?"

"Where to? I thought we were going to start dancing here?"

"We will tomorrow night, when you come to my tower instead of his turret."

"Oh dear!" Ava exclaimed. "I might just stay in bed all day and ignore both of you."

"Did he kiss you?"

"Maybe."

He clenched his fist, shaking it above his head. "Damn that Wallace!" he yelled, causing her to laugh again. "So, I have twenty-four hours to change your mind?"

"I haven't made up my mind."

"Good. Let's go."

Nathan led Ava down to the beach, away from the commotion and lights of the hotel and Tent City. They walked along the shore in the dark.

"Where are we going anyway?" Ava asked.

"A little bit further. It's a surprise."

"I thought you didn't know I was coming?"

"I didn't. I took a leap of faith."

They reached a clearing in the sand where wood was stacked in a pile and blankets were laid out. There was a basket was covered with a cloth. Nathan took matches from his pocket and lit a piece of paper, placing it in the woodpile. Before long, the fire caught and the logs began to smoke, pop, and burn.

Ava sat on the blankets, watching Nathan tend to the fire. She flashed a smile, but he couldn't see it.

"There, that'll work," he said, taking a seat next to Ava. "Let's see what we have in the basket, shall we?" He pulled out a bottle of wine and some desserts. "I stole the desserts from the Crown Room—don't tell anybody!"

She giggled as he poured them both a glass of wine.

"I'm the classiest guest they've ever had." He took a long sip of wine. "Now, for the entertainment this evening. This is where you play your violin for me while I lean back and enjoy my wine." His dark eyes danced.

"Oh, I see . . . I'm meant to *entertain* you?" Ava said, amused.

"Of course! I couldn't imagine anything better than drinking wine by a fire and watching the most beautiful woman in the world play her violin for me."

Ava relented. She opened the case and removed the violin. She took another sip of wine. She felt it warm her body like the blazing fire nearby. And she began to play.

Nathan leaned back, with his arms behind his head, and watched Ava. He was dazzled by the way the firelight flickered over her features. She played a somber tune that carried out over the calm ocean.

An hour later, they were laughing, having finished the bottle of wine. Ava felt light-headed and silly. She couldn't stop laughing as Nathan told her tales of his fishing disasters.

"You really got knocked to the deck by an oversized tuna?" she asked.

"I did—I swear it! It jumped in the boat and landed on me and pinned me down. It took three men to free me!"

"That is the most ridiculous thing I've ever heard."

"True story. I could have died but I said, 'I must live . . . for Ava!' And I pulled through."

"Now I know you're lying!"

"I'm *not*. It was a miracle I survived!"

When their laughter subsided, Nathan turned serious. He looked into Ava's eyes, and she held his gaze. His face inches from hers when he said, "I want you to think about your answer to Wallace—because I want you to marry me instead."

Ava held her breath, seeing the look of pain in Nathan's eyes.

"I know you have been in love with Wallace forever," he said. "But I was in love with you first. From the moment I saw you—when Twilah chased me in the train and you kept the door open for me to escape her."

Ava was about to speak, but Nathan silenced her with a kiss. It was a warm, passionate kiss, and she could feel his possessiveness as he wrapped his arms around her. Her mind swirled, fuzzy from wine. She had never experienced this intimate side of Nathan.

When he released her, she was in a daze. The awkward boy she had known long ago was gone. The Nathan staring into her eyes was a young man who was determined to make her *his*.

Nathan raked his fingers through his hair in frustration, clearly affected by their first kiss. "Tomorrow night, I'll be waiting for you in *our* tower," he said firmly. "Choose me before the fireworks end." Before Ava could speak, he added, "And during the day, I'll be at Sacred Heart, praying on my knees in case you make up your mind sooner."

They both burst into tipsy laughter again.

Chapter 53

July 4, 1900

Two new advertisements ran in papers across the country. Pamphlets swirled on gusty drafts as trains chugged into their stations. Stacks were displayed neatly near ticket windows and left behind on benches. Every passenger who happened upon one was left longing for California sunshine and ocean air. The first of the most recent brochures read:

Hotel del Coronado
The Most Delightful of all Seaside Resorts. Open all the Year
Unrivaled for: he amount of personal comfort and enjoyment supplied to guests by a liberal management. Well provided tables and exquisite service, which cause the belief that it is equal is nowhere to be found.
THE NEW SALT WATER SWIMMING TANKS
Under a glass roof are the finest and most elegant in California, having large, sunny dressing rooms and every convenience attached. Constant streams of hot and cold salt water flowing into the tanks. These baths are very strengthening.
SURF BATHING
On a splendid sandy beach, with more regular breakers, water ten degrees warmer than Santa Cruz and no undertow.
THE FAMOUS CORONADO WATER
Which has established such and excellent for the amazing, quick and

curative action on the kidneys and bladder, is the only water used at the hotel.

HUNTING AND FISHING

Game is plentiful. Barracuda and Spanish mackerel are now beginning to take very lively. This is the sportsman's great resort. Rowboats and yachts in great numbers and lovers of this sport can enjoy it fully in the bay.

THE CLIMATE IS

Mild, soft and even with perpetual sunshine. No cold spells, no heated terms here. Pleasant days, cool nights, hunting, fishing, surf bathing, boating, driving, enjoying life in a hundred ways.

Ava sipped her coffee and smiled. She liked the new advertisement. She particularly enjoyed the comparison to Santa Cruz and the claim that Coronado's water was warmer. She guessed there was competition with the Hotel Del Monte in Monterey, or nearby Santa Cruz, so she was pleased Colonel Holabird had tackled the issue directly.

She next read the second brochure:

This Magnificent Hotel

Is already as famous for its perfect and careful management, also for the amount of physical comfort and enjoyment it furnishes, as for its immense size, its fine situation and its lovely surroundings. Everything is provided for which heart can desire.

A testimonial from W. H. Mason, MD, a professor of physiology from Buffalo, New York claimed: "Complete restfulness and refreshing enjoyment can be had, unrivaled anywhere." He added that Coronado's "Pure and mild atmosphere, equable temperature, dry climate, refreshing westerly breezes together with its mineral water may be regarded as a regular 'Elixir of Life.' Every breeze is laden with health and every prospect pleases."

Ava began to wonder whether Colonel Holabird had paid the professor for his glowing testament. After she read his most recent proclamation, she made a mental note not to visit Buffalo in winter or summer: 'No cold snaps, no clammy fogs, nor heated terms occur here, where the climate causes a sensation of continuous pleasure."

Next Ava read the Hotel del Coronado's new postcard. It included a sketch of the hotel in the upper left corner, a sunbathing woman in the lower right corner, and people walking along the pier on the lower left. The greeting on the front of the card stated in bold letters: *Something about Coronado Beach, California / A unique corner of the earth—Charles Dudley Warner*

There certainly is something about Coronado, Ava thought, and an endorsement from Charles Dudley Warner, a well-known essayist, novelist, and avid traveler, was almost as good as the presidential seal of approval. San Diegans had been so pleased with Warner's favorable endorsement of their city, they named three streets after him in Point Loma: Charles, Dudley, and Warner Streets. Mr. Warner fondly acclaimed Coronado as "a semi-tropical flower-garden by the sea," with only the Timeo Terrace at Taormina, Sicily, as a comparison. Colonel Holabird had been wise to capitalize on Mr. Warner's fame and good opinion of Coronado in his most recent brochures.

Ava stood before the mirror of her vanity and flattened the pleats of her blue dress. She pinned on a red-bow pendant and placed a white cloche on her head. *Festive and fitting flourishes for our nation's Independence Day,* she thought. She left her room in a hurry to pick up the Hawkins children. She had promised to take them to the Fourth of July parade and then to the saltwater plunge, unless they changed their minds and opted to surf bathe instead.

The parade started at 10:00 a.m. and made its way down Orange Avenue. It continued around the flowerbed at Star Park Circle and then proceeded past the hotel to the Silver Strand, where the guests in Tent City could cheer it on. Mr. Spreckels, sitting behind the wheel of his automobile with his wife beside him, led the parade, honking the car's horn repeatedly. Next were horse-drawn coaches with the Babcocks, Storys, Hortons, and Holabirds. The ladies smiled and waved, all wearing broad hats with a mass of red-white-and-blue feathers piled upon them. Ava saw a young lady among them that looked like Beatrice, of all people, but she couldn't be sure. *It can't be her*, Ava thought. *Beatrice lives in Belgium.* Or at least that's where she was living the last time someone mentioned her.

The marching band followed the coaches, trumpets blaring and cymbals clanging to the rhythm of the bass and snare drums. A tuba blared like a foghorn.

Navy sailors marched in lockstep behind the color guard, carrying the American flag. Their boots were polished to a high shine; their uniforms were bright white. Wallace was among them, wearing a brimmed hat that signaled his rank as an officer. When he spotted Ava in the crowd, he broke protocol to turn his head and wink. She gaped, surprised he would take such a risk. He looked as handsome as ever, and Ava felt she would never tire of admiring him in his uniform.

The navy units marched on, followed by the many island clubs, including: the boating club, fishing club, bowling club, book readers' club, and lyceum club. Ava whistled when she saw her fellow members of the Good Time Club pass by.

Coronado's only policeman, Officer Palmer, walked among the crowd, surveying the revelers with a keen eye. Everyone knew he carried two cards in his pocket. One that stated: Please Quiet Your Children and another that read: Please Remove Your Children. Everyone knew Officer Palmer wouldn't use his cards on the day of the parade, but he was watchful nevertheless.

Ava gave the Hawkins children a warning look. They quieted until Officer Palmer strolled by with his hands clasped behind his back, then the children began to hoot and holler again, waving their streamers and small flags. Confetti rained down on them, released from balloons overhead. Ava doubted there could be a place more spirited than Coronado on the Fourth of July. The excitement almost made her forget about the impasse she struggled with. *Almost.* By day's end, two young men she loved dearly expected an answer from her.

"Are you all right, Miss Ava?" Clara Belle asked.

Snapping back from her thoughts, Ava smiled. "Yes, dear! I'm sorry— I was lost in thought. Shall we go to the plunge or the beach next?"

"Both," replied Clarke and Simon.

"Both it is."

❧⚬❦

On the beach, children dug holes in the sand, jumped into waves, and chased after sea gulls. The hotel's photographer, Mr. Hawthorne, had a jolly party of young men and women lined up to take a photograph with the hotel behind them. The men wore dark one-piece bathing suits, and the women black dresses, stockings, shoes, and hats. They all stood in ankle-deep water. Unlike most subjects, who stared into the camera's lens like frozen statues, this group grinned, laughed, and carried on. They draped their arms across each other's shoulders in a long chain for the picture. One woman at the end folded her arms to signal proud independence.

"Just in time as always," Mr. Hawthorne said, asking Ava to hold the flash while he disappeared under the camera's cloak.

"What a merry party this is!" Ava replied. "I'd like to put this picture in the paper, Mr. Hawthorne. May I?"

"Three, two, one, cheers!" he called out. Most of the subjects weren't looking at the camera when the flash popped and smoked. "I'll be sure to get you a copy."

❧⚬❦

It turned out the ocean was too chilly for Clara Belle, Clarke, and Simon, despite Colonel Holabird's claims, so they opted to build a sand castle instead. While Ava worked her hands through the sand, she thought about Wallace and Nathan. *Why do I have to choose? Why does it have to be now? Should I consider my decision another way? Who can I tolerate the least?* She almost laughed aloud at this thought. *Probably Wallace*, she decided. He had a way of making her so angry sometimes.

A wave rolled in and destroyed their sand castle, prompting their decision to head for the saltwater plunge. It was indoors and filled with jolly swimmers bobbing and splashing about. Some brave souls dove off tall diving boards. The room echoed with laughter and lively conversation.

Luckily, all three Hawkins children could swim. Ava watched them from the side of the pool. She clapped for them, waved distractedly while thinking of what she would decide later that evening.

Owen surprised her—she had no notion he was headed for the plunge, too—by jumping into the pool and splashing her. In retaliation, Ava ordered her three charges to dunk him at every turn. Chaos ensued, and she was reduced to giggles while Owen pleaded for air and mercy.

To Ava's delight, Grace arrived for a swim as well. "So tell me! I'm desperate for news of your handsome suitors!" Grace said, sitting down beside her.

"You were right," Ava replied, "They are both actively sweeping me off my feet. I'm expected to decide between the two this evening."

Grace clapped excitedly. "Who will it be, then? The elegant naval officer or the scrapper who became the handsome fish wrangler? You have a difficult choice."

"I know. It doesn't help that I kissed them *both* yesterday."

"You did not!" Grace threw her head back with a laugh.

"I did," Ava admitted. "I belong in the Stingaree district! I didn't ask for them to kiss me, the situation just lent itself that way."

"You don't belong in the Stingaree!" Grace protested. "So, how did you feel? Therein lies your answer."

"I felt like fainting. On both occasions."

"Oh, Ava, you are hopeless!"

"What is to be done?" Ava pleaded.

"I can't answer that for you. You have to follow your heart and not worry about the rest. Someone will be heartbroken, that's unavoidable."

"But that's awful!"

"They don't write ballads about love and heartbreak for nothing. Take some time this afternoon to be alone and sort your thoughts. Who suits you best? Who has your heart? The right choice will present itself."

"I wish it wasn't so complicated."

ॐॐ

Nathan knelt in front of the tabernacle, his hands clasped in prayer, his eyes closed. He prayed that Ava would choose him. He knew the odds were against him—no woman could resist the appeal of Wallace. He was refined, handsome, educated, and a respected naval officer from an influential family. Clinging to hope, Nathan made the sign of the cross and left the church.

He walked down Orange Avenue back to the hotel. On a park bench under a tree near the library, he saw a familiar-looking young woman reading a book.

"Beatrice?" he asked, incredulous.

"Nathan?" she said, rising to greet him.

"I didn't know you were in town!"

"I have been all week. I've been looking for Wallace," she replied, embracing him. "Have you seen him?"

"All the time. Why?"

"Sit and talk with me. Maybe you can shed some light on a few things for me."

∂∞∽

Ava walked down to the jetty and hopped among the massive gray rocks until she came upon a flat one. She sat for a long while, watching the waves build and topple into whitewash. Waves coming in at an angle crashed into the jetty, sending up a powerful spray of water and lingering mist. A pelican soared low, hovering just above the water's surface and rarely flapping it's wings. Ava waited for her favorite sequence to occur: the pelican rose, dove headfirst, submerged, then resurfaced, flapping its wings as it bobbed on the water. *An awkward but perfect hunter*, Ava thought.

She pulled Wallace and Nathan's postcards from her satchel, turning each one over in her hands. She had read them hundreds of times. She knew every curve of their writing, every crack in each photo, every frayed edge. Her mind wandered through memories long filed away. She recalled them as mere boys on the day she'd first met them. Nathan running from the ostrich, Wallace asleep in the Pullman car. She relived the last day the three of them sailed lazily in the sun together, without a care in the world. Things were so simple then. She thought of them now as grown men, smiling and reaching out their hands to her. She remembered their kisses.

She put the postcards away and watched the waves. They built up in long, parallel lines, waiting to transition from swell to arching tunnels of water. She watched each wave become a thin, foamy sheet of water reaching up the beach, leaving behind darkened, gold-flecked sand. She watched the sandpipers chase the receding waves, dipping their long beaks into the sand in search of food. Ava wished she could sit on the familiar, solid rocks forever rather than face any decision. She was content to just watch the sandpipers run. The sun began to soften. In an hour, it would start its descent behind the crest of Point Loma and set on the horizon. Ava rose at last—it was time to get ready.

Chapter 54

In her room, Ava dressed for dinner, slipping into an ivory tea dress. A knock at her door startled her.

"It's your mother," a voice called from behind the door.

Ava rushed to let her in, embracing her tightly. "I'm so glad to see you, Mother!"

"Looks like I've come just in time." She had Ava sit in front of the vanity so she could pin up her hair. "Both boys stopped by to speak with your father today. Funny, I still call them boys."

"They did?" Ava said. Gazing at her reflection in the vanity's mirror, she looked surprised, then stricken. "What do I do, Mother?"

"When I married your father, I knew in my gut that he was the right man for me. I had a few suitors myself back in the day." She smiled warmly at her daughter, seeing the two of them reflected in the mirror.

"*Gut* is such a coarse word." Ava frowned as Mother tugged on her hair.

Her mother laughed softly. "Then use your *heart* instead. I'd trust my gut more than my heart, though. Anyway, they each asked your father for his consent."

"Did Father give it?"

"He did, to both of them." Mother secured the last pin in her hair. "They're both fine gentlemen and worthy of you. Your father told them you would have to sort it out among yourselves."

"Oh dear! I feel ill." Ava's expression soured.

"You'll make the right choice. Go with your heart . . . and your gut."

"That's the problem, Mother, my gut, my heart, and my brain all tell me different things."

"They don't all have to agree to be called love. Go, and know that we love you."

ം✕ు

In the Crown Room, Ava joined Mr. and Mrs. Holabird as their dinner guest. They were perfect diversions to offset her inner conflict. The table conversation was lively, and Ava sipped wine readily, listening and laughing with the others. She looked around the room but did not see Nathan or Wallace. There were far too many people present to know where they might be sitting, if they were here at all.

After dinner, she thanked the Holabirds, who had long treated her like a daughter. "Are you all right, dear?" Mrs. Holabird asked. "You seem a little preoccupied."

"I confess that I am and I apologize. I have a big decision to make, and although I think I've decided, I worry for the feelings of others."

"You are blessed with a good mind, and I'm certain you'll make a wise choice."

Ava forced a smile. *What are the odds she'd say that? Brain over heart and gut.*

Ava said her farewells and made her way across the busy rotunda, stepping outside into the silent courtyard. She needed fresh air to clear her head. To avoid being seen, she walked among the citrus trees, staying beneath the foliage. The sun was setting, and the fireworks would soon begin. She peeked up at the top of the ballroom turret. The widow's walk looked empty, but it was hard to tell for sure from her limited vantage point. Nathan's square tower was shadowed in darkness, and she could see only its roof. Ava took a deep breath. There could be no second guesses. Could she be happy knowing she had caused pain to one of her dearest friends? What if she denied them both and avoided causing any pain at all?

368

Then *she* would surely suffer. She suppressed the thought. Her heart was racing, her breathing shallow. She made her decision and departed from the courtyard.

Chapter 55

Ava entered the noisy hotel. She walked to the center of the rotunda and lingered, contemplating her final decision. Merry guests leaving the Crown Room circled around her like riders spinning on a dizzying carousel. Ladies looped elbows with their male companions, clutching at their pearls or diamond broaches or fox stoles with their gloved hands. Their laughter and trilling voices echoed off the walls and up the balustrade to the second-floor balcony, where curious bystanders watched and listened. Ava inhaled deeply, closing her eyes. Her choice weighed heavily upon her. There could be no changing her mind once the damage was done. Around and around the guests circled and laughed, tipsy and oblivious to her heartache in their carefree world.

At last, Ava opened her eyes. She turned to face the elevator that would take her to the top floor and to the hallway that led to Nathan's tower. She took a step toward it but stopped. Her eyebrows furrowed and emotion welled up within her. Fighting back tears, she turned on her heels and followed the boisterous crowd down the hallway to the ballroom instead. The spider clock in the hallway chimed nine times as she passed. The summer sun should have set by now, with the sky dimming into darkness. The fireworks would start at any moment.

The ballroom filled with guests for the party that would continue well into the night. Ava maneuvered around several waiters serving champagne as she made her way through the crowd. She was handed a flute and decided to drink the bubbly wine before going up to the turret. She needed to calm her nerves.

Luckily, Ava made it to the staircase on the opposite side of the room without being stopped by anybody she knew. She climbed the stairs to the second-floor balcony and glimpsed down upon the orchestra playing onstage and the couples swirling on the dance floor. With such a pressing matter to attend to, she couldn't linger to watch the dancers.

The spiral staircase in the turret seemed narrower and longer than she remembered. It seemed to stretch out above her with no end. With her heart thudding in her chest, Ava reached the top and stepped out onto the widow's walk. Wallace was standing with his back to her, staring at the moon. When he heard her footsteps, he turned and rushed to her, wrapping his arms around her.

"Oh, Ava, you came! I'm so happy!"

Ava burst into tears in his arms.

"Why are you crying?" He released her and stared into her eyes, gently wiping away her. "Don't cry. I love you! We can marry right away, as soon as I return next month."

Ava opened her mouth to speak, but a bitter voice hissed behind her. "You cannot marry him because he's engaged to *me*." Beatrice glared at them, her eyes burning with fury. Wallace had stiffened at the sound of her voice.

Ava looked from Wallace him to Beatrice in confusion. "I don't understand? Is this true?"

"I didn't agree to this, Beatrice, and you know it!" Wallace countered.

"You signed a document of intent that my father set before you. Or do you not recall?"

Ava gasped, horrified.

"Ava, let me explain!" Wallace begged, gently taking hold of her shoulders. "My parents made marital arrangements with the Claypooles. It wasn't something I agreed to, or wanted, and you know that, Beatrice!" He shot her an angry look.

"Did you sign it, Wallace?" Ava asked, incredulous.

Beatrice smirked, placing her hands on her hips in a strident pose.

"I did," he admitted, "but let me explain! I only signed it to ensure that my father would allow me to join the navy so I could come back for you. I knew if you would marry me, that document would become worthless!"

"It's still legally binding!" Beatrice reminded him.

Ava turned pale. "You told me you joined the navy against your father's wishes and you had lost your inheritance."

"I did. All of that is true. My father manipulated me. After I signed the engagement letter, he changed his mind and forbade me to join the navy. I forged his signature and joined anyway. I *am* disinherited and I don't care. I only want to be with you, Ava. You have to believe me!" he pleaded. "I'm coming back on commission to be stationed here in Coronado permanently. I was waiting to tell you tonight."

"But you lied to me?" Ava's voice rasped.

"I know. And I'm sorry. There was no other way."

Beatrice stood fuming, Wallace clung to hope, and Ava was stricken, gripping the guardrail. A massive boom thundered above them, followed by a bright flash and brilliant clusters of light in the sky. Applause rose from the ballroom below as the fireworks bloomed, fizzled, and dripped in streams of fire into the bay.

Ava inhaled deeply, remembering to breathe. "Wallace, you have to honor your agreement. I have to go. I'm sorry!"

"Wait! Ava, please!" he begged, "Don't go! I promise I can fix this!"

She left the two of them, racing from the widow's walk and down the staircase. Kicking off her shoes, she carried them as she hurried around the balcony. The crowd below pressed against the ballroom windows, watching the show. Ava ran across the empty dance floor as the fireworks continued to boom outside. They were firing in rapid succession now—the finale had started and she had to hurry.

Ava ran down the hallway to the lobby and into the open elevator. She called out for the fifth floor to Mr. Reddington, who flipped the lever and slammed the metal gate closed. The elevator rose slowly. Ava watched the floor numbers illuminate one by one on the panel above the door. *Faster!*

she wanted to scream. When at last the elevator stopped at the fifth floor and Mr. Reddington pulled the gate open, she bolted, calling out her thanks over her shoulder. He shook his head. "Why is everyone always in such a hurry?" he muttered, closing the gate again. "What's the rush?"

Ava ran down the hallway, shoved open the door to the tower, and took the stairs two at a time. She dropped her shoes to hold up her dress so she could move faster. She ran out onto the deck as the last firework lit up the sky, followed by a final boom. She raced to the rail, looking around frantically. The balcony was empty. Nathan wasn't in the tower.

"Oh no!" she cried, bereft and gasping for breath. "No! No! No!" The silence was deafening on the heels of the fireworks display. The smell of gunpowder lingered in the air. Ava began to weep. Her shoulders shook uncontrollably as she sobbed. She had missed him. Nathan had already gone, feeling rejected and lowly. *If only he had waited a moment longer . . . If only I had made the right decision. Did he see me on the widow's walk?* The turret wasn't very far across the courtyard and if the wind was right, he might have heard them, too. But the flags always blow south in Coronado, which meant their voices had been carried away with the wind. Leaning against the rail, Ava lowered her head on her forearms. She floundered in a fresh wave of sobs.

"Don't cry," a soothing voice said.

Ava turned quickly to find Nathan standing in the shadows in the far corner.

"Nathan?" she replied, incredulous.

He walked toward her and put his arms around her. A fresh wave of grief washed over Ava, and she burst into more tears.

"It's going to be all right," he said, comforting her.

"But I went to the turret!" she wailed, crying against his shoulder.

He kissed the top of her head. "I know. I saw you."

"You did?" Her voice cracked and she looked confused. "Then why are you still here?"

"Because sometimes the biggest fish gets away . . . And then you get another one on the line, and when you haul it in, you know it was meant to be."

"You're talking *about fishing?*"

He gazed into her glistening eyes, "It may take you a while to realize that the one that got away was the lesser fish. Even if he was the better-looking fish."

Ava gaped.

"If you don't like my fishing scenario, I can make up something with an ostrich?" He broke into a wide grin.

"Nathan! This isn't a joking matter!" She eyed him warily.

"I know! I'm sorry," he replied. "So, did he ask you to marry him again?"

"Sort of. He implied that we would marry right away." Ava looked toward the turret looming beyond the courtyard. "But there's something you should know."

"I can't imagine what?"

Ava turned to face him. "I didn't choose him."

Nathan's tone turned serious. "Wait, what do you mean? You went over there—I saw you up there."

"I know. I did. I thought Wallace deserved to know in person that I was choosing you."

"What did you just say?"

"I went to tell Wallace that as much as I loved him, and always have, my heart is yours."

"It *is?* You told him *that?*"

"I tried to. I got emotional once I saw him, and before I got a chance to tell him, Beatrice showed up and said they are engaged. I didn't think it was important to explain at that point, then the fireworks started and I ran out of time."

"You really chose *me* over him?" Nathan's voice was raspy.

"I did."

Nathan ran his hands through his hair, looking deeply distressed. "Since when, can I ask?"

Ava wasn't sure why he looked so miserable. "I, um, I guess it happened a long time ago," she stammered. "When you sang to me onstage."

Nathan looked dumbfounded, then he threw his hands up in praise. "Thank you Guillermo!" he cried.

"Who's Guillermo?" Ava said, utterly lost.

"I thought you came here because of Beatrice said. . . Oh, never mind!" Nathan drew her close and kissed her, and Ava knew with every fiber in her being that the right man was holding her.

"Will you marry me, then, and make me the happiest fisherman that ever lived?" he asked.

"As long as you don't talk about fishing during our wedding vows— then, maybe. Or ostriches."

Nathan laughed heartily. "Wallace was right, you *are* fractious!" He picked Ava up and twirled her around, making her shriek with laughter that carried across the hotel grounds.

⇜⇝

Wallace cradled his head in his hands. He sat on the widow's walk of the turret with his legs dangling over the edge, an empty bottle of champagne in one hand. If he could change it all, he would. He had let Ava down when she deserved so much more. Why did he think his plan would work? He had taken a fool's gamble and lost. It served him right. He pulled a diamond ring from his pocket. Its facets were dull and lifeless without a light to shine on them—just as his life would be without Ava. The sound of her laughter from the tower nearby still rang in his ears.

Chapter 56

Two months later

Peach-colored clouds streaked across the sky in wispy, striated layers. Waves lapped along the shore while sea gulls hovered in a light breeze, curiously observing the wedding guests below. Mr. Babcock was especially pleased to be in attendance. "I do so love weddings!" he said, beaming. "You know the great Aristotle wisely said, 'Love is composed of a single soul inhabiting two bodies.'"

"Very wise indeed" said Mr. Spreckels.

Mr. Babcock turned to Colonel Holabird, who sat to his left. "I feel like my own daughter is marrying today."

"As do I. I may weep more than the ladies," Colonel Holabird confessed.

"It's all just as you claimed in your brochure, Colonel, Coronado provides everything the heart can desire. Even love."

"You may be on to something, Babcock. Perhaps we should promote it as an island destination where one can fall in love."

"Shall we call it Cupid's Coronado?" Mr. Babcock joked.

"Cupid strikes anyone who sets foot on this island, to be sure. We could guarantee love with Coronado's charms."

"I'll let you in on a little secret. Soon our little paradise island will be on the world stage as vitally important for our nation's defense," Mr.

Babcock confided. "The United States Navy is coming to town indefinitely."

"What an honor!" Colonel Holabird declared. "Although it looks like I'll be out of the brochure business," he added somberly.

"Good man, our job here is finished. We've done it!"

Pachelbel's Canon in D Major on guitar. His mariachi band stood behind him, holding their instruments and waiting for their cue. The guests rose and turned to watch the wedding procession move down the aisle. Four flower girls tossed pink rose petals high in the air, watching them flutter to the sand. Grace and Sarah followed them, urging them along.

Four men proceeded to the altar and faced all those who had gathered and now waited for the bride: a pastor wearing vestments, Owen and Nathan in tuxedos, and the best man, Wallace, in the white uniform of a naval officer.

Ava squeezed her father's arm nervously.

"You look beautiful, my dear—allow me to be the first to tell you. Secondly, don't trip in the sand."

"Thank you, Father! Please catch me if I fall," she pleaded.

"It's time." He placed his hand over hers and smiled down at his lovely daughter. The crowd gasped as she approached, wearing an ivory lace gown with long sleeves and a wreath of flowers over a sheer veil. Lydia followed closely behind, smoothing her sister's long train.

Nathan beamed as his bride approached. Wallace smiled despite his sorrowful eyes.

Sarah and Ava's mother dabbed at tears in the front row. Beside them sat Mrs. Bosworth, Ava's violin teacher from long ago in Cynthiana, and Mrs. Slaughter, who had sewn her own gown to echo the latest fashion from Paris. In rows behind them were the Holabirds, Hortons, Babcocks, Storys, Mr. Gruendike, and the Spreckels family. Staff from the hotel and the *San Diego Union* filled in the final rows. Everyone gave Ava a nod as she passed by.

On Nathan's side of the aisle were his father, Mr. Beckman; Mr. Wen

Lee; Gus Thompson and his son, Willard; and their extended families. To Ava's delight, she spotted the Comtesse du Boulanger and Clancy, who held his cowboy hat to his chest. Beside them stood Jesse Shepard. Ava managed a quick wave to him, so pleased he could make the special occasion. Members of the by-invitation-only Glorietta Club sat next to the rebuttal group, the Good Time Club, which anyone could join. Beatrice was among the Glorietta Club members, and she looked away dismissively when Ava passed by.

As Ava approached the altar, she flashed a smile at Wallace and Owen, then turned her attention to Nathan. Grace held Ava's pink bouquet while Lydia lifted her long veil, stepping aside to witness the marriage vows.

Nathan's face lit up as he stared at his beautiful bride.

The pastor addressed the crowd with an opening prayer and clasped the bride's and groom's hands together. The crowd quieted, and Nathan and Ava exchanged vows.

"I, Nathan Beckman, take you, Ava Sophia Hennessey, to be my lawful wedded wife, in sickness and in health, for richer of for poorer, until death do us part." Nathan spoke the words meaningfully and slowly. The ladies in the audience sniffled and passed around tissues. Mr. Holabird blew his nose.

Ava's voice replied softly as she repeated her vows, following the pastor's lead. "I, Ava Sophia Hennessey, take you, Nathan Beckman, to be my lawful wedded husband, in sickness and in health, for richer or for poorer, until death do us part." Tears welled up in their eyes, and they squeezed each other's hands. Wallace quickly wiped his cheek before handing over the rings to be placed on their trembling fingers.

With a broad smile, the pastor nodded gently to the two of them. "Then, by the power vested in me, I hereby pronounce you . . . husband and wife."

When Nathan kissed Ava, applause erupted and horns from the mariachis blared. The men started singing "Avalita." Nathan scooped Ava up in his arms and carried her down the aisle. Mr. Hawthorne snapped a photograph as rice rained down on the laughing couple.

The Hotel del Coronado loomed behind them, bathed in the golden hues of sunset. Whimsical, magnificent, and dazzling in all its appointments. A testament to vision, courage, and dedication. An iconic landmark that would inspire and delight for generations to come—and a sparkling jewel in the Crown City by the sea.

About the Author

Jennifer M. Franks is an author, mother, Navy wife, adventure traveler, animal lover, concert enthusiast, avid reader and Flamenco guitar player. She writes in genres that include travel memoir, fiction and historical fiction. She grew up abroad and home schooled herself in the jungles of Indonesia, Nigeria, India and Venezuela. She currently lives in Coronado, California with her family and dreams of writing a story in every major genre. Her novels include:

Crown City by the Sea, The Lotus Blossom, Wild Card Willie and the Pony Express, He Shall be Peace, and a short story *The Healing of the Paralytic.*

Acknowledgments

There are many people who have helped me along the way in the creation of *Crown City by the Sea*. I thank my family and friends for their support and encouragement. My writing workshop ladies, Cornelia Feye and Tamara Merrill, and Konstellation Press for publishing my work.

My incredible editor, Robin Cruise with Red Pencil Consulting (EditorWriterPubpro.com).

There are several ladies at the Coronado Historical Association I'd like to thank: Lori Boulanger, my Hotel Del Coronado tour guide and author of many resourceful articles about the history of Coronado. Also, Vickie Stone, Registrar and Curator of Collections for helping me sort through vintage images.

At the Coronado Cultural Arts Commission, thank you Kelly Purvis for your help and support. Leslie Crawford, Editor of *Crown City Magazine*, and author of *Images of America Coronado,* a great book and resource. Thank you for your guidance.

Gina Petrone with the Hotel Del Coronado Heritage Department.
Candice Hooper, Exhibits and Special Collections at the City of Coronado Public Library. Adam Burkhart, Special Collections and University Archives at San Diego State Library. The wonderful Penny Rothschild of Emerald C Gallery.

I'd like to also thank my advance readers:
Amy Steward, Raina Barthelme, Gae Coulston, Margaret Franks, Amy Bosworth, Andrea Slaughter, Lori Boulanger.

I owe you all a debt of gratitude for your help in categories ranging from publishing, editing, vintage photograph support, fact checking, guidance and encouragement. Thank you!

Bibliography

Carlin, Katharine and Brandes, Ray. *Coronado The Enchanted Island*
3rd edition, Coronado Historical Association, 1998

Crawford, Leslie Hubbard. *Images of America Coronado*
Arcadia Publishing, Charleston, South Carolina 2010

Hendrickson, Nancy. *San Diego Then and Now*
Thunder Bay Press. San Diego, California 2003

Beautiful Stranger. The Ghost of Kate Morgan and the Hotel Del Coronado.
Hotel Del Coronado Heritage Department, 2002

San Diego Historical Society Research Archives Coroner's Inquest (RT. 69), F59-2.

San Diego Historical Society Quarterly, Spring Summer 1987, Volume 33, Numbers 2 & 3. Jesse Shepard and the Spark of Genius by Clare Crane

Mengers, Douglas W. *Images of Rail: San Diego Trolleys*
Arcadia Publishing, Charleston, South Carolina 2017

Scharf, Thomas L., et. al. *The Villa Montezuma,*
San Diego Historical Society, 1955

Strong, Theodore van Dyke. *The City and County of San Diego.* Leberthon and Taylor, 1888, San Diego, California (W.H. Holabird)

Newspapers:
San Diego Union, November 30, 1892 "By Her Own Hand"
Coronado Mercury-1887-1896, Coronado Public Library collection

Websites:
Coronadohistory.org; Coronado Historical Association and Coronado Museum: A Timeline of Coronado History
SanDiegohistory.org

CPSIA information can be obtained
at www.ICGtesting.com
Printed in the USA
LVHW112318181218
601006LV00002B/270/P